It's That Time Again
by Adrian Cousins

Copyright © 2024 Adrian Cousins

All rights reserved. This book or any portion thereof may not be reproduced or used in any manner whatsoever without the author's express written permission except for the use of brief quotations in a book review.

This book is a work of fiction. Names, characters, businesses, schools, places, locales, and incidents are either products of the author's imagination or used in a fictitious manner. Any resemblance to actual persons, living or dead, or actual events is purely coincidental.

www.adriancousins.co.uk

...

Also by Adrian Cousins

The Jason Apsley Series

Jason Apsley's Second Chance

Ahead of his Time

Force of Time

Beyond his Time

Calling Time

Borrowed Time

Deana Demon or Diva Series

It's Payback Time

Death Becomes Them

Dead Goode

It's That Time Again

Deana – Demon or Diva Series Boxset

The Frank Stone Series

Eye of Time

Blink of her Eye

Before you dive in …

Hello, and thank you for purchasing this book, the fourth in the Deana – Demon or Diva series. Although all books in this series are separate stories and can be read as standalone novels, I heartily recommend reading through the series to fully appreciate Deana and Terry. Starting with *It's Payback Time*, before *Death Becomes Them*, and then *Dead Goode*.

Already up to speed with our ghostly duo? Great … crack on, swipe your Kindle or turn the page. Deana is back … bringing some festive cheer like only our ghostly diva knows how …

Prologue

Summer 2016

Walking in the Air

"No, please, I'll get you your money," he pleaded, tasting the blood that leaked from his split lip whilst trying to ignore his throbbing gums and the many now-loose teeth his tongue probed. "I know my father had hidden assets … somewhere. I just need a few days … a couple of weeks, max."

"Boss, shall I smack him again?" Bazza asked, his balled right fist poised mid-air as he glared at the whimpering man whose limbs he'd earlier cable-tied to the chair.

"Nah, give yourself a break, big man." Wayne Gower, the head of the Gower family – a notorious outfit that for decades ruled the Broxworth Estate, controlled Fairfield's drug, intimidation and protection rackets – placed his hand on Bazza's arm, indicating he should lower his fist.

"Boss?" Bazza glanced at Wayne, a smidge confused as to why he hadn't been given the go-ahead to further tenderise the weasel's already fractured nose.

"Go make the tea, Baz." Wayne placed his hand on his henchman's chest, encouraging the Neanderthal lump to step back. "Go on, three sugars for me, and go easy on the milk." After Bazza shuffled his six-feet-four, twenty-stone frame away as instructed, Wayne jabbed his cigarette towards the man's face that, after half an hour of becoming well acquainted with Bazza's ring-festooned, sledge-hammer-esque fist, now resembled something akin to the aftermath left on a fishmonger's filleting slab. "You fancy some tea? Not that he looks the sort who could, but Bazza makes a blinding cuppa."

The man fervently shook his head while forcing his back against the chair to gain a few centimetres from the glowing end of the advancing lit cigarette.

"Talking of blinding, I could just stick this in your eye. What d'you reckon? Shall I?"

"No … please, no."

"Is that a no to a blinding or a no to one of Bazza's famous brews?"

"Please, no. N-no to both," he stammered.

"Oh, really? You sure? We got PG, not that supermarket own-label shite." Wayne mocked. "Well, okay, I guess that jaw of yours ain't gonna move so easy for a while. How 'bout I get Bazza to pop a straw in it for you, eh?" Wayne smirked as he withdrew the cigarette from where he'd halted his advance an inch from the git's eye before clamping it between his lips and closing his left eye to avoid the rising blue smoke. After pausing for effect, he drew heartily on his cigarette.

"Please. I'll get you your money."

Wayne sighed heavily before leaning intimidatingly towards the muppet, the man who thought he could default on his loan payments, before blowing a plume of smoke at his pulverised face.

Due to the swelling that had all but closed his left eye, said muppet swivelled his head around when Wayne shifted his stance and thus out of his line of vision of his one good eye. He wished he hadn't, now convulsing when witnessing the horror of his tormentor placing the lit end of the cigarette millimetres from his cable-tied wrist.

"Please ... I'll get the money," he snivelled, feeling the heat of the cigarette, witnessing the horror of the hairs on his arm melting.

"See ... well, no, don't s'pose you can really, can you? Baz has done a right good job on that eye of yours. I could burn a hole in your wrist or ... when I've finished my fag, stub it out in your other eye. What d'you reckon, eh? Course, then you'll deffo be blind 'cos from where I'm standing, that left eye ain't looking too clever. So, how's that sound?"

"Wayne ... please ..." He dropped his head when accepting pleading wasn't going to work with a man who appeared to be enjoying the 'entertainment'. As his tears rolled and the shakes ravaged his body, he contemplated what was about to happen. Wayne Gower and his associates, although managing to escape justice, were purported to have tortured and murdered six Albanians who thought they could muscle in on their operation. Presumably, Wayne wouldn't hesitate to inflict the same fate upon him.

He was a broken man, facing certain death.

"Oh, come on, man up," Wayne exasperatedly huffed, shifting the cigarette away before burning the whimpering loser. "Ah, shit, nothing worse than having to watch a grown man blubber." After taking another drag on his cigarette and keeping his focus on the whimpering man, Wayne shouted through to the kitchen. "Baz, nothing worse than watching a grown man cry, eh?"

"No, boss. Nothing worse than that," Baz hollered above the whistle of the boiling kettle.

Wayne grinned and winked at the man ravaged with uncontrollable shakes. "Hey, keep this strictly between you and me," he whispered. "Baz, although he's a hefty, big lump, he always blubs like a baby … y'know, just like good old Rocky after going the distance with Apollo Creed, calling out that timid bird's name, *'Adrian',*" he mimicked Rocky's Philly tones. "Yeah, blubs just like that when that kid's Christmas movie's on the telly … ah, now what's it called?"

"Wayne, I can—"

"No, don't tell me," Wayne mockingly held his palm up. "It's on the tip of my tongue." He swivelled his head to shout at the open doorway. "Baz, what's that Christmas film that always makes you blub?"

"The Snowman, boss," came the reply from the kitchen, accompanied by the clanging of spoons on china.

"That's it!" Wayne clicked his fingers before placing his nose millimetres from the man who owed him a significant amount of cash. "The frigging Snowman. It's the ending, see. When the snowman melts, that gets poor Bazza every time."

Wayne straightened up and took a long drag on his cigarette, allowing the smoke to funnel from his nostrils before continuing.

"So, you watch the footie last night? Those muppets losing to Iceland in the Euros. Now, I can understand that's enough to reduce a man to tears. I mean, back in the day, Gazza gave it a good go during the World Cup, didn't he? You should have seen poor Bazza up at the pub last night ... blubbing his eyes out, he was. Well, after he'd kicked the shit out of four pricks and put his fist through that fancy new wide-screen TV they'd installed a couple of weeks back. The landlord was well miffed ... but sensibly, he told Bazza not to worry about it. Got his head screwed on, has that landlord. So, apart from watching England play like muppets or The Snowman melting, and unless you're like Bazza, Rocky or Gazza, geezers don't cry. That's for whingeing birds and babies."

The trembling man offered no reply. Instead, continued to give off the appearance of a man suffering the effects of being tasered.

"So, how do I get through to you ... that thick skull of yours, to make you understand the severity of your predicament, eh? I'm wondering if I stub my fag out on your wrist ... that might help you wake up and smell the coffee. Although Baz is making a brew. I don't drink coffee, you see."

"No ... no, I will ... I'll get your money."

"Yeah, so you keep saying. Thing is, you blubbering, stinking lump of shit, I don't believe you. Now, I'm half tempted to get Baz to break your neck, but then I deffo ain't gonna get me cash. So, this is how we're gonna move things forward."

The man squirmed in the chair, straining his wrist against the restraints, as he whimpered an illegible reply. His chin trembled as he became incapable of halting the flow of tears as they poured down his cheeks, stinging the blooded welts and lacerations caused by Bazza's rings.

"Ah, Baz," Wayne hollered over his shoulder. "The git's not only gone and pissed himself."

"Oh, yeah, so he has," Bazza chuckled as he padded through with two mugs of tea, handing one to Wayne. "Good job I lobbed that plastic sheet down, boss."

"Yeah, reckon so." Wayne chinked his mug to Bazza's. "Cheers. Always said you make a blinding cuppa." He slugged a quaff of tea, smacked his lips and focused on the man who appeared still to be urinating. "See, Bazza, although pretty good at making tea and dead handy when it comes to pummelling gits like you, really doesn't understand the subtle nuances of torture. Ain't that right, Bazza?"

"Spot on, boss. Err … what's nuances, boss?"

"Never you mind, big man." Wayne grinned at his henchman before scowling at his quarry. "Now, where was I? Oh, yeah, the subtleties of torture, the threat of which is sometimes a touch more effective than the actual act … what d'you reckon?"

"Wayne … you have to believe me. I can get your money."

"Yeah, so you keep telling me. Same old shite, week after week. Sorry, fella, I'm a fair bloke, but you're really stretching my patience."

"I just need some more time—"

"As I said, I'm a fair bloke. Don't you agree, Baz?"

"I do, boss. Fair and patient, you are, boss."

"See, Baz knows what a nice bloke I am. However, where you're concerned, niceties are over. Now, that new girlfriend of yours ... not much to look at, but I wouldn't mind—"

"No ... anyway, we're not together anymore—"

"Like I give a shit. So, knobhead, unless you stump up half within the next seven days ... then the rest by the end of the month, I'm gonna cover that slag who's dumped you with fag burns. And just for fun, you're gonna watch me do it before I do the same to you."

The man with wet trousers tried but failed to swallow.

"And so you understand how utterly painful that will be for her and you ... here's a taster ..." Wayne grinned as he paused before stubbing his cigarette on the man's wrist.

After a guttural scream, the sort traditionally reserved for patients undergoing anaesthetic-free extensive dental surgery, the man fell silent.

Wayne shot a surprised look at his henchman. "Blimey, Baz, has he fallen asleep?"

"Don't fink so, boss. I fink the git's fainted. Can I get me buzz saw and chop him up now?"

"No, Baz. Sorry, mate, I need this dick all in one piece for now. When I have the cash, you can wave your saw around to your heart's content."

"Cheers, boss," Bazza grinned before taking a hearty slug of tea.

Part 1

1

December 2016

Baby, It's Cold Outside

"Mr Walton. Miss De Ath will be ready for you in about ten minutes. Sorry to have kept you waiting. It's always the same at Christmas, as I'm sure you can imagine."

Terry glanced up from the dog-eared magazine he'd perused for the last half an hour while slumping on the worn, tan, leather Chesterfield sofa in the plush reception area outside Miss De Ath's office. After months of waiting to finally meet her, he guessed another few minutes wouldn't matter.

Anyway, he was dead, so it wasn't like he had stuff to do, places to go, or people to see. However, he would like to move on from wherever this was and be reunited with his wife, Sharon.

"Mr Walton?" Susan, Miss De Ath's tortoiseshell-bespectacled secretary, asked when noticing Terry appeared somewhat perplexed. Her raised eyebrows formed an arc in perfect symmetry with the curve of the frames.

"Oh, yes, righto … err, thanks."

"As I said, I'm sorry for the long wait. We've had a bit of a rush on, what with that hurricane in the Caribbean and that bout of dysentery which recently ravaged parts of Asia, the death toll has spiked somewhat. Not to mention that dreadful business with that Ebola epidemic that's been rumbling along since a couple of years back … we're still dealing with the intake of some of those, would you believe?"

"Yes, I can imagine … ehm, could I ask—"

"It's been quite awful. Most of us are working double shifts just to complete the initial process of slotting the dead into the correct categories … not how I want to spend Christmas, I can tell you."

"No, I'm sure … do you … we, I should say, still celebrate Christmas, then?"

"Of course, why on earth wouldn't we?"

"Well, just that we're all dead, that's all."

"Oh, I see. Yes, absolutely, course we do. Just because we're dead doesn't mean we miss out on Chrimbo. It's our office party tonight, and I'm really looking forward to it because I've got an inkling that my boyfriend plans to propose. We must behave this year, though. Last year, when doing karaoke, Charlie and I got a bit sloshed when singing that Dean Martin song."

"Right, well, congratulations … assuming he does. Sorry, I take it you and your other half must have died very young."

"Well …" Susan paused, taking a quick furtive glance around the oak-panelled waiting room before continuing. "We're not really supposed to say. You know, our deaths being private and all that," she whispered. "However, since you asked, and you look a decent sort, I'll tell you. I died at the age of twenty-two … blooming plane crash in '71, would you believe? Just my luck, everyone survived, bar me! I mean, what are the odds, eh?" she chuckled. "I suppose I'm a rather fab advert for wearing your seatbelt. To be honest with you, I always thought it a bit of a faff. How wrong was I!" she guffawed.

"Oh … sorry—"

"Oh, no, don't," Susan wafted away Terry's sympathy with a wave of her hand, causing a bauble from the miniature Christmas tree positioned next to her typewriter to swing back and forth. "Please, it all worked out for the best. My boyfriend, Charlie, died when HMS Hood sank in '41. When I arrived here, a little shell-shocked, to say the least, he took me under his wing, so to speak. Charlie's not like my previous boyfriends. I s'pose that's due to him being from a different generation. He's a proper gent, you know."

"Yes … I can imagine … ehm, could I ask—"

"I see from your file …" she paused and blushed. "Sorry, I know I shouldn't, but I took a sneak peek. You won't tell Miss De Ath, will you? She really doesn't tolerate that sort of thing."

"No, don't worry, I won't—"

"Thanks. So, you died at the ripe old age of thirty-three in '83, I see. Heart attack. That's unfortunate. And you've been back with us since June this year. I must say, you're rather lucky to be seen this quickly. You must be special, or you've royally pissed someone off," she guffawed again, which morphed into a protracted whine when noticing Terry's furrowed brow. "Sorry."

"For what?"

"You don't know, do you?"

"Know what?"

"I can't say. I'm just surprised how speedily you're being seen."

"Really? I've been waiting months!"

"Mr Walton, that really isn't very long, I can assure you."

"Oh, right. I have to say, this is all rather new to me. I wasn't aware I was dead until this year—"

"You were what we call a sleeper … those held in limbo until needed, sort of thing."

"Sleeper … limbo?"

"That's what we call the dead who we haven't assigned. You're lucky because I know of quite a few cases going all the way back to the fifties, which, would you believe, are still awaiting sign-off."

"Sorry, I didn't catch your name." Terry dropped the magazine on the coffee table and nipped over to the young girl's desk before perching his bottom on the edge.

"Susan."

"Okay, Susan, I don't suppose you could fill in some gaps for me, could you? It's just since I arrived in the summer, everyone here, wherever the hell this is, has been somewhat tight-lipped about what happens next. I would like to move on and catch up with my wife, Sharon, you see?"

"Blimey, you can't say that word around here!"

"What word?"

"Hell!" she hissed.

"Right … course. Is this actually heaven, then? It's just that I keep asking, but no one seems inclined to let me know what's going on."

"No, silly. Oh, dear, you really are in the dark, aren't you?" Susan snickered, covering her mouth to prevent herself from performing a belly laugh. "This is …" Susan paused to clear her throat and straighten the bow at the neck of her blouse. "This is the assessment centre."

"The assessment centre?" Terry parroted.

"You know, I think it's thoroughly rotten that they keep you all in the dark. Look, if I tell you, you must promise not to say you heard it from me, okay?"

Terry nodded.

Since completing his three missions, as Deana had called them, which basically panned out to be undertakings to save his three children – offspring whose existence he'd been blissfully unaware of during his living years – from falling foul to some wholly despicable characters, he'd been kicking his heels around in a detention centre awaiting processing. Months had passed and, apart from playing board games, cards, and the occasional game of ping-pong with the other 'detainees', there had been little to relieve the boredom. Also, information had been on the scant side.

"Promise? Say, it."

"Yes! I promise," Terry exasperatedly replied.

"Okay. So, the short version, because I'm sure Miss De Ath will call you through soon."

Terry nodded, rolling his hand around to encourage her to get on with it.

"When we die, we're held in some sort of suspension until being categorised. Well, apart from the top two and bottom two per cent, that is. Believe you me, that can take an inordinately lengthy amount of time. As I said, death seems to be popular at the moment, so we've got a shockingly long backlog to deal with. The bodies are piling up like you wouldn't believe. Actually, if the truth be known, we failed to hit our targets for decades. Ever since the Second World War, in fact. Charlie said that's the reason for the backlog … y'know, because of the massive spike in admissions in the '40s—"

"Is this the short version?"

"Sorry, Charlie's always saying I'm a right old chatterbox," giggled Susan. "He's such a character, you know. So, where was I?"

"We'd got to the bit about dying, backlogs, bodies piling up, targets, and something about the top two per cent. What did that last bit mean?"

"The very best and the very worst go through 'clearing' with immediate effect, either up to Heaven or, you know …" Susan paused, then mouthed, "Down there."

"Oh."

"Oh, indeed. So, our target is to process every death within fifty years. After assessment, those who score above sixty-one point seven per cent are afforded passage through to Heaven. Those below thirty-one point four per cent are banished ..." Susan paused, dipped her head, peered over her spectacles, and lowered her voice a couple of octaves. "Down below to that unmentionable place."

"Hell?" Terry quizzed with a raised eyebrow.

"Shush!" Susan shot a look at Miss De Ath's door before chewing her lip and nodding. "Yeah, down there. Apparently, it's absolutely awful. I know a few of the lads and lasses who've managed to appeal their banishment, thus returning to take up positions manning the phones in the Call Centre. They'll probably be stuck here forever because it's unlikely they'll amass enough points to go upstairs. But, when all is said and done, that has to be better than all eternity down there. You should hear some of the horror stories they have to tell."

"I'll take your word for it. So, can you earn percentage points here, then?"

"Oh, yes, me and my Charlie have been saving our good-points awards. We've probably secured enough to hopefully make it upstairs when our time comes."

"Right ... so I can, too, then?"

"Of course. All souls can earn points."

"How do I find out how many I need? Y'know, how far short I am on that sixty-odd target."

"Ah, that's not data we're privy to, I'm afraid. I think The-Powers-That-Be class that as too sensitive information to divulge. Makes sense, I s'pose, because if we knew, presumably there's a fear that we'd stop being good when we hit our target."

"Yes, I see. And who exactly are The-Powers-That-Be?"

"You can't ask that!"

"Why?"

"Keeping their identity under wraps is sacrosanct. Even Miss De Ath doesn't know."

"Right … and the rest of us? Those here, not up there, or down below?"

"So, as you ask … the rest of us, which is about a third of all the dead, are in limbo while The-Powers-That-Be review our cases."

"I'm in that group, I take it?"

"You are, as am I and my Charlie. While we await their decision on where we'll end up, we're held in one of four places … all part of limbo, as we call it."

"And where exactly is that?"

"Okay, well, the vast majority who are in suspension just hang around unaware they're dead—"

"Like me since 1983?"

"Yes, that's right."

"And the rest?"

"Some are selected to be spectral guides, others are offered positions here, like me and my Charlie, and some are sent back to correct mistakes."

"Right ... like I was?"

"Yes, so it seems. I can see you were selected for three missions."

"And I take it Deana was selected to be a spectral guide, as you call it."

"Deana?"

"Deana Burton. She was my invisible guide."

"Oh, yes, probably. Because of Charlie's connections in that department, I know some, but not all, of the guides." Susan tapped her forefinger on her lips. "I'm not sure I know a Deana."

"Trust me, if you'd met her, you wouldn't forget that woman in a hurry."

"Oh, was she no good?"

"Let's just say she's an acquired taste. So, what happens today, then? This Miss De Ath is going to inform me where I'll end up, is that it? I'm about to learn my fate ... either going upstairs or downstairs for Christmas?"

Susan scrunched up her nose.

"Well?"

"No ... I've just told you. Were you not listening?"

"Yes, but I'm a bit confused."

"If you *had* been listening, cloth ears, you'd remember what I said about us, unfortunately, being decades behind in processing the dead. I accept you died thirty-three years ago. However, although it's not my place to say, I'm afraid you've got decades to go until they make that decision."

"Oh."

"I've been waiting forty-odd years, Charlie's been waiting nearly eighty, and some poor sods are almost a hundred years in limbo. Basically, over the last century, the world's population has quadrupled. Despite improvements in medical science, deaths are increasing exponentially. As fast as the higher-ups increase the size of our team to deal with the backlog, death seems to be becoming increasingly more popular."

"Right … I'm confused. I thought you said the processing backlog only stretched back to the fifties."

"No, you Silly-Billy," Susan rolled her eyes, the high-powered lenses causing her eyes to appear bulbous. "That's the initial assessment to attribute a percentage award. Those who've been good go up, and those who've been bad go down."

"Oh."

"The rest of us just wait, either—"

"Yes, I get it. Staying dead, becoming a guide, completing missions, or holding a position here at the assessment centre."

"See," she grinned, "you were listening. Now, I get to see all the committee meeting minutes because Miss De Ath sits on the EDC. There's a right old flap about the poor performance regarding our KPIs. Would you believe they're even muting the idea of scrapping the targets and holding the dead for over two hundred years just to give us a little breathing space?"

"Sorry, you lost me at EDC and KPI—"

"Excessive Death Committee and our Key Performance Indicators … our targets which we're monumentally failing to hit."

"Course, silly me. So what is today's meeting about—"

"Oh … looks like she's ready for you." Susan interrupted before holding down the illuminated flashing white button on her intercom. "Miss De Ath?"

"Susan, I'm ready for Mr Walton."

"Very good. I'll send him through." Susan released the button and nodded to Miss De Ath's office door, indicating Terry should make haste. "Remember, mum's the word on what we just discussed," she hissed as Terry approached the door, his hand poised to grab the handle.

"Course, no problem. This Miss De Ath, apart from sitting on that death committee, what's her role here?"

"Miss De Ath? As it states on the door, she's the Head of Missions. Far from it for me to say, but I suspect you're about to be reassigned. If I was a betting girl, which I'm not because that would dock points I can ill afford to lose, I'd surmise it's Chrimbo back in the land of the living for you, Mr Walton."

2

Fairytale of New York

"No, I'm sorry, but that is unacceptable. Totally lamentable. I flatly refuse to go anywhere near that woman again. Period. You listen to me, young man—"

"Mrs Burton," the bumptious owner of the male voice at the other end of the line calmly interjected, cutting Deana short. "I am over one hundred years old, so I think I may have passed the point when I can be referred to as a young man—"

"I don't give a flying whatever how old you damn well are or how long ago you rather wonderfully met your demise," Deana interrupted, hearing the supercilious call centre agent at the other end of the line groan. Although a touch peeved by his impertinence, she bashed on, her fury and choler reaching heights usually reserved for her ex-husbands. "Now, listen here. I will not dance to your tune or be forced to perform like some circus monkey—"

"That is as maybe. Of course, Mrs Burton, that's your choice. If you so wish, we can terminate your contract forthwith. However, whilst you are still contractually obligated to perform your spectral guide duties, can I remind you that my superiors, and myself, for that matter, do not take kindly to threats—"

"Oh, go to hell!"

"Mrs Burton, although I've been dead for the best part of fifty years, the vast majority of which I spent in that very place, I have absolutely no intention of returning there. I can assure you it's quite unpleasant. So, just to confirm, if you no longer wish to comply with your given missions, I can process a dissolution docket and recommend that your contract be terminated. Henceforth, of course, resulting in you passing through to your final destination. Although I must warn you, there's a dreadful backlog snarling up the processing centre at the moment, so you could be waiting for some time."

"Oh,"

"Oh, indeed, Mrs Burton. Think on!"

"Excuse me—"

"I've taken the liberty to peruse your file. Unfortunately for you, it appears you're still some way off from amassing the points total required to avoid spending the remainder of your death years down in the aforementioned place where you rather rudely just instructed me to go."

"No, that can't be possible—"

"I'm afraid so."

"Oh ... well, how bad is it down there? Could I select somewhere else, perhaps? If I'm being honest, ending up on a cloud with a harp playing angel for company doesn't really do it for me. Is there a middle ground? Not Hell, but somewhere in between where perhaps I can still partake in a spot of pleasure? I'm a woman with needs, you see."

"Mrs Burton, I'm not at liberty to say. We're not a travel agent; you can't pick and choose where you end up. I'm afraid it doesn't work like that. Now, despite your rudeness, I'm prepared to offer a word to the wise …"

Deana huffed and exaggeratedly rolled her eyes when the voice paused.

"Let me be candid. Hell is blisteringly unpleasant … far worse than a two-star all-inclusive resort in some dodgy end of the Caribbean full of screaming, dirty, thoroughly objectionable children. And despite the heat, which is as awful as the living fear, you'll not be afforded the opportunity to top up your tan, that much I can assure you. Also, the company isn't great either. Until I managed to successfully win my appeal, I had to endure the indignity of sharing bunk beds with Idi Amin. Most unpleasant. Apart from the man's history of ethnic persecution, extrajudicial killings, corruption, and economic mismanagement, his flatulence is nothing short of hellaciously repugnant."

"Oh … well, if I have to perform another mission, can it please not be with that awful woman, Petunia? I can't say I enjoyed her company … most disagreeable, if the truth be known. And, I'll have you know, she wasn't much fun."

"You're not there to have fun, Mrs Burton. You're there as a spectral guide to ensure successful missions."

"Yes, well, as I stated in my report, the failure of said mission was wholly down to Petunia's shortcomings. I was totally blameless. It's unacceptable that I have to guide that vacuous, gormless old battleaxe. Anyway, I prefer men. I'm more suited to assisting ghosts of the male persuasion."

"So I've heard," the agent muttered.

"Excuse me?"

"Nothing, Mrs Burton," he haughtily sang before re-employing his usual phlegmatic timbre. "Now, I'm sorry, but your next mission, as stated, will be assisting Petunia again. And please, can you ensure a successful outcome this time, otherwise—"

"This is insufferable!"

"Yes, I'm sure. Now, I've calculated that perhaps one or two successful missions, and I stress successful, something that you haven't excelled at, I might add, may notch your points total to the required level to avoid enjoying all eternity in the company of the evil down in the netherworld. As I said, nasty lot down there."

"Some of my missions were very successful!"

"Success is relative, Mrs Burton. Page nine of the report in front of me suggests a few, and I stress a few, outcomes were favourable. However, your performance was, at best, pedestrian."

"Pedestrian?"

"Average … mediocre, if you like."

"I don't damn well like. And I'm not an imbecile … I'm well aware of what you're inferring with the term pedestrian. But I can honestly say I've never been accused of being mediocre. This is an outrage …" Deana paused when hearing the agent huff. "Look, I'm sorry, but I demand to speak to your superior."

"Mrs Burton, I am the team leader. I can assure you speaking with the duty manager will not result in a change to your assigned mission."

"Well, we'll see, shall we? I demand to be put through to the duty manager. I'll accept another mission, but not with Petunia. Are you aware the woman is thunderously dull, inexplicably stupid, and voted for Margaret Thatcher? I'm a Guardian reader, and my darling late husband, Dickie, was a leading light in the Labour party. I really can't be seen with the likes of Petunia Featherington."

"Mrs Burton, can I remind you that you're invisible? Apart from Petunia Featherington, no one can see you. Also, we don't differentiate on political sway. We're all dead when all is said and done, and politics no longer hold any meaning."

"Yes, alright. But, please, not Ponderous-Petunia," Deana whined. "Can't I have a man this time? Preferably a toned, muscly sort. As I said, I'm a woman with needs. There must be someone who fits that description, who requires the services of a gorgeous, ghostly guide. Or, if not, a woman who perhaps might also enjoy the fairer sex? I'm partial to both, you see."

"Mrs Burton," the agent huffed.

"Please, call me Deana."

"I'm sorry, Mrs Burton, but protocol demands certain formalities are adhered to. We will maintain the use of formal address if you please. Now, can I remind you that fraternising with other spectral guides, something I see on the report you and the dead Miss Travers have been indulging in, or with any of your dead subjects, is only serving to lower your points total. Something, I might add, you really can't afford to be doing unless you *do* want to end up sharing a bunk bed with Idi Amin and the likes."

"That is as maybe, but I have needs. Anyway, Clara Travers and I have struck up a friendship."

"So I see. However, Miss Travers has also been warned … she must focus on her mission, as you must yours."

"Alright, don't go on. I can assure you, there is absolutely no danger of Petunia and I doing … doing—"

"I can imagine, thank you. Now, I take it you agree to your mission, then?"

"Oh, ruddy hell, if I must. Although, being as it is Christmas, couldn't you just … perhaps … misfile something and change my assignment? I will be super grateful."

"Mrs Burton—"

"I'm sure I can offer you some recompense for your good deed. I know you mentioned something about being dead for however many years, but I'm quite certain that even over that extended period of time you've never met a woman quite like me … I'm unique," Deana dropped her tone a couple of octaves before continuing. "Men drool over me. You won't regret it."

"Mrs Burton, are you suggesting I bend the rules to offer you a favourable alternative mission in exchange for sex?"

"A little coarsely put, but essentially, yes. I'm desperate, you see?"

"Mrs Burton, I must stop you there—"

"I must say, I never thought I'd have to resort to prostitution. However, needs must. One must put one's body on the line in times of great peril. This being such a time. If you ever have the misfortune of bumping into Petunia, you'll understand where I'm coming from. Perhaps this is an arrangement we could discuss further? Iron out a few details, as such. Hmmm?"

"I've been warned about you, but I didn't think the rumours—"

"What rumours?"

"Let's just say there's chatter among us agents up here about your apparent looseness."

"I'm not sure I'm liking your pejorative tone."

"I'm sorry to hear that, Mrs Burton. However—"

"At least prostitution is a profession which is reasonably easy to perform and negates the requirement for further tuition. Of course, I come from an HR background and always champion the need for workplace training. Not that I'm fully au fait regarding the ins and outs, no pun intended, but my newly acquired daughter-in-law, Courteney, is highly experienced in the adult entertainment industry. I'm quite sure the little tramp could impart a few tips if required. Anyway, at the end of the day, we all know how to 'choke the chicken' and play 'hide the sausage' when all is said and done."

"Are you done?"

"Done what?"

"Your pitch, if that's what it was, about offering favours, or bribes, for an unauthorised change in allotted mission."

"Yes. Did it work?"

"No. I'm afraid you have me mistaken. And can I remind you who you work for? Unlike politicians, we don't kowtow to threats, bribery, coercion, or any other tactics to gain a favourable position."

"No, of course. But ... it is Christmas."

The agent huffed.

"Please. Pretty please," Deana begged, employing her well-practiced, alluring tone.

"Alright, Mrs Burton. Seeing as it's the season of goodwill, let me take a moment to review the missions that have dropped into my in-tray this morning and see if we can't find you something more suitable. However, I must stress this is highly irregular. I'll pop you on hold for a moment and be back with you in a jiffy."

"Thank you, most kind. I would like to apologise for wishing you back to Hell. As you say, it is Christmas after all ... and my outburst was most uncharitable."

"Apology accepted. I won't be a moment."

Deana sipped her wine as she waited, humming along to The Pogues and Kirsty MacColl's festive classic, which The-Powers-That-Be had chosen as one of the tunes to replace *Abide With Me* as their interlude, on-hold music for the Christmas period. It was undoubtedly a damn sight better than the usual festive saccharine-infused ear vomit perpetually pumped out on the airwaves.

Since dying earlier in the year and following the completion of her spectral guidance duties assisting Terry on three missions to help his gaggle of offspring, The-Powers-That-Be had assigned Deana four further missions, culminating in the debacle with Ponderous-Petunia. Whilst waiting, jiggling her leg in tune to the music, Deana sang the lyrics, thinking how apt they were when musing about that dreadful woman. Scumbag and faggot, she may not have been, but maggot she most certainly was. If the choice boiled down to either another mission with that curmudgeonly old hag or Christmas lunch in the company of history's most evil with Beelzebub carving the turkey down in the fires of Hell, she would plump for the latter.

However, sharing bunk beds with Mr Amin and his apparent flatulence issues didn't appeal. Also, by the very fact that the Devil ran the show down there, Deana thought it unlikely there would be too much festive cheer going around to celebrate his nemesis's birthday.

"Mrs Burton?"

"Yes, I'm still here."

"Sorry to keep you on hold. As I'm sure you can imagine, this is always a busy time of the year. Christmas brings out the worst in people, I'm afraid. Apart from being a time of goodwill to all men—"

"And women."

"Yes, quite—"

"The misogynistic attitudes of your generation are long gone, I'll have you know. I'm a woman in her prime—"

"Late fifties—"

"As I said, in my prime. I've lived through decades when men thought they ruled the world. However, the twenty-first century will be the watershed moment when we girls fight back and take control. Apart from the obvious, men are superfluous creatures."

"Obvious?"

"Pleasure … all girls should have a couple of muscly hunks to play with when feeling the need. I must say, something I'm well overdue."

"I'm sure … I'm beginning to understand how you weren't overly fond of the long-ago deceased Petunia Featherington."

"Indeed. Now, what do you have for me? While waiting, I concluded that if my only option is supping Dubonnet and lemonade on Christmas Day in the company of the vexatious pesky Petunia, I will tender my resignation forthwith. Although there is always the idiom that the grass is greener to consider, I'll risk sipping the Devil's drink with the evil lord himself. At least there is likely to be some debauched sex party on offer, even if I have to mingle with a few murderers."

"Devil's drink?"

"Coffee … I assumed The-Powers-That-Be would demand a certain level of intelligence from all their employees, no? My darling Dickie had a first from Cambridge, you know. Sixteenth century … when the aroma of a mysterious elixir wafted through the city of Venice, the great and the good, whom I imagine hold some sway in your organisation, thought the humble coffee bean the work of the Devil. As I said, men can be so stupid. Actually, on that subject, he being an exception to the rule, could you provide me with an update on my darling Dickie? Is he alright? Does he miss me? Could you let him know that I'll catch up with him soon and, in the meantime, let him know I'm fine with the notion of him keeping himself entertained with a few fallen angels as long as he's ready to pleasure me as soon as I show up?"

"Mrs Burton, we're not a messenger service."

"Oh."

"Now, the good news, I have another spectre who I'm willing to assign to Mrs Featherington—"

"Marvellous!" she chortled. "I pity the poor sod who gets that assignment."

"Hmmm."

"So, is that it? Am I done? Contract termination, and down to the fires of Hell?"

"No, Mrs Burton. I've had a bit of a conflab with the duty manager, and he and I are in agreement that you're not ready to pass over just yet. Now, there are a few missions hot off the press, so to speak, which I can offer you first refusal."

"Go on," she purred.

Deana sipped her wine, praying one of these missions involved some young, muscley, fit, horny, dead hunk who would fall for her womanly charms. Although Clara was keeping her thoroughly entertained, Deana sometimes missed the attention of a man.

"We have Geraldine Butterworth, a Trappist nun from the Order of Cistercians of the Strict Observance, dead since 1957. A lovely lady who will need the services of a spectral guide to deal with a mother superior who's not toeing the line. Gone rogue is the term on the report. An unusual case because nuns are usually afforded instant passage through to Heaven. However, before taking her vows, Geraldine had a chequered past and thus is a few points short."

"Oh, poor girl. Whatever, but I don't really do nuns. They're not really my thing."

"No, I see that. Okay, next, we have Cecil Prentice."

"I'm listening." A man. Now that sounded better, thought Deana. Cecil suggested he could be older than she would prefer, but she could crack out one of Dickie's blue pills if required.

"Cecil, dead since 1973, a little infirm due to being in his nineties, but he needs to return to the land of the living to assist his great-grandson, Jackson, aged nine, who's in a spot of bother at his boarding school."

"I'm not wild about children. There … they're so callow and, well, childish."

"Hmmm … you're being very picky. Let me see what else I have."

While sipping her wine, Deana detected the sound of papers being shuffled along with the agent's repeated 'no' mutterings as he presumably discarded missions due to deeming them unsuitable and not matching her skill set. If a nun and private-school-tutored snotty child were considered appropriate, she dreaded to think what those apparent incongruous missions could entail.

"No … no, sorry, but that's it. The nun, schoolboy, or Mrs Featherington."

"Oh … really?"

"Well, I have one other, but being assigned to you is inappropriate."

"How so?"

"The mission is for someone who's already passed through and has to return to fix further issues. We don't get many of these, and those missions are usually reserved for our more experienced, successful guides."

"I've completed seven. Doesn't that count for anything? How many do I need to complete to be deemed experienced?"

"Usually ten. All of which we prefer to be successful. Unfortunately, you have a few failures under your belt."

"Yes, alright, please, there is no need to sermonise."

"Also, I'm afraid there's a note on file stipulating you are not to be assigned."

"Excuse me? Why on earth … hello … you still there …" Deana paused when hearing Steeleye Span harmonise their version of the Latin Gaudete, realising she'd been placed on hold. "How ruddy rude!"

Deana drummed her recently painted nails on the arm of the sofa whilst she waited, pondering the depressing thought of Petunia, a trip to Hell, or, if awaiting a new assignment, the possibility of spending Christmas in solitude. Although she'd endured many a dour festive season in the company of her six turgid ex-husbands, the very idea of seclusion during the party season stoked her monophobia. Notwithstanding that most of those aforementioned turgid gits had accused her of suffering from a histrionic personality disorder, Deana accepted she was a woman who had certain needs. She prayed Clara wouldn't be tied up with her mission and could keep her company.

Of course, although Ziggy, her stepson, currently in his surfing commune in Australia, appeared to be dragging his heels regarding the settling of her and Dickie's estate, the house would soon be sold during the process of probate. At that point, being a ghost with no fixed abode, she presumed that situation would expedite her transfer to the other side. Whether being immediately transferred to be with her darling Dickie, or an indeterminate amount of time in purgatory to purify her soul, who knew? However, despite the prospect of pulling a cracker by herself whilst watching *The Sound of Music*, for reasons she couldn't quite put her finger on, Deana wasn't ready to take the next step.

"Sorry about that. I just wanted to check with the duty manager. The note was placed on file because the dead man in question stipulated as part of the agreement to return he wouldn't be saddled with you as his guide."

"Why on earth would he say that? I can assure you I'm not acquainted with many male ghosts, more's the pity, so why would they have a reason to blackball me?"

"Well, my understanding is he considered it inappropriate."

"Why?" she shrilled.

"I could take a wild stab in the dark."

"Sorry?"

"Mrs Burton. My line manager has agreed to overrule the request and assign this mission to you. Think yourself lucky. I can only assume the duty manager must be in a good mood today because he was insufferable yesterday. So much so, I was half tempted to table a transfer request back to that cage with Idi Amin."

"Oh, okay. So my mission is to guide who, exactly?"

"We've agreed to offer you another mission with Terry Walton."

"Really? Terence? How lovely! Don't tell me the poor man has more offspring who've ended up in a bit of a pickle," she chortled.

"No, Mr Walton only sired three children. This mission is to correct an issue he may be responsible for causing during one of his previous three."

"Oh … really? What an earth—"

"Mrs Burton, I can't divulge the details at the moment. Mr Walton is being brought up to speed as we speak. Rather than sending you the information, we'll let Mr Walton fill you in."

"Oh, I do hope so," Deana purred.

"Hmmm, can I—"

"Oh, I'm so excited. This is going to be such fun!"

"Mrs Burton, can I remind you, you're not there to have fun. Also, you apparently, for whatever reason, although I can probably guess, have a few broken bridges to mend where Mr Walton is concerned. And, not forgetting, we are expecting a successful outcome. Although the duty manager appears to be full of festive cheer, probably due to starting early on the sherbets before our Christmas bash later tonight, he was clear that this is your last chance. You must succeed. Otherwise, you will be transferred to the lower levels when you pass through."

"Of course. I must say you've been super helpful; I really do appreciate it."

"Yes, well, please make sure there are no hitches. I wish you all the best and a very merry Christmas to you."

"And to you, too. Oh, where is Terry … when will he return?"

"He's in a meeting with one of the mission directors, but he'll be back with you soon."

"Marvellous, you've made my day."

"Can I just check if your living arrangements are still satisfactory?"

"Absolutely. Probate is moving at a frighteningly slow pace, so I'm perfectly fine where I am."

"Very good. I expect Mr Walton to be back with you by the morning. As I said, Mr Walton will have the brief, but time is of the essence on this one."

"Don't trouble your little head. You can depend on me."

3

Lonely This Christmas

"Miss Keelan?"

I vaguely detected someone calling my name. However, since two days ago, I seem to exist in a permanent fog, unable to function at the basic level of a normal human being. Not that I could classify myself as such, even at the best of times.

Unlike the vast majority of the population, Christmas was the time of year I dreaded the most. Although, it hadn't always been like that.

My earliest memories of Christmas, probably from the age of six or seven, were full of joy. Even up to my early thirties, I'd always looked forward to those few days with my family. The laughter, the exchange of modest presents, and my father's singing after a few too many whiskeys were cherished memories.

However, as the years rolled by after losing my parents, with no close family, lacking close friends, no partner, and thus no children, the season of goodwill to all men had morphed into misery. The endless TV shows depicting joyful family get-togethers, interminable cookery shows demonstrating new and innovative ways to stuff and roast a bird, plus the regulation rolling out of *Love Actually*, only served to confirm my pathetic, isolated existence.

I'm painfully lonely. Sad, eh?

Incidentally, Sarah, Laura Linney's character in that film, is a woman I can identify with … albeit without benefiting from her obvious beauty, the institutionalised brother, not being American and not in love with a hunk in the office, but single.

Always single.

Forever single and with no family since my mother passed ten years ago.

Despite Andy Williams' claim that 'it's the most wonderful time of the year', something I recall M&S enforcing a few years back with their adverts, I considered the ever-increasing already protracted yuletide celebrations nothing short of a living hell.

As the countdown ramps up after Armistice Day when the supermarkets splatter the aisles with last year's dusty, dog-eared decorations, the radio perpetually pumps out those schmaltzy Mariah Carey, Slade, and Chris Rea tunes, to name but a few, causing the nation to fall into Chrimbo delirium, I begin the process of distancing myself, shrinking further back into my protective shell.

Until two days ago, I thought this year might be different. In fact, it would be fair to say that I was looking forward to Christmas again and, for once, excited.

What a fool.

As I performed every Sunday, my usual routine on the big day involved serving festive cheer to those less fortunate than me at Fairfield's homeless shelter. Not that I can claim any righteous calling like the rest of the volunteers, but simply to avoid being on my own.

Notwithstanding my socially awkward demeanour, an infuriating trait severely hampering my ability to make friends, the clientele who used the shelter didn't judge me. Unlike 'normal' folk, street dwellers didn't regard me as Janice, the shy, maybe dull, perhaps a smidge desperate woman best avoided.

However, despite my volunteering exploits being a whole lot better than spending the day alone, I feared Christmas this year could be worse than usual. And believe you me, that's really saying something.

Whilst patiently waiting to be seen, my apathetic gazing settled on a twenty-something woman hauling along a pushchair with two pre-school-aged toddlers in tow, attempting to negotiate the misbehaving sliding doors when entering the bank's foyer. After expertly fiddling with several levers on the buggy – the sort of contraption you needed a small mortgage to fund the purchase from Mothercare and a PhD in engineering to understand the finer details of how to operate – she barked at her two boisterous children, placated the screaming baby in a pushchair with a few shushes and cooing noises, continued to hold a conversation with whoever on the phone pinned between her shoulder and ear, and fumble for her bankcard before stepping up to the cashpoint machine. Although she appeared royally pissed off when harangued by her children, I had her pegged as the sort who, come the eve of the big day when all preparations were near completion and the wine flowed, would agree with Mr Williams.

I'd give anything to swap places with her. And despite how she appeared today, probably close to throttling her offspring, I'm pretty sure she wouldn't agree to the swap if she was afforded a glimpse of my life.

"Miss Keelan?"

I shot my head around when hearing my name.

"You are Miss Keelan?"

"Oh, sorry, yes, that's me. Sorry, I was miles away." I raised my hand tentatively, reciprocating the smile the suited gent offered, before his ushering hand suggested I should stand.

Although appearing young enough to be the son I didn't have, his dapper attire befitted his position of Assistant Customer Service Manager, which his gold, glinting badge suggested. And they say policemen are getting younger.

"Nathan Bridges," he offered his hand, and a benevolent smile laced with hints of derision. "Sorry to keep you waiting."

"Oh, no, that's alright," I lied, releasing the shake before trotting to keep up with his wide gait. I couldn't help noticing his highly polished, pointed black Chelsea boots, which scythed through the air that harboured a distinct stench of greed as he sped through to one of the private glass-fronted offices at the rear of my bank. A clinical room devoid of any festive decoration, and its sole purpose as a space where bank officials ruined lives.

"Take a seat." Again, using that presumably well-practised hand gesture, he waved to the dark-blue, on-brand-coloured chair before taking up position on the other side of the desk.

Whilst he settled in, adjusting the perfect Windsor knot of his tie and swished the mouse, my eyes were drawn to the leaflet stand positioned on my side of the desk. Specifically, the pamphlet headed up 'Scams Awareness for Seniors'.

I could detect my heart rate rise and my tongue desiccate. Any saliva left, now in full retreat as I feared the worst. The picture of the troubled pensioner depicted on that leaflet appeared to almost be mocking me. Their wagging finger taunting that I, Janice Keelan, a forty-one-year-old self-proclaimed loser, could be such a credulous fool.

"Okay, Miss Keelan. Can you provide photo ID, please?"

"Oh, yes, my passport. I have a brand new one because I'm off to California for Christmas … ehm, well, maybe not." I winced at his deadpan expression before plucking the burgundy-coloured passport from my handbag and sliding it across the desk.

Akin to an officious border control clerk, he flicked his eyes back and forth from the photo page to me, repeating that process every few seconds. Although my passport photo wasn't the most flattering snap ever taken – as were most, due to my photogenic qualities rarely bashing in an appearance – the sullen mugshot expression depicted on the penultimate page suited my mood.

"And proof of address?" he asked, reapplying that scornful look, which was probably fair enough if my fears were to be realised. Notwithstanding Nathan's highly polished, urbane, although machine-like, bank-official demeanour, I imagined he regarded me with the same contempt as I presumed that pensioner depicted on the scam leaflet might if they knew my story.

Despite the belief you could never fall foul of such a ridiculous and elaborate con if that is what it was – such as you hear about on social media and in those Sunday supplements, recalling earlier this year a woman relaying her tragic story on daytime TV – and although I was still clinging to hope that what appeared to have transpired, hadn't, I knew I must prepare myself for the worst.

I placed my council tax bill on the desk, a folded one-page document Nathan perused without touching. I took his nod as confirmation that I'd passed all security checks, and he was happy that I was who I said I was.

Janice Keelan, the stupid woman.

"Okay. Thank you." Nathan swivelled the monitor around and plucked up a branded dark-blue pen to use as a pointer before copying my sideways lean when trying to see the screen.

While I waited for Nathan to clear his throat, I ran my hand through my ponytail. An action, odd tic, if you like, I performed when feeling uneasy. Something I performed far too often.

"Via internet banking, you transferred the total of your savings account to your current account at four minutes to midnight on the 12th of December. Twenty thousand, four hundred and seventy-one pounds and thirty-one pence."

I nodded, agreeing that I had performed that act ten minutes after finishing my call with Chad.

"Thus, leaving this account empty."

I nodded again.

Nathan tapped the screen with the blue pen sporting the bank's slogan, *'Britain's Friendly Bank'*, which I thought he might need reminding of, indicating the zero balance.

"Yes, I'm aware the balance is zero."

Nathan performed a couple of mouse clicks, switching screens to display my current account. Although I already knew the balance, seeing the figure caused my palms to become clammy despite the room temperature being only a few degrees above the on-average single-digit outside temperature for December.

"The next day, aptly the 13th," he offered a whimsical smile. "You transferred twenty thousand pounds via a money transfer company from your current account."

"Yes, Chad asked me to use that service because he said it was quicker."

"Hmmm."

"Is that not correct, then?"

"Technically, yes, I suppose so. Although, of course, that transfer could have been made through us here at the bank, which means we could have applied certain checks and safeguards. You transferred the money to …"

"Chad Ruger."

"I see. By mistake?"

"I'm beginning to believe so."

"Hmmm. Can I draw your attention to your balance?" Nathan tapped the screen with his improvised pointer. "After a few standing orders and other card payments, your balance is now overdrawn to the tune of one thousand, four hundred and eight pounds and sixty-seven pence. Of course, that's over the agreed limit, so there are also the daily twenty-five-pound banking charges to consider. I'm afraid you can't use your card, and we cannot honour any standing orders until your overdraft is within the agreed limits."

"Yes," I nodded. "The gentleman I spoke to earlier said as much."

"Your accounts are frozen."

"Yes, I know, but the reason I asked to see you is because I wanted to know what could be done about that transfer. As I asked the gentleman on the phone this morning, can that be reversed? Can I get my money back?"

"Miss Keelan, you transferred the money from your account via a money transfer company. Unfortunately, due to that method of payment, that transaction isn't covered by the CRM codes."

"CR … sorry, what was that?"

"Basically, the code of practice banks have to protect customers from financial loss due to fraud or scams … we have leaflets which you might find helpful." Nathan pointed at the stand to my left.

"A bit late, I think."

"Hmmm, probably. However, you might like to take one for future reference. You know, if you plan to make transfers in the future."

"That's not very likely because I don't have any money."

"No, of course. I take it you believe you have made a mistake regarding this transaction?"

"Yes. As I just said so. Well, I think … no, I've definitely, ehm, probably made a mistake. An error of judgment."

"Oh, I see. Have you contacted Mr Ruger to discuss the error?"

"I've tried, but I can't get hold of him."

"I'm sorry to hear that."

"I think I may be a victim of a scam."

"Have you contacted the police?"

"No … should I?"

"I can't really advise, but if a crime has been committed—"

"Well, not really. I've become friendly with Chad … Chad Ruger, we chat online …" I paused and winced when I detected Nathan roll his eyes. Not exactly a professional reaction and I doubted eye-rolling was part of the bank's workplace training manuals. However, I guess it was to be expected. "Chad asked me to lend him some cash for a couple of days, and he would then pay me back with interest. He was in a tight spot, you see. All his assets were tied up, and he needed a loan to complete a deal."

"A deal."

"Yes, a deal."

"Twenty thousand pounds?"

"Yes. He's a very wealthy man … works in the oil industry, but had a cash flow problem—"

"Cash flow?" Nathan parroted.

"That's what he said."

"Twenty thousand pounds seals oil deals, does it?"

"Well, I don't know. But Chad said rather than him securing a short-term loan, if I lend him the money, then I could benefit from the interest rather than some thieving bank."

"Banks are not thieves, Miss Keelan."

"Oh, no, I wasn't suggesting … not you. Not this bank." Despite my embarrassment, dry mouth, and feeling the need to run, I bashed on. "You see, Chad just thought it would help me out. You know, the interest would provide some spending money for my trip, so I didn't need to dip into my savings."

"Trip?"

"Yes, that's what he said. He's paid for my flight to visit him in California for Christmas. He's an American."

"I see. And when should Mr Ruger have reimbursed you?"

"Two days ago."

"And you can no longer contact him?"

"No." I dropped my eyes and shook my head. "My emails just bounce. He always set up the Skype calls, so … well, without an email address that works, I can't contact him."

"Right. I'm sorry for your situation. But, as I said, we can't recover the transferred funds."

"Is that it, then?"

"Oh, no, we need your account back in order, as I just told you. Can you transfer other funds to cover your unauthorised overdraft?"

I chewed my lip and shook my head, willing with every last ounce of fortitude not to cry. Despite being in the company of an employee of 'Britain's Friendly Bank', I got the distinct impression Nathan was not the sort to offer comfort to a stupid woman.

"How about family or friends? Could they perhaps help you?"

I shook my head, unable to reply, fearing that opening my mouth would lead to the emittance of an embarrassing howl. I didn't have any family, and I found making friends … well, let's say, difficult. And much as I'd tried and, oh boy, had I tried, my awkward shyness always seemed to get in the way. Because of this, I tried to overcompensate, leaving said potential friend running for the hills.

"I see from your account that your salary payments are … somewhat erratic, shall I say? Do you expect to receive a payment soon?"

"Ehm … no, I'm temping at the moment. Unfortunately, work has all but dried up. I haven't been paid since October."

"So I see."

"I do secretarial work, office administration, reception desk duties, that sort of thing. I've signed up to a couple of agencies further afield, but it seems everyone's on cutbacks at the moment."

"Oh, right. Hmmm—"

"I don't suppose you have any vacancies here? Just a thought."

"No, Miss Keelan. Sorry."

"Yes, of course. It was worth asking, though. I'm good with numbers, see. I presume all your staff, and you, I suspect, are required to be good at maths to work in a bank. I can type, too, you know. I'm super reliable, in fact—"

"Miss Keelan." Nathan used his pen to tap the desk to enforce his interruption of what I knew to be my inane, boring drivel.

"Sorry." On the rare occasions when I managed to shimmy away from that protective wall of shyness, usually in moments of high stress, I would allow my mouth to run away at ten to the dozen and thus bore to death anyone in earshot.

"You do understand that the debt must be repaid?"

"Yes," I squeaked.

"Right, I think it's best I escalate this situation to my manager. If she's free, are you okay with seeing her now? It's just that I think it's best we get the ball rolling quickly on this."

"Of course. Sorry, but what does that involve … y'know, getting the ball rolling?"

"A plan for debt recovery."

"Yes, but what does that mean? What's going to happen?"

"That's for my manager to decide. However, I do need to inform you that failure to settle your account satisfactorily could lead to a CCJ being levied against you. If we're unable to recover the funds, that situation might lead to the seizure of assets."

"Bailiffs?"

"Possibly."

"Oh, my God."

"Miss Keelan, let's not get ahead of ourselves. I'm sure there are options available."

"Like?" I squeaked.

"Let me get my manager."

"Please, what options?"

"Well …" Nathan paused as he stood, drumming his fingers on the back of his chair. "Perhaps you could apply for a modest increase to your mortgage?"

"I rent."

"Oh. Hmmm. What about assets? Do you have a car you could sell?"

"No … I never learned to drive. Silly, really, but the timing was never right for me to take lessons."

"O–kay," he replied, emphasising both syllables, suggesting he'd also run out of ideas. "Let me see if my manager is free."

"Right. Will you be calling the police?"

"Miss Keelan, as I said, let's not get ahead of ourselves. This isn't a police matter. The worst that's going to happen is you could be declared bankrupt."

"Oh." I huffed. "And homeless … I can't pay the rent, and my landlord isn't overly tolerant regarding late payments. My rent was due yesterday. I take it that standing order won't be paid?"

"No, sorry, Miss Keelan. Unfortunately, we've frozen your accounts. Please excuse me while I track down our Customer Services Manager."

As the glass door opened, I caught the chorus of the tune being piped by the 'friendly bank' to entertain their customers.

Mud … I was knee-deep in the stuff and sinking fast.

Lonely and cold really didn't do my situation justice. Come a week on Sunday, I could be queuing with the regulars at the homeless shelter, not serving roast turkey and mushy, over-boiled Brussels.

4

Supermarket Spooks

"I'm a little disappointed in you, Terence." After taking a sip of coffee, Deana knelt and jabbed Terry's arm with her red, manicured, pointed nail while he slept soundly in the spare bed where he'd reappeared that morning. Just as that agent at The-Powers-That-Be Call Centre had stated he would after Deana had suggested popping her favourite dead partner there just in case she was otherwise engaged in her own bed. Which, as it happens, she had been. Although always up for a threesome, a dead Terry rematerialising whilst she and Clara were in the throes of enjoying themselves might have spoilt the moment.

"Come on, stop playing dead. Although, my darling, that's exactly what you are," she chortled. "Anyway, I thought we made a good team, you and me, no? Hmmm? Like strawberries and cream, mistletoe and wine, that sort of thing?" Deana poked his arm again. "Hello, earth calling Terence."

Although still asleep, Terry shifted from lying on his back onto his side, facing Deana, tugging the quilt close to halt the shivers that seemed to have ravaged his body. Despite his comatose state, his subconsciousness detected he wasn't alone.

"As I was saying, I'm disappointed with your churlish rebuff of my services. Why on earth you felt the need to stipulate that you didn't require my ghostly guidance for this mission is utterly beyond me. I'm quite put out about it all. I was saying to Clara only last night how terribly disheartened I am by your rebuttal. Miffed, Terry. Miffed."

Terry mumbled illegibly while attempting to cocoon himself in the quilt. Now feeling chilled to the bone.

"Come on, you. Wakey-wakey, Terry." Deana pinched his nostrils together in an attempt to wake him. "Terence, stop with all this playing dead nonsense. I know you can hear me. Just because you are dead doesn't mean you can lie there corpse-like all morning. Presumably, we have work to be getting on with. That supercilious agent I argued with yesterday was thoroughly rotten. Throwing around his unfounded, frankly outrageous accusations regarding my apparent pedestrian performance in the spectral guide department. Rude, Terry. The man was utterly rude and a bit too lippy for my liking. I'll have you know, I'm not going to be accused of mediocrity again … so, come on, wake up."

Deana took another sip before placing her mug on the bedside table. "Okay, well, you horny little monster, you. I'm sure this will stir you from that slumber," she snickered.

While still on her knees, lifting the hem of her silk dressing gown to ensure she didn't snag the delicate material, she shimmied sideways, thus positioning herself in line with his midriff. Sporting a wicked grin, she lifted the quilt and raised an alluring eyebrow at his naked form before placing her hand between his legs.

"Good morning, darling," she purred.

"Jesus! Frigging hell, what the hell are you doing?" Terry hollered as he pinged open his eyes before chaotically scrambling up the bed, using his heels to gain purchase on the bedsheet.

"Ah, there you are, darling. Wide awake at last."

"You … you touched me. You were touching me."

"I was stroking you awake, that's all. Don't look so horrified. I would often awaken my darling Dickie in that sensuous way. My rubbing hand action was his early wake-up call when he had an early start. Dickie often needed to attend important breakfast meetings in Cambridge, so I'd rub him awake to ensure the dear boy wasn't late. He said it was the most natural way to wake up … nothing like a rush of blood and a raging stiffy to launch you bright-eyed and bushy-tailed into a new day."

"Stiffy?"

"Hard-on. Erection, darling. I'm quite sure you know what a stiffy is."

"Yes … but—"

"A man of your experience and pedigree is well accustomed to offering up many a stiffy in his time, I'm sure. I imagine you were quite adept in that department. One more if you'd allowed me to carry on for a moment longer."

"Christ … I can't believe I'm actually back with you."

"Yes, darling, you have me again. Now, before you start all that nonsense regarding your constant rebuffing of my very generous advances, whilst you've been wherever ... up there, I suppose," Deana wafted her hand above her head. "I've been fortunate enough to become acquainted with a rather delicious, sybarite ghost who appreciates what I have to offer."

"Sybarite?"

"Yes, darling. Like me, Clara is devoted to luxury and pleasure. Nothing better than bedding a kindred spirit, no pun intended."

"Oh."

"So, despite your obvious manly qualities, which I just had the pleasure of rubbing and am more than happy to offer a repeat performance if you so wish, I am now what you'd call a satisfied woman."

"Jesus."

"No ... although I suspect worldly, I imagine that's not an activity he and I are ever likely to indulge in. Anyway, even if he fancied indulging in a spot of pleasure, I'm not sure I'm a fan of the long hair and beard, if I'm honest."

Terry's mouth sagged.

"Darling, you look ... well, horrified."

"I am. I'm not what you would call religious, but that's a shocking thing to say."

"Oh, really. Jesus was a man, after all. I know there's nothing in the Good Book to suggest he might want to indulge, but the poor boy hadn't met me, had he? It's just biology when all is said and done."

"You're—"

"Unbelievable," she snickered. "I know, darling. Oh, this is so much fun. You and me, the A-Team back together again," she chortled while excitedly clapping her hands.

"Bloody hell," Terry muttered when again cocooning himself in the quilt. "Can you at least put the heating on? I'm frozen."

"Sorry, darling, no can do. Although Ziggy is rather wonderfully dragging his heels with the probate thingy, the gas has been cut off because the house is supposedly unoccupied. Anyway, you're cold because you've just returned from the dead. You're still dead, but you get my drift. You'll soon warm up. Surely you remember when you woke in that hotel room in the spring? You were shivering then, but you soon came around."

"Orff?"

"Sorry?"

"You pronounced off as 'orff'."

"Oh … so? Have we been apart for so long that you've already forgotten what lovely diction I possess? Enunciation is important, darling. People need to know you're well-heeled. It's essential in life … and death, for that matter, to project the right image. Standards, darling, standards. Which mustn't be undone by common fish-wife parlance. Façon de parler … correct diction is vital to ensure one moves gracefully in the right circles."

Terry puffed out his cheeks.

"Anyway, I was saying how totally opprobrious you were regarding not wishing to be teamed up with me again. What's all that about, hmmm?" Deana asked as she perched on the bed, rubbing Terry's quilt-covered knee.

"I just thought, perhaps, I might … ehm—"

"What?"

"Well, you were a bit full-on, as I remember."

"Oh, so that's it, is it? You didn't want me as your guide because of my hedonistic desires, hmmm? How remiss of me for not remembering your pious monk act. Anyway, darling, as I was just telling you, you no longer need to worry on that front because Clara and I are quite content with our little arrangement."

"And who exactly is this Clara?"

"Oh, you wait 'til you meet her. She'll be around later. Gorgeous, and what a lush in bed. She's dead, of course, just like us. See, Clara is a spectral guide like me … we spotted each other in Sainsbury's, of all places."

"Food shopping?"

"No, darling. I can no longer shop because I'm dead and invisible, remember?"

"Yes, woman, I'm fully aware you're dead and invisible, but what were you—"

"Stop interrupting. So, there I was on Halloween, bored witless, I might say, flinging packets of biscuits around just to amuse myself, and there she was doing the exact same thing in the cereal aisle next door. Flinging around her oats," she chuckled. "Oh, we had a giggle. Our little ghostly act actually made the front page of the Chronicle, would you believe? 'Supermarket Spooks' was the rather prosaic headline. Not hugely imaginative, but I guess it's only the local rag, so talented reporters are few and far between."

"Is that allowed? Biscuit flinging?"

"No … we both got a reprimand for that little jaunt. Anyway, supermarket dating is all the rage. It's the new clubbing."

"Really? The store I managed wasn't that sort of place. We sold food, not acted as a place to hook up."

"Hmmm … I may have forgotten that little checkout supervisor's name, but didn't you say something about banging the girl's brains out in the electrical services cupboard behind the checkouts?"

"That was different."

"I don't see how. Anyway, the world has moved on since your day. Get with it, Terence. Singles nights amongst the ready meals and using fruit codes to signal your preferences is the way to pick up your next ride."

"Fruit codes?"

"Yes, darling. An upside-down pineapple positioned at the front of your trolley indicates you're swingers looking for new couples. Dickie and I met some lovely people that way. Such a thrill. And, of course, there's the standard drive-by peach drop … plopping a ripe peach in someone's basket just lets them know you want them."

"Is this for real?"

"Course … heavens, although you've dabbled in many an affair when alive, it seems you really did live a sheltered life, dear boy."

"Well, in my day—"

"The dark ages of the seventies."

"If you say so—"

"I do so."

"The normal way to let a girl know you fancied her was to ask them out on a date. And what if peaches are out of season … what then?"

"Oh … I don't know. Good question."

"Passion fruits?"

"Very droll, I'm sure. No, it's always been peaches. I suppose Dickie and I only dabbled in the summer."

"Are you making this up?"

"No, darling. It's a bit like the Polari code, or handkerchief code, which gay men had to resort to using when the bigots ran the world and persecuted those poor chaps for just loving another man."

"You've lost me, as usual."

"Men would wear different coloured handkerchiefs or bandanas to indicate they were up for some fun. A secret code."

"I'll take your word for it. What's fancy handkerchiefs got to do with Clara?"

"Oh, yes, as I was saying before we digressed. Clara's like me … on ghostly guide duty. She's teamed up with a right old dolorous git at the moment, the poor love. Scrooge, she calls him. The-Powers-That-Be dispatched the grunge of a man, who died in '98 after a motorcycle accident, on a mission to ruin his wife's second husband, who's not the most caring of men, apparently."

"And … and you and her—"

"Yes, darling. We're enjoying each other's company. Of course, I miss the pleasure of a real sausage, but she's such a lush and a real dab hand with a vibrator."

"Right … if you say so."

"I do so, Terence. I do so. And I'm sorry but, before you get any ideas, she's not into group sex. You're just going to have to sleep on your own. Which is a pity, but it's just how it is. Somewhat surprisingly, I'm rather touched regarding her desire not to want to share me."

"What a relief," Terry mumbled.

"Muttering, Terry? I've told you umpteen times about muttering. Anyway, what have you been up to for the last few months? Did you get to see your dead little Sharon? Whispering sweet nothings to each other up there while lounging around on a big fluffy cloud, were we?"

"No. I've been playing Monopoly and ping-pong."

"Oh, how dull. Strip Monopoly is alright, I suppose. Played that a few times … instead of paying fines for landing on another player's property, you remove clothing. Problem is, it all takes too long to end up naked. Strip snap is better. Why on earth were you playing games?"

"Oh, some ruddy backlog has caused the entire system to become snarled up."

"Like a traffic jam?"

"Yeah ... apparently, there are too many people dying, so the entire process is in some sort of crisis. I, along with thousands, millions probably, have been held in what they call processing."

"Oh, how utterly awful for you, darling." Deana rubbed his knee and pouted. "You poor thing."

"And you? While I've been awaiting the decision regarding whether they send me up or down, and apart from your ghostly food-flinging antics in supermarkets with Clara, what have you been up to?"

"Ah, yes, that's just reminded me. I haven't had a good food fight for ages. Dickie and I used to host our 'Summer Fruits and Cream' soirées in the garden every second Saturday in July. It was regarded by all our acquaintances as the most erotic party of the season."

"You flung strawberries and cream at each other."

"Yes, darling. Clothes off, then writhe around in a selection of summer fruits and cream. Fairfield's version of *La Tomatina*. Of course, one year, Dreary Drake ... you remember that gnarled old prude from up the road?"

Terry nodded, recalling the incident when the invisible Deana tormented the poor woman with a sign of the Leviathan cross.

"Yes, I'm sure you do. So, that starchy old maid made a complaint to the police, which resulted in two red-faced constables zipping around and coming face to face with their chief inspector, who, at the time, was covered in berry juice with a close friend of mine slathering him in squirty chocolate sauce whilst squishing ripe blueberries up his bottom. You should have seen it … hilarious it was."

Terry puffed out his cheeks before rubbing his hands over his face. "Why me … why do I have to end up with her?" he mumbled.

"You're muttering again, Terence. What's the matter with you, eh? Come on, buck up. For the last seven months, while you've been loafing about playing games, I've been hard at it. Nose to the grindstone. Mission after mission, and I can honestly say, none have been much fun."

Terry parted his fingers, spying Deana through the gaps.

"The last hideous one involving Ponderous-Petunia. Shocking woman, I can tell you. Would you believe she actually admitted and was proud of the fact that she voted for Margaret Thatcher?"

"So did I. Best Prime Minister this country's ever had."

"Oh, please, no. I was forgetting you're also one of those brown-shirt right-wing capitalists from the nasty party. Now darling, despite your delusions about politics and that merciless attitude to your fellow citizens, let's not fall out over it. So, come on, why have they sent you back? Not that I'm complaining … it's rather wonderful to see you again. I'll admit, despite my friendship with Clara, I've missed you."

"Really?"

"Yes, really, my darling. We're like strawberries and cream."

"Are we back to food fights?"

"No, I'm saying we go well together."

"Ham and eggs."

"Exactly, darling. If we must degrade the analogy to trucker's greasy spoon level."

"Okay, so according to some officious woman, De Ath, who's head of missions—"

"Oh, her. That woman and I have history, shall we say. We had a tête-à-tête just after I died. I can tell you, Terence, she received the rough edge of my tongue."

"I can imagine. Anyway, De Ath and her cronies decided to ping me back. Although I'm not wild about the idea, at least I'll get a break from being stuck in that detention centre for years, potentially decades."

"Playing ping-pong with your new dead friends."

"Yeah."

"And this new mission … what have we got, then? What despicable grunge do we need to scare the bejesus out of this time? For some reason, I seem not to be in favour with that lot up there. That horrid agent I spoke to yesterday said you would have the details this time."

"Well … apparently, on one of our missions in the spring, we caused this situation and now have to put it right."

5

It's a Fine Life

"Janice … oi, hen, buck up. We need to get a wiggle on here. Remember, Maggy's off with the lurgy again, so we're a woman down. I wouldn't mind betting we'll be damn busy today, what with it being so bitter out there and threatening to snow. I need those tatties peeling today. Come on, lovey, at your dawdling rate, you'll still be peeling that same spud come Christmas. Then there'll be nae a blithe yule coming from me, I can tell you."

I glanced up from the half-peeled potato resting in my hand to be faced with Dawn, not the friendliest of the three cooks who took turns to rustle up a roast of sorts at Fairfield's All Saints Refuge 'soup kitchen' each Sunday, glaring at me whilst animatedly waving a spatula in my face.

"Sorry, Dawn," I mumbled, restarting the vegetable peeling, my usual task on a Sunday morning. Although reasonably proficient at following a recipe and knew my way around a kitchen, I was rarely promoted to the lofty position of chef despite being one of the most reliable volunteers.

"Far from it being any of my business, but I'd say those puffy red eyes of yours have nothing to do with your onion dicing earlier. You had that oh-woe-is-me look about you when we opened up this morning. Man trouble, no doubt."

"Something like that," I huffed, which wasn't a total lie. I wish it was just man trouble, as Dawn suggested in that fading Glaswegian accent now softened by a Hertfordshire twang following years of living down south. I didn't know her life story, but the bustling woman made of stern stock, benefiting from a whopping bosom and a low centre of gravity, had settled in Fairfield when her husband relocated to this part of the world to work at Vauxhall Motors' Luton Plant sometime back in the late 1960s.

"You're too old to have man trouble," she barked over the sound of clanging baking tins she'd walloped on the oven's hot plate. "You have to train them. Men are simple things … fools. They need a firm hand and lists … detailed lists to keep them in check. Otherwise, hen, they'll cause you all sorts of bother. You hear me? Men need lists."

"Oh," I sniffed.

"My Bobby, when he was alive, although a pain in the backside, knew how to behave because I trained him. I gave him a list of jobs and reminders every single day. And I was careful not to allow him too much time down the bookies or propping up the public bar of the White Horse. Whatever your man is up to, get a hold of the situation. Lists, hen, that's my suggestion. Keep their minds occupied so their heads don't drift and contemplate libertine thoughts."

"Yes … good idea."

"Is this a new boyfriend of yours? I haven't heard you mention a man before. I'd begun to wonder if you were one of those lesbians. I hear it's all the rage these days. Gotta say, although I'm not that way inclined, it kinda makes sense 'cos us women don't need lists, do we?"

"No."

"Right, just need to boil those tatties, and I think we're ready."

"Sorry, Dawn, my mind is elsewhere today."

"Och, give it here." Dawn snatched the peeler. "Go on, I'll do these. You make me a wee cuppa."

I hesitated, a half-peeled Maris Piper still in my grip.

"Go on … tea. Two sugars, my deary." Dawn relieved my hand of the potato and continued. "Remember, I've got two girls just about your age. What with my late Bobby and their dopey husbands, I know all about man trouble. So, what's this fella of yours done, then? Don't tell me … because he didn't have a list, his mind has drifted, and he's been sniffing around some bisom, eh?" Dawn, peeler in hand, paused as she waited for me to glance at her after I'd grabbed the kettle.

"Sorry … bisom?"

"Tart. Hussy. A wanton woman."

"Oh, I see."

"Is that it? Played away, has he?"

While filling the kettle, I pondered whether to enlighten Dawn about my situation, which, since the bank visit on Friday afternoon, had taken a significant turn for the worse.

The customer service manager, Nathan Bridges' boss, was so lovely. Whether her service skills were a product of maturity, wisdom, or just being a woman, I don't know. However, despite the threats Nathan had levied not being retracted, she delivered an assessment of my dire situation with empathy, resulting in me almost apologising to her for putting the bank in that situation caused by my credulous gullibility when being sucked in by Chad Ruger's lies.

Not for a few years now, but I'd previously dabbled in the dating app scene. At first, starting an online dialogue with someone seemed so much easier when I didn't have to face them. Of course, that all went belly up when a few men I'd chatted with suggested we meet for a date. I'd break out in hives just thinking about it. The two I'd managed to go through with – the other four I'd chickened out of before arriving at the pub, one due to being physically sick and thus pebble-dashing the gangway on the bus – could only be described as excruciatingly painful.

Both dates, although a few years older than me, were attractive, attentive, and engaging. Whether just patter, both reckoned my profile picture didn't do me justice. Both acted as perfect gentlemen and, initially, both appeared super keen. Not that I was afforded long to make that assessment because my ruddy shyness muscled in, tied my tongue in knots, initiated debilitating stomach cramps, and delivered what I presume could only be described as a humiliating, protracted, menopausal-styled hot flush, all leading to me ending up spending most of the date in the ladies. Safe to say, it's difficult to form any kind of affinity or relationship with someone when you're suffering chronic diarrhoea, hidden away behind a locked door of a toilet cubicle.

I dropped the dating app as a viable option to find love soon after the second incident. The final straw being when I eventually re-emerged to discover my date had given up waiting, resulting in suffering those smirking, knowing looks as I completed the walk of shame from the bar to the car park. The jilted woman with the stinking bowel issue.

In fact, I gave up all thoughts of dating until Chad sent me a friend request on Facebook. Look, I'm not a total idiot ... I know some people are not real. Fake profiles and all that. Also, I'm usually extremely wary of strangers appearing out of the blue, wanting to make friends.

I'd spent my whole life behind my protective, non-trusting defence shield – right from primary school, hugging the chain-linked fence that circumnavigated the playground as I beady-eyed the other children, when convinced they were all disciples of Satan's, intent on causing me harm – determined no one would wheedle their way in, gain my trust and then hurt me.

However, thirty-odd years after hugging fences during break times, dressed in white socks and pigtails, Chad Ruger, whoever he really was – now suspected he wasn't an executive in the oil industry and definitely not the owner of an ocean-view villa overlooking the Pacific on the idyllic coastline in Monterey – had carved through my defences with the ease of a sharpened knife through the breast of a succulent Thanksgiving turkey.

Clever sod.

Prone to suffering from the occasional flatulence issues when facing high-stress situations but lacking the big personality, not a widow or shower-curtain-ring saleswoman,

I could claim a certain affinity to Del Griffith. Friendless, totally alone and, if what my landlord suggested when bellowing threats through my letterbox yesterday morning was to play out this week, soon to be homeless. Why I thought of John Candy's character was probably down to spending Saturday night demolishing the best part of two bottles of cheap supermarket red and a catering pack of garlic bread when watching that film whilst nursing a box of Kleenex.

Talking of homeless, that's precisely how that clever sod scythed through my defences with such ease. Chad Ruger, not John Candy, just for clarity. Not that I could be classed as a habitual user of social media, finding the gushy posts from acquaintances and celebs about their utterly perfect life all too much to take, plus having little or any interest in posting myself, my few forays into uploading pictures was usually reserved for sharing information about All Saints Refuge.

Chad Ruger, the clever sod, replied to one such post, saying how he also supported his local homeless charity after his brother tragically lost his life following years of drug abuse and sleeping rough. I'd given a thumbs-up response but didn't reply, not giving it a second thought.

A couple of days later, with an accompanying picture of himself, Chad added an update detailing how losing his brother had changed his outlook on life. Now reasonably comfortable, in his early forties with no family to support, and in the memory of his brother, he'd decided to throw himself into helping those less fortunate. This time, probably because his picture appeared similar to Cliff Thorburn, my late father's favourite snooker player and, like him, being an attractive man benefiting from a friendly face, I'd replied. All I'd typed was how inspirational I thought his story was, plus I'd thanked him for sharing.

A few days later, we were chatting via Skype. Then, weeks after, I agreed to spend Christmas with him in Monterey, Chad kindly purchasing my economy ticket. Then, within less than a few months … I know, stupid woman, I'd, unbelievably, loaned him my life's savings when he needed a short-term loan to help him through a 'cash flow' issue.

Until the wee hours of Saturday morning, after the ten minutes spent conducting some investigative surfing regarding all things Cliff Thorburn, a part of me still clung to the idea that Chad wasn't fake. Maybe he'd been involved in an accident, his phone was broken, and he now lay in a hospital bed. Of course, that didn't explain why his Facebook profile no longer existed or the email reply I received from an empathic lady at Monterey County Union Rescue Mission, who politely stated she had no idea who Chad Ruger was.

Suppose I'd invested those ten minutes of internet surfing a few months back. In that case, I'd still be a sad, lonely spinster – not a term I particularly warmed to – but at least I wouldn't class myself as stupid.

The internet is awash with photos of the 1980s snooker superstar, who apparently became the first player to make a 147-maximum break during the world championships. One such image just happened to be identical to the one Chad posted of himself. A dapper man dressed in a tuxedo, sporting a cheerful grin when receiving an award. A works thing, he'd said. I guess with a couple of clicks on Photoshop, the background and trophy changed, and I was suckered in.

Notwithstanding that Dawn wasn't the sort who I'd usually confide in, but what had I got to lose by telling her about my woes? She'd asked, which most didn't. I guessed the worst that could happen would be this parochial, peremptory woman, who, when employing her judgemental, belittling manner, would confirm my stupidity credentials and probably advise me to make a list.

"Dawn."

"I'm still here, hen … peeling these tatties. Thirsty and ready to listen."

"Yes, sorry, tea's on its way."

"Come on, tell all. I know I can come across like a right-old harridan … my two sons-in-law, both wimps, God knows what my girls were thinking when they married those idiots, are terrified of me. Weak men, but that's by the by. Now, listen, hen, I'm nae as fearsome as I seem. Remember, I get by on a meagre pension, but rather than get a paid job, I chose to give up two days a week to cook for those less fortunate than me. I have a good heart and an open ear."

I placed her tea next to the pot of peeled potatoes and took a couple of deep breaths to ready myself. Apart from the senior staff in my bank's customer service team, Dawn was going to be the first person to hear my tragic story.

Thirty minutes later, two more cups of tea brewed and drunk, potatoes boiled and pulverised by Dawn's ham-fists wielding the masher, then creamed and ready to serve, I'd completed relaying my tale of woe. When recounting, out loud and not in my head, what had transpired since the summer, the catalogue of credulous decisions on my part sounded significantly worse.

Stupid woman didn't come close.

Apart from what I took to be withering looks, Dawn hadn't interrupted my flow, which turned into a torrent once I got going. Not that it helped, but I needed to unburden.

"You have got yourself in a wee pickle."

"Yeah … that's one word to describe it. I expect you think me stupid."

"Gullible and maybe a little unworldly, but I wouldnae call ye stupid."

"Hmmm … well, sorry to burden you with my woes." I puffed out my cheeks and checked my watch before grabbing a clean pinny. "Right, I'd better go and open up. I hate the thought of them all lined up, stamping their feet to fend off the cold."

"Give it a minute. Now, have ye talked to our father?"

"Oh, sorry, Dawn, I'm not what you'd call the religious type." Head bowed, I tied the pinny straps with a bow. "My late father used to spout, 'Without religion, there'd be no wars'," I parodied in a baritone voice when glancing up, offering Dawn a pained, tight smile. "Sorry, don't mean to offend. I s'pose praying might now be my only option to prevent me from ending up on the other side of the counter each Sunday." I nodded to the refectory where the lost souls of Fairfield would soon congregate to sample Dawn's fare before retreating to their sleeping bags nestled in shop doorways or enjoying the icy-wind-shielding properties afforded by the side of a Biffa bin.

"Och, nae him up there. I gave up praying when my Bobby was alive. I mean Father Dowding … up at All Saints."

"Oh … who?"

"He's the new vicar, taken over from Harold, who retired in September. An odd'un, if you ask me, and he's got some mighty strange ideas, but I reckon his heart's in the right place."

"Oh … no, but why—"

"'Cos, hen, he's involved with the women's refuge. That place on Chapelfield Road. Now, I think it's for women who've escaped a violent relationship, but I reckon he could swing it for ye to get a place. I'd offer ye a bed at my place, but I only got me a one bed, and the council don't allow tenants taking in lodgers."

"Oh, that is kind, but I'm not homeless yet. I'm hoping I can hold the landlord off for a few weeks. Come the new year, I'm sure I'll find a job … any job," the last two words more of a mutter to myself.

"I'm sure you will," Dawn mumbled, seemingly more engrossed in lifting lids on the industrial-sized bain-marie, checking we were all set. "Anyway, just in case it don't go your way, I'll put in a word with his nibs. The man's terrified of me, so I'm sure he'll come around when I explain your situation. Always good to have a backup plan. That's what I say. I don't reckon it's that pleasant up there, but it's better than the streets."

"Oh, no, thank you. There's no need—"

"Course, there's a need. That landlord of yours is a man, eh?"

"Ehm … yeah."

"There you go, then. What did I tell ye ... men are idiots. Now, go on ... you better let the horde in."

"Okay ... wait for the stampede," I threw over my shoulder in a far cheerier tone than how I felt.

After firing back the top and bottom bolts and swinging open the door, fully expecting to see Harry Wilks toothless, gurning mug facing me – Gummy-Harry always being the head of the queue – I was somewhat surprised to witness a fracas.

Notwithstanding that many of our clientele either sported criminal records, were addicted to class-A drugs, alcoholics not interested in the services AA had to offer, suffered from mental disorders, were just damned unlucky, or all of the above, they would, without fail, fall into line – no pun intended – when it came to queuing for their Sunday lunch. The offer of a free meal tended to quell any disagreement they may harbour towards each other. Most being able to leave their personal troubles – caused and exacerbated by one or more of the aforementioned issues that left them trapped in ever-decreasing circles – at the door.

However, not today, because a Cliff Thorburn lookalike, albeit younger than Chad's fake picture but sporting that famous chevron moustache, appeared embroiled in an argument with Gummy-Harry Wilks and a few of the old boy's peers.

"Ehm ... what's going on?" Due to the tone of my question being nothing more than a polite enquiry, coupled with Gummy-Harry, Super-Glue-Steve and Turpentine-Tom shouting and gesticulating at 'Cliff', my question fell on deaf ears.

I'd had enough.

I could scream.

I'd reached the point when I felt the need to vent my spleen, and I didn't particularly care who was on the receiving end.

"Excuse me. Stop this. Stop!" I bellowed.

The three who didn't look like a famous snooker player, their filthy attire better suited to be on the backs of those extras in the Dickensian Three Cripples Public House, plus him with the moustache, ignored my bellow, favouring raised fists and an exchange of verbal threats. Although, for some bizarre reason, Turpentine-Tom seemed to stagger sideways, clutching his face. Odd, because clearly, from my vantage point at the top of the three stone steps, I could see no one had laid a finger on him.

"Oi!"

That got their attention, plus the thirty-or-so rubberneckers still holding some sort of line formation to my left, albeit now slightly wavey.

Also, I now sported a sore throat.

"Him!" Gummy-Harry pointed at 'Cliff'. "He was trying to push in."

Super-Glue-Steve and Turpentine-Tom nodded in agreement, along with most of those patiently waiting in the now-reformed queue. There was something terribly British about it. Nudity, smoking on a bus, and even sexual activity in a public place would only result in a raised eyebrow and a pronounced tut. But queue jumping, well, that was a capital offence.

"Is that right?" I unintentionally haughtily enquired, feeling like a chastising school ma'am while waiting for 'Cliff' to reply.

"It is," Gummy-Harry butted in. "He reckons he knows you and wasn't trying to queue jump. A frigging lie if there ever was one."

6

Performing a Harry Worth

"Harvey Nicks, darling. One of the few premium department stores left, I'm afraid. Dickie purchased this exquisite ensemble for me last Christmas … right down to the boots. The boy had such an eye for detail. Although it's an Alexander McQueen, I wouldn't normally wear the same threads for two seasons. However, this is what you would call a timeless piece, you know? Of course, he's now dead, like you and me, darling."

"Who? What are you on about?"

"You asked about my gorgeous coat. So, your 'who' question is referring to the shop where my coat was purchased or Mr McQueen?"

"I know what Harvey Nichols is."

"Oh, darling, Alexander McQueen was one of the most famous couturier and fashion designers ever. Gay men are so much better at haute couture than women, don't you think? It must be in their DNA."

"As I said, I have no idea what you're on about."

"Never mind. I'm just saying I'm having to wear last season's attire because shopping is tricky these days."

"The price for being dead and invisible, no doubt."

"Hey, get this …" Deana paused to lower her voice. "This new swish boutique in the High Street was displaying a stunning mustard halter-neck dress in the window … part of their new autumn collection. A must-have frock if ever there was one. First time I've shoplifted and, I can tell you, what a thrill. Course, there were a few odd looks from the shop assistants as the figure-hugging garment floated off the rail before disappearing into my handbag. Rather fortunate because some woman was eyeing it up, and they only had one size ten. Should have seen her face. What an absolute picture," she chortled. "Of course, the only disadvantage of shoplifting is you can't very well try the garments on before taking them."

"Shoplifting! You … stealing."

"Needs must, darling. Needs must."

"Huh. Shoplifters were the scourge of society when I was alive. When we caught them thieving sods pilfering in my shop, we stuck the boot in, I can tell you."

"Very Dickensian of you, darling. No doubt you and your supermarket muscle men didn't enquire about their circumstances and the societal injustices that forced them into a life of crime but chose to act like bovver boys … brutes, I suspect, before slapping them in irons and having them hauled away in a Black Mariah."

"I have no idea where you get these namby-pamby lefty views from. But what I do know … you look like Mrs Claus in that get-up."

"I know," she purred, two-handedly clinging to Terry's biceps as they strolled through town on Sunday morning. "The luscious red velvet and white fur collars and cuffs make it the perfect festive attire."

"Santa's little helper."

"That's me, darling. Of course, when I say collar and cuffs, I'm referring to my coat, not whether my pubes match my hair colouring. Which, of course, they would if I had any. Pubes, not hair, if you see what I mean," Deana snickered.

Terry tutted.

"The fur is faux, of course. We must consider the plight of those little furry minks and chinchillas. My darling Dickie was an avid anti-blood-sport campaigner. Good on him, I say. Course, I didn't get involved. Traipsing across the countryside sabotaging illegal fox hunts dressed in an anorak and a pair of gum boots really wasn't my sort of thing. But I cheered him on from the sidelines. Metaphorically speaking, of course."

"Fox hunting is illegal?"

"Yes, darling. The lovely Mr Blair banned it years ago."

"That … that lefty loon, Labour Prime Minister, you bang on about."

"Oh, don't be such a festive grunge. I'm not getting into an argument about politics again. Anyway, although claiming I look like a sexy Mrs Claws, I presume you approve of my coat."

"It's a bit full-on. If you weren't invisible, I think you'd be attracting attention in your Santa suit."

"Oh, darling, it's so much more than a Santa suit," she purred. "Of course, I have a sexy red number in the wardrobe, which is exactly as you imagine, I'm sure ... a skimpy little silk thing leaving little to the imagination. However, dear boy, now my Dickie is waiting for me on a celestial fluffy cloud, said sexy outfit is solely reserved for my Clara's eyes. Don't protest, but I'm exclusively hers now."

"Thank frig for that," Terry muttered through a cough.

"Don't mutter, Terence." Deana checked her stride, causing Terry to halt and turn around.

"What now?"

"I'm just adjusting my attire, darling. A girl must take pride in her look."

"You're invisible."

"That doesn't excuse not keeping one's appearance perfecto." Deana peered at her reflection in a greetings-card shop window, fiddling with her fur collar and straightening her belt. "Not that I would freely admit I've ever entered such an establishment but, last year, I purchased this black clinch belt from that awful clothing store beginning with P. It's perfect for this coat because it pinches in my waist and accentuates my rather alluring hourglass figure."

"If you say so."

"I do so."

"Come on, woman, we need to get a move on."

"Hold up there," Deana nipped to the corner of the window before performing a 'Harry Worth', giggling as she did when the parting of her 'Santa' coat revealed her dangerously short dress and knee-length boots. An act leaving little to the imagination as her levitating star jump reflection displayed more leg and thigh than could be considered decent.

"Jesus, woman, what are you doing? I can see what you had for breakfast."

"Oh, lucky you, darling. I'm having fun. That's what cheery folk do at Christmas. My father would always perform a 'Harry Worth' to make my brother and I giggle."

"I'm made up for you. Now, can we get going, please?" Terry hissed as Deana performed two more 'star jumps', purposefully waving her leg forward and out to up the outrageous stakes.

"Alright, Mr Grinch. I'm coming," Deana threw Terry a look, a raised eyebrow to accompany her narrowed eyes. "You're a Grunge, Terence. I want to have fun. Lots of, I might add. God knows I'm due some after three weeks with Ponderous-Petunia. Now, cheer up. If the Grinch can see his way clear to love Chrimbo, so can you." Deana retook his arm and fell into step as they headed towards the less salubrious end of town. "So, what was this woman's name again?"

"Janice Keelan."

"Ah, yes, that's it. Never been too keen on the name Janice. There was this horrid girl at school with the same name. Right nasty little shit she was. Bullied me rotten, she did."

"Really?"

"Yes, really. I wasn't always so confident and forthright, you know?"

"I can't imagine you anything but."

"Butter wouldn't melt was me when in knee-high socks and a grey gymslip."

"What happened?"

"Puberty, darling. I became a woman. Soon discovering the pleasure my womanly curves have to offer."

"Hmmm. Come on, I think it's this way." Terry nudged Deana into a side street. "Used to be the old Methodist chapel, back in the day. Now it's a soup kitchen."

"And this Janice … according to The-Powers-That-Be, we're responsible for her situation."

"That's what that De Ath woman reckoned."

"And they didn't divulge anything else, apart from the fact we've apparently caused some problem for the woman when solving one of your offspring's little issues?"

"Damian is your son, too."

"Quite right. Our boy seems settled with that little tart Courteney. Unfortunately, I caught up with old Sidders again last week. Like the proverbial rotten penny, the old grunge popped around again like a lost puppy. Apparently, The-Powers-That-Be are hunting him down … he's a spook on the run."

"I imagine that lot up there are none too chuffed about his murdering spree."

"No, probably not. Although the dolorous old bore did help us out on that mission. I sent him packing, of course. Anyway, while trying to evade capture, old Sidders has been keeping tabs on our boy. He mentioned that Damian's actually gone ahead and married the girl, and they now have a child on the way."

"Oh, that's good news. I liked Courteney."

"Yes … would that be her potty mouth or the fact there's no denying she's rather easy on the eye?"

"Well, I just think she'll be good for our boy. Hey, we're going to be grandparents."

"Hmmm. Anyway, despite the girl's less-than-savoury past, you're probably right. All's well, that ends well."

"I just hope he's not the cause of this Janice woman's issues."

"Oh, Lord no. Let's hope not."

"Or Kim or Ginny, for that matter."

"No, absolutely, darling."

"But, as Miss De Ath said, one of our missions caused the issue with this Janice woman. So, I suppose there has to be some connection to one of them."

"Yes, darling. It's all very cryptic."

"How are my two daughters?"

"Tickety-boo. I've not kept close to what's happening, but I know Kimmy is with her dashing Italian boyfriend. And Ginny is all loved up with that rather hunky policeman."

"That's good. They all deserved to be happy."

"They most certainly do. Anyway, this De Ath woman said nothing else? No clues to point us in the right direction?"

"'Fraid not. You'll know better than me that they can be a bit tight-lipped."

"Yes … quite so. I did question their reluctance to supply full disclosure on a previous mission, and the response was curt, at best. Apparently, we have to prove our worth rather than having everything handed to us on a plate. One imperious agent incredulously suggested that spectral acts were nothing but child's play, and anyone was capable of making moaning noises like a ghost."

"I imagine you set him straight."

"Of course, darling. No man speaks to me in such a way, dead or alive. I firmly but politely informed the tenebrous dead grot that being an effective ghost took precision planning and high levels of skill and natural talent. All of which I demonstrate my prowess in that particular field of spookery."

Terry side-eyed her, smirking as he guided Deana to make a left at the next corner.

"Degree level, Terence. Before you even think about mocking me, I'm a PhD doctorate-level spook."

"Apart from when your performance is pedestrian."

"Hmmm. Yes, well, I'd rather forget that shocking accusation, if you don't mind? Remember, although Clara and I are an item, I want to have fun during this mission, darling. It is Christmas, after all."

"I'll try my best. I suppose it'll be better than another game of Monopoly. It'll be too soon if I never get told to go back to Old Kent Road again."

"I preferred advance to Mayfair … more befitting my social standing. Oh, talking of which, going by the state of that gaggle of bedraggled, stinking hobos, I suggest this isn't Mayfair but the soup kitchen where this Janice girl volunteers. A sloth of tramps … the snaking line of the great unwashed."

"That a line straight out of your lefty, socialist, caring society songbook, is it?"

"Sorry?" Deana halted, pulling Terry back. "What are you talking about?"

"Stinking hobos ... the great unwashed. Not exactly the mantra you like to bash out regarding how we must all chip in and do our bit to help the common man."

"Oh ... well, I was just pointing out that those poor chaps and chapesses clearly indicate this is where we'll find the girl. I had no intention of denigrating those less fortunate, just merely pointing out that their attire and general bedraggled appearances suggest we've arrived. And, as I told you, I'm not discussing politics with you. I'm super proud of my socialist principles ... something I fully believe will support attaining the points total required to avoid spending all perpetuity in the company of Satan. Somewhere where you will end up unless you start softening the edges of your fascist ideology."

"Socialism," Terry tutted, disparagingly shaking his head at Deana. "Come on, let's get on with it."

"Hmmm ... I'm not liking your tone, Terence. Remember, it's Christmas. Now, what's the plan?" Deana retook his arm, indicating they should head towards the line of rough sleepers, all with bowed heads while stamping their feet to ward off the biting chill.

"The plan, dear Santa's little helper ... I'm going to strike up a conversation with Janice and see if I can identify how she's connected to Kim, Damian, or Ginny."

"Your three children. All of whom we saved during our three previous missions."

"Indeed."

"And how exactly do you plan to get her talking, hmmm?"

"By employing my razor-sharp wit and charm."

"And pray, what do you expect me to do while you dazzle the girl with your repartee and persiflage?"

"Mingle … see what you can pick up from any of the natives."

"Oh, yuk … scurvy and rickets, by the look of that lot."

"And don't think, just because you say so, as in the political discussion is closed, but I refer you to a quote by Mrs Thatcher … the problem with socialism is that you eventually run out of other people's money. The woman was an inspiration. The product of your lefty beliefs is high rates of progressive taxation, causing the dismantlement of business enterprise, loss of jobs for the common man, and ultimately leading to queues of unfortunates looking for handouts like this lot."

"Piffle! You're going to hell, Terence. The precise place I expect *she* is right now while enjoying tea and cakes with old Nick himself."

"Whatever. Now, wait there while I go and assess the lie of the land. Looks like this place isn't open yet, so I'll see if we can nip in for a chat before this lot piles in."

"Off you go. I'll wait in the wings, looking gorgeous," Deana shouted after him as Terry trotted to the front of the line.

"Hello there," Terry cheerily addressed a gurning man. Due to his weathered skin, salt-and-pepper beard, and stooped posture, suggesting the man at the front of the queue was a seasoned street dweller, Terry found it tricky to pin down his age.

"You got a spare smoke?" he growled.

"Say I give you the packet ..." Terry paused as he rummaged in his coat pocket, a cashmere overcoat borrowed from Deana's darling Dickie's wardrobe, before extracting a packet of Marlboro. Although he'd given up since the summer – due to a complete smoking ban enforced while in 'limbo' – like any ex-smoker, it hadn't taken much to start again when spotting Deana's cigarettes on the kitchen windowsill.

"Yeah, okay ... what's the catch, then?"

"The catch, my friend ... uh-huh, hang on," Terry pulled his hand back when the chap reached for the packet. "I just need to nip in front of the queue to have a word with a lady inside."

"Queue jump?"

"Well, I'm not here for—"

"I've been 'ere for over an hour, mate. Freezing my bollocks off. We don't allow queue jumping," his lisping growl accompanied by spit due to a lack of teeth. "You, with your fancy coat, can wait your turn." Akin to a lizard's tongue, his arm shot forward and made a grab for the cigarettes in Terry's raised hand.

Before he knew what had occurred, Terry found himself in a tussle with the three men holding the podium positions in the queue: Gold, the gummy chap, digging his nails into Terry's skin while attempting to relieve Terry of the packet of smokes. Silver, a man with disturbing red eyes, grappling with Terry's free arm. And Bronze, a younger chap with a constant sniff, who attempted a spot of eye gouging when muscling into the gap between his compatriots.

"Terry, darling, from where I'm standing, it appears that wit and charm you mentioned earlier isn't cutting the mustard with these three.

Why don't you let go of the cigarettes, hmmm?" Deana, now circling the four men embroiled in what could only be described as a street brawl, halted behind Bronze. "Darling, are you alright in there? Or would you appreciate some support from your ghostly, socialist guide?"

"Christ, don't just stand there. Do something!" Terry hissed while attempting to extradite himself from the clutches of Gold and Silver.

"Oh, you sound just like Dick Dastardly, darling," she snickered like Muttley.

"Deana!"

"Alright, calm yourself. Not that I'm one for inflicting pain on those less fortunate, but needs must in times of crisis. I'll perform my Harry Potter invisible cloak routine ... see if that sorts this little issue your charm and wit have landed you in."

"Whatever," Terry grunted, trying to avoid the eye gouger and maintain his balance on the icy tarmac.

"Please accept my antecedent apology for this." Deana then walloped Bronze's right ear with her raised gloved hand. The well-timed strike effectively halted his attempt to gouge Terry's eye as he staggered sideways, clutching his ear while spinning chaotically around when trying to identify the perpetrator.

"What the ... who?" Bronze crinkled his forehead, confused that the line of 'rubbernecking' compatriots were all at least a couple of yards away, and it appeared none were close enough to be guilty of the wallop that his glowing red ear could attest to.

"I'm so sorry about that. I truly empathise with your plight, but roughing up my Terry is beastly and unacceptable." Deana waved her gloved hand at the man, who now accusingly scanned the line of

rubberneckers breaking ranks from their queuing positions. "You do realise I'll have to get my sheepskin gloves dry-cleaned. Lord knows what might have been deposited on them off that filthy face of yours."

"Oi!"

"Oh, by golly." Deana spun around to put a face to who'd rather uncouthly bellowed 'Oi'. "Good grief, Terence, I do hope this isn't Janice. What a rough loudmouthed fishwife. Very befitting of such an establishment, I'm sure."

"Him!" the gummy chap exclaimed. "He was trying to push in," he added when letting go of Terry's arm in favour of jabbing an accusing digit.

"Is that right?" the fishwife woman asked. Deana thought in a slightly less fishwife-ish tone.

"It is," the gummy chap confirmed. "He reckons he knows you and wasn't trying to queue jump. A frigging lie if there ever was one."

"Oh, darling, here we go. This woman wearing that ridiculous Elf-on-the-shelf pinny must be this Janice woman. I have to say, not that I want to portray my bitchy side, but this unfortunate girl is nothing but frightfully bland. She actually, and somewhat unbelievably, I have to say, makes your plain little Kimmy seem almost appealing to the eye."

While there seemed to be some sort of Mexican standoff – Gold, Silver and Bronze holding position, encircling Terry – Deana nipped up two steps to inspect the woman at close quarters, who now seemed to be clearing her throat after her boorish hollering.

"To be balanced about it, she's blessed with a divine skin tone which belies her age. And, I wouldn't be surprised if there's a half-decent figure

hiding under those awful rags which I suspect come from that unmentionable 'P' shop, if not the scouts' jumble sale."

"Look, there's been a misunderstanding," Terry threw in, keeping a wary eye on his attackers as he gifted the cigarettes to the gummy bloke. "I don't want to butt in, but could I just have five minutes of your time … you might find it beneficial."

"Really? Who are you? What d'you want?"

"Oh, ruddy hell, talk about halitosis!" Deana, who'd been up close and personal, sporting a pinched face when inspecting who she believed to be this Janice woman, hopped back down the two steps. "She might have some alluring qualities, but her ruddy breath could strip paint! That revolting expulsion should be bottled and used as a military-grade chemical weapon."

"Ehm …" Terry paused his reply to her perfectly reasonable question when distracted by Deana's exaggerated hand wafting.

"She certainly doesn't need to worry about vampires coming near."

"My name is Terry, and I might be in a position to … well, to—"

"Careful, darling, let's have none of your silly claims about being a dead guardian angel. I take it your charm and wit isn't exactly firing on all cylinders today?"

"Janice, can we come in now?" the gummy chap enquired after counting the cigarettes in the gifted packet, offering two each to Silver and Bronze.

"Yes, sorry, Harry. We're ready."

Deana joined Terry as they watched the woman usher in the waiting line. "Darling, you seem a little dumbstruck. I thought you had a plan?"

Before Terry could answer, the woman who'd stopped the hand ushering when the queue morphed from an orderly line to something of a stampede pointed at him.

"Is this about Chad? It's just … it's just, you look a bit like him. The moustache. Y'know, the retro Cliff Thorburn look."

"Oh, how funny. You do a bit, darling. Why on earth you've allowed that bushy caterpillar to regrow, I have no idea. I told you before, highly unfashionable and affords you that shockingly outdated '70s porn star look."

7

Please, Sir, I Want Some More

"Chad?" the man who introduced himself as Terry asked.

For a split second, I'd wondered if this dapper chap could be Chad. Meaning my knight in shining armour had come good, not conned me out of my life savings, was actually real, and hadn't answered his phone or emails because his phone and laptop had been in flight mode when zipping across the pond.

I know, a stupid thought from a stupid woman.

Unless that journey went via the moon, it only took about eleven hours to fly from California, not five days. Also, this bloke was probably ten years younger than Chad, who'd claimed to be in his early forties. And, not forgetting, he'd introduced himself as Terry.

"Do you know something about him? Chad, that is," I asked, keeping my stupidity flowing. Although an obviously ridiculous question, the ever-fading hope that I hadn't been taken for a fool still hung in there by its fingernails. As 'they' say, it's the hope that kills you.

"No, sorry, I don't know a Chad."

"Hmmm ... the plot thickens. Chad. Interesting name." Deana tapped her gloved finger to her lips before whisking it away when remembering where it had been. *"An American name, I suggest, darling."*

"No shit."

I glanced in the direction where, following a pregnant pause, he'd shot out a 'no shit' comment after stating he didn't know of a Chad.

"Alright, tetchy Terence. I'm merely just trying to perform my ghostly guide duties, such as providing information and short synopses of the situation when required. Now, as I said, I suspect there is an issue with whoever this Chad is. Our first clue in our burlesque whodunnit mission. I refer to the absurdity, not the striptease variety, of course."

"Right, sorry, of course, you don't know a Chad. I suspect no one does," I mumbled when Terry turned to face me again. That 'hope' now dancing on my grave. To add to the aforementioned issues, when pondering that Terry couldn't be Chad, I realised this bloke didn't possess an American accent either. Oh, Janice, my mind screamed, admonishing my desperate and frankly witless thoughts.

"Just ... if you've got a moment?"

"Not really," I nodded to the line funnelling past. "Look, what's this about?" I asked, stepping aside to make room for one of our regulars. A lady whose name, I'm ashamed to say, I didn't know, and we volunteers hadn't attributed a moniker because, despite her size, she was quiet and unassuming. Not that we called Harry, Gummy-Harry or Steve, Super-Glue Steve to be nasty, but due to this lady only being able to fit through the door by shimmying sideways, it would mean any nickname afforded the poor woman would probably be unkind when referring to her ample frame.

"Let's just say that I'm aware you might need some help."

"Terry? What's the plan? You don't have a good track record in these sorts of conversations. I'm concerned you're going to blow it with some stupid claim that you're a guardian angel. Which you are, but not hugely believable, I might suggest."

"Oh, right. That's very kind of you. Sorry, as far as I know, we're not looking for any more volunteers. If you speak to Helen at All Saints … I'm not sure of her actual title, but I know she helps out there. This refuge for the homeless is affiliated with that Church. I'm sure she could let you know if there are any other charitable organisations you could support." I stepped sideways as Pervy-Perry shuffled past. Not that Perry was large-framed and thus needed to afford him adequate space, but he was known for wandering hands, so any woman was best to stay at least a yard from his reach. "Was it just for Christmas you were looking to volunteer for, or more long-term?" I asked this Terry bloke, stepping back up the steps, safe in the knowledge I was well clear of Perry's strike range.

"Oh, no," he shook his head and held up a defensive palm. "Apologies. I haven't explained myself well enough," he nervously chuckled. "I wasn't looking to volunteer—"

"How's that wit and charm of yours coming along, darling?" Deana quipped, pawing at his biceps again. "I must say, Old Garlic-Breath here doesn't appear overly enchanted by your patter."

"Sorry, I'm not sure what you're asking. Look, I must get on." I offered a tight smile at the man who I thought could play the part of a young Cliff Thorburn if they ever make a film of his life story, before ushering in the last in line and heading back to assist Dawn, who I expect wouldn't hold her tongue regarding her displeasure that I'd left her to serve lunch on her own.

"It's Janice Keelan, yes?" Terry called after me.

Halted in my tracks by his question, I swivelled around and narrowed my eyes at him. Besides being confused about how he knew my name, his odd, somewhat exaggerated arm movements and mutterings surprised me.

"Terence, please don't swat me like a fly. Ask politely if you want me to let go of your arm."

"Ehm ... yeah ... how d'you ... who are you?" I asked, stepping tentatively back towards the open door.

"That's difficult to say."

"Really?" I bit back with an uncharacteristically sharp tongue.

"Yeah ... um, for now, let's just say that I'm aware you've landed in a difficult situation. A bit of a pickle."

"Pickle," I parroted.

"Yeah ... pickle."

"Good God, if this is your charm and wit, I'm amazed you ever managed to woo any woman. I seem to remember you being a little more forthright back in that hotel room in '83. If you're not boring her half to death, you're definitely boring the knickers off me! Not that I'm wearing any, of course."

"Janice!" boomed Dawn above the chatter inside the refectory.

"Oh, I've got to go." I bolted back inside, a smidge concerned about who that man was, how he knew my name, and his 'pickle' comment, but the wrath of Dawn was a greater pull. "Sorry, Dawn, I'm here," I panted when barrelling into the kitchen.

"Where the hell … och, never mind, you take that side," Dawn nodded to the vegetable pots and the serving spoons that lay strewn at odd angles where she'd flung them while frantically zipping back and forth when piling up Gummy-Harry and Super-Glue-Steve's plates, who both now shuffled away to grab a seat. As per usual, Harry Wilks had gobbled most of the offerings whilst on the move. His plate would be half empty by the time he'd parked the seat of his stained combats onto one of the eclectic mix of donated chairs.

Grabbing two utensils, mash ladle in my right and perforated spoon for the carrots in my left, I quickly fell into my well-practised routine of synchronised plate-filling, enabling us to pick up the pace, move the line through, and put a halt to the grumblings regarding slow service now emanating from the back of the queue.

"What were ye doing out the front?" Dawn enquired as she expertly dolloped spoonfuls of braising-steak stew. "You'll catch ye death out there in this weather."

"I was chatting with some bloke."

"I'd have thought once bitten twice shy might have tempered your enthusiasm in that respect, hen."

"Oh no, it wasn't like that—"

"Och, it wasn't Father Dowding, I take it? He's been threatening to pop in for a few weeks now."

"No, I don't think so. Of course, I've never met the man, but I can't say he looked much like a vicar."

Whilst in full flow with my mash and carrot ladling, I pondered who that Terry bloke could be and if he was still outside waiting to talk to me. My mind raced through the possibilities: a 'heavy' employed by my sadistic landlord, a bailiff serving an eviction notice, or a private investigator hired by my bank to gather information on my activities. Well, that polite customer services manager had been pretty clear when employing her silent assassin-styled smile after informing me that the money owed would need to be recovered. Hmmm, perhaps I'd lost all sense of proportion. Whoever the chevron-moustached chap was, he knew nothing of the man who'd conned me.

"Thank the Lord for small mercies. I wouldnae want Father Dowding to visit today. Not while we're short-handed and in this mess." Dawn hollered her reply over the scraping cutlery and chatter before wagging her ladle at Red-Box-Ray, a well-known rough sleeper who'd claimed the old telephone box down by the river after BT decommissioned it some years back. When the company attempted to oust Ray, there'd been an online petition with thousands of the town's folk saying he was part of the community, many donating curtains and other soft furnishings to help Ray spruce it up. Someone had even donated him a foot-high battery-operated fibre-optic Christmas tree this year. I'd often wonder how the old boy managed in the tight space and whether he slept upright or curled in a ball. "Raymond, like everyone else, ye only getting one spoonful," she advised Ray, jutting her chin forward to enforce her point as he held his plate up, Oliver-Twist-please-sir-I-want-some-more style.

"Why?" I asked.

Dawn shot me a look.

"Oh, no, I mean, why was Father Dowding planning on coming in?" I clarified when walloping a hearty dollop of creamed mash onto Ray's plate. A mixture of fear that I could soon be joining him on the other side of the counter and his heart-melting Mark-Lester-doe-eyes being the cause of my extra-large serving.

"New broom, I think, hen. Showing his face to the troops. Old Father Mackie never took much interest, but this laddie has his finger in every pie. We need to make sure we're shipshape 'cos I suspect he'll be in next week with it being Christmas Day."

Although Dawn had earlier suggested Father Dowding was terrified of her, I mused how he'd clearly made an impression on the formidable woman who favoured portraying her harridan old witch qualities instead of that kind-hearted nature that lurked beneath the surface.

"Not seen your face before, laddie." I heard Dawn call out to one of the stragglers as I ferried a few empty stainless-steel pots to the sink. "Grab yourself a wee plate … we've just enough left for you. Fine coat you've got, I must say."

With my hand in the sink preparing to start the cleanup, I shot a look over my shoulder when connecting Dawn's comment and that man wearing an expensive overcoat from earlier.

"No, I'm not here for … I'm not homeless, I'm …"

"Technically, you are, darling. By the very nature of being dead, all ghosts are homeless. Well, if you discount a wooden box six feet under, that is."

"I just want a word with Janice, if I may?"

"I must say, it stinks in here. Most unpleasant. I can't determine if that's the lingering stench of Old Garlic-breath, the clientele, whatever that sludge is sloshing about in that serving dish, or a combination of all three."

"Well, I'm not her keeper." Dawn raised an eyebrow at me. "I take it this is the fella who courted your attention earlier?"

"Oh, you again. I'm kinda busy, I'm afraid." I turned and wiped my hands on my pinny, frowning at Dawn when this Terry bloke became distracted by the remnants of Dawn's stew and performed that odd hand waving from earlier.

"Deana … stop it," he hissed.

Dawn shot me a look before turning back to Terry. "Who you talking to there, laddie? You know if …" Dawn's sentence trailed away when, like Terry, she also became distracted by the serving dish. "Mary, mother of Jesus," she muttered, making the sign of the cross.

"Yuk!" Deana exclaimed, pulling a face after licking her finger. "Lord knows what ghastly stock she's shoved in this. Nigella, she isn't, that's for sure. But the Devil's food it is! A rancid feculent pot of slop that's probably poisoned the lot of them."

"Stop it!" Terry hissed again.

Whatever strange affliction had gripped this man was his business. However, with the hem of my pinny still in my hands, I padded over to see what had caused Dawn's jaw to sag as she gawped at the remnants of the pot of stew and repeatedly crossed herself.

"Dawn, you alright?" I peered at what appeared to be where someone or something had written in the dregs of the gravy with their finger. "Oh ... how ... weird."

Deana! The Demon Diva

"Who on earth wrote that in there?" although a reasonable question to ask, I didn't expect anyone to answer.

"Sorry, darling ... just couldn't help myself. Oh, look at them two. They look like they've seen a ghost. Well, come to think of it, they have. You, my darling," she tittered.

"Laddie, who stuck their finger in my stew?" Dawn asked, head bowed, seemingly unable to tear her eyes from the gravy writing.

"You really don't want to know," Terry huffed.

"Well, if it wasn't me and it wasn't you ... I think we're going to need Father Dowding ... there's an evil spirit about."

"Oh, darling, this could be an issue if this woman with the largest pair of Cupid's kettle drums I've ever laid my eye upon is planning on summoning up some cleric to exorcise the place. According to my Clara, some, although not many, I hasten to add, persons of the cloth, to coin a phrase to cover all faiths, can actually see us ghostly guides. Clara, the darling girl, experienced a frightfully awkward situation on a previous mission when a local imam spotted her. There was a proper old to-do, and she got bumped off that mission on to another. The love has obviously been avoiding the mosque and the surrounding streets ever since. I think, Terence, this may be an impromptu time for a tactical retreat."

8

Ooh ... You Are Awful

"Hello, Dawn ... blimey O'Riley, it looks like it's all go in here," the man who'd barrelled in chuckled as he scanned around the noisy refectory. "Full house, I see. Oh, I don't think you've met my daughter Ellen." He laid a hand on the girl's shoulder and peered down at her. "Ellen, say hello to Dawn."

The girl with a button nose and eyes sadder than mine, and that's really saying something, offered a look to her father that suggested the request to open her mouth horrified her.

"Come on, Silly-Billy, say hello," he encouraged. However, I detected a hint of irritation at having to ask the girl twice.

"Hello," Ellen squeaked, offering a shy smile to the floor as she blushed and continued to fiddle with the drawstrings on her anorak.

"Bashful is our Ellen—"

"Oh, Father Dowding, as if summoned by our Lord himself, you're just in time." Dawn laid her hand on her chest and puffed out her red-veined cheeks.

"Are you alright, Dawn? You're looking a little flustered. Not like you, I must say?"

"Dawn, I'm not sure we should mention—"

"Ah, you must be … don't tell me, Janet, yes?" Father Dowding interrupted me, thrusting out his hand.

"It's Janice," I corrected him in a whisper borrowed from Ellen while running my hand through my ponytail before taking his proffered hand, somewhat surprised by his iron-fist grip and pronounced forthright shake. I offered a pained smile similar to his daughter's in response to his blithe grin to use one of Dawn's favoured descriptions.

Those few seconds in his company suggested Father Dowding was one of those lucky people full of mirth who could see the positive in any given situation, irrespective of how dire. I guess that's the raison d'être for being a vicar, along with faith, of course.

Lucky sod.

As Dawn had earlier suggested, if I decide to confide in him regarding my current debacle of a situation, thus securing a bed up at the women's refuge if my landlord followed through with his threats of eviction, I had him pegged as the sort who harboured that ability to discover that elusive silver lining in that somewhat nebulous, ominously foreboding cloud which cloaked my life.

While the handshake continued a few seconds longer than was usually acceptable when being introduced to a stranger, I contemplated that maybe Dawn's suggestion held some merit. If this man could inject some positivity and perhaps root out some tiny glimmer of hope to guide me forward, then it was probably worth the risk of burdening a second person with my tale of woe. Although, despite rapidly running out of options, turning to any faith wasn't my thing ... yet.

As he released my hand, I noticed Dawn surreptitiously swish the ladle to eradicate the evidence of evil spirits, if that's what it was. I can only assume she'd decided not to raise the subject due to him visiting with his young daughter in tow. The Hello Kitty fan, just noticing her on-brand hair slide, appeared too fragile to be part of a conversation about demons with a penchant for gravy writing.

Not very Christmassy, eh?

It was frigging odd, though. I mean, who is Deana? An oddness that coincided with the strange man with that moustache.

Hmmm.

"Thank you so much, Janet, for your support," Father Dowding boomed in a rich baritone voice, each word enunciated with a clarity that bespoke education and intelligence, breaking my thoughts free from demons and divas. "I was only saying to Dawn last week that it's down to the kind hearts of the volunteers offering their time and favour to the cause that we're able to support those less fortunate."

"Oh, err ..." I ran my hand through my ponytail again. "No ... I mean, yes, no problem. Anyway, I enjoy it. I like doing it." After trotting out that drivel, blushing at my 'I like doing it' comment, I decided not to correct him regarding my name. I mean, what did it matter?

"Are you looking forward to Christmas, Ellen?" Dawn asked, morphing into Mrs Doubtfire mode to presumably not scare the poor child half to death. By the looks of it, that wouldn't be too difficult to achieve.

Ellen nodded but didn't look up, shuffling her pink 'Hello Kitty' rubber boots. An involuntary motion, tic if you like, that I suspected to be a by-product of her shyness. The poor girl looked as comfortable in strangers' company as yours truly.

"Sorry, Dawn," Father Dowding whispered. "It's tough, you know. What with it being the first Christmas since … well, you know."

"Aye … I'm sure, Father, you'll all make it special for the wee lassie."

"No need for formalities, Dawn. Call me Niall when I'm free from those blessed, uncomfortable dog collars. Wearing those damn things is like being trussed up in a straitjacket," he chuckled. "Of course, some call me all sorts, but best not repeated around little ears, eh?" he grinned while placing his hands on the side of his daughter's head.

I considered Dawn's earlier comment to be an exaggeration or a blatant lie. I struggled to see how anyone could intimidate this man. Despite Dawn's bellicose demeanour, her claim that Father Dowding was terrified of her belied what stood before me.

Some people project a certain aura. A confidence you're either born with or was thrashed into you at some public school. His not posh but eloquent diction suggested he'd attended something of that ilk. Niall afforded the look of the upper classes. Those sorts whose aplomb wasn't brash or ostentatious but the quiet assurance of a man who moved through life with the ease of one who knows that the ground will always rise to meet his step. Whether there was a deliberate carelessness to his just-out-of-bed appearance, suggesting he was above the trivialities of meticulous grooming, or he was just oblivious, I couldn't tell.

Nevertheless, it was clear Niall was a man entirely at ease in his own skin, unburdened by the expectations of society.

"I must say I like your Christmas jumper." In wonder and somewhat surprised by the connotation of the wording, I read aloud the slogan written underneath a grinning Rudolph, blushing like the depicted picture of the cartoon reindeer's face as I did. "At Christmas … vicars do it with amazing grace."

"Oh, yes, rather fun, don't you think?" He petted his daughter's luscious, long, almost jet-black hair, presumably inherited from the mother's side due to Niall's unruly mop being that nondescript mouse colour most are blessed with, including me.

"Yes, I s'pose," I nervously tittered, noticing Dawn's sour-face disapproval of said festive attire.

Niall nudged his daughter. "Ellen, tell Dawn and Janet who you thought that lady was we just bumped into."

Ellen looked up at her father and shook her head.

"Go on," he encouraged.

"You can whisper it to me if you like?" Dawn suggested when bending over the counter, her walloping frontage spreading sideways as her whopping chest, which probably required scaffolding supports, forced her tunic to the precipice of splitting when smothering a significant portion of the still-warm bain-marie.

Ellen shook her head and glanced down at her boots.

"Sorry, Dawn," Niall mouthed, petting his daughter's hair again. "She doesn't speak much."

"Och, the poor love."

"Ellen thought that lady was Mrs Father Christmas," he chuckled.

"What lady would that be?" Dawn asked without looking up.

"That's what I was going to ask you. Intrigued … and I must say I'm a little surprised to see a couple like that coming out of here, of all places."

"What couple?" I asked as Dawn shot a quizzical look up at Niall.

"The couple who were just leaving," Niall gestured to the door by way of jabbing a finger over his shoulder. "The woman in the red coat hanging onto the arm of some bloke sporting a wicked eighties-style moustache. Very retro …" Niall lowered his voice a couple of octaves and leaned forward before continuing. "I shouldn't say, but the woman dressed in that Santa coat was showing a bit too much leg if you get my drift."

"A man with a moustache … like Cliff Thorburn, or Magnum … Tom Selleck?"

"Yes, that's him. As you say, just like them two. My father, God bless his ʻsoul, loved the old snooker. Dracula Ray Reardon, Grinder Thorburn, Terry Griffiths, the Griff from the Valleys, and not forgetting the Hurricane, himself, good old Higgins."

"And he was arm in arm with a woman dressed in a Santa coat?"

"Yes, as I say, red with white collar and cuffs, but the slit at the front perhaps a little too revealing. The woman will catch her death wandering around with all that … that, well, you know … naked thigh on show. If she wasn't so well-heeled looking, I'd have said she was a working girl, if you catch my drift."

"Oh, Father, please," Dawn admonished him.

Niall held up an apologetic hand.

"Not in front of the wee lassie and not from your mouth, please."

"Apologies. What were they in here for? I must say the chap was wearing a coat that looked to me like it must have cost a few quid. I can't imagine they were in need of charity."

"Cheers, Dawny, nice bit of scran that," Gummy-Harry called out as he popped his licked-clean plate onto the trolley provided before extracting a cigarette from the packet gifted by that man with the moustache. Who, apparently, unless the vicar was hallucinating, which he must have been, left here with a woman dressed in a Santa suit. "Perhaps I can grab a Christmas kiss and cuddle for me afters next week, eh? Make an old boy happy finding those two bazookas in my Christmas stocking." He offered a wink and a pronounced gurn.

"Harry Wilks, ye be getting nothing of the sort. Be off with ye, man."

With a shoulder shrug and a couple of hearty sniffs before heading to the door, Harry inspected his tailor-made smoke as if it be the consolation prize after Dawn had made it abundantly clear with her rebuke and hand wafting that there'd be no festive smooching.

"Now, mind how ye go there, Harry."

"Hello, there. I'm Father Dowding from All Saints. Nice to meet you." Niall stepped into his path, thrusting out that forthright arm of his.

"Oh, ehm … vicar, you say?" Harry, appearing uncomfortable, either due to being in the company of the man who obviously didn't mix in his social circle, or because Niall just happened to be a man of the cloth, or perhaps both, nervously took the proffered hand whilst glancing at Dawn for support. "Look, sorry, vicar, I … ehm … I wasn't being … well, I was rude. Sorry, Dawny."

"Och, don't fret. Not much can offend me … as a bonny lass from Glasgae, I've heard my fair share of words and suggestions to make a fair maiden blush, I can tell ye."

"I don't think you meant anything by it, did you, Harry?" Niall clamped both hands around Harry's, offering that mirthful grin.

"No, Father … apologies."

"As I thought. I'm sure you'll be respectful from now on." Although Niall still held that warming smile, his tone wasn't suggesting but demanding that Harry change his attitude in the presence of females, not to mention the shrinking violet still inspecting the toes of her boots. Not that I thought Ellen would understand the term bazookas that Gummy-Harry was referring to. I wondered if I should introduce Niall to Pervy-Perry.

"Yeah, course."

"Good man. That's what I thought you'd say."

I spotted Harry's Adam's apple jump. I had a sneaking suspicion there would be less lip from Gummy-Harry over the coming weeks.

"So, tell me, young Harry, how are we doing here … at the refuge?"

"Ehm …" Harry glanced down and winced at his crushed fingers still held vice-like by our chirpy cleric's hands. "Yeah, great. Dawny … ehm, Dawn makes a cracking bit of scran. Well, all the cooks do." Harry nodded at me. "And Janice keeps us all in check, that she does. Put that bloke in the fancy coat in his place with no bother."

"Good to hear. Good to hear." Niall released his hand grip before slapping Harry's shoulder with the gusto that Dick Emery's Mandy would employ before telling whoever that they were awful, but she liked them. Another one of my father's favourites. However, the comic's portrayal of the vicar sporting the impressive oversized gnashers couldn't be more diametrically opposed to the man who I struggled to even offer a stab-in-the-dark guess at his age.

Despite his daughter being of primary school age, I struggled to fathom which generation the vicar was a product of. Niall Dowding was one of those people who looked somewhere between thirty and fifty when they were in their twenties and probably would appear very similar in a couple of decades.

I'm aware the desire to wait and start a family later in life has become very on-trend. Women were increasingly more likely to wait until their thirties, and men often into their forties. For starters, Meryl Streep was in her forties when she gave birth to her fourth child. Mick Jagger had been siring offspring for decades, producing another when in his seventies only this year. A significant increase in the average age since my parents' generation. Most of whom, including my mother, started a family when in their early twenties.

Not that it mattered in Niall's case, but I was curious. Also, I liked to keep abreast of trends when clinging to a thread of hope that my hankering to be a mother could be realised before being considered too old or when my biological clock refused to play ball.

A ticking time bomb in my case. Plus, the slightly tricky issue of being unattached. Traversing the equally on-trend route of adoption or artificial insemination as a means to motherhood didn't particularly appeal. Also, I doubted that would be a sensible move in my current situation.

"Janice … your name is Janice?" Niall asked after Gummy-Harry performed a swift exit.

I nodded, offering a tight smile, thinking I'd better crack on with pot washing before Dawn barked her instructions or, God forbid, gave me a list.

"Oh, bugger, sorry, I think I called you Janet. Please accept my apologies. Being a vicar, I'm supposed to listen," he chuckled. "Clearly, I didn't do too well on that front."

Dawn performed a lemon-sucking wince at the vicar's choice of word but chose not to pick him up on the invective.

Instead, she glanced at me whilst surreptitiously nodding at Niall.

"Hen, that wee chat you were gonna have. I can entertain the lassie for a few minutes."

"Oh, no, I don't think there's any need—"

"Father," Dawn interrupted my plea not to be the centre of attention. "Janice needs a wee word. Perhaps I can keep the lassie entertained for a few minutes?"

"Of course."

"Oh, no, please, there's really no need. I'm fine—"

"Och, come on. You've been nigh on useless all day, what with all that mithering. It canna do no harm, lassie. As I said, it's always good to have a backup plan."

"Sounds intriguing. Nothing to do with that couple who were here, I take it? You know? That woman dressed as Mrs Claus and the dapper gent."

"Oh, no. Err ... although that was odd. The man said he needed to talk to me and then promptly skedaddled without saying another word."

"You don't know them, then?"

"Them? Sorry, he was on his own. There wasn't a woman with him."

"The lady I mentioned, who was hanging on his arm."

"No ... he was on his own."

"Oh ... you must have seen her." Niall pursed his lips and narrowed his eyes. "That is very odd because Ellen and I nearly bumped into them both on the doorstep. Isn't that right, poppet?"

Ellen raised those doleful eyes and nodded.

"Well, Father, I can assure you there was no such woman in here with that man or otherwise. I think the description you gave would make that woman quite memorable."

"Yes, she was pretty unforgettable," he chuckled. "Oh, well, Ellen and I must be seeing things. Perhaps she was the *Ghost of Christmas Yet to Come* … dropping in to offer a vision of the future to young Harry!" he offered that mirthful grin as Dawn and I glanced down to the congealing gravy, the 'a' in the word diva still visible.

"Or a demon … a succubus, perhaps," Dawn muttered.

9

Ashes to Ashes

"Sorry," I huffed before cupping my cheeks in my palms as I rested my elbows on the table. "I'm damn sure you didn't come here today to listen to a stupid woman recount her tale of woe." I offered a tight smile to conclude my protracted, bore-the-arse-off-anyone twenty-minute monologue of all things Janice Keelan.

Despite saying earlier that he hadn't performed well on the listening stakes, Niall employed an attentiveness that offered an air of sincerity which, like me, would make any interlocutor feel valued.

"You're very brave, Janice."

"Brave? Frigging stupid, more like."

"No, not stupid. That was quite courageous of you."

I knitted my brow.

"I mean, I can see how hard that must have been to talk through what's happened to you."

"Oh … yes, well, I've become quite skilled at it now, what with boring the arse off Dawn this morning. Oh, sorry for the arse comment."

Niall smirked.

"Sorry."

"Not in front of Ellen or the bishop … although I've heard some choice words flow from his mouth where the Most Reverend and The General Synod are concerned, I have been known to utter the odd expletive."

"She's a real cutie. How old?" Niall followed my gaze towards the kitchen where 'Mrs Doubtfire' entertained the little girl with handfuls of washing-up bubbles.

"Eight and a half."

"Oh, to be that age with no troubles," I mumbled.

"She's got her cross to bear, the little mite."

"Oh?" I asked, swivelling around to face him.

With a dismissive hand wave, Niall wafted away my surprise that little Miss Hello Kitty could have anything to worry about other than what her father would say to the heaps of bubbles Dawn had expertly stacked on her head. After her dour persona from earlier, it was lovely to see the girl giggle.

"Now, I'm sure it won't come to it, but leave it with me. Dawn was quite correct in suggesting I hold some sway at the women's refuge. The manager, Margo, was very accommodating when one of my parishioners found herself homeless with a newborn in tow. Shocking story … after months of inflicting physical and mental torture on the woman, her partner booted her out and left the poor girl and her one-month-old with nowhere to go."

"Oh, awful. Sorry, that makes my problems sound pathetic. My situation is all self-inflicted."

"I don't think so. By the sounds of it, you've been taken for a ride by a highly skilled con artist. The blame for your situation cannot be laid at your door."

"I never thought I could be fooled so easily. You hear these stories, but not for one moment would I ever have believed I could fall for something like that. A combination of gullible and desperate, I suppose. I mean, Chad, or whatever his real name is, paid my airfare. I'm supposed to fly on Tuesday morning. Not that I will be now, of course."

"It's all part of their con. They prey on the vulnerable and are ingenious with it. I imagine that airfare of a few hundred pounds was an investment. He knew that would add to the lie the awful man was concocting."

"Yes, I see that now. So, is that what I am ... vulnerable? I'm so pathetic that Chad could see my vulnerability and went for it."

"Janice," Niall paused as he laid his hand on mine when spotting my chin wobble. "They work on percentages. I'm sure they target hundreds, hoping to wheedle their way into the few they catch off guard. All of us have those times in our lives when we're susceptible, and they know casting their net wide will snare enough poor sods to con."

I shrugged before glancing through the window to avoid eye contact with Niall, fearing my tears weren't too far away. That benevolent expression he now sported, which I caught a glimpse of before averting my eyes, I suspected would usually be reserved for mourners after reading aloud from The Book of Common Prayer. Whether he meant it or not, Niall harboured a countenance that radiated pity for the stupid woman opposite. That look which kind-hearted folk offer as they hand over a few coins to the very sort who'd, all but two, had now left the refectory.

"So, as I said, don't worry. You won't end up on the streets like these poor souls."

"Thank you." I flitted my eyes back to offer a tight smile before returning my gaze through the window, focusing on the bins and heaps of cardboard piled up at the back of the shops, which a few of our regulars sifted through as they selected new, dry bedding. Perhaps a snapshot of a scene of my future life. "As you say, I doubt it will come to that. I'm sure I can hold the landlord off for a few weeks. After Christmas, there's bound to be plenty of job opportunities." A positive statement that belied my fears about the future.

"And you haven't reported this to the police yet?"

I shook my head. "I don't see the point."

"Hmmm. I think you should."

"Yes, probably. But I'm embarrassed, and I'm not sure what good it will do. I'd imagine the police already have their hands full chasing thieves and murderers. So, hunting down a man to whom I willingly gifted my life savings wouldn't be high on their list of priorities."

"Maybe. It might be an idea to contact Citizens Advice, though. I'm not au fait with tenancy laws, but at least someone there can ensure you know your rights in case your landlord isn't too accommodating."

"Yes, I could do. That's not a bad idea."

"And … look, not wishing to pry, but the bank?"

"Oh, God, the bank. The woman I dealt with was lovely, but at the end of the day, my situation isn't her fault. My accounts are frozen, so for the moment, I'm living day to day. I have what's in my purse to get by on ... after that, well, I have no idea what I'm supposed to do. Of course, I have to repay the debt. I just told them I'll try to cobble the money together from friends."

"Can you?"

"Oh, no. That was a little white lie to buy me some time. I don't really have friends like that. Not the sort who can lend money."

"No, that's a lot to ask of anyone."

"I don't really have friends, to be honest."

"Oh ... I'm surprised."

"Always found it hard ... socially awkward is the term, I think."

"You don't seem like that to me."

"You're easy to talk to."

"Ah, that's the top requirement for the job, you see. I wouldn't be very effective if I couldn't talk to my flock."

"I'm not in your flock."

"That doesn't matter. I'm not just here for that poor lot who choose to suffer my Sunday sermons."

"Are they that bad?"

"Awful. Shocking things."

"I'm sure they're not."

"Come along next Saturday, Christmas Eve, and you'll see how bad they are."

"Why are you a … a—"

"Vicar in a small market town."

"Yes."

"Long story. Which really isn't very interesting. Safe to say, though, spouting the Sunday sermon isn't really my thing. That's all a bit last century. I see myself as more of a community worker, like supporting here, for example. I certainly don't see my job as a preacher. You could say, I'm more of the vicar who supports, not sermonises. So, on that note, apart from ensuring you're not homeless, is there anything else I can help with?"

"No, I don't think so."

"Do you have a plan to keep the bank at arm's length?"

"No … I'm planning on nipping up to the food bank tomorrow just to help stretch my finances. I'm burying my head in the sand on the bank issue. I find wine helps, too."

"Janice, that's not going—"

"I know," I interrupted him. Although he said he wasn't into delivering sermons, I suspected he was about to sermonise that alcohol wasn't the answer. Which, of course, I knew. However, my plan for the next few nights was to plough my way through my stash of cheap plonk before, maybe, turning to Turpentine-Tom's favourite tipple. A bottle of which I'm sure was stashed on a rickety shelf in the shed.

"I'm sorry. I'm not here to lecture. All I'm saying is don't put off the bank issue. Citizens Advice, as I suggested, is as good a starting place as any."

I nodded.

Niall took a moment to ponder, tapping his pinched lips with his index finger. "And this Magnum lookalike who came to talk to you today, what's his part in all this?"

"Oh, probably nothing. I don't actually know. As I said, he shot off just a second before you turned up."

"You don't think he's connected to the man who conned you?"

"I don't see how. Anyway, after I'd stupidly transferred my life savings to the man, he's become a ghost. There's nothing else to rinse from me, so I suspect the git's moved on to his next victim."

"And the woman? The one you didn't see."

"Well, no ... I still don't understand how a woman in a Santa coat could be stepping out the door when you entered. I mean, she wasn't there. You sure she wasn't already outside when you and Ellen turned up?"

"No," he chuckled. "Honestly, and vicars don't lie. She was walking away from the counter with that man when we came in. I had to step aside at the door to let them pass."

"Well, Dawn and I didn't see her. That's got to be almost impossible."

"She was there. As plain as day, I can assure you. Although there was nothing plain about her."

"No, so you said. It's weird, though. Terry, that's what he said his name was, said something about offering to help. I thought he was looking to volunteer, but he said he wasn't."

"You said he knew your name?"

"Yes."

"Maybe he does want to help, then?"

"Well, maybe. That doesn't make any sense, though. I've only told you and Dawn about my predicament. Oh, and my bank, but they're not going to send some Good Samaritan on a mission to help, are they? So, how would he know I'm in a pickle? That's the word he used … pickle."

"I think you'll just have to wait and see if he contacts you again." Niall pulled out his phone from his jeans pocket. "You want to give me your number? If he does contact you and you feel the need to have someone with you, I'm happy to step into the breach. No pressure, of course. Just a thought," he nervously grinned after adding the last sentence when clocking my surprise.

"Oh … alright, why not. Go on, then. If that's not too much trouble?"

"Course not." Niall opened up his contacts before sliding his phone across the table. "Pop your details in there, and I'll text you so you have mine. Honestly, call me anytime."

"Daddy, can we go now?" I heard Ellen call out as she approached the table whilst my finger hovered above the screen when my newly discovered, non-trusting persona waved a metaphorical red flag. However, I continued when telling myself Niall was a man of the cloth, not a con man.

"Sorry, Father, I took my eye off her for one second," panted Dawn as she shimmied her hips through the chicane of abandoned chairs when in hot pursuit of the girl who still sported remnants of her Mild-Green-Fairly-Liquid halo.

"Yes, Ellen, we can." Niall wrapped his arm around his daughter's waist before looking up at the flustered Dawn. "Thanks, Dawn. Janice and I were just finishing up, anyway."

"Nae bother. She's a lovely wee lassie, this one."

"Daddy."

"Yes, sweetheart."

"Look," Ellen pointed through the window. "There's Mrs Father Christmas again."

10

A Dead Norwegian Blue

"Leave it, Deana. I really don't want to have to listen to any more of your excuses. This is precisely why I told that lot … that ruddy woman, De Ath, I wanted a new guide. The reason we got ourselves in such a tight spot when helping Kim, Damian, and Ginny is because of your ridiculous capers and inability to behave. You're like a spoilt child who has to be the centre of attention."

"You finished, darling?"

"No! No. I. Have. Not!" Terry stamped his foot.

"Who's the petulant child now, then? Hmmm?"

"Oh, for Christ's sake, woman. Why on earth did you write your name in that gravy? We were getting somewhere, then you … you," Terry swivelled around from where he'd been leaning on the wall, gazing across the river, to jab a finger at Deana. "You just had to start playing games. Now we've wasted a whole day, and the chance that Janice woman's likely to speak to me again is, I imagine, somewhat on the ruddy low side."

"You're very grumpy, Terence." While lounging on a bench, the gap in her coat revealing her bare legs, Deana tipped her head back and sighed. "Peevish, darling. Very peevish."

"Caused by you."

"Is it the dead thing that's making you like this? All that waiting around, playing Monopoly and ping-pong with your dead friends for months on end, that's caused you to become such an irascible bore? You used to be fun." Deana tipped her head forward. "Certainly, I can say with some authority you had some spunk about you when alive. Now, it's just morose, dead Terry. I'm sick as a parrot, wondering if another mission with Ponderous-Petunia might actually be more fun."

"Be my guest. I'm quite happy to go it alone."

"Apart from an insulting suggestion, you know that's not how it works. You must have a spectral guide. It's the rules. And, grumpy guts, you're lucky to have me."

"Really?"

"Yes, really."

"Well, if I'm 'lucky', as you put it," Terry performed air quotes as he pushed away from the wall to step towards Deana. "Why the hell do you see fit to prat about when we're supposed to be completing a mission? A mission that we must fulfil to correct the issue we've caused … apparently. Although, I'm at pains to see how."

"Yes, I've been thinking about that." Deana patted the bench seat beside her. "Come sit, darling."

"No, thank you."

"Suit yourself. It's just the weedy-looking man standing not twenty yards to your left is filming your antics as you gesticulate and holler at an empty bench seat. No skin off my nose, darling, but continue in this vein, and I suspect you'll attract quite a crowd. You never know, you might even make the front page of the Chronicle or, if you're super lucky, a clip at the end of the six o'clock news."

Terry, still with his arms outstretched, the pose he'd held when venting his displeasure at Deana, swivelled his head to spot the man walking towards him, holding up his phone.

"If you remember back to the spring, specifically the day we solved your little Kimmy's issue, when that line of traffic stopped to film your antics near the Broxworth, I wouldn't mind betting you're about to make your second foray into a starring role on social media. So, darling, I suggest you think on. If you're hellbent on highlighting my shortcomings, I might very well be left with no choice but to take retaliatory action and dob you in to The-Powers-That-Be regarding this celeb status you're courting. A status that is most certainly prohibited and makes my supermarket custard-cream-flinging antics appear almost trifling in comparison."

"D'you mind not pointing that thing at me?" Terry barked at the man, who, while continuing to film, took another couple of steps forward, flicking his eyes back and forth between the screen and Terry.

"This nutter, for anyone who can remember that far back, who looks like that Yosser Hugues from *Boys from the Blackstuff*, is shouting and waving his arms around at an empty park bench."

"Who you talking to?" Terry asked.

"I should be asking you that. I'm adding commentary to the clip. We're live on YouTube. Don't let me stop you, mate. This is frigging hilarious."

"Naff off!"

"Hey, say, 'Gissa job'. Can you do it in a scouse accent? It'll just make it more authentic."

Terry shot Deana a look.

"Darling, it's Yosser Huges's catchphrase. I'm sure that show was on before you decided to die on me."

"Yes, I can remember, thank you! I'm trying to understand why this ... this dick is filming me."

"Ah, fantastic," he chuckled. "Keep it going, pal. Perhaps you could say who you're talking to? Y'know, bring some context to the clip about who you reckon is sitting on that bench."

Terry stepped purposefully towards the man holding his phone aloft, causing him to take evasive action by way of a few backward hops.

"Trust me, you really don't want to know," Terry hissed, while jabbing his finger repeatedly. "Sitting on that bench is a dead woman dressed as Mrs Christmas. A diva, a spook, a damned right pain in the frigging arse, who is so ruddy annoying it's enough to make a man contemplate suicide. Something I would willingly commit if I wasn't already dead because being in her company is totally insufferable. She's a sex-crazed fifty-something ghost who's hell-bent on pratting about, ruining my mission to save a woman from something or other that I have no idea what it is. And another thing—"

"Not anymore, I'm not, Terence." Deana barked as she stood beside him.

"Okay, so you're not sitting on the bench, but you're still a total—"

"My 'not anymore' comment was about us. Specifically, our ex-working relationship, and not my precise whereabouts. However, as you seem determined to make a fool of yourself, I'd better perform my spectral guide duties and thus prevent an unpleasant situation. Which, I'm quite sure, will be frowned upon by that lot up there."

Terry made to counter but said nothing as his jaw flapped when unable to find the words while the man continued to film.

Deana sprang into action. She snatched the phone from the man's grip and tossed it into the river. In one swift movement during that nanosecond, when the chap tried to compute what had happened while watching his phone cartwheel over the wall and give off an audible plop, she parted the front flaps of her coat and raised her bare knee.

"What the fu ... augh!"

"Sorry about that." Deana lowered her leg after her raised knee had connected with his nether regions, effectively stopping his protests when incapacitating the man, thus leaving him bent double, wheezing and panting in pain, before turning on Terry. *"So, that's what you think, is it? A sex-crazed pain in the arse spook annoying enough to drive men to suicide. Ruddy charming, Terence. I hereby inform you that we are done. I will contact you-know-who and inform them that our partnership must be terminated with immediate effect. To be honest, I don't give two shits what action they take. If I'm banished to a life of purgatory down with Old Nick whilst bunking up with Idi Amin, then so be it. However, think on Terence because I suggest our failure to work as a team will do*

little in assisting your quest to be reunited with your pathetic, precious little Sharon."

After giving the wheezing chap a fleeting glance to check he was no longer a problem, Terry hot-footed after Deana, who, with her nose in the air, marched off in the direction of the bus stop. Despite the dead woman's infuriating behaviour, he knew she'd made a valid point. If The-Powers-That-Be were made aware of any issues that could affect his points total, that would be a problem. As he chased after her, Terry recalled Miss De Ath's secretary's comment about some of the dead spending decades awaiting placement. The possibility of another twenty or thirty years playing board games didn't bear thinking about.

"Deana!"

"I suggest you stop shouting my name."

"Deana!"

"Old Crushed-Testicles is out of the picture now he's writhing around on the pavement, caressing his privates. However, there are a few people knocking about on the other side of the road who might start to wonder if you're the local nutter if you insist on bellowing my name," she shot over her shoulder when nipping across the road. Forgetting she was invisible, Deana offered the middle finger gesture to a driver who didn't seem to have the courtesy to stop at a Belisha beacon crossing.

"Ruddy hell," Terry muttered as he chased after her.

"The damage is done," she hissed as Terry caught up and fell into step.

"Can we perhaps discuss—"

"There's nothing to be said." Deana halted her jaunt, spun around, and faced Terry. "You've made your position quite clear. I must say, my darling Dickie would never have spoken to me in such a way. And there I was, always wondering if you were the one who got away. Could we have had a life together, raised Damian, and been like normal folk? So, it appears my decades of pondering were all in vain because it's become quite apparent that I dodged a bullet when your heart gave in due to being unable to keep up with my indefatigable and unforgettable, energetic performance in that hotel room."

"Can we talk?" he hissed between clamped teeth, trying his darndest not to draw attention to himself. It seemed everyone carried these camera phones in this era. He suspected that if he started another conversation with thin air, the half-a-dozen or so patrons standing outside the Red Lion Pub opposite smoking would soon notice and presumably begin filming.

"If that conversation starts with an apology."

"Alright, alright," Terry hissed with his hand clamped over his mouth.

Deana raised an eyebrow.

"I'm sorry."

Deana thumped her hands on her hips, holding that facial expression.

"I'm very sorry, and I won't say anything like that ever again."

"Hmmm, that will have to do, I suppose."

"Right. Can we discuss our next move?" Terry nodded to the pub. "A pint wouldn't go amiss. As well as a smoking ban, they're a touch economical on the alcohol front up in limbo."

"If you think I'm going to sit in a scummy public house surrounded by this town's great unwashed while watching you guzzle pints of lager, you're very much mistaken. No, Terence, definitely not. You can take my arm and walk me back to the bus stop. We'll discuss our next move back at home."

As instructed, Terry allowed Bossy-Boots-Deana to loop her arm through his before they retraced their steps, heading for the High Street.

"What d'you mean, like normal folk?" Terry asked after a few minutes of silence.

"Sorry?"

"You said you'd often wondered if we could have been together like normal folk."

"Oh … well, you know, ordinary people who raise children, go to the supermarket on Saturday mornings, wash cars on Sunday mornings, enjoy two weeks in some scummy Spanish beach resort every August, argue on Christmas day, that sort of thing."

"I can't see you in that scenario."

"No, probably not. So, assuming we're friends again, what's the plan?"

"Okay, so we need to work out what's happened to Janice and how we are responsible."

"Yes, darling. I think that's obvious. But the plan?"

"Well, as that refuge place is only just around the corner, I think I'll go and talk to her again."

"Alright. And I promise to behave."

"Oh, no. I need to go it alone. And remember, if that woman has summoned the local priest to exorcise evil spirits, it might be prudent for you to hang back. We can't risk you being spotted if this thing about men of the cloth being able to see spooks is a possibility."

"Oh … hmmm, yes, alright. It's only some who can apparently spot us. But you're probably right. Best to be prudent in these situations. Can I just ask that you don't hang around there for too long? You see, I get bored easily. When that happens, I'm liable to get up to mischief. And we wouldn't want that, darling, would we?"

"No … no, we wouldn't," Terry huffed. "Right, it's just up there. Perhaps it's best that you don't come any further. There's that row of knick-knack shops over …" Terry paused to allow a couple to pass, not wishing to be labelled a nutter again. "You could do some window shopping and I'll meet you there when I've finished up with Janice. Just hope she's still there. Otherwise, we'll have to find out where she lives."

"Yes, alright. I can't say they're the sort of establishments I would normally be seen in. However, seeing as this is a crisis situation, coupled with the saving grace that I'm invisible, I suppose I can take one for the team and peruse their cheap, tacky wares."

"Very decent of you."

"Please don't be sarcastic, darling. Now, I'm quite sure those turgid little emporiums don't stock designer apparel, but do you need me to pick you up anything? You need underwear or a pack of razors to sort that spikey fuzz that's reappeared under your nose."

"Err … no, I'm good, thanks. Anyway, you're invisible, remember?"

"Shoplifting, darling. I've become quite proficient. It's a lot easier than one might think, you know?"

"You said you'd behave. And I believe your spook status might offer you an advantage over most shoplifters. I can honestly say we didn't apprehend one invisible shoplifter during my time at Freshcom's."

"Yes, handy this death thing."

"Christ, please don't cause a ruddy scene. Just amuse yourself for half an hour without giving half the town a reason to start believing the ghost of Christmas has bowled up looking to grab a few last-minute stocking fillers."

"Excuse me! Excuse the intrusion, but can I have a quick word?" hollered a man trotting towards Terry, waving his right arm to get his attention.

"Oh, bugger. Don't tell me this is another one of these portable phone camera idiots who's spotted me talking," Terry mumbled. "Why is everyone obsessed with filming? In my day, you only got the cine camera out on special occasions. And that's only if you were minted. Our neighbour had one and used to boast about it before boring us half to death with his dreadful home movies. If I remember, the only relief was when the projector blew the bulb. Which, fortunately for us, was a regular occurrence."

"I'm sure. Back in the day of the blackouts and the three-day working week. You know, Dickie and I loved making home movies. Not the sort of thing you'd show your granny, though," she snickered.

"Amateur porn movies, I suppose," Terry tutted.

"There was nothing amateurish about our erotic scenes, I can assure you. Everyone makes home porn movies these days. In fact, everyone films everything. I'm quite sure if camera phones were a thing back in 1912, rather than try to save themselves, those poor souls drowning on the Titanic would have all filmed their demise before sinking to their watery graves."

"Hi there, sorry to bellow," the man waving slowed from a trot to a walking pace as he made up the ground. "Might I have a word with you both?"

"Both? What d'you mean both?" Terry blurted.

"Oh, hell, darling, can he actually see me?"

11

Highway to Heaven

"Ellen. Who is your father talking to?" I asked, a hint of disbelief in my tone as the three of us peered through the window. With her forehead planted on the glass, Ellen, sandwiched between Dawn and me, took a moment to answer as the three of us watched events unfold after Niall had bolted out the door when we'd spotted that man who called himself Terry strolling back towards the refuge.

Because of Niall's haste to catch up with the odd man, we'd only touched on the subject of the apparent woman dressed as Mrs Christmas, who wasn't there as far as Dawn and I were concerned. A frankly bizarre conversation where Ellen and Niall insisted this Terry bloke wasn't alone, and Dawn and I questioned their sanity.

"I don't know," Ellen mumbled, in a tone children employed when believing they'd been accused of something.

"Okay, but your father is talking to a man, yes?"

"And the lady."

"What lady, Ellen?"

"The lady who I think must be Father Christmas's wife?" Ellen replied, her nose touching the window, her breath misting the glass.

Dawn and I exchanged a look.

"Ellen?" I asked, waiting for her to look up. "The lady in the Santa suit … is she talking to your daddy right now? Like right this minute?"

"It's a Santa coat. Is Daddy letting her know what I want for Christmas?"

"It's what I wish for. Not what I want," Dawn corrected the girl. Her tone slipping into that harsh Glaswegian phonation, causing her correction to come across as a scolding.

Ellen shrugged her shoulders without turning around to look up at Dawn.

"He might be," I mumbled. "And you say Mrs Christmas is standing beside the man wearing the long, dark coat?"

Ellen nodded before returning to watch the proceedings a hundred yards or so further down the street.

"What woman?" I mouthed at Dawn.

"I have no idea, hen. I know my eyesight isn't what it used to be …"

"Or we're both losing the plot." I finished the sentence for her.

"Aye."

"Ellen?" I thought I'd clarify one more time and ask about this phantom. "You're telling Dawn and me that next to the man talking to your daddy is a woman in a red coat?"

"Yes. She's right there." Ellen poked a finger at the window, the force of her confirmation at complete odds with her earlier display of shyness.

With her rubicund right cheek pressed to the glass, Dawn mumbled incoherently. Although I didn't catch the words, the tone suggested she was offering up a prayer of some sort.

"Dawn, can you mind Ellen for a sec?"

"Yes, hen. Be careful." Dawn petted the girl's long dark hair whilst still straining to ogle what was occurring with the woman who wasn't there. "I'm not liking this. Today is turning out to be mighty strange."

After leaving Ellen and Dawn in their ogling positions, I flung my pinny onto the nearest table before scooting out to the street. If, when I caught up with Niall, he claimed the woman in the red coat was there, then I would probably have to accept the stress of the last week had taken its toll on me. Instead of job hunting and visiting the food bank, I considered booking a double appointment at the doctor's might be required.

I'm aware that stress can cause hallucinations, but having the effect of not seeing apparent realities was a new one on me. I suspected a single five-minute appointment wouldn't be nearly enough time for my doctor to assess my mental well-being. However, it was probably enough time to have me sectioned. What Dawn's excuse was, well, that was anyone's guess.

After trotting down the steps, wrapping my arms around me as I felt the winter chill of the early afternoon, I hot-footed down the hill to where Niall and Terry appeared to be embroiled in some sort of heated exchange. Niall gesticulating at something further down the street toward the river, and Terry vehemently shaking his head.

"Look, fella, I really don't want to come across as rude, but claiming I'm seeing things is ridiculous. Who was that woman, and why are you saying she didn't exist? I saw her," Niall barked. "She's just scooted off down to the shops in the arcade."

"What's going on?" I called out as I approached.

Niall swivelled around. "Janice, you must have seen her."

"The woman in the red coat who doesn't exist?"

"What ... you must—"

"See, as I've been telling you," Terry grinned. "There's no one here but me."

"No, this is ridiculous," Niall blustered.

"Terry ... it is Terry, yes?"

"It is."

"What's going on? You seem to know of me, and you turned up earlier claiming you want to offer some help because I'm in a pickle, as you put it. Then, as soon as the vicar arrives, you make a run for it."

"Ah ... you're a man of the cloth, then?" Terry asked Niall, ignoring my question.

"I'm the vicar of All Saints Church. Man of the cloth might be considered an outdated term these days. But what's that got to do with anything?"

"Well, it explains what's just happened."

"What has just happened?" I interjected.

"Err … I can't really say. It's complicated. Sort of."

"Look, Mr …"

"Walton."

"Well, Mr Walton, this may be none of my business. However, Janice has asked for my assistance, and I fully intend to offer my help. She's been through a difficult time of late, and I'm now wondering if you showing up here today with that woman, whose skedaddle suggests skulduggery at play, has something to do with her situation." Although a vicar, so should be displaying a measure of agreeableness, harmony and sensitivity, Niall employed quite a menacing tone as he leaned into Terry before turning to me. "Janice, I don't want to overstep the mark, but are you alright if I push this bloke for answers?"

"Oh, err … yeah. Okay, thanks. If you've got the time, that is. Although I'm still a bit bemused about the Mrs Christmas woman."

"Aren't we all," Terry muttered.

"Sorry?" Niall barked, shooting his head back to face Terry.

"Nothing. Look, sorry, this isn't panning out quite as I'd planned."

"Niall," I grabbed his elbow. "Leave it. I don't want to cause a scene. I'm sure you have somewhere to be, and I expect Ellen is becoming bored."

"No, it's alright. I think you need some answers from this bloke." Niall turned to glance back up at the refuge where his daughter's and Dawn's faces could be spotted pressed against the window. "Oh, is Ellen alright?"

"Darling," Deana called out as she scooted around the corner. *"I've decided to come out of hiding. I think it's best we understand how this man can see me. I must say, he's a bit of a dish, if not lacking the attentions of a comb. That said, the bed-hair look always gets me horny."*

"No!" Terry hissed, swivelling around.

"Oh, it does, darling, I promise you. Messy hair is such a turn-on. Now, of course, I'm aware that showing myself might be super risky, but what have we got to lose?" Deana panted as she took hold of Terry's biceps.

"Yes, Ellen's fine …" pausing momentarily when distracted by Terry blurting out 'no' for no apparent reason. I continued, now pondering if he was one of those poor sods afflicted by Tourette's syndrome. "Ellen's with Dawn. Everyone's gone now, so it's just them two. Look, should you be somewhere? You don't have to … get … involved …" I paused again and knitted my brow when noticing Terry start that odd arm movement and somewhat bizarrely mouthing silently to his left.

"Janice?" Niall prompted me.

"Oh, Jesus, woman, you're—"

"Unbelievable. I know, darling. If nothing else, this will be fun," Deana chortled. *"Stop flailing your arms about and let me nuzzle up close."*

"Janice?" Niall asked again, presumably wondering what had caused me to stop mid-flow. When I didn't respond, he swivelled around on his heels before hopping backwards as if faced with some hideous demon. "Her! Where the hell did she—"

"Who?"

"Her!" Niall jabbed a finger to Terry's left.

"Niall, there's no one there."

"Janice! Look … there … the woman dressed as Mrs Christmas."

"Niall, this isn't funny."

"Oh, this is hilarious. I wonder how this dashing chap can see me. I was led to believe that particular talent was reserved for a select few of the religious persuasion and some small children, of course. The latter being a frightfully disconcerting situation."

"He's a vicar."

"Ah, I see. Oh, what a dreadful waste. But that does explain how he can see me. Clara, the little minx, was right all along."

"Sorry, who are you talking to?" I somewhat exasperatedly questioned.

Terry didn't answer me. Instead, the man with that retro moustache, who I now wondered if I'd met before today, focussed on the vicar as Niall tentatively reached out to Terry's left before shaking what appeared to be an invisible hand.

"Delighted to make your acquaintance. Now, I'm sure you're wondering why on earth this poor girl is claiming she can't see me. Simple fact is, I'm dead. I'm a ghost. An angel in the true sense of the word, but most certainly not someone who could be described as virtuous. Chaste is not a label that could be attached to me—"

"Understatement of the century."

"Yes, thank you, Terence. Please don't mutter or interrupt."

"I … can see her, touch her … but—"

"Niall?" I laid my hand on his outstretched forearm, fearing the man was having some sort of seizure.

"She's almost translucent," he mumbled. "Shimmering like an apparition in the sunlight."

"Oh, what a chat-up line." Deana guffawed. "I've heard them all now. What a cad!"

"Niall!" I pulled on his arm, which harboured a rigidity as if he held onto something solid, not just dangling mid-air as was apparent.

"Oh. I don't think the poor chap can hear me." Deana let go of Niall's hand, leaving the man motionless while still holding his hand out as if freeze-framed in position. "I wonder if that's because this luscious vicar isn't considered pious enough. Perhaps sufficiently righteous to see me, but not ranked high enough on the religious scale to enjoy the full suite of my delights. Shame, really, because my eloquent diction is one of my favoured qualities that comes in a close second to my wonderfully pert boobs."

"Niall, what are you doing?" I hissed, letting go before stepping back while rubbing my arms. I presumed my goosebumps were because of the near-freezing temperature and not due to this frankly bizarre situation. If it wasn't for the fact that Dawn knew him, I'd have Niall pegged to be as equally nutty as the man claiming he could help me out of my pickle.

"Darling, old Garlic-Breath looks like she might catch her death out here. Be a gent and offer her your coat."

"Janice. You look frozen stiff," Terry broke the silence when Niall failed to reply. "Here, take my coat," he suggested, shrugging out of the expensive garment as he stepped around the comatose Niall to offer it up for me to slot my arms into the sleeves.

"Thanks ... err, what's going on?"

"Okay, well, in for a penny, as they say. Now Deana has decided, unilaterally, I might add, to put us in this situation, I might as well come out with it."

"Come out with what? And who's Deana?"

"Standing there ..." Terry pointed to a few feet in front of me. "Is Deana. She's dressed in a red coat that apparently Steve McQueen designed—"

"Oh, Terry, you dummy. Alexander McQueen, darling. I really don't think the Cooler King was into haute couture, do you? Hmmm?"

"She said something again. Why can't I hear her?" Niall blurted when coming out of his inert state before frowning at me. "Why can't you see her?"

"Because there's no one there!"

"Janice! She's here." Niall waved his hand up and down. "Are you blind?"

"No ... and to be honest with both of you, I've just about had my fill of all this shite. Whatever game you two are playing—"

"Woah ... hang on there," Terry interrupted. "The reason you can see her is because you are of a religious persuasion. Apparently, that affords you the ability to see the dead," Terry nodded at Niall before turning to me. "And the reason you can't is for that very reason. Deana, who is standing right there, is dead. She's a ghost. An angel, if you like."

"Oh, darling, you say the sweetest things," Deana purred.

"Oh, give me strength—"

"I touched an angel," Niall mumbled.

"What? Don't be such a credulous idiot. Sorry, Niall, I don't mean to be rude, but please … oh," I paused when detecting something touching my hand. When I tried to pull away, the invisible force gripped my fingers, holding on tight. I shot a look at Niall.

"That angel is holding your hand."

"Nice to meet you, Garlic-Breath. You know, if it wasn't for your pungent, revolting halitosis, I could find you quite alluring. There's something irresistible about that button nose of yours, and I must say, your skin is quite divine, my girl. I'm into women just as much as men. Us bisexuals have the best of both worlds, you know. A prolonged swilling of mouthwash and you never know, you could get lucky."

"What did she say?" Niall asked.

"Trust me, you really don't want to know," muttered Terry.

"This can't be happening," I mumbled, trying, but failing, to pull my hand back.

"Angels are actually real, then?" Niall asked Terry.

"I'm surprised a man of your profession would be asking that."

"I take your point, but … well, I don't know what I thought. Of course, I preach the teachings of our Lord, but actually witnessing … well, you know."

"I think I do. And yes, angels are real. We're here to help Janice."

"We?"

"Yes, I'm dead too. I'm also an angel, just a visible one. It's kinda complicated."

"Clarence Odbody," Niall mumbled.

"Yes, sort of," Terry grinned.

"Highway to Heaven," I muttered, thinking of that somewhat cheesy show from the '80s rather than the guardian angel from that '40s Christmas film, still fully aware that something held onto my hand, causing the hairs on the back of my neck to fizz. Whether I wanted to believe the unbelievable or not – taking into account my rather lofty gullibility rating, considering how easily Chad Ruger had duped me – I had to consider this peculiar event was just another elaborate con. I, Janice, the stupid woman, was again falling for the trickery of the wicked who preyed on the vulnerable.

Great. That made me doubly stupid and vulnerable.

Despite my mumblings about '80s TV shows, I considered the latter the more likely explanation, rather than believing the more pleasant scenario that the 'Boss' had sent a couple of guardian angels to help me out of a tight spot. Or pickle, as Terry, the man claiming he was dead, had called it.

When employing a sharp tug, I extracted my hand from the 'angel's' grip and thrust both hands into the coat pockets as I stepped backwards to distance myself from the 'thing'. My right hand curled around what felt like a card tucked in the bottom of the pocket. After extracting and flipping it around, I realised it was a business card. The name printed on the front cleared the fog from my brain, enabling me to remember why Terry appeared familiar.

"You!" I thrust my arm out, waving the business card at him. "You're Richard Burton. I knew I'd seen you before."

"Oh ... now this is odd. Although both you and my darling Dickie are yummy, delicious hunks, you look absolutely nothing like each other. Why on earth would Garlic-Breath think you're my poor dead husband?"

12

Lady in Red

"Do it again. Again, again. Pleeeese," Ellen whiningly pleaded as she excitedly hopped up and down on her chair. Her beaming pleasure was a sight to behold as the little, previously melancholy girl displayed her gappy-toothed grin.

Whether Dawn had just had enough, claims from Niall and Ellen about this apparent woman dressed in a Santa coat becoming all too much, or her announcement that she was already late for afternoon tea at her eldest daughters, who knew? However, as soon as Niall and I, along with dead Terry and that 'thing' which had earlier groped my hand, traipsed back inside the refuge, Dawn made herself scarce after instructing me to lock up when we left.

"Go on, Deana, spin them again," Ellen squealed in delight as the cutlery, specifically two spoons, again magically stood on end on the table and spun around of their own volition. Or, as Ellen claimed, a woman dressed as Mrs Father Christmas, who, according to Terry – the bloke who claimed to be dead – was an angel, performed the spinning of said cheap silverware.

"Niall … can you still see her?" I hissed while watching the spoons rotate and the giggling Ellen. Her delight presumably caused by the fact that I couldn't see the woman.

"No … she's disappeared."

"What?" I shot him a look. "I thought you said you could see this … this thing, this lady in red."

"I could when we were outside, but I can't now," he mumbled while vacantly staring at the spoons.

"That, dear boy, is because you've allowed the rational part of your mind to push away your beliefs. Apparently, according to my gorgeous, sexy Clara, who's also an angel, she reckons men of your persuasion … you know, you religious types, can see the likes of us if you're super devout. You start doubting our existence, and we will fade, I'm afraid to say."

"Daddy, Deana said you must believe she's here. Otherwise, you won't be able to see her. It's a bit like believing in Father Christmas."

"The thing spoke?" I blurted.

"Ellen, dearest. You are a sweetie, and you will no doubt break some hearts when you grow up, be a love and ask Janice to stop calling me a thing. I'm a gorgeous, sexy angel. I assume she's not trying to be rude, but I'm not liking being called a thing, that much I can tell you."

"Are you Mrs Christmas?"

"No, dear."

"But you're wearing Santa's coat."

"It's haute couture, sweetie," Deana corrected Ellen whilst keeping the spoons spinning. "Now, come on, please ask your father's friend to stop calling me a thing."

"Ellen … is the lady talking to you?" Niall asked, his voice breaking. That previous confident timbre reduced to a choirboyish soprano squeal.

"You can't hear or see her, then?" I asked, rolling my eyes and admonishing myself for uttering such a ridiculous statement.

However, whether this was an elaborate con cooked up by Niall and Terry, I doubted Ellen would be part of that. That said, children had been used for much worse, like chimney sweeping, and then there were those evil kids like Sid from *Toy Story*, not to mention *Damien Thorn*. However, this Hello Kitty superfan just didn't seem to fit that mould. Anyway, unless I was hallucinating, caused by the stress of the past few days resulting in the rational part of my brain shutting down, there were two spoons spinning on the table, and nothing I could see could be attributed to the perpetual momentum. As far as I could remember, from physics classes in school, that was an impossible phenomenon. Something, some force, had to be causing the spoons to spin.

An angel dressed in a revealing red coat? Ridiculous. However, I had to accept that something had held my hand. Whether I was turning into a fruitloop or not, I'm damn sure I didn't imagine that.

"Ellen?" Niall repeated.

"Yes, Daddy. Deana said you must believe she's real … then you can see her. She also said something about being sexy, I think. What does that mean?"

Niall shot me a look.

"She—"

"My name is Deana. Not, she," Deana interrupted Ellen. *"I'm not the cat's mother."*

"Ehm … Deana asked if the lady can stop calling her a thing. She said she's a … ehm—"

"A gorgeous, sexy angel."

"She said she's not Mrs Christmas. She's a sexy angel. And she's not the cat's mother."

"Well said. Don't forget the gorgeous part," Deana threw in whilst giving the spoons another swizzle.

"Oh, and she's gorgeous, too."

"Ellen—"

"That's what Deana said. She's a gorgeous, sexy angel."

"Very sexy."

"Very sexy angel," Ellen confirmed with a pronounced nod before glancing back at the wall just above the still-spinning spoons. "Deana?"

"Yes, deary."

"What does very sexy mean?"

"Ah … you'll find out in a few years. Many a young man will be calling you that, I suspect."

"Deana."

"Yes, deary."

"Do you like Hello Kitty?"

"Absolutely … I'm sure I do. She sounds delightful."

"Deana?"

"Yes, deary."

"Do you know my mummy?"

When Ellen uttered that 'mummy' word, Niall shot his hand to his mouth.

"Niall?" I grabbed his elbow. "What is it?" Due to only hearing one half of the apparent conversation between the little girl and this invisible angel thingy dressed as the lady in red, I wondered if *Angel* was Niall's nickname for his wife, and Ellen had picked up upon it. Or … his wife was dead, and Niall had told his daughter that 'Mummy' was now an angel in Heaven.

"Oh, no, my sweet. I don't think I do. Is your mummy an angel, too?"

"Yes," Ellen nodded profusely. "Daddy said she is."

"Ellen," hissed Niall. "Does … does she know Mummy?"

"No, Daddy. Deana said she doesn't."

"Do you have a cleaner?" Terry asked when padding back into the refectory after using the facilities.

"Sorry?" I quizzed while still trying to get my head around that an apparent angel had mentioned the words sexy and gorgeous, along with contemplating the state of play regarding Niall's wife.

"Well, it's just that whoever used the toilet before me may not benefit from the healthiest of guts. The pan looks like it's gonna need some industrial cleaning. A hose and shovel might come in handy as a start."

"Oh, great. That's my job. I wouldn't mind betting that was Super-Glue-Steve. We've had him pegged as the phantom pooper for some weeks."

"Super-Glue-Steve?" Niall and Terry asked in unison.

"Oh, sorry. That's a moniker for Steve. He's partial to glue sniffing."

"Okay, shall we get down to business, then?" Terry suggested when clapping his hands together before rubbing them as if moulding Plasticine.

"Ellen, can you come here, please?" Standing by the window, the furthest point away from the 'thing', Niall held out his hand to beckon his daughter. "Until we know what's actually happening here, I want you by my side."

Ellen pulled a face.

"Ellen, I think it's best you do as your father asks. We'll play some more games in a minute when everyone here believes I'm real."

"Ellen," Niall barked, exaggeratingly beckoning with an outstretched hand to encourage his daughter.

"Go on. And tell that dashing father of yours that I'm a good angel. I'm here to help the lady who insists on calling me a thing."

"Ellen, is she still talking? And please, come over here," Niall asked as Ellen begrudgingly slid off her chair to comply with her father's demands.

"Deana said that she's a good angel," Terry stated before muttering to himself. "Although that's somewhat tenuous and depends on the context."

"I heard that, Terence."

"Deana's come to help this lady," Ellen chimed in, taking her father's hand in one while pointing at me with the other.

"She has. We both have."

"You'd better explain," I raised an eyebrow at the man who claimed to be dead. "You call yourself Terry, but I know you as Richard Burton as per your business card."

"Darling, while you were pointing your pecker at the porcelain, I remembered where I've seen this woman before."

"Where? Where from?" Terry asked the two still-spinning spoons that suddenly clattered to the table as if the force which propelled them had instantly dissipated.

"Back in the spring, during our first mission to help your little Kimmy. If you recall, we visited your father-in-law at that care home, and this woman was the receptionist."

"You sure?" Terry asked, looking at me.

"Am I sure about what?" I asked, shooting a look at Niall and Ellen for backup. Sensibly, Niall had moved into protection mode, gripping his daughter as if Satan himself stood before us. Which, I guess, was possible if you believed in all that malarkey. Being a vicar, I supposed he would.

"I was talking to Deana," Terry qualified while still looking at me.

"Course you were," I sarcastically fired back.

"I am quite sure, darling. I seem to remember the woman was a bit of a gossip and clearly smitten by the chat-up patter that you trotted out as we conned our way in ... you calling yourself Richard Burton, as per my darling Dickie."

"Oh, that's her, is it? I'm not sure I gave the woman a second look."

"Excuse me, but—"

"Sorry, can you give me a second, please?" Terry interrupted, cutting me short with a raised palm. "I can't hold a conversation with Deana and you at the same time."

Dumbfounded by the absurdity of the statement, I complied, wondering if it was time to call a halt to proceedings and ask this Terry bloke and his angel-thingy friend to leave.

"Yes, well, I know what men are like. You probably wouldn't remember her because, as far as men and window shopping goes, she's not that alluring. You were throwing her bedroom eyes so we could con our way in, if you remember?"

"Well …" Terry turned around again to give me the once up and down. "I think you're being a little uncharitable," he stated as he swivelled around to address the table with the now inert spoons. "I wouldn't say that—"

"Say what?" I shrieked, throwing my hands in the air. "And why did you look at me like that?"

"Ehm …"

"Deana said—"

"Ellen, sweetie. This is not a conversation for children. Now, as my father used to say, children are to be seen, not heard. Be a good girl for Deana and cover your ears. Otherwise, I might have to speak with Father Christmas about you. You wouldn't want that, would you?"

Niall, like me, presuming the 'thing' was speaking to his daughter, focused on Ellen as she shrunk behind his legs, shaking her head before holding her hands over her ears.

"Good girl. You know you have to be good for Santa before Christmas."

Ellen nodded.

"Deana," hissed Terry.

"Darling, I'm merely making sure the girl doesn't hear anything that little ears shouldn't. As I was saying, you wouldn't recall meeting Janice because the poor woman is not what you would call memorable. I'm sorry, that's just how it is. It's a built-in mechanism in the male brain ... chest and legs first, then bum and face, with eyes last. Simple biology, my darling. Men must reproduce, so their vision is trained to look and remember the sexy bits first. An area this girl is sorely lacking."

"Whatever. But I can't understand how we could have caused an issue with this woman as that De Ath woman claims. We only met her the once."

"I know, darling, it does seem rather odd. But it's definitely her. She wore glasses back then, but maybe she's opted for contact lenses. Despite her acceptable figure and rather luscious skin tone, I'm afraid to say that the poor girl's no oil painting. A bit like your somewhat bland-looking Kimmy. We can't all be gorgeous like me, I suppose. Shame, really, but at least the saddo is trying to improve her appearance. Specs make a girl look like Velma Dinkley."

Niall and I exchanged a look as the man, claiming to be dead and holding a conversation with someone called Deana, appeared to be following the invisible thing with his eyes, this angel – who claimed to be sexy and gorgeous, which I considered a rather odd claim from a winged messenger from God – that had presumably moved from the table and now stood by the serving counter.

As Niall and I locked eyes, the gravy-writing incident from earlier came to the fore, causing me to swivel around and point to where I believed the 'thing' now to be standing.

"You ... wherever you are. You dipped your finger in the gravy."

"Oh, gravy, was it? It tasted like slurry to me. A dollop of unmentionable straight out of the septic tank. Totally yucky." Deana pulled a face and feigned gagging.

"She did, but she's very sorry for spooking you. Deana said the gravy tasted divine," Terry stated, swivelling around and offering me a grin.

"No, she didn't," chimed in Ellen, as she poked her head around her father's waist where Niall had tried to secure her. "Deana said it was yucky."

"No, I did not. Don't lie, Terence."

"Really? I'd be surprised …" I paused as Terry winced and glanced back at the counter. "I said, I'd be surprised because I've always considered Dawn's gravy to be on the tart side. Not that it's my place to say, but I keep telling her to add a pinch of sugar. See, I'm just the dogsbody around here."

"See! Yucky, Terence."

"Erm … actually, I lied," Terry grimaced. "Sorry, Deana wasn't overly complimentary about the gravy."

"Well, that doesn't surprise me. But whether I'm going completely off my rocker, or there is actually a sexy angel somewhere over there, d'you want to start explaining yourself? The last time I met you, you claimed to be called Richard Burton."

Because of the iconic name, I remembered this bloke when he rocked up in the spring to visit one of the residents at Waverly Care Home. I was the part-time receptionist at the time, only leaving that post when the manageress, Miss Shrives, and I had a disagreement, culminating in the officious old battleaxe suggesting I find alternative employment. Easier said than done, I might add.

Terry pursed his lips and nodded.

"Well?"

"I lied. Sorry about that."

"I'm aware of that, but why?"

"Long story, I'm afraid."

"Well, Terry, or whatever your real name is, I've got plenty of time on my hands. So, I'm all ears, as they say. And while you're at it, d'you wanna explain why you claim to be Richard Burton, carrying around business cards to that effect? Fakes, I suspect, which are all part of some elaborate con. Jesus, why do I seem to attract them? Chad, now you. Well, listen up, because I've had enough …" I paused as my rising inflexion, shrill of a woman at the end of her tether, if you like, caused Terry to take evasive action and step back a pace, encouraging me to jab an aggressive index finger at him. As I peered down the barrel of my finger, I lowered my voice to a hiss. "If you plan to con me, you're gonna be sorely disappointed because Chad Ruger's already been there, got the t-shirt, eaten the pie, and stolen my life savings!"

"Darling," Deana waved a knife at Terry. "How's that wit and charm of yours coming along? Need any help? Hmmm?"

"Janice … there's a knife hovering in the air," Niall exclaimed, tugging on Ellen's coat-hood to haul her back behind him after she'd strayed forward.

"Oh … and while you're explaining who you are and what you want, d'you wanna tell me how the hell you can do that?"

163

I swivelled my jabbing finger toward the levitating knife. "This trickery."

"Deana, please put the knife down. And as for my wit and charm, I'm getting there."

"Seems like it, darling. I think whilst you've been playing ping-pong for months on end, you've lost your touch with the ladies."

Terry tutted, I presume, in response to something the lady in red must have said. Niall, Ellen and I all jumped in fright as the knife dropped from the air and clanged onto the bain-marie as Terry had instructed.

"Please don't tut. You know I find it so childish and unnecessary."

"Janice, I'll explain everything. But I need you to keep an open mind. Now, do you remember Kim Meyer?"

"Terry, darling, I don't want to be a party pooper, but please, let's not take this conversation too far down the ridiculous route, shall we? Hmmm?"

"Yes, I know Kim. I haven't seen her for over six months, but what's she … oh, hang on, I remember, now. You came to the care home to visit old Clive. Clive Bradshaw, Kim's grandfather—"

"That's right."

"You know Kim, then?"

"Kim's my daughter."

"Oh, terrific!"

"Really?" I sarcastically fired back. "And I presume you still claim to be dead? Even though you're standing right here in front of me."

"Correct. I'm dead. Have been since 1983."

"Right, course you have," I muttered before rolling my eyes.

"Unfortunately, I suffered a heart attack a few months before Kim was born."

"Just after we made love, darling. When we created our love child, Damian. Very selfish of you to die in that moment, I must say."

"Whatever, but what's Kim got to do with me? And I know you said about keeping an open mind, but please, do you really expect me to believe … oh, this is stupid." I turned and shot an exasperated look at Niall. "Please tell me you're not in on this because I've just about had my fill. I really don't think I can take much more."

"No …" Niall shook his head before raising an arm to point behind me toward the kitchen. "Heavens above, would you look at that," he muttered, his eyes dilating to the size of saucers.

Despite clearly seeing his fear, the quivering arm and the paling of his complexion being telltale signs, and considering his earlier display of what I would regard as a robust and stoic-like persona, with great trepidation, I swivelled my head back to face the kitchen.

"Oh. My. God."

Part 2

13

November 2016

The Angel of Death

"Sorry to keep you waiting, old chap. There's an awful flap on at the moment. The 'suits' … that's the bigwigs, are chucking directives around like damn confetti. Happens every year when we get near to the silly season. Christmas really does seem to bring the worst out of the living. Goodwill to all men, my arse," he chuckled before dramatically slumping into his leather Chesterfield swivel chair.

Still somewhat perplexed, Pete hovered in front of the desk while repeatedly rubbing his hand back and forth over his bald head. Who the 'suits' or bigwigs were was utterly beyond him. In fact, he was none the wiser regarding the identity of the heavy-framed Eric Sykes-styled bespectacled man now gurning when rifling through an in-tray stacked with paperwork at least a foot high.

"Sit, man, sit. You're making the damn place look untidy."

"Oh, okay. Err … what's—"

"All in good time. All in good time, Peter. Ah, here it is."

"What?"

"Oh, no, bugger. That's not it." The man, who still hadn't introduced himself, lobbed the manila file to the floor on top of a heap of discarded files before rifling through the stack in the in-tray with renewed gusto, causing the top four inches of papers to slide and thus cascade to the floor. "Take a seat … there's a good fellow," he muttered, grimacing as he attempted to extract a file from the bottom two inches.

Pete eased himself into a leather-seated Cesca-style chair before steadying himself by gripping the arms when detecting the back starting to give way. When satisfied it could take his weight, Pete released his grip and surveyed the office from his leaned-back position. Although clad in ornate wooden panelling, oozing an air of opulence of perhaps a fancy solicitor's, Pete struggled to see how his presence could make the place untidier than it already was. To add to the mess strewn across the threadbare royal-blue carpet, the floor-to-ceiling bookcases, overflowing with box files and loose papers, suggested total chaos.

"Ah, got you, you little bastard," he hissed as he slowly drew the file from the stack, wincing like you might when at the business end of a game of Jenga or Kerplunk.

"Look, sorry, mate, could I—"

"Oh, sorry, who are you?" With the file in hand, the man peered up at Pete as if he'd been teleported into his office.

Pete frowned. "What d'you mean, who am I? You asked me to come here."

"Oh, yes, sorry, got distracted," he chuckled. "You're Peter Jones. Correct?"

"Pete Smith."

"Oh, same thing."

"What?"

"Jones, Smith, it's all the same at the end of the day, isn't it? You know that many Joneses and Smiths trundle through here each year, it can all get a smidge confusing."

"Oh ... well, I'm Pete Smith."

"Right, Peter, let's get down to it—"

"It's Pete. Only my mother called me Peter. And who are you?" Pete rubbed his hand across his scalp, worried and a little bewildered, as if now he'd become the unwitting stooge in a Monty Python sketch.

"Oh, didn't I introduce myself?"

"No." Pete continued rubbing his scalp. "Why am I here?"

"Ah, I see. Do you mean as in here in my office or here residing in 'limbo', as we like to call it?"

"Here ... your office."

"I presume you're fully aware that you're dead?"

"Yeah! Course I am. Ever since that bitch murdered me."

"Mrs Burton? Deana Burton."

"That's her."

"To be fair and balanced about it, you did kill the woman, her husband, and Mr and Mrs Clayton when you rolled your damn great lorry over their car on the M1 motorway back in the spring."

"Well, yeah," Pete shrugged. "That was an accident."

"From what I read, you were playing online gaming slots on your mobile telephone at the time. Death by dangerous driving, I would call that."

"Yeah, whatever."

"Did you win?"

"What?" Peter frowned, halting the scalp-rubbing with his hand positioned on his crown.

"Did you win the game you were playing when you killed those four people? Come on, Peter, keep up, there's a good chap. Otherwise, we'll be here all damn day. I've got a tee-off time booked for this afternoon."

"Oh … um, I can't remember."

"Right, so as I was saying—"

"Look, mate, you gonna tell me who you are?"

"Yes, sorry. Name's Graves. I'm heading up a new task force the bigwigs want in place and firing on all cylinders sharpish. PDQ is the term. Well, when I say new, we've put together these sorts of operations before. Still, like all new initiatives, they tend to wane after time. Operation Payback, we're calling this one. All rather hush-hush, so I'll need to rely on your discretion."

"What's this operation got to do with me? And another thing …" Pete paused when Graves held up a finger to interrupt him before flipping open the file, pursing his lips and peering down at the front sheet.

"Do you suffer from a condition?"

"Sorry?"

"A skin condition? Like eczema or psoriasis?"

"No."

"In that case, be a good fellow and refrain from rubbing your head. I'm trying to read, and you're putting me off."

"Oh."

"Yes, here it is. So, your case manager has recommended that you be seconded to this operation. It seems she believes you may have the right skill set we've been on the lookout for."

"Oh."

"Yes, as each new batch of the dead gets processed through clearing, a right sodding debacle, that is, I can tell you. Never seen such a dreadful backlog. Anyway, our case handlers keep an eye out for the right sort."

"Oh."

"Of course, the usual sort we go for is ex-army. Special forces, types. However, we've always found them rather gung-ho and a bit too Rambo-ish. Chaps like yourself tend to work out better."

"What do you mean, chaps like me?"

"Thuggish. Blessed with a bit of muscle, can handle themselves, lacking intelligence, and will comply without feeling the need to question constantly when given instructions."

"Oh."

"You do say, 'oh' a lot, don't you, Peter? Not that I'm complaining, per se, but it does get a touch boring." Graves checked his watch. "Good grief, is that the time? Okay, yes, you'll do. We'll arrange your transfer with immediate effect and start your training."

"For what?"

"Sorry, you've lost me, old chap."

"What am I being trained for?"

"I thought I was clear, no? Operation Payback."

"Yeah, but what is that?"

"Hush-hush, as I said a moment ago. Peter, come on, wakey-wakey."

"Right. This operation is … well, I take it that I do whatever, then go through to the Pearly Gates?"

"Good grief, man. There's no such thing. Really, Peter … that's the stuff of children's storybook fantasies. There aren't twelve pearl gates with St Peter guarding the entrance to Heaven."

"Oh."

"You'll be assigned to this operation for more or less all eternity. Unless, of course, you don't perform to the required standard. I suggest you knuckle down, get on with it, and count your blessings. You haven't exactly got what I'd call a good track record, have you, Peter?"

"What d'you mean?"

"Well, let's list a few, shall we?" Graves flipped over a couple of pages before stabbing a digit on the page headed up

'Negative Points Tally'. "A long list, this one. A hell of a rap sheet, as our American cousins like to say."

Pete frowned before restarting his head-rubbing.

"So, I see from your record that not only do you have death by dangerous driving under your belt, there's drug smuggling, plus the charge of causing an affray when a member of the Frontliners gang loosely affiliated to Tottenham Hotspur Football Club. And that's not overlooking the stealing cheques from your dear old mother's chequebook. I presume the last one on that list you probably thought no one, including Mrs Smith, ever knew about. Wrong Peter. We knew as well as your mother. Her only crime was not raising you with a firm enough hand."

"Oh."

"Oh, indeed. Anyway, all that, and the rest of this list, which I haven't got the time or the inclination to read through, means failure to perform your duties to the required standard, and it'll be a protracted stay in Hell for you. I don't want to put a dampener on the conversation, but it's pretty awful down there. The living rightly fear that place."

"Oh."

"You're a lucky chap."

"And what exactly will my duties be?"

"Collection and disposal."

Pete halted his head-rubbing and parted his lips.

"Two per cent of all those who die are so wicked we don't waste time assessing them. That sort we whizz straight through the clearing process into the bowels of Hell. So, you'll be a courier for our operations manager. You will efficiently collect your targets, some still alive, I might add, and dispose of them appropriately, as per your training. Your new job will be sort of a bin man. Collecting rubbish and disposing. Now, I don't want to appear rude, but I do have a tee-off time booked with some of the lads."

"Are you telling me there's a golf course up here?"

"Good grief, man. Of course, there is. As I regularly informed my dear wife, back in the days when I was still alive, without golf, there's not much point to living. She remarried, you know. Decent sort, but he's a bowler. So, she's gone from being a golfing widow to a bowls widow. Kind of poetic, don't you think?" he chuckled while closing Pete's file before lobbing it onto the top of the stack precariously balanced on the in-tray. "Now, run along. Your handler will take you through to meet your new boss. Odd chap, but nevertheless a half-decent fellow."

Pete remained seated.

"It's time to go, my good fellow." Graves shooed him with both hands.

Pete scrambled ungainly from the chair before padding towards the heavy oak door. When gripping the handle, he turned to face Graves.

"Who will I be working for?"

"Mr Reaper. Not much of a conversationalist, although a damn good golfer. Got an enviable handicap of just two, would you believe?"

"Mr Reaper?"

"Yes, that's him. He prefers to be called Grim, though. I'd bear that in mind if I were you. He can be a moody sort when the dead upset him."

"Oh."

14

December 2016

Crack Open the Bolly and Stolly

Despite the hand-grabbing incident, spinning spoons and a levitating knife, not to mention Ellen's insistence that we were in the company of a sexy angel wearing red, what I witnessed in the kitchen on the other side of the servery seemed to have transported me from reality into the set of an animated Pixar movie. So much so, as I gaped open-mouthed at the scene in front of me, if the green, one-eyed Mike Wazowski and his best pal, Sully, the sizable cyan-blue hairy monster sporting dinner-plate-sized purple spots, hopped out of the larder intent on catching our screams – that Niall and I were undoubtedly on the cusp of omitting – I wouldn't have been overly surprised.

While Terry hung his head, presuming he was used to these sorts of events – a spectacle better suited for an episode of *Bewitched* – Niall and I watched in awe as what appeared to be a tornado systematically rifled through the kitchen cupboards, drawers and the industrial-sized stainless-steel fridge. My eyes bulged as my head involuntarily tipped forward when various Tupperware pots floated mid-air, hovering for a second or two before the lids magically lifted.

"Oh, good grief!" Deana exclaimed, copping a whiff of something unpleasant when lifting the lid of the third container she held stacked in her left hand. "Even a drove of starving pigs would turn their snouts up at that."

"Deana, this isn't helping much."

"Darling, I'm just having a shufty while you apply that misplaced wit and charm of yours. If you need any help, just ask." Deana tentatively lowered her nose and sniffed the content of the open pot before pulling away and grimacing. "You know, I'm surprised any of those poor tramps turn up here for their meals because I would have thought anything foraged from the bottom of a stinking dumpster would harbour greater nutritional value than this God-awful pigs' swill. Less likely to give them food poisoning as well."

"I'm trying to get to the bottom of what our mission entails. You, with your ghostly acts, those *Wicked Witch of the West* antics, are only serving to distract Janice."

"Oh … yes, I see your point. Sorry darling, I just thought I'd have a nose around. It's all rather enlightening. I must say I've never encountered a place like this … you know, not being the kind of establishment that someone of my social standing would typically be seen dead in," she chortled. "Although … I am very dead."

"Look, if I need you to fling stuff around, I'll let you know. But for now, d'you think you could stop these antics and behave so we can work out how the hell we help Janice out of whatever mess you and I have apparently caused?"

"Alright. I'm sorry, darling. It's just that I, unfortunately, harbour an extremely low boredom threshold. It's probably the reason I worked my way through so many husbands. All of whom, apart from my luscious Dickie, could bore the knickers off a corpse. Well, poor choice of words because I won't be dropping my drawers for any of those turgid gits, dead or alive."

"Your many husbands' lacklustre performances are well documented," Terry huffed. "The fact their prowess in the bedroom department didn't move the earth for you—"

"Move the earth! Christ, the vast majority couldn't even rock the headboard, and only the sheets gave a little ripple. I wouldn't have minded if they'd just managed to stir my clitoris, so moving the earth was never going to happen!"

Terry huffed again, shaking his head dismissively.

While still holding my focus on levitating Tupperware boxes, I tried to rid the vision of my mother holding such parties back in the '70s. Evenings when my father's angst came to the fore caused by having to look after me while a gaggle of women invaded the lounge to swoon over a display of various-sized plastic storage boxes. Going by the glow on my mother's cheeks afterwards, I suspect there would have been a few glasses of Blue Nun consumed and probably some swapped risqué stories about their husbands whilst the Tupperware fanatics demurred their loose tongues.

"Oh, darling, don't get that totally unnecessary, droopy, porn-star moustache of yours all tied up in knots." Deana lobbed the Tupperware pots back where they came from before flinging the fridge door shut. *"What's the plan, then? I can't see Jaded-Janice here, the gormless woman with an open mouth, swallowing the guardian angel line you were about*

to trot out, so I venture you're going to have to come up with something a smidge more tangible."

"That's what I was trying to do before you started your Elvira impression."

"Blithe Spirit, darling, quite apt—"

"Yes, well, d'you think we could—"

"Oh, I loved that play. Noël Coward was such a brilliant playwright. I believe Joanna Lumley played Elvira on stage around the time you decided to die. Although clearly not in my league regarding gorgeousness, we heralded a certain similarity in our younger days. That said, I see myself as more of an Emma Peel sort, really. As in both ravishing sex icons, devastatingly witty, and look absolutely fabulous in a leather catsuit."

"Talking of which, I think the Patsy Stone character might be a more appropriate comparison."

"Hmmm. Yes, I seem to recall you made that accusation back in the spring when it was all I could do to drag you away from watching the damn television. Anyone would think that there was nothing worth watching in your day. And as for your accusation that I and that debauched character have any similarities, it's nothing short of rude. Rude, you hear, Terence? Now, I attest I like the odd ciggy and can be partial to a large VAT and drop of Bolly. Still, I'm not going to waste any more of my breath countering that effrontery."

"Blithe Spirit," I mumbled, shooting a look at Niall. "He said Elvira and then Patsy from *Absolutely Fabulous*," I hissed. "I'm not sure what Joanna Lumley's character has to do with this, but d'you think there really are spirits in the kitchen?"

Although an utterly barmy question to pose to a vicar or anyone for that matter, there were happenings afoot that suggested the paranormal: Ellen had maintained this gravy-licking woman in red was here with us, something definitely held my hand when we were outside, unless this Terry bloke was in the same league as David Copperfield or Paul Daniels, the scene in the kitchen could only be caused by spirits from the other side, such as an Elvira type, and unless this Terry bloke was a complete nutter, he seemed to be holding a conversation with thin air.

"I … I," Niall, white-knuckle gripping onto Ellen's hood as if her life depended on it, shot me a look. "I don't know, but I've never seen anything like it," Niall nodded to the window, gesturing that we should take a step back from Terry.

"Janice, look, sorry about all this, and I'm aware this is all a bit odd—"

"Terry, or whatever your name is, I need a moment to talk to Niall in private. D'you mind?"

"Oh … of course," he grinned before shrugging and glancing back at the servery.

"What do we do now?" I hissed as we retreated to the window.

"To be honest with you, I don't know, but I'm not happy being here with … with whatever is in that kitchen. Especially as I have Ellen with me."

"No, I see your point. You should go."

"I don't think I can leave you alone with him … this Terry bloke. I'm not sure he's all there. I mean—"

"Deana!" Terry hissed, causing Niall and me to shoot a look in his direction before continuing our whispered conversation.

"D'you think this Deana is actually here? I mean, you claimed to be able to see her when we were outside."

"Sorry, Janice, I have absolutely no idea. I did see her ... but—"

"But what?"

"Well, I'm starting to wonder if I imagined it. I lost my wife in the summer—"

"Oh, I'm so sorry."

"Ovarian cancer. Mercifully, it was quick."

"How awful."

"Yes ... but I often converse with her as if she's here with me. Perhaps my subconscious is conjuring up images that aren't real."

"Elvira," I muttered.

"It's a bit like that. Although, unlike the Charles Condomine character in the play, I can't actually see my dead wife."

"No, I understand. I sometimes talk to my mother."

"She's dead?"

"Oh, yes, long ago."

"So sorry."

"What about Ellen?" I nodded to the girl who stood between us, gazing up at nothing in particular as if held in some sort of odd trance. "Your daughter is adamant this Deana is here ... even holding a conversation with her."

Niall pursed his lips and pondered that thought as he stroked his daughter's hair while I continued.

"She can't be imagining the same vision, too. Can she? You both said you saw a woman who looked like Mrs Christmas. I mean, what are the odds that you both are imagining the same thing? Ghost, apparition, or whatever."

"Yes, I know—"

"As I said earlier, I'm not a believer. Sorry, I've inherited my father's view of religion. But you … you believe in God—"

"Of course."

"So, you believe in angels. Life after death. The resurrection."

"Yes, regarding our Lord Jesus Christ. Not a woman dressed as Mrs Christmas."

"No … so angels aren't real in your eyes, then?"

"Janice, I'm a vicar. I believe in the Almighty, The Son of God, the Holy Spirit. Still, I'm not going to start claiming the dead walk around rifling through kitchen cupboards wearing the sort of attire one might see a loose woman parade around in."

"Loose woman, charming. There's nothing wrong with tastefully showing a bit of leg. If you've got it, flaunt it."

"What's happening here then? The work of the Devil? Is *he* real?"

"Apparently, he is. I was talking to a chap from The-Powers-That-Be call centre only the other day who's actually met him. He reckoned Old Nick was a right shifty sort."

"The devil is a force of evil. I don't actually believe there's this hideous beast with horns sitting on a throne of fire. It's not literal. It's an ethereal wickedness or antagonistic but impersonal power which we must resist. I ask all to reject evil, not renounce it. The latter suggests the existence of a being of some sort. There's a subtle difference. It's a huge topic of discussion amongst my peers. Some, shall we say more conservative, prefer renounce to reject. Of course, that's not the teaching of the Book of Common Prayer, but that's my take on it. Being a realist in the modern world, if you see."

"Blimey, talk about drivelling on in answer to a simple question. A straightforward yes or no would have sufficed. Little does our man of the cloth know, but Old Nick is very much in existence, apparently."

"So, could this be the Devil's work or just some elaborate trickery?"

"Oh, Janice, I don't know. The only thing I do know is something's not quite on the level. I think we should get this Terry chap out of here, lock up, and go home."

"Yes, you're probably right. I'm sure there must be a rational explanation. But what about what this Terry said a moment ago? Y'know, when he was talking to this angel, that ghost thingy that ripped through the kitchen cupboards."

"Sorry?"

"He said that they had to help me out of the mess I'm in that they, him and this invisible Deana thingy, apparently caused. They must have some connection to Chad, the man who conned me out of all that money."

"My mummy always said listening to other peoples' private conversations was rude."

"Your mummy was quite correct, deary." Deana peered down at Ellen, distracted from the conversation she'd been earwigging. "However, until

your father and Janice accept I am real and here to assist, Terry and I need to hear what is being said."

"Ellen?" Niall asked.

"Oh, God," I grabbed Niall's arm and hopped sideways. "Is *it* here … standing next to us?"

"*It! Terence, what's the matter with this damn girl? Thingy, it, not exactly terms of endearment.*"

"Deana is standing right beside you, exactly where Ellen is pointing," Terry confirmed as he stepped closer.

"Ellen?" Niall asked, shooting a glare at his daughter.

"Yes, Daddy, Deana is there. I can touch her."

"*Darling, I think this calls for an unchained melody moment. Not that I plan to get all dirty with clay on a pottery wheel … incidentally, a movie scene my darling Dickie and I reenacted one evening, much to our guests' delight, during one of our erotic sex soirées a couple of summers back. Dickie's raging stiffy being the metaphorical pot, if you get my drift, when frolicking in a mud pool primarily employed for a spot of erotic, sexy nude mud wrestling … but I mean, I'm going to have to touch these non-believers and convince them I'm here and real.*"

"Yes, probably." Terry rolled his eyes.

"I'm just saying, darling."

"With him being a man of God, it's a good job they can't hear you, that's all I can say," muttered Terry.

"What did *it* say?" I blurted, recoiling when feeling something graze against my cheek before allowing what felt like a warm hand to touch me again.

"*She really does have wonderfully smooth skin. Wasted on a girl like this. And Terence, please ask her not to keep referring to me as an it.*"

"Trust me, you really don't want to know. Oh, on a separate note, Deana respectfully asks if you could stop calling her it."

"The dishy vicar needs a shave. His cheek feels all prickly. Although, at least, he doesn't have the urge to sport a silly porn-star-styled moustache." Deana purred as she stroked the two shocked faces.

"Daddy, what's a porn star and … and what's a raging stiffy?"

15

Hev Yew Gotta Loight Boy

"I'm feeling uneasy about not knowing where she is," I hissed at Terry, shifting forward on the sofa as my eyes flitted around the room, trying to locate the invisible woman.

"Boo!"

"It all feels a bit creepy. Can't she be wrapped in bandages like the Invisible Man? Then at least I'd know where she is," I asked, nursing a large glass of wine while ensconced in an armchair in the sitting room at the vicarage.

"I'm behind you! Oh, no, I'm not. Oh, yes, I am," Deana chortled after employing two distinct tones to play out her pantomime-esque sketch.

"Deana, grow up!"

"Oh, Christ, she's behind me?" I blurted when following Terry's gaze, frozen with fear, not daring to move when bug-eyeing Terry as he relaxed in what appeared to be a comfy, albeit tatty, armchair opposite.

"Sorry, darling. It's just that Jaded-Janice's silly comments are becoming all so tedious. At least the dashing vicar seems to have accepted my existence."

"Just park your backside, take a load off and drink your wine."

"Park my backside! Darling, pur-lease, if you're going to refer to my pert cheeks, then it's my luscious derrière, if you don't mind."

"Please, just sit and behave," Terry pleaded. "After your antics at the soup kitchen and that poor child asking what a raging stiffy meant, not to mention her enquiry regarding porn stars, perhaps it's time you left this to me to sort out."

"Alright, Tetchy-Terence. I'm not used to being around children, that's all. When alive, children and my paths didn't often cross. As we both know, I wasn't that close to our Damian, so children are a complete mystery to me."

"Going by the tales of your debauched garden parties, I'm not overly surprised. Please, Deana, let me handle this because at least we're now getting somewhere."

Due to being only able to hear one side of the conversation and keen to know the precise location of this Deana woman, I played head tennis between Terry and the general direction he seemed to be looking, presuming his focus was on this angel when talking. I say angel, but the subject of their conversation, namely erections, mucky films, and swingers' parties, led me to ponder that Deana didn't fit the mould of the teachings in the Good Book. Not that I'm overly au fait with the Bible, but I can't remember those sorts of stories at Sunday School where angels were mentioned.

"Okay," Deana sighed before flopping into an armchair and dramatically crossing her legs, Kenny Everett's Cupid Stunt style.

Although following the frankly bizarre experience at the refuge, witnessing the seat pad depress in the armchair next to

Terry, and a wineglass levitate still took my breath away. At least I knew where this thing, or whatever, was now positioned. However, I couldn't help but wonder how the wine consumed became invisible as Deana, the ghostly angel, if that's what she was, glugged back her Pinot.

A few years back, I'd stupidly attended one of those ridiculous clairvoyant events at the local theatre. I say ridiculous, probably because the spiritualist, self-proclaimed medium, didn't experience visitations from my mother, just connections with a fright of ghosts related to a select few who just happened to be conveniently seated in the front row. To say I felt cheated was an understatement.

Anyway, my mother had always been a believer, attending shows by the famous Doris Stokes at the London Palladium in the late '80s. So, after Mother passed, I'd thought, why not … I'd give it a whirl. When embarking on this fool's errand, still mourning the loss of my mother and feeling there were many unsaid words between us, I'd got sucked into the idea that I could perhaps hold a conversation with her from the 'other side' and clear the air, so to speak. If the clairvoyant, charlatan, more like – or the Madame Arcati character, to use the Blithe Spirit analogy from earlier – just happened to make contact with Mother, I'd hoped to come to terms with my grief. Although I'd known it was a show, therefore entertainment and probably not authentic, I'd been clutching at straws to grab any opportunity that might help me move forward.

Now, here at Niall's home, and whether the wine I was holding was blessed or not – unsure if that would make any difference – the 'entertainment' before me could only mean one of two things were afoot: ghosts-cum-guardian angels were actually a thing, or Niall, Ellen and I had simultaneously lost it.

Based on the fact that I considered it unlikely that all three of us were hallucinating, and despite the utter absurdity of the last few hours, I erred towards the first explanation. To bolster my fortitude while waiting for Niall to return after popping Ellen around to the neighbours for safekeeping, I glugged my wine, grabbed a refill and slugged that one, too.

"Oh, dear, darling. D'you think Jaded-Janice might be an alcoholic? I'm always up for a glass or two. As they say, it's five o'clock somewhere, but the girl doesn't half appear able to put them away."

"I imagine it's all a bit of a shock for the girl."

"Did she say something?" I asked, making a grab for the bottle.

"Deana was just suggesting you might want to go easy on the wine."

"Really?" I sarcastically fired back. "Easy for her to say. I might suggest it's not exactly that easy to come to terms with the idea that I'm sitting here drinking with dead people." I tipped the bottle up when my glass reached half full, thinking this ghostly woman may have made a valid point. Getting bladdered when invited back to the vicarage might not be such a great idea. "Anyway, if you're dead, as well as this Deana woman, how come I can see you? If you're a ghost, aren't you supposed to be see-through … translucent, or whatever?" I questioned, followed up with a nervous giggle, uttered either involuntarily caused by the effects of alcohol or embarrassment due to conducting a wholly daft conversation.

"That's a good question. Sorry, I'm not totally sure, just that it has something to do with needing to be visible to those we've been assigned to help."

"Right … and why is she … Deana, invisible? Well, apart from the fact Ellen can apparently see her."

"I'm not sure about that either, I'm afraid. Deana's my guide. Apparently, due to their innocence, some children can see her."

"And Niall … although, for some reason, he claims not to be able to see her anymore." I held my glass to my lips but paused due to feeling slightly woozy. Not that I was a lightweight when it came to consuming wine but, even for me, four o'clock was a smidge early in the day to get wasted despite how tempting that idea seemed.

"As I said earlier, men of the cloth can also see some of the guides."

"And when you say, 'those you've come back to help', I take it I'm not the first?"

"No."

I bulged my eyes to indicate his one-word answer really didn't cut it before flicking them at the levitating wine glass hovering about three feet above the chair to Terry's left. If I didn't know differently, I could be the stooge on an episode of *Rentaghost.*

"Do you want to expand on that?" I asked.

"Darling, come on, buck up. I'm with Jaded-Janice on this one. We can't wait for the vicar to return, so let's cut to the chase, shall we? It's time to go all in … spill the beans about who we are and why we're here. In a vicarage of all places." Deana turned to glance at the Christmas tree,

pulling a face as she did so. "Can't say I think much of the tree. Artificial old tat, hmmm! Dickie and I always went for a real tree. So much more festive, don't you think? Although Clara's seven-inch strap-on three-speed delight hits the spot, you can't beat the real thing ... phallic delights and trees." Deana flicked a bauble as she sipped her wine whilst jiggling her right leg before turning to offer Terry an alluring pout.

Terry rolled his eyes regarding Deana's references to whatever she and her ghostly spooky friend got up to in the bedroom.

"I just don't know how you manage to seamlessly shift from Christmas trees to dildos in the same sentence."

"It's a skill, darling."

"Hmmm. As for moving the conversation on, I'm getting there."

"Getting there! Back in the day, so was British Rail. That is until your friends in the nasty party sold it off. Privatisation ... lining the pockets of fat cats, I might add. Another one of that lot's lunatic policies. Now look at it ... total disaster. Our rail system is akin to a third-world country."

While Terry held a conversation with the invisible ghost waving around a wineglass, my eyes were drawn to a red, glittering bauble that now swayed back and forth on the amateurishly decorated tree.

I assumed Niall didn't possess an eye for detail or Ellen had arranged the decorations based on the fact the vast majority were hanging on lower branches. Also, whilst focused on the hypnotic swinging of said bauble, I presumed this Deana, the dead woman, had flicked it, and its wild toing and froing wasn't as a result of a freak gust of wind that had singled out that one decoration to set swinging. However, something Terry said caught my attention.

"Sorry … did you just say … err …" I lowered my voice to a whisper. "Dildo."

"Ehm … I was repeating something Deana said."

"An angel said dildo?"

"She's not your average angel."

"Yogi Bear's not your average bear, but I must say I'm a bit surprised that an angel would mention that word. What on earth was that in reference to?"

"We were discussing British Rail."

"Really?" I asked in a somewhat surprised tone when struggling to see how dildos and trains could form part of the same conversation.

Only last year, I witnessed a fracas when a bigoted old pillock made a scene about a woman breastfeeding, so I can't imagine what he would have made of a dildo, whatever the owner might be doing with it whilst commuting. Train journeys can be a smidge boring, but … I shook my head, ridding the vision.

"Well, we got onto the subject after discussing real and artificial trees."

"Is this relevant?"

"No, not at all. Deana was suggesting—"

I swivelled my focus to the levitating wineglass, assuming Terry's pause and sideways glance meant Deana had interrupted him.

"I'm just saying, darling, that's all. If you get on with it, then, before I die again, this time as a result of boredom ... termination by tedium ... we might actually discover what the hell we're doing in a vicarage. Not somewhere I would usually be seen, I might add. Although, there was one occasion when a rather coy curate of somewhere or other ... a church of some description which Dickie and I visited to see the vicar about getting married ... the poor understudy became a little flustered when copping an eyeful of a bit of leg. My fault, I suppose, for wearing a daringly short leather miniskirt." Deana waved her glass at Terry. *"If you're blessed with luscious, comely legs like mine, you just have to show them off."*

"So I see. It's a good job that Ellen's not here. You're showing a touch too much flesh that could be considered decent, especially when considering where we are," Terry tutted as Deana hitched the hem of her dress up another couple of inches, licking her top lip for added effect. "And another thing, I recall British Rail was a complete disaster, so I'm damn sure the commuting public fare a damn sight better than in my day. It was in the papers nearly every day ... dirty, smelly, late trains, strikes, and dried-up sandwiches."

"Apart from the Guardian, you shouldn't trust what the papers say."

"You an authority on the subject, are you?"

"Dickie was. He knew all about the press. Mirror readers think they run the country. Guardian readers should run the country. The Times readers actually do run the country ... poorly, I might add. The Daily Mail is read by the wives of those who run the country ... poorly, as I just said. The Financial Times is read by people who own the country, the Morning Star is read by those who think the country ought to be run by another country, and the Daily Telegraph is read by people who think it is. Oh, and the Sunday Sport is read by those vertically challenged men who can't reach the top shelf but enjoy a good wank at the weekend."

"My God, where did that drivel come from?"

"The right Honourable Jim Hacker, I'm led to believe," tittered Deana. "I'm paraphrasing, of course."

"Who the hell is this Hacker bloke?"

"Never you mind … a television sitcom. Maybe you were already dead by then. Who knows? You were lying in that grave for quite some time. Actually, I don't think he actually said the word wank. That's a direct quote from me."

"Christ, you're—"

"Unbelievable. I know, darling. It's such fun being with me. Now, come on. Let's be having you, to quote Delia."

"Who's Delia?"

"Doesn't matter, darling. It's a football, cookery thing. Something to do with that footie team from that very strange place in Norfolk. Not that I've ventured that far north. I assume it's all chewing straw and singing postmen. Now, let's put a jiggle on and get Jaded-Janice to stop gawping at this tacky excuse of a tree and probe the girl so we can discover whatever we're here for."

"Singing Postman … have you got a light boy?" chuckled Terry. "Christ, I remember that awful song. I reckon I was at school at the time. Probably early sixties."

"I have no idea. Can we move it along, please, darling? Preferably, before Jaded-Janice ends up paralytic on the sofa."

"Sorry, did you say you were at school in the early sixties?" I ask Terry after taking another hearty gulp of Pinot.

"I was. Born 1951. Died of a heart attack in '83—"

"While pleasuring my pussy."

I shot my eyes left to copy Terry when he paused. I assume the angel had said something, and Terry's expression suggested he wasn't overly chuffed with the interruption.

"As I was saying, I died in 1983."

"Yes, before I spent five minutes giving you a hand job in preparation for round two. Only to discover my tugging efforts were in vain when you couldn't get a stiffy because you were already dead. Lord knows I've dabbled in all sorts, with all sorts, but you're the only corpse's pecker I've ever given a good hearty tug on, I can tell you."

"I'm buried over the road in All Saints. I've been there for thirty-three years until I was chosen for a mission to help my daughter, Kim."

"Kim Meyer?"

"That's right—"

"I spotted that report in the Chronicle about her stepfather being arrested for a string of sexual crimes dating back to the early '70s."

"Sam Meyer. He was my best man when I married Kim's mother. After I died, Sharon unfortunately married Sam."

"Your precious little Sharon," Deana heckled from the sidelines. *"Dead Sharon!"*

"Your mithering is not required," Terry fired at the empty chair.

I shot a look at the seat pad to ensure the depression in the leather still existed. Not that I heralded concerns that this Deana could cause me harm, but felt the need to know her location.

"Mithering! Blimey, that's a big word for you, Terence. I presume you also played a spot of Scrabble as well as Monopoly and ping-pong while lounging around with your dead mates for all those months stuck up there in limbo."

Terry tutted.

Deana stuck out her tongue and scrunched up her nose.

"Just behave. Amuse yourself for a moment … on second thoughts, don't take that literally—"

"Shall I strip? Give the vicar a thrill when he comes back. Just think, if he's now starting to believe again … not the Lord, but in me, the dashing boy could cop a vision of pure beauty when I'm writhing around naked on the hearthrug. Hmmm. What d'you think?"

Terry shook his head and frowned before facing me.

"What did she say?"

"It's irrelevant. Now, as I was saying, I was returned from the dead to help my daughter. Sam Meyer had to pay for his crimes and what he did to Kim."

"What did he do?"

"I'd rather not say. But in the end, Sam got his comeuppance, and Kim is now happily living with her boyfriend."

"Vinny. I introduced them. I should have kept in touch, but you know how these things are. We weren't really friends, as such. We just used to chat when Kim visited Clive, her grandfather. Who, if all this is to be believed, was your father-in-law."

"Correct."

"Kim mentioned her real father died before she was born. I feel utterly stupid asking this ... but are you actually her dead father?"

"I am."

"And Kim knows ... believes you've returned from the dead?"

"I don't know. We didn't part on good terms. I suspect Kim struggled to accept who I claimed to be, despite offering up enough evidence."

"Yes, I'm sure." Without glancing her way, I pointed at the empty chair. "Deana was with you when you helped Kim?"

"She was," Terry nodded. "Also, when we helped my other two children, Damian and Ginny."

"And they believed who you are?"

"Again, I don't know. See, the thing is, on those three missions, no one could see Deana. This is different because Ellen can see her, as Niall did briefly, too. I'm unsure why we didn't think of this during those missions, but you must admit, Deana touched your hand earlier. You felt her."

"I did," I mumbled, my hand involuntarily rubbing my cheek where the 'thing' had touched me. Although that had definitely happened, I still couldn't shake the feeling that I was being taken for a fool ... again.

"Right, sorry about that," announced Niall as he barrelled into the lounge. "Ellen's playing with her friend next door, and Lucy and Scott, my neighbours, have suggested a sleepover ... oh," Niall paused, his eyebrows shooting upwards when glancing towards the bay window behind

Terry. "I can see her again. No longer the lady in red … but perhaps auditioning for a part in Calendar Girls."

"Calendar Girls?" I quizzed, shooting a look at the bay window, then to Terry, who'd swivelled around, now holding his head in his hands, then back to Niall, who appeared mesmerised by whatever he and Terry could see, but I couldn't.

"Sorry, vicar, I have an insatiable urge to be naked. I hope you don't mind. As for your reference to said members of the WI, I, dear boy, am more Playboy centrefold material … as your fixated gaze can attest to," Deana chortled before placing the tips of her index fingers on her nipples just to impart some modicum of decency.

16

Mistletoe and Wine

"Darling, is this going to take much longer?" Deana groaned, dressed again, now lying sprawled on the sofa after her exhibitionist jaunt around the tree when impersonating a nymph. "I'm aware explaining who we are is part of persuading Jaded-Janice to fess up to whatever pickle the girl's landed herself in, but I'm a woman who needs to be entertained. I'm sinking into this outdated MFI sofa, as well as the depths of despair while you prattle on for hours about life after death. Bor–ing!"

Following the apparent incident of an angel striptease, and after Terry went off on one at this Deana woman regarding her behaviour, which, if Niall was to be believed regarding her nudity, was fair enough, the visible one of the dead duo recounted his life story after he died … if that makes any sense. Even for Niall, accepting life after death, as in this limbo place, The-Powers-That-Be who decide our fate, and the missions that some of the dead are asked to complete, was a stretch to believe.

However, believe I did. And, it appeared, so did Niall.

The naked angel had again shown her presence with another round of hand stroking and, after she'd reapplied her clothing,

I'd patted her down, airport-security-operative style, which confirmed an invisible presence stood before me.

Bizarre.

Perhaps Doris Stokes and those Madame Arcati types weren't all charlatans. Although I'm still convinced the medium, psychic woman who I paid good money to see was definitely on the dodgy side.

"Look, Terry, I'm struggling to get my head around all this. Are you saying you and Deana are buried here … at All Saints Church?"

"We are," Terry confirmed with a pronounced solemn nod. "My grave is to the left of the main entrance, row seven, fifth from the end. You can't miss my plot. It's the one that no bugger tends to."

"They do now, darling. Your little Kimmy and that rather exotic Italian boyfriend of hers have been nose to the grindstone, hard at work bringing your final resting place into tip-top condition."

"Oh," Terry grinned to his left, clearly pleased with what something the invisible angel must have said. "Deana's buried just a bit further down on the right … in a double plot with her husband."

"How old is Deana?" I asked. "How long has she been dead? Oh, and I presume her husband to be much older than her?"

"Depends which husband. I can't remember their names due to being too many of them—"

"Darling, remember my little ditty I recite to remember the order I married them. ISMAAAR. Ian, Sidney, Mark, Alan, Adrian, Alex, and Richard. Ian Screwed Mark After Adrian Analed Richard … ISMAAAR. Of course, they didn't perform those acts because they were

never together in the same place simultaneously. Conjures up a vivid picture, though, don't you think?" tittered Deana.

"Oh, blimey, how many husbands did she have?"

"Seven."

"Seven," I parroted, my eyes bulging.

"Good Lord," muttered Niall before scrubbing his hand over his face and then shooting a look at the far end of the settee.

"Yes, seven, vicar. Men find me irresistible, and I suffer from a frighteningly low boredom threshold. It's a lethal combination that means my life was often in the company of one of your lot and then quickly followed up with an audience of thieving lawyers." Deana offered a finger wave and a smirk.

"Some are dead ... one of whom I've met during our mission to help our son, Damian. Deana's buried with her seventh husband, Richard, who I believe was quite a few years younger than her. Both died in a road accident earlier this year. As for her age—"

"Careful, darling. My foot is strategically positioned inches from your meat and two veg. You know it's not good form to speculate about a woman's age."

"Deana is ..." Terry shot a look left before continuing. "She's a mature woman, I guess you could say."

"Hmmm!"

"Right," Niall glanced towards the end of the settee again before addressing Terry. "So, if this isn't too daft a question. Where are your bodies? I take it you're not in the grave because you're here ... right in front of us."

"That's a fair question. To be honest, I'm not quite sure how that works. I mean, when up in limbo for all those months, the officials were somewhat tight-lipped on imparting information. Everything was on a need-to-know basis."

"Heaven and Hell actually exist, then?"

"A somewhat surprising question coming from a man like yourself," stated Terry, whose odd hand movements were apparently due to him massaging Deana's invisible feet.

"Well, I hear you, but as I was saying to Janice earlier, I'm a believer. When all is said and done, it's part of my job," he chuckled. "I'm more at the pragmatic end of the spectrum where Christianity is concerned. Let's face it, a quarter of the world's population are Muslims, and a fair chunk are non-believers. In my mind, what some may call infidels and heretics are all our fellow man."

"And woman! Fellow woman. Why do men always refer to the population as our fellow man? This is the twenty-first century, you hear, you dishy vicar?"

"Deana …" Terry glanced to his left, frowning at the invisible angel. "Please be quiet."

"Sorry, darling. I'm just saying, that's all. Now, carry on, I don't want you to stop. I must say you excel in the foot massaging department. You're almost as proficient as my darling Dickie."

"So, can I get this straight? These people … the spirits up there … wherever," I waved my hand at the ceiling. "They've sent you to help me. As in, get me out of my current pickle, which is all your fault."

"Yes, apparently so."

"But you don't know Chad, the man who conned me, and you have no idea who he is or how my situation is connected to these missions you performed in the spring when assisting your three children?"

"Correct again."

"Right. Not exactly the X-Files, is it? I mean, Mulder and Scully at least had a decent brief about what they were investigating, even if it was supernatural."

"I don't know what that is, sorry."

"Err … the X-Files. Everyone's seen the X-Files."

"Sorry, is this a film? I've been dead, remember? Although I managed to catch up on a fair few movies during the spring, up in limbo, the TV lounge was always a bit overcrowded for my liking, so I haven't watched much telly recently."

"Oh … sorry, course. Yes, it was a TV series about supernatural happenings. Mostly bad guys and the agents fighting evil. Do they actually have a TV lounge up there? Do you get all the channels without a subscription? I can't afford Sky, so I have to make do with a Freeview box."

"You know, I met Gillian Anderson once. I must say her obvious beauty totally captivated me. Dickie was mesmerised. I said he should have a crack at her, but he lost his bottle. The woman's blessed with wonderfully high cheekbones. I wouldn't have minded myself, you know. Disappointingly, though, I think she's straight."

Terry glanced left again.

"Sorry, Terry, we can't hear what Deana is saying," stated Niall.

"You can still see her?" I asked, laying my hand on Niall's knee to grab his attention, instantly wishing I hadn't due to concerns that he might construe that act as being overfamiliar. Not that I'm a touchy-feely sort, but since meeting him only a few hours ago, I regarded him as a friend. Maybe that was silly, but I didn't have many. Probably zero.

"I can. She's right there." Niall nodded to the sofa before giving my hand a comforting squeeze, which I took as an act of solace that he would often employ when consoling a parishioner. "Lying on the settee, no longer flashing her wares," he raised an eyebrow before continuing. "Of course, there's nothing wrong with nudity, per se, as long as it's not flaunted in an improper manner. At the end of the day, I suppose it's just our natural form. Lord knows what the Bishop would say if I told him I had a naked ghost on my sofa," he chortled.

"I can strip again if he so desires. To be honest, it's awfully warm in here. I couldn't say with any certainty if I've enjoyed the company of a vicar at one of our pool parties … you know, our summer soirées that Dickie and I hosted, but I'm quite taken with the dishy boy."

"Sorry, as I mentioned, you'll have to let us know what Deana said so she can be part of the conversation."

"Err …" Terry glanced left again.

"Go on, darling. I dare you," snickered Deana.

"Trust me, it wasn't relevant. Now, back to this Chad bloke. I think you'd better bring us up to speed so Deana and I can try to piece together how we might have inadvertently caused this issue when completing our earlier missions."

Despite unburdening myself to Dawn and Niall earlier, giving a run-through of the headlines regarding the events of the past few months that pertained to all things Chad Ruger still had the effect of causing me to inwardly wince at my utter stupidity. The more times I relayed the story, the more I failed to believe I could have been so easily duped.

Janice, the stupid woman.

After recounting my tale of woe, I employed an exaggerated wince, awaiting the ghosts' scorn.

"My good Lord, the woman's denser than an old maiden's minge. How on earth could anyone be so foolish? I tell you, Terence, we've landed ourselves a right dippy one here."

"What did Deana say?" asked Niall.

"She was just saying how awful that must have been. She's very sorry to hear about what's happened and is determined to move Heaven and Earth to help Janice."

"Piffle. The woman's about as sharp as a polished marble. Anyone that daft deserves all they get. Dozy mare."

"Oh … well," I paused to look at the far end of the sofa, assuming the depression in the cushion would be the position of the angel's head. "Thank you, Deana. It really has been an upsetting time. I feel rather stupid for being sucked in by him." Despite fully believing the angel existed, it wasn't lost on me the absurdity of talking to a cushion.

"Hey," Niall took my hand and gave it that vicar-esque type squeeze. "You're not stupid, just unlucky. As I said earlier, these con men are professionals. Evil men who've perfected their wicked trade."

I offered a tight smile in response, squeezing his fingers to thank him for his kind words. If I knew where Deana's hand was, perhaps I would do the same for her. Her kind words were certainly appreciated, irrespective of whether she and this Terry bloke could actually help me recover the money or not.

"Darling, Chad Ruger is clearly not Chad Ruger. He must be connected in some way to Little Kimmy, Damian, or Ginny. He's someone who, through the act of saving those three, we've inadvertently forced into a situation that's led them into conning this witless woman. I think we need to make a list."

"I think you're right." Terry nodded at the cushion before facing me and the man whose hand I still gripped. I hoped Niall didn't mind, but the physical contact seemed to impart a strength that had ebbed away over the last week. "We need to make a list."

"Oh, you sound like Dawn."

"Dawn?"

"The cook at the refuge. She likes lists."

"The gravy killer, I presume."

"Yes, well, as Deana just suggested. Chad Ruger, clearly not his real name, must be someone we've crossed paths with back in the spring. Whatever we did to save my kids, someone who ended up on the sticky end of our actions must have diversified into becoming a con man."

"That, darling, could end up being a long list … probably long enough to rival Schindler's."

"Do you have any idea who that might be?" Niall asked.

"No, as Deana just said, that could be a long list. Unfortunately, Kim, Damian and Ginny found themselves in tight spots with some wholly despicable sods trying to ruin their lives."

"But you were able to help them, right?"

"Yes, Janice. As we will for you. Okay, I think it's fairly safe to say Deana and I need to come up with a list of the most likely candidates, and then we can formulate a plan from there."

"And just to be clear, whatever that plan involves, I assume your actions will be on the right side of the law?"

"Of course, Father. As I mentioned earlier, both Deana and I have to improve our points total so we don't end up in Hell. Apparently, we're both some way short of the amount required."

"Oh, yes, I see … I wonder how many points I have?" I pondered. "I mean, I've been pretty good, I think. Oh, I did steal my best friend's pink fluffy pencil case when at primary school. That's long before I swiped her Sheena Easton LP. She wouldn't let me borrow it, see. There was that time when I sort of borrowed but didn't pay back the one pound fifty I stole from my mother's purse to buy Cliff Richard's Christmas number-one single." I tapped my lips as I trawled through my memory for other naughty acts that may come back to bite me when I'm up there being assessed. "Oh, hell, there's the eavesdropping into the private telephone calls of Miss Shrives, the care home manager. That really was awful. I don't know what I was thinking." I turned to Niall. "Sorry, I was talking out loud. You don't do confessions … that sort of thing, do you? I'm just wondering if that might help. Thinking about it, I'm sure there are a few more iffy things I might have to own up to. I mean, one time in …" I paused and winced at the memory.

"One time, in band camp, perhaps? Christ all-bloody-mighty, talk about droning on."

"One time, in college, I sort of, silly really, snogged my Maths lecturer. He was at fault, too, of course. But we didn't, you know …" I paused to lower my voice. "We didn't go any further, if you know what I mean." When clocking Niall's bemused expression, I blushed, now wondering why I'd divulged that unnecessary tit-bit. Something I'd never previously uttered to anyone. Perhaps this man made me feel safe. Safe to be me and free from the fear of being judged.

"I presume a blind lecturer or the man was desperate. Jaded-Janice isn't exactly a master criminal or wanton hussy, is she? Certainly, no Bonnie Parker, that's for sure. If that's the extent of her misdemeanours, I imagine her points total could rival that of Mother Teresa! I bet she's a virgin, too. Jaded-Janice, not Mother Teresa. Well, both."

Niall waved a finger at Deana while raising an eyebrow at Terry.

"Oh, Deana was just suggesting it might be time for a cup of tea, perhaps? Maybe a mince pie, too, if there are any going spare?"

17

The Female of the Species

"Come on, darling, let's start compiling this list. Now the dizzy mare and the dashing vicar are out of the way, we can get the ball rolling." Deana took a bite of her mince pie, catching an errant crumb at the side of her mouth with her index finger before continuing. "I want to solve this mystery sharpish, preferably within the next couple of days. Then, perhaps that lot up there will let us enjoy Christmas together. You, me and the delectable Clara can relax, play a few party games, and make merriment. Might even let you join in on a game of nude Twister if you like."

"I think you're being a smidge unkind about this girl." Terry repeatedly clicked the Parker pen when pondering the next name to add to the list on the notepad provided by the vicar before he and Janice took a trip next door to drop off an overnight bag for Ellen.

Deana sighed before popping the half-eaten pie in her mouth.

"Not that I want to get into a drawn-out debate about it, but you've been quite the mischievous one today. And regardless of this Janice woman's naivety, we're here to help her, not constantly highlight her many shortcomings. That's not to mention the earlier stripping and pole-dance antics with the damn Christmas tree."

"Yes, sorry, darling. You're quite right. See, the last few months, time with Ponderous-Petunia, has literally sucked the life out of me. Being back together, the A-Team, has rejuvenated my sense of adventure. You really do bring the best out in me, you know."

"This is your best?"

Deana smirked.

"Christ …"

"I know, darling, I'm unbelievable. Okay, you peevish little thing, you … read the list to me while I lie here looking gorgeous. I'll chip in if I think of anyone you've missed."

"Shall I feed you grapes while you lie there?" Terry sarcastically fired back.

"Like in a triclinium … as scantily clad goddesses being fed delicacies by slaves."

"I have no idea what you're on about. As per bloody usual."

"A triclinium is a dining room with reclining sofas. Chaise longue type thingies where the great and the good, Roman goddesses are pampered and enjoy wine and other delicacies."

"Right, if you say so."

"I do so. Come on, relay that list."

"Okay," Terry puffed out his cheeks. "I've penned them chronologically. Starting from our first mission."

"Very good."

"So, first up is my old mate and best man, Sam Meyer."

"Oh, horrid man. Rotting in prison, thankfully. I do so hope some evil beastly brute with a thunderously enormous, whopping willy gives him a good rogering up the rear alley. That will teach the little pervert."

"Quite. Well put, by the way."

"Thank you, darling. I do have a way with words. Apart from my wonderfully pert boobs, it's my most alluring quality."

"Sam is unlikely to be our man because he's incarcerated."

"Agreed. Who's next?"

"Joseph Meyer, Kim's half-brother."

"Oh, lordy lord. Him! Your precious little Sharon's son."

"Yeah, unfortunately. Joseph wouldn't have been born if I hadn't died."

"Spilt milk, darling. Don't dwell on your death. It's not good for your health. Although, being as you're already dead, I suppose it doesn't matter. Now, Joseph Meyer ... one wholly despicable specimen of a man. A douchebag, if ever there was one. He has to be a prime suspect. We ruined him ... the git lost everything. I've not heard what happened to him after his father's arrest, so he could be floating around. Also, I imagine he's got a fair few axes to grind."

"I agree. Next is Daniel Maypole."

"The jeweller who tried to con little Kimmy?"

"The very same."

"Oh, yes, slimy little weasel, that one. That day in his shop when I spooked him with my *Wicked Witch of the West* antics was such fun," she snickered.

"Yes, well, he didn't exactly come out of that situation smelling of roses, as I recall."

"No, you're spot on, darling. Maypole Jewellers has held a presence in the High Street for decades. However, the business folded soon after he levied false claims about Kim stealing from him. It's deplorable how many long-standing businesses and institutions are going to the wall. Still, weak men rightly get their comeuppance."

"The man was a compulsive gambler. He has to be high on our list of suspects. Gamblers are as desperate as drug addicts to get their next fix. Daniel Maypole would presumably resort to any method to lay his hands on some cash."

"His shop was boarded up for months … but I spotted in the Chronicle just the other day that it's now reopened as a vape shop."

"A what?"

"Vape … electronic cigarettes. It's all the rage, darling."

"Oh."

"I have to say it's all rather ridiculous. Those right-wing fascists, that lot in the nasty party you so adore, have jacked up the price of cigarettes, plastered the packaging with pictures of dead people and black lungs, and now hidden them behind locked cabinets in the shops in an attempt to discourage children from starting the habit. Nothing wrong with the odd ciggy, I say. Puts hairs on your chest. Well, men's chests."

"I'm not sure that's been medically proven."

"No, anyway, for a few years, the fascist's policies worked. Smokers became social lepers, and kids no longer considered smoking to be cool. Then what do they do ... don't answer, I'll tell you what they do. The stupid government actively court the vaping producers to open shops selling brightly coloured plastic sticks, most of which wouldn't look out of place as a Christmas tree decoration ... probably better than the tat on the vicar's tree. Anyway, these vapes are packed full of nicotine disguised as a sweet mango flavour. I mean, how ridiculous, darling, it's regression at its finest. Vapes are the new mobile phone, as in the population are glued to them ... try to take a vaper's stick away, and they regress into a baby wailing for their dummy."

"Just a point of order before getting back to our list. I seem to remember you saying that smoking in a public place was banned in 2007 ... a time when I believe the country was run by those nanny-state-loving lefty loons you so adore."

"Hmmm. Touché, darling, touché. Who's next?"

"Next is Portly-Pete. The man who killed you and, in turn, you murdered."

"Oh, yes, that Neanderthal lump of gristle. He's dead, and my dead bestie, Odette, has the heathen on a tight leash."

"Yes, okay, we can scrub him." Terry drew a line through his name. "That's it for Kim's mission, so on to Damian's. First up is Lee Parish."

"Well, a con man who's perfectly suited for this type of skulduggery. However, the rotter's dead. My Sidders crushed his skull with a candlestick in the vestibule to use a Cluedo-esque term."

"Hmmm. Good point."

"Although, to your point, darling, we can't rule anyone out based on the fact they've stopped breathing."

"We'll keep him in mind. What about old Sidders himself?"

"Again, dead, but as we just said, that doesn't necessarily mean we can rule him out. However, I'm not sure Sidders has the guile for this sort of thing."

"Agreed. So, next, I have Bridget, the evil woman who conned Damian before Sidders dropped her off a balcony. I think we'll assume she's out of the frame due to being a woman and dead. I think we need to focus on men and the living."

"Agreed."

"So, Nathan Bragg. Bridget's half-brother. Although he came good in the end, by all accounts, he was a shifty, sly sort."

"Yes, add him in. That said, the man did the right thing by our boy, so perhaps he's not high on our list."

"I think you're right. Okay, then there's one of your other husbands, Alex Bond, Nathan's stepfather. Which number was he?"

Deana counted out on her fingers. "Ian, Sidders, Mark, Alan, Adrian, Alex, then my darling Dickie … Ian screwed Mark after Adrian analed Richard. Yes, that's right, analed stands for Alex. He was number six."

"Right."

"No, I think we can cross Alex off the list. He's a wealthy man in his own right. Although a turgid git like the other five, con man antics aren't in his playbook."

"Okay, I'll bow to your greater knowledge."

"You do that."

"Next, we have a man whose name remains a mystery. Damian and Courteney referred to him as Gold Tooth. A bent copper."

"Oh, yes, well done, darling. I'd forgotten about that sod. We don't know what happened to him, do we? I presume he's still up to no good. If he was in cahoots with Lee Parish, then I imagine the nasty bastard has connections to a plethora of other low-life felons. We'd better add him to the list."

Terry nodded as he underscored the moniker.

"This is fun, darling." Deana nuzzled her cheek to Terry's arm after flipping her legs off the settee. "I do so enjoy our little sessions when we get the old grey cells whirring. Almost as good as sex."

Terry side-eyed his dead partner, raising an eyebrow.

"Well, that might be overstating it a smidge. But fun, all the same. Who's next, you clever boy?" she asked, giving his biceps a rub.

"Karl Greene. Courteney's ex. The drug dealer she stiffed."

"Hmmm. I'm not sure Mr Greene would have the nouse for this sort of operation. We only met him the once, and I'd say he was more the head-butting thug type. Also, he's in Brixton Prison, serving life for murder. With a bit of luck, sharing a cell and enjoying the delights of Sam Meyer's hairy bottom."

"That conjures up a rather disturbing image. And to think, Mr Greene once had the lovely Courteney to cuddle up to."

"Yes, alright. Don't overplay it. I can't deny Damian's girl is easy on the eye … she benefits from similar beauteous genes as myself. I, of course, am significantly more alluring."

"Of course."

"Thank you, darling. It's good that we agree. I'm so sorry that you're missing out … you know, what with me now fully bought into the lesbian lifestyle. If I was still of a mind to entertain playing hide the sausage, yours would be the first to sizzle my senses."

Terry rolled his eyes but sensibly chose not to remind the woman that he had no desire to hide his sausage where she was concerned. Of course, there was a day when he would have happily obliged, as he did the day he died. However, his sole focus was to amass the required points to be reunited with Sharon. Assuming his wife was on the upper level and would be of a mind to take him back after his dallying with many a willing participant of the opposite sex when alive.

"And then lastly, for Damian's mission, we have Fred Hallam."

"Oh, yes, Inch-High-Perverted-Private-Eye himself. As I said, when we rummaged around in that festering cesspool of an office of his, I have no issue with porn, per se. However, there's tasteful, consensually produced erotica that my darling Dickie and I would often create. Then there's the exploitive filth that man seemed totally obsessed with."

"Hmmm. Those pictures on his computer thingamajig were certainly hard-core. Definitely under-the-counter jobs compared to the stash of Fiesta and Knave mags I used to keep in the shed."

"Filth, Terry. Pure filth. That's what that man had secreted on his laptop. The little perv should be castrated. As for your stash, those tacky publications packed full of pictures of obese, au natural readers' wives, that's very low-brow, I must say."

"Sharon wouldn't allow them in the house."

"Quite right. Now, Hallam was in all sorts of bother. A failing business and a drinking habit. He is definitely high up on our list."

"Agreed. Okay, that's it for Damian's mission. Next, we have those we encountered when solving my Ginny's issues. First up, and my personal favourite for con man of the year, is Alistair Strachan. Her ex-husband."

"Oh, yes, what a shifty, conniving, detestable degenerate. I had the snivelling weasel pegged as one of those inadequate flash gits who think they're God's gift but are anything but. I witnessed the unfiltered version of the pathetic excuse of a man when rifling through his office that day. A small man, I suspect, in every sense of that meaning, with anger management issues probably caused by misogynistic beliefs inherited by his lamentable father. Also, going by the copious amount of body spray he must smother himself in, I suspect Alistair is one of those stupid, deluded buffoons who actually believe the adverts that suggest that immersing themselves in a chemical fog of 'eau de too much' actually makes them irresistible to the opposite sex. I wouldn't mind betting he's the sort who wanks in front of the mirror to enforce his delusional imbecilic self-appreciation, even though I suspect the reprobate probably can't masturbate for toffee."

"Safe to say you didn't warm to him?"

"Correct. We didn't like Alistair Strachan, did we?"

"We most certainly did not. Despite your suggestion regarding his lack of hand-to-sausage coordination, I think Alistair has all the attributions required to pull off an elaborate con."

"Agreed. And, something you're probably unaware of … after Ginny left his accountancy firm, the idiot racked up eye-watering debts. Thus, the business fortunes took a significant turn for the worse, resulting in Alistair declaring bankruptcy in the autumn."

"Did he now?"

"He did. Strachan Accountants is no longer. Plenty of time to diversify into running cons and choking the chicken in front of the mirror."

"I can imagine."

"I'd rather not, darling."

"Yeah, not sure which is worse … thinking of Alistair or what Karl and Sam might be getting up to in their shared cell."

"Don't dwell on that thought, darling. It'll give you indigestion. Right, who's next?"

"His father, Mel Strachan."

"Dead. Next?"

"DCI Kevin Reeves."

"Hmmm. Probably not aware of our involvement and also very dead."

"I think we can discount Ginny's parents, Paul and Lizzy Goode. I mean, they're both dead, too."

"Agreed. There really are a lot of dead people, aren't there, darling."

"According to that De Ath woman's secretary, death has become so popular that the process of assigning the masses to either Heaven or Hell has become completely snarled up."

"So you said, darling. What a mess they're in. You'd think The-Powers-That-Be would be more organised, wouldn't you? I bet it's run by a man."

"God?"

"I would imagine he's probably the Chairman. A non-executive sort of position. I'm referring to the CEO. Of course, if they put a woman in charge, no doubt the utter debacle would be sorted in a jiffy."

"If you say so."

"I do so. Now, in my capacity as your spectral guide for this mission, shall I provide a short synopsis of our findings?"

Terry offered a pained grimace in reply.

"Hmmm, I know that look, Terence."

"I'm all ears."

"I should think so. Okay, we have compiled a list—"

"We?"

"Yes, we, darling. I accept you penned it, but it most certainly was a joint effort."

"Right," Terry offered a po-faced nod.

"Hmmm. We're going to have to deal with your petulance, Terence. This cavilling attitude you seem to have returned with really isn't welcome. I'm aware I'm not perfect …

although almost … but I don't appreciate this testy undercurrent you harbour that's simmering below the surface. I'm not just some troubadour here to entertain. Far from it, I'm an integral part of the team to ensure we deliver a successful outcome to the mission. Now, pin those lugholes back and listen up while I offer a concise précis of our discussion."

Terry raised an eyebrow as Deana took a moment to gather her thoughts, drumming her red, glossy-painted nails across his knee.

"Okay. Here goes. We have a person, probably male, based on the fact Janice has conversed with said perpetrator. However, that doesn't necessarily rule out that the man she spoke with isn't just the stooge in an elaborate operation run by a fiendish female. The fairer sex is immeasurably more cunning than the male—"

"Deadlier."

"Quite. Now, stop interrupting my flow. As I was saying, there could be a woman behind this. However, we only have one on our list. That beastly Bridget, and we know she's dead. Expertly despatched over a fifth-floor Parisian hotel balcony by good old, lacklustre Sidders. We also know that in our previous missions to save little Kimmy, our wonderful boy, Damian, and the rather annoyingly exquisite Ginny, we, that's you and I, must have crossed paths with said nasty bastard at some point. Meaning, they most certainly are not American, so they must have employed the accent to play the part."

"A synopsis is supposed to be brief, is it not?"

"As I said earlier, we'll tackle your peevish attitude later. I might see if Clara can knock this querulous mood out of you."

Deana lowered her voice to husky tones before continuing. "The girl is blessed with a vast array of talents."

"Right." Terry rolled his eyes.

"So, I continue, ensuring my account covers all the salient points. When referring to my earlier point, it's probably right to assume that we are hunting a man. Something I've excelled at for many a good year," Deana snickered while rubbing Terry's knee. "Of which we have twelve prime suspects. I shall list them in ascending order, starting with the most unlikely and thus culminating with those in pole position for the nefarious rotter of the year award."

"Go for it," Terry grinned.

"Lee Parish. Sidders. Portly-Pete. Mel Strachan. All dead, so bottom of our list. Karl Greene. Sam Meyer. Both despicable reprobates are currently enjoying the hospitality provided by our monarch, hence the reason for placing them at the lower end of the list, just above the dead. Then Nathan Brag and Gold Tooth, the bent copper. At the top of the tree, we have Fred Hallam. Alistair Strachan, Joseph Meyer and our front-runner, Daniel Maypole."

Terry pursed his lips and nodded. "I agree, but have Alistair as the front runner."

"No, darling. Top four at best. Trust me, Daniel Maypole … pole position."

"If you say so."

"I do so. Okay, as far as the plan of attack. Although you're quite wrong, we start with Alistair to appease you. Tomorrow, we hunt him down, see what he's up to, and scare the bejesus out of him. If he's our man, we ask him for Janice's life savings."

"And if he's not prepared to play ball?"

"He can go the same way as his father. You hold him down, and I'll suffocate the git with a carrier bag. I have a Fortnum and Mason carrier that's just the right size for his big head and robust enough for carrying out a spot of murder."

"Not sure the second part of that plan works for me. I'm trying to improve my points, not fritter them away."

"Oh. Yes, good point, darling. After dispatching Portly-Pete into the afterlife, I've acquired quite a taste for murder. I can quite easily see how serial killers get the bug and thus find it difficult to stop. It's almost addictive."

"You're going to Hell, woman."

"Quite possibly. For now, Terence, here, perched around a cosy fire in the vicarage while enjoying the festive fare on offer, I'm very much in the land of the living and possibly Janice's only hope.

18

Roll Away The Stone

"I hope you didn't mind me asking you to join me. It's just I thought it would be a good excuse to have a natter about what's going on without those two ghosts ... angels, or whoever they are, listening in."

"No, course not." I ran my ponytail through my hand. "I thought that was why. Niall ..." I paused, waiting for him to turn and face me as I leaned against the open door to his daughter's bedroom, watching Niall pack Ellen's overnight bag, ready for her sleepover at her bestie's next door.

If any company needed a lesson on how to sell a brand, they could do a lot worse than learning from the owners of Hello Kitty. Ellen's bedroom was a shrine to the character, from the lampshade to the quilt cover, clock, and even her slippers and dressing gown. For a fleeting moment, considering the large bedroom, the plethora of toys and goodies, and the comforts that the five-bedroom Edwardian vicarage had to offer, I thought Ellen to be a fortunate girl. Then, of course, I remembered the poor little love had lost her mother. No amount of materialistic, branded 'comfort blankets' could replace the love of a lost parent.

"Janice, you alright?" Niall asked, looking up while continuing to stuff Ellen's on-brand backpack with her on-brand PJs.

"Are we going mad?" With both hands, I stretched my hair back and retied my scrunchie. Not that I needed to, but it's just what I do.

"Hmmm." Niall straightened up, allowing the overflowing, stuffed full to the gunwales backpack to topple over on the quilt cover. "The fact that we have two angels … dead people, compiling a list of who might have conned you, perched on my sofa scoffing a packet of Mr Kipling's mince pies and sipping PG Tips."

"Err … yeah."

"I don't know. Maybe. Probably. Who knows? That's partly why I persuaded Ellen to stay next door for tonight."

"Because evil is lurking at the door? Or stripping naked and prancing around your Christmas tree? Or both?"

"Something like that. If it wasn't impossible, apart from when solving historical cold cases, I'd consider requesting to have their bodies exhumed."

"Are their graves where Terry said they are?"

"I don't know but, after dropping Ellen's bag next door, I fully intend to grab a torch and take a peek."

"Bit creepy."

"Rummaging around in a graveyard in the dark?"

I nodded in response as Niall retrieved Ellen's bag and fought with the zip.

"Ghosts …" Niall huffed and checked himself before continuing. "Well, okay, maybe not ghosts, but monsters and the dead crawling out of graves aren't real. That's the stuff of horror movies. Graveyards are probably the safest place to be at night. Folk get murdered in their beds, and city streets can be dangerous places. The days of resurrectionists and Burke and Hare are long gone. The only company you'll find in a graveyard after dark are a few nocturnal animals and the whispering wind in the trees. Even in South London, the street dwellers and smackheads didn't venture into graveyards after dark. The dead don't come back to life."

"Jesus?"

Niall offered me a smirk, halting his wrestling match with the zip. Due to the bulging backpack, a bout he was losing. "With one exception."

"One?"

"As you said, the Son of God."

"Well, unless we're both delusional, there's three … Jesus, a man with a wickedly retro chevron moustache called Terry Walton, and an apparent nymphomaniac called Deana Burton. I can't comment on the first, but the other two are currently downstairs in your front room."

"I know."

"Maybe we are going mad."

"That would be a slightly more believable answer to what's happened."

"Hmmm …. not that I think you'll get much more in that bag, but have you got everything Ellen needs?"

"I think so. I'm not too proficient on the packing front. My wife was the suitcase packer, not me."

"I can see," I chuckled. "You got her toothbrush?"

"Oh, bugger, no. Could you grab it for me? It's the—"

"Hello Kitty one?" I threw over my shoulder as I turned and padded across the landing toward what I presumed to be the bathroom.

"Spot on. How did you know that?"

"Call it women's intuition," I hollered, grabbing the on-brand brush and noticing three in the jar. Either a third person lived here, or Niall hadn't brought himself to the point of letting go of the woman whose photos liberally plastered on the mantlepiece and atop the piano's fallboard – suggesting Mrs Vicar had been the pianist – positioned in the front room, clearly showing the vicar of All Saints was punching above his weight where his wife was concerned. Long dark hair, high cheekbones, and flipping gorgeous. Not that it mattered. Just my insecurities bashing in an appearance to put me down. An all-too-regular event.

"Could you also grab—"

"Her hairbrush?" I completed his sentence as I entered her bedroom, holding out both items.

"Oh, great, thanks."

"Shall I do it?" I asked, nodding to the bag and Niall's ham-fisted attempts to rip the zip apart.

"Could you?"

"Course."

While I emptied the bag, deciding to fold her clothes neatly before repacking, Niall padded over to the window, which offered views of the church and that creepy graveyard. Although not relishing a jaunt along the pathways that weaved through the headstones, I also didn't fancy the idea of being in the company of two ghosts without Niall by my side. So, Hobson's choice … after popping Ellen's backpack around to the neighbours, I would be embarking on a stroll amongst the dead who presumably hadn't left their final resting place. Not that I'm a believer, but I might suggest Niall carries a cross as well as the torch. Better to be safe than sorry.

"Ellen hasn't come to terms with her loss."

I didn't comment; instead, I focused on folding Ellen's jimjams.

"She doesn't understand why God would let her mummy die."

"It must be tough for her. At that age, it's impossible to understand."

Still facing the window, Niall didn't reply, his reflection offering a frown.

"What about you?"

Niall swivelled his head. The fact that he didn't answer caused me to pause the repacking.

"Oh, sorry, that was rude of me. It's none of my business."

"No … not at all. It's fine. And yes, I have … you have to, don't you? The only reason I haven't donated Julie's clothes and sorted through her bits and bobs and general paraphernalia ... the bathroom cabinets are still full of her makeup ... is for Ellen's sake."

"Perhaps if you did, it might help Ellen move on."

"That's a very good point. You're probably right. I try not to talk about Julie ... I don't want to upset Ellen."

"You should talk about your wife with Ellen. She needs to hear you mention her mother ... so she knows you miss her as much as she does. Remember the good times and keep those memories alive. But perhaps ... look, not wishing to butt into your private life, but the constant reminders of her mother's things probably aren't helping Ellen. I know it's totally different, but when I lost my mother, the fresh start helped me move on."

"I think I should have seen you when I asked for help instead of the nigh-on useless bereavement counsellor the church offered," he smirked. "Five sessions, and all I got from him was a suggestion to be like curtains."

"Curtains?" I parroted, frowning and pausing again while folding Ellen's pink dressing gown, thinking I would have loved this at her age. It certainly stole a march on my old Care Bear version. Despite my parents' assumptions, I'd never been into the 1980s phenomena.

"Pull myself together ... curtains."

"Oh, ... really? He said that?"

"Not in as many words. However, he suggested because I'm a vicar, I should be able to cope."

"Vicar or not, you're still a person, like the rest of us."

"Unlike those two downstairs."

"Yeah. Anyway, I'm not sure I'm qualified. I'm an unemployed administrator-cum-receptionist lacking in life experience. To be honest, I've spent years worrying about others, not myself. I know I come across as a gossip, but I'm not. I think it's just my way of ignoring my own issues ... y'know, focusing on others. If that makes sense, which it probably doesn't. See, here I go again, rambling."

"It does make sense."

"Really? Are you just doing your understanding vicar routine?"

Niall snorted a chuckle, grinned and shook his head.

"Sorry, didn't mean to suggest—"

"Janice ... I understand. For what it's worth, apart from being in the company of them two downstairs, I've enjoyed this afternoon. Being with you. In *your* company."

"Oh," I blushed, lowering my gaze to finish the repacking. "Me too," I whispered.

"I don't have many friends here, so it's nice to be able to chat ... talk about ..." Niall shook his head. "Sorry, we need to focus on you and how we can get your life back on track."

"I'd presumed you'd have lots of friends. Y'know, being a vicar."

"We had loads back in London." Niall rubbed his chin, grimacing, before continuing. "It's kinda weird, really. After losing Julie, they all seem to have disappeared. I think most just don't know what to say, so take the easy option and avoid me. Which is relatively easy for them because we don't live there anymore. Nothing quite like a death to use as a convenient excuse to avoid someone, eh?"

"Oh … sorry, that's a shame. Why did you come to Fairfield in the first place?"

"I asked for a transfer, for Ellen's sake. Her primary school was pretty poor, and Ofsted rated all four high schools in the catchment area as inadequate. Also, Julie was worried about the area Ellen was growing up in. When they offered me the position here at All Saints, Julie and I thought it would be the start of a new life. A life away from London, where we could settle and Ellen could grow up away from the inner-city issues my old parishioners battled with daily. Gang violence, drug abuse, muggings, antisocial behaviour, all that angst left in our past—"

"You haven't visited the Broxworth Estate then?" I interrupted as I zipped up her bag and held it aloft for inspection.

"Thank you. As I said, I'm not known for my bag-packing skills. And, yes, I'm aware of the Broxworth. It's not in my parish, thank the blooming Lord. I know that may sound uncharitable, but I've served my time in places—"

"Not at all. You don't have to feel guilty about not wanting that place." I waved my hand to waft away his excuses after placing the backpack on the bed. "That dump's won Britain's Most Violent Estate award more times than not."

"Blimey, is there such an award?"

"No, probably not. But if there were, I reckon any estate in the country worse than the Broxworth would be nailed on to win such an award. Apart from someone whose name escapes me, who won gold at the 2012 Olympics, and the IRA bombing of the Bell Pub in '77, it's what the town's famous for. Whenever someone asks where I come from, when I say

Fairfield, I always clarify, not from the Broxworth. You can see it in their eyes as soon as you mention the town."

"Shall we pop that next door?" Niall nodded at the backpack. "Then I'll grab a torch from the garage, and we'll nip over to the church and see if we can spot their graves."

"Even if their graves are there, that doesn't mean those two downstairs are actually them, does it? They could have just picked their names as a cover story."

"No, but we can't deny Deana is in my front room. You can't see her, but we both know she's there."

"As barmy as it is, yes."

"Shall we?" Niall grabbed Ellen's backpack.

"Hang on." I plucked my phone from my jeans pocket, opened up Facebook, and, a couple of taps later, came across a picture of a woman who I thought fit Niall's description of the woman prancing around in front of the window earlier. Although dressed in a bikini, so not naked, this lady perched on a stool at what appeared to be a beach bar sported the same name, and the page had 'remembering' tagged at the top. I swivelled my phone around and held it up for Niall to inspect. "Is that the invisible woman?"

"Err … may I?" Niall asked when reaching for my phone. "Difficult to say with any certainty. But … yes, I reckon it is."

"Then the angel-cum-ghost, or whatever she is, the woman scoffing mince pies in your front room, is the real deal. Deana Burton is dead. And I wouldn't mind betting her grave is exactly where Terry said it would be."

Niall raised an eyebrow when handing back my phone. "What about Terry? Has he got a Facebook profile?"

"Hang on, I'll check."

"Although, if he's been dead for thirty-God-knows-how-many years, then I presume he hasn't."

I nodded as I searched through my phone. With what seemed like an endless stream of Terry and Terence Walton's profiles on offer, it took me a while to search through them.

"Anything?" Niall asked when ten seconds of my scrolling had elapsed.

"Sorry, there's loads of them. Discounting the females—"

"What?"

"Terry is also a woman's name."

"Oh … yeah, course."

"And …" I paused when noticing a profile that could be him, squinting at the screen and tapping into the details. "No, that's not him … this bloke comes from Oklahoma."

"Who does?" Niall asked, dropping Ellen's backpack on the bed and stepping closer.

"No … doesn't matter. I thought one looked like Terry, but it's not. I'd say the bloke downstairs with dead Deana is English. Most of these live in the United States."

"On Waltons' Mountain in Virginia, perhaps?"

"Oh, I loved the Waltons," I chuckled, continuing the never-ending scroll. They say the average person scrolls the height of the Eiffel Tower each day. At this rate, I reckon I was on for scaling the Empire State or even that new One World Trade Centre they'd just thrown up to replace the Twin Towers in Lower Manhattan. Not that I'd ever been there or America full stop. Of course, until a few days ago, I assumed

I was about to embark on my first States side visit. "Stupid woman," I muttered.

"Sorry?"

"Oh, ignore me."

"Anything? Anyone who looks like him?"

"Nope."

"So, he doesn't exist, as we suspected."

"Looks that way ... oh, this could be him." Again, I squinted at the screen to study the profile picture while Niall shimmed to my side to be able to see. "Oh, no, that's not him. This bloke is much older."

"No, that's not him. That man's in his fifties," Niall muttered when studying the profile.

When our cheeks touched, we both almost simultaneously hopped sideways, resulting in me stubbing my big toe on the foot of the metal bed frame.

"Shit! Frig, that hurt."

"I'm so sorry."

"No ..." I shook my head while scrunching my eyes closed and gritting my teeth as I flopped on the bed. "Sh–it that really hurt."

"You alright?" With his hands outstretched, appearing unsure whether to step closer, Niall hovered in a stooped position. "D'you want me to rub it?"

I shot him a surprised look.

"No, sorry. Inappropriate."

"Nice offer, but I think I'll cope," I hissed through gritted teeth, as if that would help stem the pain.

"Let me at least take a look?"

"It's fine. Honestly, it's fine. I only stubbed it." I batted away his advance with a waft of my hand.

"Janice, you're bleeding."

While still pulling that pained expression, I lifted my foot to inspect the damage. As Niall had suggested, my pink polka dot sock had a growing red dot to complement the white ones that were there by design.

"Hang on, I'll get the Savlon and a plaster."

"Oh, don't worry, it'll be fine in a minute," I called after him as I attempted to wiggle my toe without panting. Although I wouldn't class myself as a complete wuss, there was no denying that a stubbed toe could be excruciatingly painful. As for my panting, I guess if I ever got lucky enough to become pregnant, there'd be a fair bit of gas and air consumed when it came to the business end after nine months.

"Here we go. Whip your sock off." Niall offered a sopping flannel before placing a first aid kit on the carpet.

"Oh," I grimaced, not wanting to bare my toes.

"What?"

"I've got a … well, a weird foot."

"Weird?"

"Yeah, weird."

"What kind of weird? You got six toes? Goliath purportedly may have had six toes. Although that didn't end well for him."

"Who?"

"In the Bible."

"Oh. I'll take your word for it."

"And it was mooted that Marilyn Monroe also had an extra digit. I think that theory was debunked, though. Hey, it's widely considered that people blessed with an extra digit are gifted with extra sensory capabilities. And, I also know—"

"Niall …"

"Sorry. You don't have six toes, I take it?"

"Correct, I don't. It's embarrassing, though."

"Okay, well, not to worry. Here's the flannel and there should be plasters and some cream in there." Niall tapped the first aid box. "I'll leave you to it."

"My toenails are all a different colour."

"Oh." Niall, now on his haunches, raised an eyebrow. I thought Niall looked confused, which was fair enough.

"I was trying out ten different colours to see which one I liked best. As a rule, I don't normally paint my toenails, but I thought for … oh, it doesn't matter."

"For Chad? When planning to see your illusive American friend, you decided to apply nail polish?"

"Yeah. Pathetic, I know."

"Come on, before you bleed to death, take that sock off. Which toe have you stubbed?

"My big toe. The purple one."

"Purple nail polish, or purple through bruising."

"Probably both," I muttered, gingerly extracting my foot from the sock.

"Blimey, you really whacked that, didn't you? You've split the nail right down."

I winced as Niall held my foot and applied the flannel, cradling it around my toe to stem the blood flow.

"Do as I have done to you, as it states in the Good Book. Blimey, the sights you see behind closed doors," chuckled Deana as she hovered in the doorway, taking in the scene of Janice perched on the bed and the vicar, with his back to the door, cradling the piteous woman's foot in his lap. "Not that I class myself as a Mary Magdalene type per se, but I wonder if the dishy vicar washed my feet, would all my little misdemeanours be excused by The-Powers-That-Be?"

"Niall … I don't know why, but it feels like we're not alone, as if there's someone … something in the room with us."

19

The Hateful Eight

"There, it's this one. Look. Exactly where Terry said. I think he mentioned it wasn't well tended to. Going by that pot of Cyclamen by the headstone, I'd suggest someone does on a regular basis. Also, the grave hasn't been desecrated, so it doesn't look as if anything has crept out of there in the last thirty-odd years or any evidence to suggest body snatchers have been busy." Niall shone the torch at the headstone's gold lettering, which stated this to be the final resting place of one Terence Stirling Sherlock Walton.

While holding onto Niall's arm, staring at the illuminated lettering as he waved the torch back and forth, I offered an involuntary shiver. Despite only being the early evening and not the witching hours during the dead of night, the lane that led down to the church remained eerily quiet. As the season's first few flakes of snow wisped and danced in the near-still air, local residents were presumably in the warmth of their homes – either enjoying a family dinner, getting ahead with the present wrapping, or poring over bank statements, admonishing themselves for the cost if it all – not wandering through a creepy graveyard trying to ascertain if a couple of corpses were missing. Specifically, the two currently enjoying the comfort afforded by the homely front room at the vicarage.

"You cold?"

"No, I'm fine."

"Creepy graveyard?"

I nodded and sniffed.

"How's the toe?"

"It's alright. Throbbing a bit."

"Stirling and Sherlock. They're unusual names."

"Maybe his parents were motor racing and detective story fanatics."

"A Case of Identity."

"Sorry?" I glanced up at him, releasing one hand from his arm to run my ponytail through it.

"Sherlock Holmes. A Case of Identity." With the beam of torchlight still playing on the grave, Niall turned to face me. "It's one of the original Sherlock Holmes stories. A tale of a crooked man with two identities, who courts a woman to swindle her fortune."

"That sounds familiar. Not that I had a fortune, but it was everything I had. I assume Terry Walton isn't Chad. Whoever the man is who swindled me is probably now swigging champagne while sunning himself somewhere expensive."

Niall rubbed my hand, offering it a comforting squeeze. "Although I'm sceptical, and that's putting it mildly, I hope this Terry Walton, the man who should be six feet under that stone slab, can work out who Chad Ruger really is."

"Then what?"

"Who knows? But as daft as it sounds, I reckon two ghosts are your best shot at getting your life's savings back."

"If someone this morning had suggested I'd be having this conversation today, standing here in the middle of a graveyard, I'd have said they were nuts."

"Agreed, me too. The Lord moves in mysterious ways, as they say."

"You think your boss has a hand in this? As Terry suggested, he's a ghost on a mission sent by the Almighty himself."

"Shall I ask him?"

"Terry or God?"

"God."

"Like a prayer?"

"Sort of."

"D'you actually get answers?"

"Not as in an email or a text, more like a thought, as if the prayer clears away the brain fog. You should try it."

"Hmmm. Not sure it's my thing. I talk to myself a lot, though. Does that count?"

"Not really."

"No, I guess not."

"The five aspects of a prayer … the third being a prayer for intercession, as in asking for his help and guidance for others. Perhaps my prayers will be answered, and we'll get a lucky break."

"Lucky break?"

"More divine intervention."

"Go for it. What have we got to lose? Just so you know, I really don't believe, so that might put a dampener on things."

"When you woke this morning, did you believe in ghosts?"

"Err … no. Fair point."

"Okay, here goes for nothing."

"Do you have to kneel?"

"No, I can pray standing up. It still works just the same."

"Right," my tone being unintentionally sarcastic, accompanied by an involuntary eye roll.

As I waited, both hands tightly gripping his arm, I glanced around the graveyard. Due to my eyes being fully adjusted to the gloom, and the visibility enhanced by the reflective qualities of the precariously fragile thin layer of snow that now formed around us, I considered the scene less *The Evil Dead* or *Blair Witch Project* and perhaps more cosy Christmas card-ish. Not that I'd seen many greeting cards depicting a hotchpotch scattering of headstones, but you get my drift.

As I continued to wait, that feeling of presence in Ellen's bedroom, which I'd experienced earlier when Niall applied first aid to my toe, now returned. Like earlier, there didn't appear to be anything physical or visible but a force or revenant. Well, unlike Ellen's bedroom, I was in the right place. Perhaps the spirits of the dead lurked at night, keeping those nocturnal creatures company. Or, maybe, due to Niall having that chat, I could sense the presence of God himself. It was nearly Christmas, after all.

"Get a grip," I muttered before looking up at Niall, who, with eyes now open, appeared to be gazing into the middle distance. "Err ... sorry to butt in, but are you done?"

"Yep. All done. Come on, shall we go check out Deana's grave?"

"What did you ask him?"

"Ah, that's a bit like divulging a birthday wish."

"Oh."

"Shall we?" Niall waved the way forward, illuminating the path towards the Church, which, at night, transformed from the quintessential village church to appear like a brutalist, monolithic edifice more akin to housing that mythical lot from Transylvania. The only things missing were a full moon and a cauldron of vampire bats swooping in and out of the belfry.

Still clinging to his arm, following the torch beam, Niall and I traipsed along the weaving path through the headstones, heading to where Terry had stated Deana was buried, only to halt our jaunt a few metres short. Where we suspected the double grave to be, following the dead man's suggested location, stood Terry.

Bizarrely, to his right, the falling snow, which had increased in intensity in the last few minutes, appeared to halt its descent mid-air as if each flake was uncertain where to land, thus taking a moment before continuing its journey to the rapidly freezing ground. Within a few seconds, those mid-air, halted flakes formed a hazy, snowy outline of a figure's head and shoulders.

"Can you see her?" Niall whispered, tilting his head down towards mine.

Due to being mesmerised, unable to tear my eyes from the forming vision in front of me, my mouth now gaping as if in awe as the eighth wonder of the world emerged from a rising fog – not that I could confidently list the other seven, one of which was probably the Hanging Gardens of Babylon, or witnessing a rerun of one of those old Ready Brek adverts, central heating for kids – I tightened my grip on Niall's arm and nodded in response.

"What's the matter with her, for God's sake? The gormless moron looks as if she's seen a ghost or is suffering from a bout of Bell's palsy. Darling, I said to you earlier, after witnessing that toe-sucking incident, I thought Jaded-Janice and Dishy-Vicar were hitting it off." Deana paused when clocking Terry's raised eyebrow. "Alright, foot washing, but I tell you, they were only one step from doing a Fergie. And now look at them, snuggled up arm in arm. A ten-minute stroll through the graveyard, and they already have that Winslet and DiCaprio look about them. It'll end just as badly, and I don't mean getting close and personal with an iceberg when cruising on their honeymoon, but that dishy boy will never lower himself to Jaded-Janice's level. I mean, did you see the pictures of his dead wife? A lush, darling, an absolute lush."

"You're holding my arm in just the same way. That doesn't mean—"

"We were lovers, darling. Albeit thirty-odd years ago. However, unlike these two, we've shared intimate moments and body fluids."

"Did you say body fluids?"

"Yes, darling. You may have forgotten, but I most certainly have not. That night in the hotel back in good old '83, you were extremely virile, I must say. You came twice, whereas I lost count of my orgasms. Gushing

in torrents like Niagara, expelling that much fluid, I was surprised I didn't become dehydrated. Of course, you would have cum thrice if you hadn't decided to snuff it."

"Christ, you don't half have a way with words."

"I do so."

"Anyway, I don't see how you can assume they are becoming intimate just because Janice and the vicar have linked arms."

"Just saying, darling. Just saying."

When Terry replied to whatever Deana must have said, specifically regarding the act of me holding Niall's arm being construed as intimate, I attempted to uncouple myself, only for Niall to hold on tight.

"It's alright," he hissed. "Hold on to me so you don't put too much weight on that toe," he clarified before facing Terry. "I'm not privy to your conversation, but Janice has a sore toe. She's holding on to me for support. So, whatever's been suggested is entirely unfounded."

Terry held up a placating hand, offering a slight bow as an apology.

"Piffle. You should have seen them earlier. Him bathing her foot, holding it like Prince-ruddy-Charming, and Cinders here, all gooey eyes. If she'd had a packet, the woman would have given the dishy boy her last Rolo."

"My good God, it's real," I hissed.

"It's? There she goes again, calling me an 'it'! Christ, I've been called some things in my time, but really … I'm reduced to an 'it'!"

"I know I felt her earlier … touched her body …"

"In your dreams, girl. Luscious skin you might be blessed with, but I'm not that desperate. Not yet, anyway."

"But seeing her is a whole new level." I shot Niall a look, my eyes wide and childlike with wonder, as I finally accepted the ridiculous. "Ghosts are actually real. I'm not going mad."

"You're not. We're not." Niall nodded at the grave to my left. "Look."

When Niall played the beam across the double-heart headstone, the gold lettering illuminated stated it to be the final resting place of Richard and Deana Burton. Unlike the vast majority of headstones we'd passed, this one was clearly new, further confirmed by the wording that stated their deaths occurred earlier this year.

"The headstone wouldn't have been my choice, of course. Ziggy, my darling Dickie's son, sorted all that and, although I do so like the boy, he does harbour questionable tastes. He's a bohemian sort, spirited away in a world off-grid down under, so to speak. Anyway, he made an effort, even though it's somewhat on the garish side."

"They were so young," I whispered, noting Deana had only been in her fifties and her husband a few years her junior. "What an absolute tragedy."

"Too right, it was. Thank you for the young comment. Much appreciated." Deana nudged Terry. *"Take note, Terence. As the girl states, I'm young."*

"The poor couple. At least they died together, which is some sort of solace, I suppose."

"Agreed, it is. Unfortunately, Portly-Bloody-Pete, in his giant pantechnicon, steamrollered the damn car. Silly sod paid the ultimate

price for his lack of concentration, though." she snickered. "Murder is such a blast."

"You followed us out here, then," Niall asked Terry, leaving me to again gawp at the manifestation of what appeared to be the outline of the human form as the snow settled and clung to her apparent Santa-styled coat.

"Darling, d'you think we could continue this dialogue back at the vicarage? I've always loved the snow, but it's rather chilly." With a gloved hand, Deana dusted her hood and shoulders.

"It's like a snow globe," I muttered.

"However, snow, like talcum powder ... by the way, copious amounts of which I plaster my naked form before slipping into my erotic, skin-tight PVC catsuit for Clara's benefit, has the effect of ruining my invisible qualities. You're supposed to be visible, but I am most certainly not."

"We weren't following you, as such," Terry replied to Niall's question while shooting a look at the ghost beside him. "I said to Deana that I thought you might pop over here and check out our graves. It's just that we've compiled our list and were ready to give you both a run-through of our findings."

"Oh, right. So, you think you might have some likely candidates who could be responsible for swindling Janice?"

"We do. Twelve in total. Eight in reality, but two or three are in pole position."

"I said he was into motor racing. Or his parents were," I muttered, still watching the snow globe effect of the ghostly Deana as she fought against the ever-increasing intensity of the falling snow. "Eight people who could have conned me ... that's a lot," still muttering when verbalising my thoughts.

"These two or three ... the ones in pole position to be the con man who swindled Janice, what's your plan? I'm just asking because, despite what they may or may not have done, I don't think I can be party to anything illegal."

"We going to scare the shit out of the bastards. So much so the snivelling little weasels will rue the day they came on my radar ... PTSD doesn't even start to cover their emotional state once I've done with them. That's, of course, assuming I don't murder the gits."

"What did she say," Niall asked.

"Deana said that we'll politely but firmly ask them to reimburse Janice."

"Oh, will that work?"

"Deana can be very persuasive."

"Like you wouldn't believe, darling."

"And who are these men?" I asked, keen to hear the true identity of the man who'd taken me for a fool. Which I clearly was.

"Okay, look, we wanted you to know we have a list and whittled it down to a few, but Deana and I think it's best you don't know their names until we've identified the actual one."

"I think that's quite right—"

"But—"

"Janice," Niall squeezed my hand when interrupting me. "I think it's best that we don't know for now. As Terry suggests, as soon as they have identified the right one, then they can tell us."

"Okay ... alright," I reluctantly nodded, accepting hearing the name of someone I didn't know served no purpose.

"Look, it's getting late, and I should probably make tracks before I miss the last bus into town. Although I can just as easily walk as it's not far."

"Yes, so should we, darling. I'm hoping Clara will be free tonight. The love reckoned she was coming towards the business end of her mission and might have a few days free to relax. Nothing better than coming home to my darling girl after a hard day of scaring the bejesus out of a few weak, detestable reprobates."

"With Ellen on a sleepover, I can drop you home. No need to get the bus and I'm certainly not going to let you walk in this weather, especially with that bruised toe." Niall waved his hand at Terry. "What about you two? You need a lift?"

"No, we're fine. Deana lives just over there," Terry gestured up the lane.

"Oh, you're local, then?"

"Indeed, near neighbours for the time being."

"Niall, that's very kind, but I don't want to put you out." I offered a tight smile to cover up my lie. The last thing I wanted to do was traipse along to the bus stop in this weather, which appeared to have set in for the night. "I've taken up enough of your time," I added in a mumble, also not relishing returning to my pitiable abode that may soon not be my home if the landlord gets his way.

"It's no issue. Anyway, it's not every day a chap gets the opportunity to meet a couple of ghosts," he chuckled. "Right, that's settled, then. Come on, we'll have a cuppa before I pull the old Landy out of the garage and fire her up."

"Landy?"

"My 1964 Land Rover. Of course, I prefer the ride Wet Nellie offers—"

"Who's Wet Nellie?"

"Blimey, darling, what a dark horse he's turned out to be. This Wet Nellie sounds like a right trollop and, by the sounds of it, he keeps her trussed up in the garage. All very dark, mysterious and Tarantino-esque."

"Wet Nellie is my Lotus Esprit. As per the Bond film. Although mine doesn't do water particularly well and is completely hopeless in the snow."

"Oh."

"I'm a petrolhead."

"Wet Nellie's not some trollop he's got tied up in his cellar, then. Good to hear. I had the vicar pegged as a Volvo man myself. Looks alright on the surface, but is safe, boring and dependable, if you see the analogy."

"I've got an old Volvo for everyday use. It's a car that probably befits the local vicar image more than the Lotus. Right, come on." After one step, Niall halted. "Hang on, I have a better idea. Silly me, why didn't I think of this earlier? With all that's going on, and Terry and Deana only up the road, so nice and close, why don't you stay at the vicarage until this is all resolved? There's plenty of room, and I'll be grateful for the company."

"Oh, vicar, very Bond-esque, I must say. You smooth operator, you. That steals a march on asking a girl to come up and see your etchings!"

20

The Girl with the Dragon Tattoo

"How long did you say Lena will be gone for?" I asked, feeling uneasy about being here, conscious I was wearing yesterday's clothes and, despite the power shower being divine – a serious step up from my clapped-out useless thing above the stained bath, which, to get wet and thus lather up under its trickling jets, required performing a dance routine that could be construed as a hybrid of the pogo and the rumba – I still didn't feel particularly fresh following a night of fitful sleep that involved a fair bit of quilt thrashing and 'sheep counting' when ensconced in Niall's spare room.

Anyway, to add to how I was feeling, it was Monday morning. Although unemployed, so no valid reason to feel down at the start of the working week, like the Boomtown Rats, I really didn't like Mondays. And to think, we were only a few weeks from Blue Monday. I'd read that the idea that day was the most depressing day of the year was considered by many as pseudoscience. Whether it was or wasn't, if I was still jobless and potentially homeless in four weeks, then I guess it would be a *Blue Monday* for me.

"She's away until the first Saturday in January. The 7th." Niall poured tea from the pot, which all seemed somewhat archaic. The man before me, who I still couldn't pin down his age, dressed in old, grey jogging bottoms and a sweatshirt – the Rocky Balboa training ensemble if you like, also sporting bed hair to suggest he'd suffered an equally disturbed night, resulting in him heralding a Tintin-esque fringe – appeared modern in many ways, but old before his time in others.

"A couple of weeks, then?"

"Yep," he nodded, pulling out the Windsor chair on the other side of the square farmhouse-style kitchen table. "Lena asked to go home early to help her mother prepare for the Wigilia Feast on Christmas Eve. That's the day they traditionally celebrate and exchange presents in Poland. Look, it's an awful presumption, but you'd be doing me a huge favour. I know it's only short-term and not something you wouldn't probably choose—"

"Not in a position to be picky, am I?"

"I know, and I wouldn't want you to feel obliged. I will obviously pay you the going rate and, together, we can keep tabs on those two spooks."

"Oh, God, them. In the cold light of day, I've started to wonder if I imagined it all."

"We didn't, though. Did we?"

"No … and I was thinking when trying to sleep. If what Terry said about the afterlife is true, that really is … well—"

"Completely and totally at odds with all the stuff the likes of me have been spouting for centuries. Changes the landscape somewhat, don't you think? It's pretty much all I've thought about since yesterday."

"Hmmm. Anyway, what about Ellen?"

"What about her?"

"Me. Here in her home."

"She'll be over the moon. I have various neighbours on the hook to take her when I'm working, but I know she isn't keen. This way, she'll be at home."

"Really?" I whined before sipping my tea and thinking this plan was way too good to be true.

"Yes, absolutely. You two were getting on famously yesterday."

"Well, I wouldn't put it quite like that. We chatted but—"

"There you go, then," Niall grinned, running his hand through his hair, affording him the Stan Laurel look.

"Yes, but … I presume Lena is trained. I don't know the first thing about childminding. Don't I have to be CRB checked, or whatever it is?"

"You would if you worked for an agency, but this is just us, friends, coming to an agreement … hopefully," the last word uttered pleadingly while he gave his boiled egg a hearty wallop with the back of a teaspoon.

"Friends? Are we friends? We've only just met."

"Course we are. You seem like a cracking good egg." Niall shot a look at his breakfast. "Good egg, get it?"

"Is that what they call a dad joke?"

"Probably. Sorry. You're giving me that look Ellen does when I fire off my awful yolks. Yolks, get it?"

"Oh, blimey. Ellen's look is one of pity, I presume. Your jokes are so poor they don't warrant a reply … that sort of look."

"Yeah … that about covers it," he chuckled while decapitating the aforementioned subject he'd just de-shelled.

"I could be a serial killer. Child molester. A pervert, or generally a badass, as they say in the movies. Are you really comfortable about entrusting your daughter into my care?"

"Are you …" Niall hoofed in half his egg, giving it a munch. "Any of those things? A badass?"

"No. But you're very trusting."

"Ah, yes, well, we all tread a fine line between trust and gullibility. Both require making yourself vulnerable to someone. Trust usually requires evidence, so you're willing to depend. Whereas gullibility is a blind leap into the unknown."

"Like me with Chad."

"Con men work on creating a veil of trust." Niall jabbed his tea spoon towards me. "That's how they operate."

"Okay, trust requires evidence. So, what evidence do you have about me?"

"I don't. On that fine line I mentioned sits gut instinct."

"And your gut instinct reckons I'm not a badass."

"Yep. Also, I like …" Niall paused, pursed his lips and winced.

"You like what?"

"You."

"Oh."

"Don't sound so surprised."

"Err …"

"Look, I'm not good at this sort of thing. But I like you. I enjoy being with you. Yesterday, apart from meeting a couple of spooks and blowing ship-sinking holes in my beliefs, was one of the best days I've had this year."

"Vicar, if that's the case, you need to get out more. People don't put me and best days in the same sentence."

"You have to stop this."

"Stop what?"

"Putting yourself down."

"Oh."

"Janice Keelan. There's nothing odd about me liking your company."

"Right. Um … that's not why you suggested I move in, is it? You a fast mover? Not that I'm saying you would fancy me, of course." I could feel my cheeks burn, hating myself for saying such a stupid thing.

Anyway, based on my gullibility, so eloquently put by Niall a moment ago, the thought that he might not be all that he seemed gave rise for concern regarding my judgement. Was moving in here for a couple of weeks as lunatic an idea as gifting Chad my life savings? What if he was a serial killer? Perhaps regularly using his sweet child as a lure to reel women in before dismembering them in the basement. For all I knew, he might have a torture chamber set up a few feet below where I sat to carry out such debauched acts.

"Sorry, I've spooked you. It's just what with all that going on, you moving in to look after Ellen and the fact that for the first time in God knows how long I've met someone who I enjoy being with, I thought it would be the perfect solution. As in, we keep tabs on those two spectres up the road, Ellen isn't palmed off to whoever, and we can become friends."

I ran my ponytail through my hand a few times, pondering if Niall could become a friend or whether I'd soon be chopped up into bite-sized chunks.

"Does this house have a basement?"

"Err … no." I could see by his expression that his mind must be whirring. "What's that—"

"Nothing. Forget it."

"Right. So, what's your gut instinct telling you?"

"My gut instinct isn't worth a jot."

Niall offered me a wry smile.

"Just to clarify, you're not a psycho murderer?"

"No. I'm just an ordinary bloke who's met a woman he believes he enjoys being with and is hoping she likes his company, too … that's all. I didn't mean to come across all heavy."

"I do enjoy your company. It's just … I've lost my confidence, and I'm struggling to trust my instincts after what's happened."

"I know. I want to help if I can."

"Thanks."

"You agree then? Move in for a couple of weeks until Lena returns."

"I don't know."

"Come on. Kill two birds, as they say."

"Talking of killing birds, what about Christmas? As in Christmas Day."

"Ah … yes, sorry, I hadn't thought about that."

"Oh, no, please, I wouldn't expect. Honestly, Niall, that's no problem."

"Sorry, I'm assuming you're saying you've already made plans?"

"Plans?"

"For Christmas Day. So you couldn't be here to look after Ellen in the morning."

"Good God," I chortled. "The only plans I've made for Christmas, as I do every year, is to stay in bed as long as I can and, for the few hours I'm awake after serving at the refuge, get royally shitfaced so I pass out and miss the rest of the damn day."

Niall, spoon held at his lips, paused mid-chew.

"Sorry, I didn't mean to blaspheme."

"No … it's not that."

"What then? Why you looking at me like that?"

"Janice, why don't you have anyone to spend Christmas with?"

"My family are all gone," I shrugged. "So it's just me."

"Friends?"

"I have a few friends, but I'm not that close that I get invited around to pull a cracker and moan about mushy sprouts."

"But they all know you're on your own, right?"

I nonchalantly shrugged before plucking up my mug to hold in front of my lips to hide what I suspected was the inevitable onslaught of a chin wobble. Of course, I've always known that friendship is a two-way street. And no one could accuse me of not trying. Too hard, probably. Notwithstanding my efforts, accepting that no one wants to spend time with you is still hard to cope with.

It hurts.

Despite knowing I'm not exactly the life and soul of a party type, I'm okay-ish per se. I can certainly tell a joke better than Niall, that's for sure.

"I'm so sorry."

"Don't. It's okay." It wasn't, but that's what you say to convince folk you're not a saddo.

"No, it's not okay. You'll stay here for Christmas Day, then? With Ellen and me? Unless …"

"Unless what?"

"Unless getting wasted is a more preferable option. No man should come between a woman and her wine when all is said and done."

"I don't really get bladdered. Just a few glasses to obliterate the day. The loneliness."

"I understand. I've been there. So, Christmas here with me?"

I blinked a couple of times when detecting a tear form, nodding as I bowed my head.

"That's settled then. I'm not a bad cook. Better in the kitchen than in the pulpit, let's put it that way. I can't guarantee mushy sprouts, though. I'm more of a Birds Eye pea sort of bloke."

"I'm not too bad in the kitchen, either. My gravy is definitely better than Dawn's."

"Then there's no reason not to. We can conjure up Christmas dinner together."

"What about family? Don't you have parents … other relatives?"

"Nope. I'm an only child. My parents are gone, so it's just me and Ellen these days. I keep in contact with Julie's mother, mostly for Ellen's sake, but we were never close. Since Julie passed, I've barely exchanged half a dozen words with Ellen's grandmother. Civil words, that is."

"Oh, that's a shame. I presume Ellen still enjoys being with her grandma."

"Not much. Based on the fact my jokes need some work, I won't attempt any Les Dawson-type quips. Still, it's probably fair to say my mother-in-law wasn't overly enamoured with her daughter's choice for a husband."

"Oh. Why on earth not?"

"I think she had ideas that Julie would marry a man more befitting her social standing."

"What d'you mean?"

"My mother-in-law is Lady Hesketh. Blue blood … some obscure distant relative to the Queen. She rattles around in a ruddy great mansion down in Kent. I never felt comfortable in the place … too Downton Abbey for me."

"Where did Julie and you meet? Oh, hell, sorry, I'm giving you the third degree. Please, ignore me."

"No, it's alright. Anyway, now we're living together … err …"

I raised an eyebrow, causing the vicar to blush.

"I don't mean like that. Sorry, that came out all wrong. You should know about the man with whom you're going to be under the same roof. That's what I mean. I wasn't suggesting … y'know …"

"Niall. … it's alright," I batted away his embarrassment with a waft of my hand. "We covered off that stuff."

"Ha, yeah. Babbling, like I do in the pulpit. I'm surprised anyone still turns up," Niall nodded at the kitchen window, presumably indicating the church. The tower of which appearing to glow in the halo produced by the rising sun. "I'm led to believe my predecessor was a skilled orator. Anyway, Julie and I met at university in '85. We were married for nearly twenty years before she had what's commonly called a geriatric pregnancy. We were lucky. Our first round of IVF blessed us with Ellen."

Although I hadn't initially noticed this when meeting him yesterday, Niall's expression changed when he mentioned his daughter's name. Tiny facial muscles moved into position to radiate a glow. I wondered what it would be like to love someone so much. While he continued to proudly offer a run-through of his daughter's life story, I performed some maths. Based on his years at university, I mused Niall must be somewhere between his late forties and early fifties. Assuming his wife was of a similar age, those photos plastered around the house suggested Julie possessed a full suite of youthful genes. They say the rich have it all, I mused. However, wealth, privilege, blue-blooded genes and beauty are no barrier to cancer.

"So, that all sounds okay, then?" Niall waved his hand in the air to gain my attention. "Janice?"

"Oh, sorry. I was miles away. What were you saying?"

"It doesn't matter. I was doing the boring parent thing. Y'know, rattling on about my offspring as if I'm the first man to have a child."

"Adam … first born being Cain."

"You know the Book of Genesis."

"No, not really. I just remember learning it at school."

"If Terry Walton's version of the afterlife is to be believed, I might have to reevaluate my beliefs."

"Seriously?"

Niall leaned back in his chair, shrugged, and opened his arms.

"Yeah, I suppose." I placed my mug on the table mat, folded my arms and leaned forward. "Okay, changing the subject. Assuming I've agreed to this arrangement—"

"You already have."

"Yes … okay, I have. So, I think you'd better let me know what I'm signing up for. I'm not known for my Mary Poppins skills and, although there's only Ellen to look after and not a brood the size of the Von Trapps, I don't want to end up traumatised hiding in the basement when unable to cope with an eight-year-old."

"Oh, you don't need to worry about Ellen. She's the sweetest kid. Honestly, she is, and that's coming from a vicar's mouth, not just her father's. I wouldn't lie to you … honesty being part of my job description. Now, on the subject of full disclosure, Ellen sometimes needs to be reminded to clean her teeth before bedtime. Also, I'm guilty of letting her not eat her greens, so you might need to roll out your hidden strict governess performance at meal times. As I mentioned, I'm a Birds Eye pea sort of bloke. Anyway, I don't have a basement."

"That's news I'm delighted to hear."

"Oh … why is not having a basement good news?"

"Never mind. Just the silly thoughts of a stupid woman."

I hoped.

21

The Imitation Game

"You're grumpy."

"I'm not grumpy."

"You are."

"I'm not."

"Are."

"Not."

"Are," Terry hissed, determined to have the last word.

"Terence. If you accuse me of being grumpy once more, I *will* be grumpy."

"See, you are."

"Christ Almighty, you're ruddy infuriating."

"Me!"

"Yes, Terence, you." Deana poked his chest as they hovered at the foot of the metal staircase that led up to Fred Hallam's office. "I attest that I may have been slightly melancholy since last night. However, you peevish little thing, you, before your accusation regarding my apparent mardiness, I wasn't the slightest bit grumpy."

Terry smirked.

"I'll accept that I'm disappointed Clara was otherwise disposed and thus couldn't come around. That's all."

"You worried she's found another spook to play with and has given you the Spanish archer?"

"No!"

Terry raised an inquisitive eyebrow.

"Oh, darling, you don't think so, do you?" Deana whined. "I do so love that girl."

"Err … I thought you loved your darling Dickie."

"I do. But I love Clara, too. I have oodles of love to offer to the right people. My ardour knows no boundaries, as my polyamorous lifestyle attests. As you well know, and could rekindle if you feel the urge."

"Hmmm."

"Alright, I won't push it. Although disappointing, I do find your desire to atone and thus woo your dead little Sharon again all rather touching. Anyway, I want my Clara back."

"You don't actually know for certain that she's dumped you."

"Dumped!"

"I'm getting the vibes that you've never been dumped before."

"Good grief, of course not. I dump, not get dumped!"

"As I thought."

"I can't be dumped. What on earth will that do to my reputation? The Deana Burtons of this world, not that there are many with my alluring qualities, call the shots in relationships. I can't have the dead, or anyone else for that matter, thinking I'm dumpable."

"No, I can see that could be distressing."

"Distressing!" she shrieked. "Distressing doesn't come close to how I'd feel. The utter shame of it. I'd never live it down. It's unheard of. I'd be the laughing stock." Deana shuddered as she laid her palm on Terry's chest before peering up at him while fluttering her eyelids. "You're going to have to be gentle with me today. I'm bruised, darling. Bruised, d'you hear?" she whispered, employing her well-practised damsel-in-distress tone.

"If you say so."

"I do so." Deana gave him a gentle, playful shove before standing back and placing her hands on her hips. "Now, Terence, I haven't given you nearly enough praise for your inspired idea. One of your better ones, I must say. You're a clever boy."

"Err … thanks."

"You're welcome. So, let's get to it. Carpe diem, Terence, carpe diem!"

"Shall we?" Terry stepped back and theatrically waved the way forward.

"Very chivalrous of you. But you first, darling. You knock on the door, and then I'll set to work scaring the shite out of that little pervert. If he's not our con man, then when I've finished with him, he'll not only require clean britches but also have no choice but to come to heel and do our bidding."

"Well said."

"Thank you, darling. Now, time is running away with us, so we must crack on. Although, as I always used to say, it's better to be late than pregnant."

Terry furrowed his brow.

"A woman's menstrual cycle."

"Oh. Very droll, as you would say."

"There's nothing droll about that monthly ordeal, I can assure you. And lateness in that regard is a worry. Especially if one's finding it tricky to accurately pinpoint which encounter might have been responsible. Nigh on impossible when you've enjoyed a few erotic parties during the weeks prior," she tittered. "Right, come on, follow me." Deana bolted up the metal steps despite previously stating she wasn't taking the lead.

"Erotic parties," Terry muttered, shaking his head as he followed. "I never got invited to erotic parties," he mumbled, wondering how he'd missed out.

Once Terry and his invisible guide had traversed the steep metal staircase, just as they had that day back in the spring when on their mission to save their son, Deana stood to one side, ready to sneak in unnoticed when Fred Hallam, the hapless private investigator, opened the door.

Of course, they hadn't seen Hallam since that day in the abandoned car showroom when Deana had performed her *Wicked Witch of the West* antics to scare the man. Which, based on the fact he didn't show up to their agreed meet at All Saints

Church a few days later, suggested she'd sufficiently spooked Hallam enough for him to lie low.

"Just a minute," came the shout after Terry gave the door a few hearty thumps with his ready-for-action clenched fist.

Terry turned up his nose.

"At least he's there, darling."

Terry nodded before thumping the door again.

"I said, give me a minute," the agitated voice bellowed. "Just a sec," now with a hint of panic in his tone.

"Perhaps the little pervert was enjoying a Monday morning session, and we've disturbed him at the point of no return. Dickie always said when you're there, you're there, and there's no turning back."

"Session?"

"You know full well what singular activities I'm referring to, and it has nothing to do with solitaire. The man has filing cabinets full of depraved mucky publications—"

"You can talk."

"Dickie and I amassed a collection of erotica. All tasteful and nothing like that gutter porn this little pervert likes to peruse."

Terry tutted and raised an eyebrow before offering Deana a disparaging look.

"Just saying, darling. Back in the spring, the man's client book wasn't exactly brimming. Idle hands are the Devil's tools, as they say. Tool being the operative word. Anyway, as Dickie would say, always good to get the working week off with a bang, eh?"

"Okay, the doors open," came a harried shout from inside the office.

"I presume he's done." Deana poked her tongue into her cheek, smirking up at Terry.

"You've cheered up."

"Come on, let's get on with it. Remember, darling, carpe diem."

After entering, Terry purposefully left the door open for a second or two to allow Deana to enter before turning around to close it.

"Morning. Sorry about that, I was just finishing off some …" Hallam paused and glanced at the battered filing cabinets. "Filing."

"Is that what they call it these days? After my last visit to this repulsive locker-room-stinking dump, I'm fully aware of the depraved publications you keep in those filing cabinets. Also, you grubby excuse of a man, those florid cheeks of yours suggest you've been up to some vigorous activity and don't suppose it involved Zumba or an energetic game of solitaire."

"No problem." Terry grimaced as he clocked the scrunched tissues precariously balanced on the top of a full wastepaper basket.

"Take a seat." Hallam gestured to the chair, the seat appearing to have once taken on the role of a cat scratching pad.

"I wouldn't, darling. What's left on the material is covered in some dubious-looking stains."

"I'll stand."

"Suit yourself," Hallam shrugged. "I take it you've tramped your way up here because you're looking to employ the services of Fairfield's premier private investigator?"

"If we had, you silly little man, we wouldn't be here. We're going to use and abuse you, not enter a financial transaction."

"Err … yeah. Look, do you remember me?"

Hallam furrowed his brow as a look of concern briefly skated across his two-day greying stubble.

"From a few months ago." Terry stepped forward before resting his clenched fists on the desk, causing Hallam to push back in his chair. "April, May time, to be precise."

"Look, pal, if I've investigated you, that was a paid transaction by whoever employed me. Your beef is with whoever paid me, not—"

"I don't have any beef, I'm just asking if you recognise me?"

"Darling, back in the spring, you didn't have that ridiculous moustache crawling around under your nose. I suspect Mr Hallam, despite his apparent detective skills, isn't that good with faces. Oh, hang on … the wide eyes and revolting stench suggesting he's skidded in his pants presumably means the penny's dropped."

"You! No, no … I want you out of here." Hallam used his heels to force his chair back on its castors while furtively scanning the room. "Is it in here?"

"It! Good grief, why does everyone think it's acceptable to call me an 'it'?" Deana exasperatedly threw her arms in the air.

"Ah, so you do recognise me."

"You … you're that bloke, err …" Hallam's Adam's apple performed a few vertical jumps as he continued shooting panic-fuelled looks around his office.

"Hallam. What are you doing?"

Hallam eased himself out of his chair and backed up to the window while tentatively peering around Terry. "That ghost you hang around with. The one that flings stuff about. Ha– have you brought her with you?" he stammered, again swallowing hard.

"Oh, dear … Inch-High looks petrified. And to think, it's only little old me who's caused the stinking lump to quiver." Now standing next to the clearly terrified man, Deana placed her palm on the glass before leaning close to his ear. *"Boo!"*

"My friend is with me. She's standing right next to you."

While keeping his head still, as if transfixed with fear, he shifted his eyes to the right.

"No, fella. The other side," Terry nodded at Deana, who'd pinched her face, scrunching up her nose in disgust as she remained only a foot to the petrified man's left.

While still holding position, not daring to move his head, Hallam exhaled, shot his eyes left and offered a nervous grin.

"Oh, lordy. Yuck!" Deana hopped back a pace and wafted the air with her hand. "And there was me thinking Janice was the one with halitosis issues. That frankly obscene breath she hoofed my way yesterday has nothing on Stinky-Pete here. What's on earth the matter with the living these days? Twice daily oral hygiene is as fundamental as regularly washing one's labia. Christ, I think I might gag."

"Who's Stinky-Pete?"

"Oh, sorry, darling. Stinky-Pete's a character in a children's movie. You were dead when that film was on at the cinema."

"Right. I guess the new Windy Miller? There was this bloke at college in the sixties who farted all the time. John Miller, nobody liked him. We called him Windy Miller after the puppet on *Camberwick Green*."

"I'm quite sure you did. You do seem to have the propensity to refer all conversations back to Watch with Mother. Were you a mummy's boy? Perhaps showing tendencies to the Oedipus complex?"

"What?"

"You harboured fantasies … desires, if you like, about your mother."

"I don't like. And, no, I did not!"

"Alright, tetchy. I was just making conversation."

"Making conversation?" Terry scoffed. "We're here to scare the shit out of him," he jabbed a finger at the man who'd turned rather pasty looking as he pressed his back against the window. "Not discuss debauched ideas about my thoughts regarding my mother. Who, as it happens, was an upstanding citizen. My mother was a decoder at Bletchley Park and played an important role in the war effort, I'll have you know."

"Alright. Calm yourself, darling. Your passionate defence of your mother is admirable. I was just asking, that's all. Now, can we focus on Stinky-Pete here?"

"Err … how come your mother was around during the war?" Hallam nervously asked while shooting worried looks to his left.

"What?" Terry barked, still frustrated by Deana's outrageous accusation.

"Calm yourself, darling. We wouldn't want you to suffer another heart attack, would we? The last one killed you, remember?"

"Well, ehm … it's just you don't look old enough to have a mother that age."

"I'm dead. I've been dead for decades."

Hallam's Adam's apple performed a jig before he offered a nervous laugh.

"Something funny?"

"No," Hallam shook his head. "You're a ghost, too?"

"I am."

"How come—"

"You can see me?"

Hallam nodded.

"It's complicated."

"Oh."

"Perhaps you could show Mr Hallam you're here with us."

"Shall I put a sheet over my head and make moaning noises? I'm quite good at that in more ways than one."

"Hilarious. No, just something so he's under no illusion."

"Hilarious. Touché, darling. Okay …" Deana drummed her lips with her fingers as she scanned the room.

"Sometime today would be good."

"Alright. God, you're tetchy."

"Look, there's no need to do anything. I believe you."

"I know," Deana grabbed a sheet of paper and snatched up a chewed pen from a pot on Hallam's desk, tittering to herself as she scrawled a

message across it before holding the page in front of the clearly petrified private investigator's face.

"Oh God … please, no."

"What did you write?"

"Here, read for yourself." Deana flipped the page around for Terry to see. "This should focus his mind."

"Really?" Terry whined. "That's a bit strong."

"Please … Please, don't cut my cock off."

"Yes, I imagine that choked chopper of yours is your best, and probably only, friend. And to clarify, I didn't write the word cock." Deana jabbed the page. "Genitalia is what I wrote. Anyway, Inch-High, be under no illusion. I will gladly separate you from your best mate if you don't play ball with us."

"Will she … cut my cock off?" Hallam's pleading eyes urged Terry to intervene.

"Genitals!"

"No … she won't, as long as we come to an acceptable agreement."

"Anything."

"I suggest you sit."

Hallam, his eyes bulging while skittishly scanning the room, didn't move.

"Sit!" Terry pointed at the chair. "I said sit, man."

"Right, okay." Hallam complied while holding up a placating palm. "She's not going to hurt me, is she?" he whimpered, nervously glancing to his left.

"Stop looking over there. She's invisible to you, so it's pointless you keep glancing that way. Anyway, she's behind you now."

Hallam tipped his head back, shooting his eyes northwards while both hands covered his privates, footballer-in-a-wall style.

"Darling, I do so love it when you're forceful. This gruff, brutish, caveman trait you occasionally bring to the surface is so yummy."

"Yummy."

"Yes, yummy. Like an aphrodisiac. Makes me horny."

"We don't have time to discuss your fetishes."

"No, quite right." Deana whipped out a plastic carrier bag from her handbag before holding it aloft. "Semper Paratus! Always ready ... I'll stay here with the bag at the ready to suffocate the smelly lump in case he's not of a mind to play ball while you, you grouchy little thing you, employ that brutish manly side to squeeze some intel from the pervert."

"You brought a carrier bag with you?"

"I did, darling. A Waitrose one, too. I can't be seen with a bag from one of those cheap supermarkets where scummy people shop. Standards, darling, standards."

"Right." Terry parked one bottom cheek on Hallam's desk, offering the man an exaggerated grin.

"What's going to happen?" Hallam squeaked.

"You're going to answer my questions."

"Okay, sure ... I can do that," Hallam nodded vigorously.

"Good. Because if I don't like your answers, my friend, who, as I said, is standing behind you holding a carrier bag, a posh one from Waitrose, no less, will suffocate you."

Hallam torpidly closed his eyes, taking a few deep breaths.

"If we're satisfied that you're not responsible, then you will use your detective skills to assist us—"

"Pro bono."

"Services you will provide for free."

"Is she still behind me?"

"She is. Ready and waiting if you don't comply."

"And when you say responsible ... for what, exactly? I heard that business back in May was all resolved. I'm no longer investigating Damian Statham."

"It is, no thanks to you."

Hallam grimaced.

"You should have shown up at our planned meeting at the church. Instead, you decided to tip off Lee Parish ... the man behind that con to ruin Damian."

"Err ... sorry. But Lee's dead now, so it's all turned out okay." Hallam's eyes widened. "Oh, you ... or her," Hallam raised his eyes to indicate Deana. "You killed Lee?"

"No," Terry shook his head. "Although you need to be aware, my ghostly friend has killed before."

"Right. Good to know, I think. Look, I know from the police investigation that Deana Burton broke into my office and stole my laptop. They found her fingerprints."

"Yes, on your stash of filthy publications, you pervert. I was perusing them to assess what sort of man you were."

"That was us. We didn't trust you, so we thought we'd have a rummage around."

"Yeah, I get that. So, I take it your friend behind me is Deana? It's just they shelved the investigation into the break-in because Deana Burton was already dead."

"She might be."

"Err ... right. Hmmm. Is there any way I could have my old laptop back? It's just that there's a fair chunk of sensitive data stored on the hard drive, which I really do need."

"Obscene, illegal porn, you depraved perv. That sort of sensitive information, I take it?"

"We'll see. For now, we have another matter to discuss."

"Like?"

"Like, have you sidelined into running scams?"

"Scams?"

"Catfishing, I'm led to believe is the term."

"Get you, darling. Very on trend."

Terry glanced up at Deana. "Last night, while you were pining for your girl, I was conducting a spot of research on your darling Dickie's computer thingamajig."

"I don't pine."

"Do. Did."

"Don't. Didn't."

"Sorry to interrupt. But what scams? I haven't run any scams. I run a legitimate business here."

"No, you don't."

"Alright, I don't. But I haven't run any scams."

"Do you know a Chad Ruger?"

"Who?"

"Ruger. A man called Chad Ruger."

"No. Never heard of him."

"Darling, over many years of learning how a man's mind works, I've developed an extremely effective BS detection system. Stinky-Pete, Inch-High, Pervy-PI, whatever we're calling him today, doesn't know that name. I suggest we cross the perv off our list and move to phase two. Or, if you have a better idea, I could just suffocate him. I enjoyed killing Portly-Pete, and I can't imagine for one tiny moment that this odious, weedy thing will be missed by anyone."

"No, we need him alive."

"Party pooper," Deana smirked.

"I'm telling the truth. I don't know that name. Please, I don't. I haven't—"

"I believe you. Stop whimpering."

"Sure … I can do that."

"So, Mr Hallam. You're going to find Chad Ruger. Well, the man who claims to be Chad Ruger, that is."

"Oh … okay. That could take some time. And there's my expenses to consider."

"I think you're missing the point. You're going to do this work for us out of the goodness of your heart. Otherwise, I will take my ghost friend off her leash."

"I'm not a dog, Terence. Or an 'it', or a 'thing', while we're on the subject."

"Also, we don't have much time. So, to make it easy for you, we have a list of likely candidates." Terry extracted the folded sheet of notepaper from his jeans pocket and slapped it on the desk. "You can start with the top three. Call it an early Christmas present."

"How can you getting me to work for nothing be classed as a gift?"

"Because, assuming you come up trumps, Deana won't separate you and your best mate, and you can then enjoy Christmas together watching porn."

"I don't watch …"

Terry cleared his throat. "We still have your old lab thingamajig—"

"Laptop, darling. It's called a laptop."

"Laptop thingamajig, remember? We could drop that off at the police station if you like? I mean, Jesus, I've seen some mucky videos in my time, but the stuff you've got on there is—"

"Okay. You've made your point."

"Good." Terry offered a tight-lipped grin. "So, you'll locate these men, and we play nicely."

"Okay, yeah, that seems fair. The top three, you say?" Hallam asked when glancing at his desk.

"Correct."

"That's easy, mate. I know exactly where you can find them."

"Really?"

"Yeah … the Broxworth Estate."

22

Rebel Without a Cause

"I can categorically state with some measure of certainty that I have never been inside one of these things before. I never realised how they rattle so. One can hardly hear oneself think. Are they supposed to be like this ... so kerflooey? I'm amazed it still runs and hasn't gone kaput," Deana bellowed.

"It's old."

"Yes, I can see that, darling," Deana lowered her voice when Hallam killed the engine. *"The liberal coating of rust suggests as much. Now, apart from the obvious repugnant stench of sweaty jockstraps and the company ensconced in the driver's seat being less than congenial, it's quite an experience. Almost fun!"* Deana, her arm around Terry, kissed his cheek.

"Don't do that!"

"Do what? I didn't do anything?" Hallam pleaded, shooting a look sideways while gripping the steering wheel.

"Not you. Deana."

"Oh."

Deana ran her hand through Terry's hair. "I'm not too heavy for you, am I, darling? Hmmm? I wouldn't want to squash your you-know-whats," she pouted.

"No, not at all." Terry winced as he shifted his bottom on the passenger seat of Hallam's knackered, it's-a-miracle-it-passed-an-MOT Transit van. The twenty-minute drive across town to the Broxworth with Deana perched on his lap had the effect of causing his sciatica to play up. If only the rattling rust bucket had a bench seat.

"Correct answer, darling. Despite my luscious womanly curves, I am but as light as a feather."

"If you say so," Terry grunted, again trying to shift in position.

"I do so."

"We could stand outside, you know?" Terry suggested, keen to shift Deana from his lap. As she tightened her hold around his neck and lay her cheek against his, Terry presumed that was a no-go.

"Were you talking to me?"

"No, Hallam. I was talking to Deana," Terry barked. "If I'm going to talk to you, I'll let you know, okay?"

"Okay."

"Just do what we're paying you to do. Now we're finally here, keep an eye out for our targets."

"You're not paying me." Hallam glanced at Terry, whose expression suggested he might want to add to that statement. "Which is, of course, totally fine."

"Darling, we can't very well stand outside in this weather, can we now? For starters, there's a ten-foot snowdrift smothering the place. Also, outside this rust bucket is the beastly Broxworth Estate full of undesirables, gypsies, tramps and thieves, to quote Cher."

"There's about an inch of snow. Hardly a drift."

"Don't split hairs, darling. Now, if you're cold, you can put your hands inside my coat if you like."

"Your Santa coat."

"Yes, if that description makes you happy."

"I'm fine, thanks. Well, my hands are," Terry grimaced, shifting in the seat again, attempting to find relief from the pain shooting down his left leg.

"Don't fidget, Terence."

"I've got sciatica."

"Lucky you."

"Not really. I would have thought one advantage of being dead was not to feel pain. Apparently not."

"You know, this reminds me of sitting on Father Christmas's knee when I was about, oh, probably six or seven. My mother took me, under duress, I might add, to his grotto in Peter Robinson's department store. Course, that's long gone now. I think they knocked it down when the twits on the council built that monstrosity of a flyover in the late sixties. Garish lump of hellish concrete … a bit like this place, really. Hmmm." Deana peered out of the window, glancing up at one of the three brutal grey tower blocks, turning her nose up as she tilted her head upwards. *"Anyway, I call the man dressed in a Santa suit Father Christmas but, of course, darling, even at that age, I knew full well he wasn't the real Santa. I mean, he stank of cigarettes and whisky, just like my Uncle*

Herbert and stinky old Hallam here." Deana turned away from drinking in the vista of hell provided by the Broxworth to nod at Hallam.

"Is there a point to this story?"

"Darling, have some patience. It's not really a story, just me reminiscing about Christmases past. Anyway, I'm getting there."

"Like British Rail?"

Hallam shot another look to his left, shaking his head when trying to imagine what conversation the two ghosts were conducting that involved sciatica and British Rail. He pursed his lips and mused that the rattling, drafty carriages back in the day could be the cause of many ailments.

"Very droll, I'm sure. So, there I was, dressed in my anorak with my mittens ... you know, the ones with a string attached that looped through the arms. I was a devil for losing things. Lost my virginity at fourteen ... did I ever tell you that? I was what you call an early bloomer. Irish traveller sort who saw himself as a bit of a James Dean type. We had a quickie behind the Dodgem cars on the last evening of the summer fair. Not bad, if I recall ... certainly didn't put me off."

"Clearly. So, what happened when you went to see Father Christmas?"

"Oh, nothing really. As I said, I didn't warm to him, and Mother scolded me for sticking my tongue out and calling him a stinky old Mac man."

"Mac man?"

"There'd been this flasher dressed in an old Mac spotted roaming around the park. Obviously, Mother forbade Simon and me from playing there. The Moors murderers had just been arrested, so, unsurprisingly, that caused Mother to become a little jittery."

"Well …" Terry puffed out his cheeks. "That's put a dampener on the conversation."

"Yes, sorry, darling. Grizzles from times past, and not very festive."

"Right, Hallam," Terry barked, causing the pasty man to shudder. "As you stated back in your office, now we're here, in this damn awful place, you'd better fill us in on how you know the top three in the hit parade live here."

"Hit parade?"

"Alistair Strachan, Joseph Meyer and Daniel Maypole. Our top three for the position of con man."

"Ah, yeah. Okay, so Maypole lost his business back in—"

"We're aware of his history. Deana and I played a small part in his downfall."

"Oh, right. You know the toad's got a bit of a gambling problem, then?"

"The gee-gees."

"Yeah, daft prat. He ran up some debts, one of which was to the bloke you have at number two in your hit parade."

"Joseph Meyer."

"That's him. So, Meyer, safe to say he's got a bit of a chequered past—"

"We know. Deana and I were involved in exposing Sam Meyer and, by association, ruining his son Joseph."

"Oh. So you know the old man's doing time, then? Historical rape cases, apparently. I tell you, the country's chock full of nonces crawling out of the woodwork. There's them Fix It and Glitter blokes, for starters."

"Terence."

"What I heard is that Sam Meyer bloke who ran those bookies," Hallam jabbed a finger at the windscreen, just below the foot-long crack that started in the top right corner and increased an inch across the screen with every speed bump negotiated. "There used to be one of their shops over there, and—"

"Hallam, hang on. Deana is talking."

"Oh."

"Darling, I know I can go off-piste on the odd occasion. What with my horrid tale when regurgitating the grizzly account of Brady and Hindley. However, do you think you could instruct Stinky-Pete here to be a little more concise?"

"Agreed. Hallam, can you cut the crap and get to the frigging point?"

"Well said, darling."

"Sure. Where was I?"

"Maypole owing Meyer a gambling debt."

"Oh, yeah. So when Sam Meyer has an epiphany and hands over his entire business to his stepdaughter—"

"Kim Meyer, my daughter."

"What?" Hallam furrowed his brow. "How the hell …"

"I'm dead, remember. I died in 1983."

"Don't confuse the man. Otherwise, he'll prattle on until Christmas, forcing us to listen to his protracted, turgid drivel. Regardless of how comfy and cosy I'm finding your lap to be, I wholeheartedly do not aspire to be stuck in this rust bucket for a moment longer than necessary."

"I keep forgetting you're dead. What's it like, then ... y'know, being dead?"

"Hallam!"

"Sorry." Hallam held up his palm and shifted to his right when clocking Terry's annoyance. "So, Meyer, Joseph, that is, he's a bit strapped for the readies and can't find Maypole 'cos the knob's gone to ground, so to speak. I've done a few jobs for Meyer and his old man in the past, so I said I'd hunt down Maypole for him if he shared the booty. Thing is, Meyer still owes me for that job."

"You found Maypole?"

"Yup, and then Meyer gets his dosh owed and cuts me out of the deal. Bastard."

"How does that place both men here? I know Maypole was struggling, but Joseph still had assets, even after Sam gifted the business to my Kim."

"Tracking Maypole to here was easy. It's the first place I sniff out when hunting down a mark that's lost everything. This shithole offers flats at relatively cheap rents and, taking into account the high murder rates, landlords are always looking for new tenants as soon as the dead ones are stretchered out. It's the drug gangs, see. The Albanian gangs have been muscling their way in for years, and the local boys ... the Gowers, don't take too kindly to their interference. Basically, it means a lot of killing."

"Are the doors to this so-called vehicle locked?"

"So you know which flat he lives in then?" Terry asked, ignoring Deana's concerns.

"No, mate. I got lucky when spotting Maypole coming out of the convenience store. Meyer did the rest."

"And Meyer? How come he's now living here?"

"Joseph's as thick as two short ones. It's Sam Meyer who runs the business. Well, he did up until he lost the plot, claimed he's had visitations from the afterlife and confessed to his crimes ... oh, the penny's dropped. It was you two."

Terry rotated his hand, encouraging Hallam to continue.

"Right, the bully-boy son, Joseph. Right knob. He obviously wasn't too chuffed about the situation, plus, as far as he was concerned, his father had gone gaga. So, the prat made a few shit decisions. Joseph's the sort who could fritter away a EuroMillions win in a week if you get my drift. Last I heard, when I was trying to get my money owed, the prick lost everything and more, so had no choice but to end up here in this dump. I tell you, the council should have bulldozed the whole damn place years ago."

"First sensible thing to come out of that little pervert's mouth."

"You don't know which block either happens to live in, do you?"

Hallam shook his head. "Sorry mate, it's a case of waiting and seeing if we spot one of them. Trouble is, no daft bastard is coming out in this weather."

"Could we ask around?"

"Darling, I'm not so sure that's such a good idea."

"You having a laugh? Jesus, mate, you don't go around asking questions in a place like this. Not unless you fancy booking fridge space up at the morgue."

"I'm already dead."

"Oh, yeah, fair point."

"Terry, darling, no. We might be dead, but I'm not feeling good vibes about that idea."

"I take it if you're dead, you can't die again. Is that how it works? You're sorta like that Highlander bloke?"

Terry pulled a face.

"Y'know, Scottish bloke with the sword."

"I have no idea what you're on about—"

"Stinky-Pete is referring to a film character, darling. I would have thought you were still alive when that came out. I may be mistaken … a seldom occurrence, but it has been known. A rather strapping immortal Scotsman flits across the Highlands, hunting other immortals. Dickie loved it. Not my type of thing … film or man, I can assure you. However, I have no issue with a man in a skirt, per se. Dickie looked fab in a rah-rah."

"What did she say?" Hallam asked when detecting the invisible woman must be speaking by how Terry cut his sentence short.

"I'm not sure." Terry furrowed his brow, trying to rid the image of Deana's late husband dressed in a skirt. "It wasn't relevant. And to answer your question, I don't know if I can die twice."

"Oh. Anyway, asking questions on this estate is a death sentence."

"What about Alistair Strachan?"

"Ah, Strachan, the bean counter. Funny thing is, I knew Strachan through his father, who'd used my services back in the day."

"Why did Mel Strachan employ you?"

"Can't say, mate, client confidentiality, and all that shite." Hallam tapped his nose. "Strachan, Alistair, the son, had the accountancy firm, did he not?"

"He did. Again, Deana and I sorted him out earlier this year when he was trying to frame my daughter."

"Kim Meyer?"

"No, my other daughter."

"Oh, right. Ehm … how many kids you got, then?"

"Ruddy good question!"

"Three, as far as I know. Damian Statham, who Lee Parish paid you to frame, is my son."

"Our son." Deana poked Terry's chest.

"Ah … now I understand … well, I think I do."

"You don't need to know the details."

"Yeah, course."

"So, Alistair Strachan."

"Okay. Knowing Strachan as I did, I had a little chuckle to myself on this job. So, some bloke asked me to conduct a surveillance job for him. Domestic surveillance … my bread and butter, you could say. It's usually women who tap up my services. Y'know, follow a cheating husband. But on this occasion, the chap asked me to follow his missus 'cos he suspected she was up to no good with another fella. Which she was. The tart was …" Hallam held up his left hand in the A-okay form before repeatedly poking his right index finger through the hole. "Doing that with Strachan."

"If she ran off with that weasel, Strachan, she must have a sight impediment, been ruddy desperate, or her husband made Joseph Merrick appear like a hunk."

"And this couple lived here?"

"Oh, no. The husband was a stockbroker in the City. They had a bob or two. I provided the evidence, and he booted her out. What the daft cow didn't know was that Strachan had royally screwed up his bean-counting business and was basically potless. They ended up here before she left him and ran off with the ex-husband's best man. Who would you believe she'd previously had an affair with? She was the sort to put it about, by all accounts."

"And Strachan is still here?"

"As far as I know. I haven't spoken to Strachan for months, and he's oblivious to the fact I'm the one who took the pictures of him and that woman he was knobbing. As I said, the woman was a right tart. I wouldn't have minded giving her a poke, though. I mean, women like that are fair game, eh?"

"Fair game! My God, what a detestable piece of shite. Please remind Inch-High that I am here, and I do not take kindly to his misogynistic attitude. Idiots like him need castrating! An operation I'm happy to perform if he feels the need to continue verbalising his vulgar views. No wonder the man has to play with himself. I mean, no woman would put up with that!"

"Hallam. I think you're forgetting there's a woman in the cab—"

"Lady!"

"A lady perched on my lap."

"Oh, sorry … I was forgetting," Hallam winced. "Just lads' talk and didn't mean to offend."

"Lads' talk! My Dickie would never have said such a thing about any woman. And, I can tell you, we encountered a few trollops in our time."

"I think it's a bit late for that. She's contemplating castration."

"Hey … please," Hallam held up his palms, pressing his back against the side window. "Look, lady, I didn't mean … oh, hang on, look. There …" Hallam, still holding that surrender position and an expression that radiated pure terror, nodded towards the convenience store. "Look, there's one of your top three."

23

The Rebel Alliance

"Oh, Christ, no. That's all I damn well need. Look, my front door is open. Jesus, I've been broken into!"

"That's your house?" Niall asked, swinging the Landy, as he called it, into the only available parking space thirty yards from my front door that stood ajar.

"It is ... although for how much longer, who knows?" I groaned, grabbing the door lever before Niall killed the engine. My attempts to hop out and scamper to my open front door were only thwarted by Niall grabbing my arm.

"Hang on. If you have, there might be someone still in there."

"Oh."

"We'll go together. Have your phone ready to call the police, but stay behind me."

"What you gonna do?"

"I'll take a look. There could be a perfectly rational explanation for why your door is open."

"Like?"

"Does anyone else have a key?"

"No."

"Do you know him?" Niall nodded to my house, specifically the man now standing on the threshold of my front door.

"Oh, you've got to be joking."

"Who's that?"

"My arsey landlord. The git's been in my house." I threw open the door and slid off the seat before my wholly inadequate footwear for these conditions sunk into the rutted snow piled up in the gutter. "Oh great," I muttered before gingerly stepping onto the pavement, already feeling the wetness seep in and soak my bloodstained, pink, polka-dot socks.

"Janice, wait."

As I hot-footed along the snow-covered path, as much as I dared in my suede ankle boots – admonishing myself for not taking a peek at the weather forecast before leaving my house yesterday morning. Although, in my defence, I thought I'd only be out for a couple of hours, not meeting two ghosts and spending the night at the vicarage – I wagged a finger at John Parish, the man in the running to be short-listed for this year's most-unaccommodating-landlord-of-the-year award.

"Janice, hang on," I heard Niall call after me as he closed the Landy's driver's door with a wallop.

"You can't break into my house," I hollered as I approached.

"Ah, Miss Keelan. Good timing."

"What d'you think you're doing? You can't just waltz in when you feel like it. This is my … oh shit!" As my left leg slid sideways on a patch of ice, I flung out my hands in preparation to save myself before the inevitable occurred when gravity won the day.

"We're going to have to get you some decent boots," Niall grunted after catching me mid-fall.

In a pose that might be better suited for a movie poster to promote *Gone with the Wind* or *The Empire Strikes Back* – preferring the latter because I really didn't want to be labelled a Scarlett O'Hara type, plus I'd always had a thing about Harrison Ford so really wouldn't mind being held in his arms – I gazed up at Niall, who looked nothing like the man who could expertly wield a whip and looked amazing in a fedora, before puffing out my cheeks.

"Thanks."

Niall didn't utter a word. As he held me in his arms, clasped tight to his chest, he continued to gaze down at me.

"Ehm … Niall? Could you—"

"Oh, sorry. Here you go. As I said, we need to get you some decent—"

"So, as I was saying, what are you doing in my home," I barked at my landlord with an uncharacteristic fervour as Niall helped me into an upright position, focusing on the man blocking the doorway as he blew into his hands and stamped his feet, rather than listening to Niall's mumblings.

"Some decent boots."

"Sorry," I spun around when detecting Niall was still talking.

"It doesn't matter. I was just saying about your footwear."

"Oh … thanks for catching me." I spun around and raised my eyebrows at John. "Well?"

"It *was* your home. Anyway, I think you'll find it's my house. I own it."

"I'm aware of that, but you—"

"Hello. I'm Niall Dowding," Niall interrupted my flow as he stepped past me and proffered his hand to John.

"So?" John shrugged as he glanced down at the outstretched hand but didn't make any effort to reciprocate, keeping his hands firmly entrenched in his coat pockets where he'd shoved them a moment ago.

"I'm a friend of Janice's. I see that you've entered her home. Did you ask her permission to do so?"

"Don't have to, mate."

"I think you'll find that you do—"

"Well, you can sue me if you like. But as Miss Keelan hasn't paid this month's rent, I suspect she probably couldn't afford a lawyer, either." John grinned as he delved into the inside pocket of his anorak and extracted an envelope before waving it in my face.

"What's that?"

"It's for you." While sporting a supercilious grin, he flipped the envelope around. "See, it has your name on the front. Happy Christmas."

With a scowl, I snatched the envelope and tore it open.

"It's a Section Twenty-One notice. Which, if you're not fully au fait with your tenancy agreement, is my right to serve you. You've got two months to vacate, which is more than reasonable considering you owe me rent. That's hopefully more than enough time for this gentleman to sell this dump." John nodded to the grinning man clasping a clipboard who now hovered on the pavement.

Clearly, for whatever reason, my landlord had decided to sell up, and Clipboard-Man's appearance slotted perfectly into the mould of an estate agent-cum-double-glazing salesman. Flashy, sporting a 'just back from Majorca' tan, a set of gleaming gnashers on loan from his blingy second-hand-car-salesman twin, and a spray-on suit that I would class as obscene if it wasn't for the position of said clipboard.

"Mr Parish?" Flashy-Git asked.

"That's me, come through," John gestured with open arms for the agent to step past Niall and me while we both scanned the letter. Three-quarters of the way down the page, my eyes seemed unable to move past the sentence regarding contacting my local authority if I believed that, as a result of this notice, I could become homeless. Of course, that had always been on the cards but, until facing the prospect of becoming one of those poor sods tagged with the 'no fixed abode' label, it hadn't felt real.

But here it was, in black and white.

"Oh, Miss Keelan. One more thing …"

I dragged my eye from that foreboding sentence and looked up when my landlord paused.

"Just in case you want to throw any more accusations at me regarding what I can or can't do with my own property, you'll find it in your agreement that I can show agents and potential buyers around at any time deemed reasonable. I deem today as reasonable. Also, the agent will be taking pictures later today, so you might want to have a tidy up and perhaps hide your knickers and any other washed-out, drab-looking underwear that you've got drying on the radiator in the front room."

I offered an upward lip curl in response to his exaggerated 'I've won' grin.

"I see you haven't put up any Christmas decorations yet. If you are planning to do so, please don't. I want potential buyers to see this little hovel in its best light, and tacky additions such as paper chains, threadbare tinsel and a moth-eaten plastic tree won't help. Much appreciated."

"Get out. I want you out of my home," I barked, fortitude and confidence in my tone rising from the hidden depths. However, as they say, back a rat into a corner.

"Janice," Niall laid his hand on my elbow. "You can't fight this. Let's just wait inside until they're done."

"Good advice."

"It's Mr Parish, yes?"

"That's me. What's it to you?"

"Can this be settled in another way? If I pay the back rent and act as guarantor for Miss Keelan, would that solve the issue?"

"Niall?" I shot him a look. "No, no way."

"Janice, hang on a sec."

"This isn't your problem."

"You can pay the back rent and the two months owed for the final period of the agreement. But that makes no difference because I'm selling up. I've had my fill of this landlord game. Too many late-paying, complaining tenants, present company included." John leaned forward to sneer down at me.

"Mr Parish, there's no need to be aggressive—"

"Aggressive? My arse. You ain't seen nothing, mate. Unless you want me to a call the Old Bill, I suggest you and your girlfriend calm down, stand back and wait till the agent's done."

"Sir, I'm not Miss Keelan's boyfriend. I'm the vicar of All Saints, here to just lend her some moral support."

"All Saints? That frigging place where some bastard bludgeoned my poor boy to death."

The news of the murder of a man at All Saints earlier this year had been the talk of the town for weeks and even made the national news. I'd felt sorry for John for losing his son in such a tragic way, despite my annoyance regarding my repeated request over weeks before his son's death to fix the leaking window in the back bedroom. Maintenance my landlord repeatedly refused to complete. A leak I'd managed with the application of a Tupperware pot wedged on the windowsill, which required weekly emptying. I bet dripcatching wasn't part of the sales spiel at one of my mother's plastic-storage-box parties.

"Oh, blimey, I heard about that. I'm new there, but I'm so sorry that was your son."

"It was. Bloody Old Bill have all but given up investigating it. Just because my son served time, they weren't interested in finding his killer. Your predecessor, old Father Mackie, silly sod, reckoned it was a ghost that killed him."

Niall and I shot each other a look, which John instantly picked up upon.

"What's that look for?"

"Why did he think it was a ghost?" I asked, shooting another look at Niall.

"Because he was a deranged old git, that's why. He was there when it happened and said it must have been a ghost. Daft apeth should have gone to Specsavers."

"It was all over the news, and I remember the vicar being interviewed, but I don't recall him suggesting anything about a ghost being responsible for Lee's death."

"Well, he did. There were three others there at the time. Two men about Lee's age and a young woman. Course, they never traced them, so the police just gave up. Infuriates me, it does. That's one of the reasons I'm selling up and moving to Spain. Soak up a bit of sun and get away from this shit." John, clearly feeling the need to vent his spleen, tapped his forehead. "I've had it up to here with this poxy country."

"I remember them appealing for those three witnesses," I mumbled much to myself than anyone else.

"Yeah, old Father Mackie reckoned one of the blokes was a bit deranged."

"Deranged?" I parroted.

"Yeah, deranged. Talking to himself and shit like that. Or maybe this ghost, who the silly sod reckoned killed my boy," John scoffed. "Anyway, what the hell has this got to do with you? I need to see how the agent's getting on. And yes, Father, whatever your name is, I will accept your offer to pay this woman's outstanding rent. She'll give you the details." Rant delivered, and an extra sneer shot my way, my soon-to-be-ex-landlord completed an about-turn and marched into my home.

"It can't be, can it?"

"Terry … and Deana, for that matter, at the church when his son was killed?"

I nodded and chewed my lip.

"It's a hell of a coincidence. I didn't know Father Mackie well, but he seemed pretty lucid to me when we handed over."

"Although a smidge on the odd side, I don't think Terry Walton looks like a killer."

"Nor do I, but then I haven't met many killers to make a comparison."

"He wouldn't be the killer, though. It would be the invisible Deana, wouldn't it? Did she look like a murderer?"

"I definitely haven't met any killer ghosts before, so I really couldn't say. But anyway, she appeared more the good-time-girl sort than a deranged killer ghost."

"The nude prancing incident?"

"Yeah," Niall nodded. "I'm struggling to marry the vision of Deana jiggling her wares at me and the image of her bludgeoning a man to death."

"I suppose. But what are we going to do?" I hissed. "If Terry and Deana are murderers—"

"Let's not jump the gun. We'll get this sorted. Then I think our ghostly duo have some questions to answer."

"And on the subject of getting this sorted. I can't allow you to pay my outstanding rent."

"Why not?"

"Because … because it's not right."

"Who says?"

"Me!"

"Look, it'll be a loan. It will get him off your back. From what I can see, your landlord's not that accommodating, and I reckon he'll hound you for what's owed. Let me sort this, then you can pay me back whenever."

"That could be a long time in the future."

"Doesn't matter."

"Why you offering to do this?" I narrowed my eyes; the alarm bells … no, scrub that, a set of klaxons were doing their thing in my head, warning me that men – despite Niall's profession – didn't offer to pay off stranger's debts without harbouring an ulterior motive.

"Because I would like to help you. Because I'm your friend. Because I like you, as I've already said over breakfast. Because it's the decent thing to do. Because I can easily afford it and because it's sodding Christmas, alright?"

"Should you say sodding and Christmas in the same sentence?" I twisted my lips and smirked. That little speech of his about 'why', punctuated with a lot of 'becauses', putting me at ease and thus no longer fearing Niall was up to no good. Perhaps, just perhaps, Niall was just a genuinely decent bloke.

"No, I'm sure I shouldn't."

"It's just a loan, though." I wagged a finger at him.

"Just a loan."

"Interest rate?"

"Zero."

"You sure?"

"No, I want thirty per cent APR."

"Oh."

"Janice, for Heaven's sake. I'm joking. Let someone inside that protective shell of yours. I understand why you're cautious, but not everyone is a con man. Let me do this for you. Anyway, your outstanding rent can't be that much, can it?"

"Six-fifty a month. Six-fifty I don't have."

"That's fine. I'll pay the bloke today, and then it's settled."

"Short-term settled. Thank you." I rubbed his arm and offered a tight smile. "I'm still going to have to move out, though. Pay the rent or not, I'm still losing my home."

"I know. We have the next two weeks sorted, and you never know, those murdering ghosts we met last night might actually get your money back."

"By killing someone? Murdering the man claiming to be Chad Ruger. Do guardian angels actually do that sort of thing?"

"I don't know. But I have a feeling we're going to find out."

24

All that Glitters is Not Gold

"Excuse me, can we have a quick word?" Terry called out when he and a panting Hallam reached the top landing of Belfast House, one of the three brutal grey concrete blocks that made up the odious estate.

"They need to fix those damn lifts," Hallam wheezed, clutching the rusting handrail before slapping his hand to the wall to steady himself, feeling nauseous after drinking in the view of the central square, five storeys below.

The fact that the dead Terry had effortlessly traversed the steps, leaving him a couple of flights behind, had afforded Hallam the opportunity to discreetly fire off a couple of texts. Insurance policies, as he saw them, which might pay dividends if his hunch was correct. For now, he'd toe the line and keep his suspicions to himself.

"Excuse me," Terry hollered again, picking up the pace when Daniel Maypole ignored his earlier shout.

"Me?" Daniel halted at his door, key in hand, offering an expression that suggested he might shit himself or just had. "Hey, I don't want any trouble."

"Hang on there. I just want a quick word," Terry scooted along the landing, trying his best not to spook Maypole, who, since Hallam had spotted earlier, he and Deana, with Hallam in tow, had followed.

"What about?" Daniel warbled, his hand resting on the inserted Yale key.

"Oh, dear, the man looks a quivering wreck, and the cretin's not even had to face me yet. Pathetic!" Deana boomed in Maypole's ear after coming to a halt, following her dash up the stairs at the other end of the block. Although Daniel didn't know it, he was now corralled between two ghosts.

Terry slapped his hand on Maypole's front door and glanced at Deana as she pinched her face when inspecting Maypole, her expression suggesting she considered what stood before her to be a festering turd, before leaning close to the man who'd now developed a hyperthermia-styled shake.

"Shall we go inside?"

"What? Why?" he whimpered. "Who are you? Who's he?" Daniel shot his eyes left as Hallam approached, crabbing along the spartan concrete landing – so uninviting even last night's festive weather had given it a wide berth – with his back against the wall and eyes closed.

"That's Inch-High-Pervert-Eye. He's a revolting toad of an excuse of a man much like yourself."

"This is my associate." Terry glanced over his shoulder. "What the hell are you doing?" he asked Hallam, who stood with his back pinned to the graffiti-covered wall.

"I'm afraid of heights. Ever since getting stuck on the two-metre diving board at Butlins in '74 … it gets worse as I get older. Just my blooming luck this bloke lives on the top floor."

"Oh, dear, poor Inch-High, afraid of heights. It's a good job the pervy PI is a short arse, then. Did I ever mention that I came first in the Holiday Princess Competition that very year in Skegness? Cock-a-hoop I was. I was only sixteen, but as I said earlier, I was an early bloomer. My high-cut crochet bikini soon saw off the competition in their dour one-piece cossies. Inch-High probably couldn't even win the knobbly knees contest."

"Sorry … but who are you? I haven't done anything and don't have anything worth taking. Please, I really don't want any trouble." Still gripping his key, Maypole flitted his eyes from Terry and the man stuck to the wall, who appeared more petrified than he did. Although for very different reasons.

"Oh, lordy, what a wretched wimp. Darling, what on earth causes some men to be so … well, inadequate? I almost, not quite, feel embarrassed for him. The man's a joke."

"Daniel, let's go inside and have a chat. You're shaking with cold, so best we go in, eh?"

"I … I don't want you to come in."

"I really don't give two shits what you want. Open the door, or I'll do it for you."

"Oh, darling, you brute, you. I do so love it when you're all mettlesome. Unlike mousey Maypole here. I wouldn't be surprised if the wimp's peed himself."

"Okay." Maypole nodded vigorously as he turned the key. "I don't have much … please, there's nothing worth taking."

"Maypole, I'm not here to steal from you. My associates and I would like a chat, that's all," Terry waved the way forward, encouraging Daniel to step inside before gesturing to Hallam that he should peel himself from the brickwork and follow so he could let Deana in before closing the door.

"Can I get you a cup of tea?" Maypole asked, stopping short of the kitchen doorway and nodding to the lounge for Hallam and Terry to go through.

"Stinks! Just like Hallam's office. The odour of adolescent boys' sweaty locker room. A few of which I ventured into in my younger days. I imagine the wimp isn't that well acquainted with deodorant and spends all day watching porn, farting and masturbating. Darling, open a window before I choke to death on the stench."

"Maypole, sit in there. We don't want any tea." Terry jabbed his finger towards the lounge, leaving Daniel under no illusion that he needed to comply. After opening the window and ensuring the nicotine-stained net curtains were back in position, Terry nodded to Hallam, who stood in front of the ancient big-box TV.

"Racing Post." Hallam, who it was agreed when in the Transit would conduct the questioning based on his years as operating as a private investigator, nodded to the sofa and the stack of newspapers. "I see you still enjoy a flutter after all that's happened."

Maypole shot his eyes left at the stack, then to Terry, who remained by the window, before nodding at Hallam.

Despite the threats levied at him from the invisible one of the two ghosts, the carrier bag and note incidents back at his office still uppermost in his mind, Hallam's worries eased a smidge now that the two spooks seemed to have moved their attention from him to the quivering man perched on the dilapidated sofa.

It appeared from the decor and furnishings that the ex-jewellery shop owner's life hadn't slid but more gone into free fall to the lowest depths. One rung up from the druggies who resided in most of the squalid flats on this estate. Now feeling less terrified, although there was always the concern about the precise location of the deranged woman ghost, Hallam pushed Maypole for answers.

"So, Maypole, how much you losing these days, then?"

"Who says I'm losing?"

"All gamblers lose. You frittered away your jewellery business that your grandfather built. I suspect the old boy's turning in his grave. I bought my missus's engagement ring from your shop. Bloody waste of money, that was," Hallam tutted. "She booted me out years ago 'cos of my affection for Johnny Walker. So, you could say I know all about addictions."

"How … how d'you know who I am?"

"I'm a private investigator—"

"Oh, God." Maypole bowed his head.

Hallam shot Terry a look, who offered a shrugged response.

"As I said, I'm a private investigator. I'm the one who tracked you down when Joseph Meyer was trying to recover money owed."

"That bastard," Maypole hissed.

"I'm not going to argue with you on that front."

"I don't owe him … I don't owe anyone." Maypole raised his head. "And I don't have to answer your questions."

Terry, still with his arms folded, took a pace forward.

"Alright, alright." Maypole held up his palm. "You don't have to get heavy."

"So, you're still gambling. How much d'you owe?" Hallam asked.

"I just said I don't."

"Had a big win, have we?"

"No … I've been on a bit of a bad run of late, but it'll come good soon."

"And where you getting the readies to service this habit?"

Maypole shot a worried look at Terry, then back to Hallam, his mouth flapping.

"Well?" Hallam asked.

"Oh, shit," Maypole hissed, burying his head between his knees before clasping his hands behind his head.

"Oh shit, what?" Terry interjected.

"Please, don't hurt me," came his muffled cry. "I know I shouldn't have taken them." Maypole gingerly lifted his head. "I'm assuming the liquidation company hired you. Look, I can get the money … promise, straight up. I have a ton placed on a nailed-on certainty. *Goodbye Stranger*, a seven-year-old that's got good form on soft going and is coming good. It only came second in its last race because it got hemmed in against the rails. If you fancy a flutter, it's running in the two-thirty at Carlisle this afternoon. Great odds … thirty-three to one, but

I know it will win." When noticing both men roll their eyes, Daniel again buried his head. "It has to win," he whispered.

"Okay, so …" Terry paused as he shot a look towards the hallway.

"Darling, I don't think the wimpy boy here is our con man. This dump has nothing of any real value in it, so I can't see what he's doing with the ill-gotten gains if he's been pretending to be Jaded-Janice's American friend," Deana called out from the bedroom. *"I've had a good rifle through his stuff, and apart from an infestation of yucky cockroaches huddled together trying to keep warm in his sock drawer, the puny excuse of a man doesn't have much to show for himself."*

Hallam, clocking that Terry appeared distracted, assuming his ghostly friend was talking, questioningly shrugged and raised his palms.

"She said there's nothing here."

"Oh," Hallam nodded. "Where is she?" he hissed.

"She, as you rudely refer to me, is here." Deana padded into the lounge. *"Darling, as I was saying, there's nothing here of any interest apart from this, which I discovered hidden under this reprobate's piss-stained mattress. I've frolicked my way around dubious bedding, sporting questionable stains in my time. Still, I have to say, I've never seen anything so revolting in my entire life. Anyway, darling, I found this bag of junk, which I thought was interesting."*

Although Fred Hallam, after the incident back in the spring, and further confirmed with what happened earlier today, had come to accept that a ghostly woman roamed around, actually seeing a levitating clear plastic bag of what appeared to be jewellery just hovering in the air caused his jaw to sag, and the need to place his hand on top of the TV for support. Fred blinked a few times to make sure he wasn't hallucinating.

"Where's who? There's no one else here," Maypole mumbled in response to Hallam's 'where is she' question before raising his head.

"This your stash, Cockroach-Boy?" Deana jiggled the bag, causing the jewellery to rattle, before spinning it around Catherine wheel-style. "Although a veritable collection of bling, all that glitters is not gold. To be accurate to the Bard of Avon, I'm sure Shakespeare coined the phrase, all that glisters is not gold, but I'm splitting hairs. And before you say otherwise, yes, it appears most is gold, but more the cheap, tacky nine-carat effluvia you used to sell in that horrid little shop of yours."

"Oh, no … not again, please …" Maypole scrambled up the sofa, his feet now on the seat pad and his back pinned to the wall Hallam-style. "This can't be happening again."

"I take it Maypole has encountered your friend before," hissed Hallam while following the golf-ball-in-flight-styled arced trajectory of the bag of bling as it spun through the air and landed on the sofa next to Maypole's feet.

"He most certainly has."

"Yes, you filthy reprobate. I'm back!"

"How can this be happening?" quivered Maypole, his eyes pleading at Terry to explain.

"What you experienced in your shop before you accused my daughter of stealing her mother's engagement ring, a ring I purchased from your father in 1981, I might add, was the actions of my dear friend and ghost, Deana."

"Ghost?"

"Yes, ghost."

"A g-ghost called Deana?"

"That's right."

"And she's here ... like, right now?"

"Currently sticking her tongue out at you ... just there on your left." Hallam and Maypole shot looks at where Terry indicated.

"How come you can see her?"

"I'm a ghost too."

"You're a ghost too?"

"Someone shoot the parrot!"

"That's what I said."

"Your daughter is Kim Meyer?"

"Correct. The woman you tried to swindle."

"But ..."

"I know ... I look about the same age as her. Without going into detail, let's just say it's complicated."

"And you?" Maypole nodded at Hallam.

"Oh, no, mate. I'm fully alive ... just a bloke trying not to be otherwise."

Maypole offered a nervous grin as he held his position, arms splayed out, pinned to the wall, and eyes tightly closed as if that last action would rid the room of the horrors.

"So, if I was a betting man like you, which I'm not, I would wager that the bag of jewellery which my friend is now sifting through ..." Terry paused to allow Maypole to peek open one eye and witness the sight of what appeared to be levitating bracelets and earrings. "Is stock you took from your business that actually belongs to the liquidators and ultimately your creditors? You've assumed they'd rumbled you, probably when you pawn this stuff to keep your habit going, and we're here to recover the, essentially speaking, stolen goods."

Maypole, still watching his free-moving jewellery, offered a single nod.

"What d'you think, darling? These earrings suit me, or are they too garish?" Deana asked, holding up said items to her ears.

Terry scrunched his nose up.

"No, you're probably right. Anyway, leave me to rummage. I'm quite enjoying myself. Do continue, darling ... you're doing a sterling job. Proud of you, sweety."

"Well, the good news for you is we have no interest in your bag of tat. However, tell me what you know about a man called Chad Ruger?"

"Who?"

"Chad Ruger."

"Never heard of him."

"You sure?"

"Deffo. Never heard of him."

"My BS detector suggests Cockroach-Boy has never heard that name. We can cross him off the list. I always maintained he wasn't the one."

Terry raised an eyebrow, wondering how Deana could so easily forget her insistence yesterday afternoon that Maypole was the con man.

"He's not your man. I smell bull from a mile off, and this guy's never heard that name before," Hallam interjected, like Maypole unable to peel his eyes from the moving jewellery.

"That's what I just said. I do so wish people would listen to me. You're just like my first six husbands. Stupid, irksome and totally irrelevant. Ah, now this bracelet isn't too bad. Costume jewellery at best, but sort of okay-ish, I suppose. Darling, I might take this piece. Will that be alright, d'you think? Clara would love it."

"A trinket to woo her back?"

"Please, don't say that. I can't bear the thought of … well, you know."

"She'll be back, I know it."

"I hope so, darling," Deana sniffed.

Terry offered a tight smile, noticing and not wishing to exploit her rare display of vulnerability, before turning to address Maypole.

"Okay, you're probably not the man we're looking for. We'll leave you in peace."

"That's it … you're going?"

"We are."

"And the ghost?"

"Yes, and the ghost."

"My bag of jewellery?"

"No, that's staying here. Although looks to me like Deana's got her heart set on a bracelet to give to her girlfriend, so you might be one item short. But, as that stuff isn't technically yours, I presume you won't mind?"

"No, that's fine … totally fine." Maypole tentatively shifted his bottom along the back of the sofa when spotting his bag of glitter appeared to have stopped wriggling like a pot of maggots. "Err … would the ghost …" he paused to look around, trying to detect her location. "Would she like another piece … just to be friendly like, and perhaps that might smooth the way to you all forgetting what you've seen here today?"

"No, I would not. Think yourself lucky I want this thing!"

"She said that's very kind of you. But, no, she doesn't want anything else."

"Okay." Maypole snatched his bag of gold, holding it tight to his chest. His gleeful expression not too far removed from that of Ron Moody's Fagin.

While in the throes of trying to wriggle free from Deana's clutches, who'd grabbed his arm and tiptoed up to kiss his cheek, Terry gestured to Hallam that it was time to leave.

"Darling, I'm just giving you a kiss to show my appreciation. Well done, you. An utterly superb performance."

"Hmmm. Come on, you bracelet thief."

"Yes, well, you can't be labelled a thief for stealing stolen goods. That's a double negative … I think. Anyway, I've got the taste for it after my forays into shoplifting," she tittered.

Terry paused in the hallway before stepping back to the lounge and peering around the door.

"Before we go. Don't suppose you know which flat in this dump we'll find your old pal, Joseph Meyer? And while we're at it, do you know Alistair Strachan?"

"I might."

"You do, or you don't?"

"I said I might. What's it worth? Information costs, you know?"

"Darling, I'm not liking his tone. Please remind Cockroach-Boy that the ghost is still here and is quite up for a spot of mischief."

"Maypole, as Deana just said, she's still here. You really don't want to upset my ghostly friend."

Hallam joined Terry, both now peering around the door.

"Look, mate, this is up to you, but I'd take heed. That woman ghost is a frigging psycho. I'd cough up the info or wave goodbye to your crown jewels, and I don't mean that bag of tat lying on your lap. More the meat and two veg positioned underneath it."

"Oh, very droll. I was going to take Inch-High to task over the psycho comment, but that was quite funny for the little pervert lap dog we've acquired."

"As Hallam said, I suggest you start talking."

"Alistair Strachan's my neighbour," Maypole pointed at the wall opposite. "We don't really talk much, but he let slip last week that he's had a windfall, quite a few grand by all accounts, and reckoned he'd be out of this dump pretty soon."

"Ah-ha … the plot thickens! Sounds to me, darling, we have our man. I knew it! That shifty little accountant was always top of my list, as I said yesterday."

"No, you didn't!"

"I did so. Come on, Terence, we have work to do and horrid little men to scare half to death."

Part 3

25

Merry Christmas, Mr Potter

"When I see that the transfer's come through to my account, then, and only then, I'll tell you what I know."

"This better be good because if you're pissing me about, Hallam, there'll be consequences."

"Don't threaten me. I gave you fair warning earlier today, which I didn't need to."

"Not out of the goodness of your heart, you didn't."

"Yeah, well, a man's gotta eat."

"Drink, in your case."

"Whatever. Anyway, what I've discovered today is worth a monkey."

"Frigging better be."

"Hang on." Hallam pinned his phone between his ear and shoulder as he wiggled the mouse and refreshed his screen on his banking website. He knew he could install the app on his phone, but he was old school, and even internet banking on his laptop pushed the boundaries for a man who preferred the feel and smell of hard cash.

However, following his jaunt to the Broxworth with those two ghosts, now back in his office, he'd spotted an opportunity to make a fast buck. So, one phone call and he was about to become five hundred quid better off. Not a bad day's work.

"Well? Is it there? I made the transfer ten minutes ago."

"Frig sake," Hallam muttered when again refreshing the screen. "No … oh, yeah, it's just dropped in."

"Right, start talking. And this better be worth hearing!"

"A threat to your life … I reckon that's a clear and present danger you should be aware of. You need to rein it in and probably should be thanking me."

"You've got your money. Now, spit it out."

"Okay … first up, I'm gonna say a name and, if you want to hear what I have discovered, you better be honest with me."

"What name?"

"Chad Ruger."

Hallam detected the man at the other end of the line take a sharp intake of breath. So, going by that reaction, he deduced that those two ghosts were on the right track. The continued silence at the other end of the line confirmed as much. As he waited for a response, Hallam grabbed his glass, still with three fingers' worth of Johnnie Walker, raised it and non-verbally offered cheers to himself. After swilling a mouthful, savouring the smokey, herbal, almost toffee notes to the taste, he grimaced due to the throat burn as he swallowed the dark amber liquid.

"Well?" Hallam asked as he again tipped his head and pinned his phone to his shoulder before grabbing the bottle. Due to this afternoon appearing to be panning out to be a good one, and because Christmas was less than a week away, not that he needed an excuse to drink, he poured himself another stiff measure.

"Where did you hear that name?"

"You know the name, then?"

"Where … who said that name?"

"Someone accused me of being Chad Ruger."

"Who?"

"I'm coming to that. Apparently, but I guess you know this already, someone has used that fake identity to con some woman out of her life savings."

"Hallam, don't play games! Spit it out, man. Who's said this to you?"

"Okay … easy tiger, calm down."

"Don't tell me to calm down!"

While rocking back and forth on his chair, Hallam held the glass aloft, allowing the undiffused light from the cobweb-smothered fluorescent tube to transform the whisky and make it appear almost alchemical. He marvelled and grinned at its amber depths flickering with hints of gold and bronze. The liquid seemed to catch the light and hold it prisoner, refracting the brightness into soft, glowing hues that shifted with every tilt of the glass. Today just got better, and it was time to up the ante.

"Hallam!"

"I'm still here. Bung me another five hundred, and I will reveal all."

"Piss off."

"I could … and then I'd be forced to reveal to those inquiring about Chad Ruger exactly who you are and where to find you. And trust me, one of them two you really don't want an audience with." Hallam swallowed another mouthful and shuddered when remembering Deana's note. "How shall I put it … she's certainly an acquired taste and, going by what she threatened to do to me, has issues with men."

"She?" he scoffed.

"Scoff all you like, mate. But the woman threatened to cut my cock off."

Another pause left Hallam wondering if he'd pushed it too far. Well, he had five hundred. So, at the end of the day, his decision to risk the wrath of the psycho ghost had been a good one.

"All right. I'll transfer it now."

Hallam afforded himself another grin. The fact this prat was happy to cough up a grand confirmed he had used that fake identity to con some woman out of her life savings and probably many more. And was sufficiently concerned about the prospect of being caught. For sure, the man had diversified from his previous business after a monumental tumble from grace earlier in the year, albeit that diversification being into a shady, if not illegal, one.

"Shall we pick up a call in a few minutes when the payment is confirmed?"

"I've made the transfer. Don't try to rinse any more from me. That's all you're getting, and I want everything you've got."

"Yeah, yeah, whatever. Just hang by your phone, and I'll call you back in a minute."

"You'd better."

Hallam killed the call, took another sip of whisky and grimaced as he refreshed his screen, waiting for the second payment. After leaving Maypole clutching his bag of bling, he and the two ghosts had failed to locate Strachan, despite Terry pounding on the man's door with enough force to wake the dead. Although, as bizarre as it was, the dead were already awake. A few minutes later, following a scoot across to the second landing of Dublin House, an equally squalid hellhole as the tower block they'd just left, Terry repeated the action on Joseph Meyer's door with the same result.

Hallam refreshed his screen again, musing that the two ghosts weren't quite as clever as they thought. Asking him to give them a lift home, thus meaning he knew where they lived, afforded him the upper hand. Despite what that ghost had threatened to do to him, Hallam hadn't been in the private investigator game for over a quarter of a century to be outwitted by the dead.

He intended to take complete control of the situation and call the shots. For starters, he could keep tabs on their movements. Plus, if an opportunity arose, which experience told him they always did, he would make his move and ensure no woman, ghost or otherwise, could leave him terrified of his own shadow. His ex-wife, after she booted him out, had a good go, but he wouldn't be put in that position again.

Notwithstanding Terry's point regarding the possibility that the dead couldn't die twice, which he accepted was a valid consideration, Hallam didn't have murder on his mind. Once this issue was resolved, he planned something much worse for the ghostly duo … exposure.

An interesting piece of useful intel he'd gleaned from the few hours in their company is that ghosts' biggest fear was their existence being discovered by the living.

Of course, he, along with Maypole and probably a few others, had already come to that conclusion – the evidence was irrefutable – but he was banking that Terry and Deana believed he, Maypole and the rest, whoever they were, wouldn't expose them because the ghosts held all the aces. However, Hallam planned to turn that situation around. And when he had, he intended to expose them on a grand scale.

While twiddling the glass around in his hand, rocking back and forth on his swivel chair, he afforded himself a moment to muse about the future. Fred Hallam, the man who proved the existence of the afterlife. He would be famous – rivalling Einstein, Newton, and even Darwin – and wealthy, deserving the attention of a few glamour models, all of whom couldn't resist a week on his yacht. No longer would he have to skulk around in the bushes or spend hours upon hours in his van trying to grab pictures of husbands to prove their infidelity to a bunch of annoying women who he wasn't at all surprised said husbands had cheated on.

Fred stretched up and snapped off the light, plunging his office into near darkness, leaving just the backlight of his laptop reflected in the window. He spun around, propped his wet, dilapidated-trainer-clad feet onto the windowsill, sipped his whisky and surveyed the alley that gave access to his shitty office. The likes of which even Jim Rockford, his idol who could only afford a trailer parked on Malibu Beach, wouldn't have considered using.

The snow had started again, settling on the lids of the Biffa bins and covering the tarmac enough to cast a pure white blanket over the plethora of daily discarded junkie's needles that carpeted the alley. That wonderful, imagined future, just within his grasp, almost spurred Hallam into performing a Jimmy-Stewart-styled dash through the streets while bellowing Merry Christmas to anyone and everyone. Soon, if a few things went his way, it could be a wonderful life.

However, first things first. With rejuvenated vigour, Hallam spun around and snatched up his phone before refreshing his laptop screen. Pleased to see that while pondering his future his bank balance had swelled by another five-hundred quid, he dialled the number of the man who he'd just spoken to. One of the two men he'd texted while panting up those flights of steps when heading for Maypole's, suggesting they needed to hastily vacate their flats. Not that he gave two shits about either, but he'd sensed an opportunity and a hunch that he could take advantage of a situation that earlier looked particularly dire for him.

A hunch that appeared to be becoming good.

"You took your time."

"It's our banking system that took its time."

"You got the transfer?"

"I did."

"Well?"

"The woman who threatened castration is the same woman who broke into my office earlier this year. She's an unusual sort—"

"What d'you mean, unusual?"

"You'll find out."

"Name!"

"Deana Burton. She's got a sidekick who goes by the name of Terry Walton." Hallam raised an eyebrow when hearing the caller hiss a couple of expletives. "I take it you've heard of them and are aware of their unusual talents?"

"You're joking me, right?"

"No, mate. I can assure you, this is no laughing matter."

"You know where I can find them?"

"Oh, no, mate, it don't work like that. I'm just giving you fair warning that they know what you've been up to. Fair to say, unless you skip town, they plan to do unmentionable things to you."

"Hallam, stop pissing about and just tell me where I can find them."

"No way. That psycho cow and her sidekick are the goose that laid the golden egg. While you're running for your life, I'm gonna make a killing."

26

Mrs de Winter

"Mrs Drake. I'm so sorry to disturb you at such a late hour."

"Good evening, vicar. Not at all. Actually, I had hoped you might be the police. Unsurprisingly, though, they are very slow to respond these days. Anyway, you're welcome to knock on my door at any time."

"Police?"

"Yes, there's an old van, the sort of dreadful thing the travelling community drive, gyppos as my Brian called them, parked at the end of the road. It's not the sort of vehicle you see around here. No doubt the occupants are up to no good."

"Oh."

"Do come in out of the snow and cold. I was just putting the kettle on, so perfect timing, vicar. Looks like we will have a white Christmas this year."

The plummy woman, who I had pegged to be in her mid-sixties, with a sour face and pinched lips, gave me a good look up and down. In contrast to the tight smile offered to Niall, her flared nostrils and raised chin suggested she wasn't overly enamoured by my presence on her doorstep.

"Oh, sorry, this is Janice … a friend of mine."

"Hi," I raised my palm and offered a finger wave in response to her po-faced sneer.

"Mrs Drake does all the flower arranging at the church and helps out with organising Sunday services," Niall qualified, probably feeling he needed to say something when Mrs Drake didn't seem that forthcoming with pleasantries where I was concerned.

"I have for the last ten years or so. Are you coming in?"

"No, thank you. Sorry, we can't stop. Janice and I—"

"I've not seen you at a service. Are you new around here or just visiting?" she barked, interrupting Niall while giving me that look that suggested the woman didn't think I was the sort to be from around here and probably suspected I was more suited to be the owner of the old van parked up the road.

"Janice is stopping over to look after Ellen while Lena's back home for Christmas."

"Oh."

"Look, as I said, we can't stop. I just wanted to pick your brains, if I may?"

"Fire away. I'll see if I can help you."

"Fabulous. You've lived here for some years, I seem to remember you saying."

"Fifteen, November just gone. My Brian was alive when we moved in. But, as you know, I lost him five years back. Of course, the house is far too big, but I'm comfortable here."

"Yes, um, do you remember a neighbour of yours who I'm led to believe lived in one of these houses? I'm just trying to locate which one. A lady called Deana."

"Oh … *her* …" When she paused, I detected a darkness skate across her face. The mention of Deana appeared to have elevated her lemon-sucking expression to new heights.

"Mrs Drake?"

"Sorry, vicar, but why on earth … my apologies. That's not for me to ask. Deana, Mrs Burton, along with her husband, used to live three doors up." When grabbing the doorframe, Mrs Drake shot me a look, which I took as her assessment as to whether it was safe to talk in my company, before furtively glancing down the street, then continued in a hushed, gossip-type tone. "Not that I'm one to speak ill of folk. However, Mr and Mrs Burton were not like the rest of us up here. This is a private road, you see. We're all well-heeled, respectable people. We, the residents of Winchmore Drive, demonstrate a level of urbanity, unlike whoever has the audacity to park that rust bucket up there. A situation our local constabulary seem to do nothing about despite the fact I made it quite clear regarding the need for urgent and swift action."

"I suspect they're busy—"

"Being too busy is not acceptable. It's about prioritisation, as my Brian would say. Anyway, Mr Burton, a … well, shall we say an odd man, was a member of the Labour Party. I had to complain to the council when, during the run-up to the last election, he had the gall to erect a Vote Labour sign in his front garden. Shocking!"

"Oh," Niall muttered, squeezing it in when Mrs Drake took a breath.

"Would you believe the council said Mr Burton was well within his rights to erect the sign, and there was nothing they could do about it? I tried to rally the neighbours to sign a petition for its removal. That didn't work, did it? No, because *that woman*, Mrs Burton, with her libertine attitudes and frankly debauched activities, put the fear of the Devil into them all. They were too terrified to side with me. That demon woman didn't intimidate me, though, I can tell you. I'm sure you'll think me wicked, but since they've gone, it's a respectable street again."

"Um … I see."

"I assume you're aware that both he and *her* are no longer with us? Both died in a road accident earlier this year. Not that I'm saying they were wicked people, but there is that saying, you reap what you sow."

I raised an eyebrow at how she managed to say the word 'her' with such venom. Based on what Niall and I knew about Deana Burton and what I was fast learning about Mrs Drake, I could see they wouldn't have been great friends and probably didn't enjoy each other's company over a cup of Mellow Birds and a Digestive during coffee mornings.

"Well, um, thanks, Mrs Drake." Niall stepped back from the doorstep onto the snow-covered gravel driveway and pointed to his left. "Three doors up, you say?"

"Yes, that's right. Number six." The slipper-clad Mrs Drake reciprocated Niall's steps back with an equal amount of steps forward. "The house is still empty. I heard it's all to do with a probate backlog. My Brian was a solicitor, and I can tell you he wouldn't have shilly-shallied about like they do today. I really can't imagine what's all the hold up. Months it's been.

Mr Burton's son, who lives in Australia, is apparently overseeing the affairs. He needs to stamp his feet and demand the solicitor gets his finger out because the garden is going to rack and ruin, making the street look unkempt. Whatever my views are regarding Mrs Burton, she did at least keep her bushes well-trimmed."

I shot Niall a look and smirked. Not that I knew, but I presume he could confirm either way after witnessing Deana prance naked nymph-like around his Christmas tree. Niall's raised eyebrow confirmed he'd picked up on my train of thought, but neither confirmed nor denied whether Mrs Burton maintained a tidy bush post-mortem.

"I'm sure it will be sorted soon, Mrs Drake. Anyway, don't get wet and cold on our account." Niall and I backed up another couple of paces, only for Mrs Drake to follow.

"I've had to call the police on several occasions, you know? Quite often, I've noticed activity there, which, of course, there shouldn't be. I'm the lead in the neighbourhood watch, you see. Lights on, movement in the garden, that sort of thing. At first, I assumed the son must have returned, but a friend of mine's daughter's neighbour's cousin, who's been temping for the firm of solicitors dealing with it all, mentioned in passing that he's still in Australia."

"Oh."

"Of course, I was concerned it might be burglars or, God forbid, squatters. Can you imagine squatters in a neighbourhood like this?" she shrilled.

"No, quite." Niall and I halted our backwards steps when reaching the gate. "Anyway, we mustn't keep you any longer. Thanks for your help, and I'll see you on Christmas Eve."

"I see that van is still there. Perhaps you could call the police … add a bit of weight to my complaint," she called after us.

"Leave it with me," Niall hollered over his shoulder as we hot-footed away.

"Sorry about that. Mrs Drake is a right old busybody, and she can drone on a bit. I floated the idea about her stepping down from her duties and letting a younger person step in."

"How did that conversation go?"

Niall raised his eyebrows at me.

"Oh, that good."

"No, it wasn't. Mrs Drake made it quite clear she would retire from her duties at the church when God said so and not a moment before."

"Couldn't you have a word?"

"With God?"

"Yeah."

"Believe me, I've tried. On this one, he's not listening."

"I hope he's listening where I'm concerned."

"We'll soon find out." Niall nodded to the Burton residence. The front of which, as described by Mrs Drake, appeared to be unkempt. Also, the house was bathed in darkness, affording it a ghostly appearance, which, considering who we thought lived there, felt kinda apt.

"I got the distinct impression that Mrs Drake wasn't Deana's number one fan."

"What gave you that idea?" Niall chuckled as we hovered by the front gate.

"Okay, now we're here, shall we knock on the front door? Ask the owner if this is where a couple of ghosts live?"

"I'm assuming it's just them two living here. I'm not expecting Lurch to open the door and offer up a 'You rang' greeting." Niall's impression of Lurch's famous catchphrase suggested he'd been an avid watcher of the show.

"What if there's actually more than just the two of them in there? The place could be packed full of spooks—"

"A ghost convention?" he smirked.

"Yeah … the Sedgwick Hotel scenario," I mumbled.

"Who you gonna call?"

"Yeah, exactly."

"I ain't afraid of no ghost."

"Oh, very good. Ghostbusters fan, are we?"

"Come on." Niall opened the gate, shooting me a look as the hinges gave off the classic horror-movie squeak.

"Christ, that about sums it up," I muttered as we approached the front door. "We're about to enter a house full of dead people who may well have murdered my landlord's son." I sighed. "Ex-landlord's son," I qualified based on the Section Twenty-One notice he'd served earlier that day. "I don't know about Lurch, but I wouldn't mind betting the Grim Reaper himself will be there to greet us."

"Well, if he is, we'll just tell him to put his scythe away because we're not ready."

"Will that work?"

"I don't know. Fortunately, I've never met the man."

"I don't think he's real."

"There you go, then."

"But the ghosts of Deana Burton and Terry Walton are."

"I think we've established that's a certainty."

"I imagine Mrs Drake wouldn't be too chuffed to hear that."

"Blimey … that's a thought," he chuckled. "Anyway …" Niall gave the door knocker a hearty rap. "These two ghosts said they were here to help you. And, as I said to Ellen when she got a bout of the collywobbles after I'd read her a scary bedtime story … all children are afraid of ghosts, but as you get older, you realise its people who are scarier."

"Some father you are! Scaring your daughter a regular routine at bedtime, is it?"

"Ellen can be a little fragile, especially after … you know … her mum—"

"Oh, Christ. Me and my big foot. Sorry," I winced.

"Oh, don't." Niall gave the knocker another couple of raps. "Life goes on, as they say. Looks to me that our two spooks are out for the evening." Niall cupped his hands around his face and peered through the panel of obscured glass to the right of the door.

"Can you see anyone?"

"Hmmm. No."

"That's assuming you can see Deana today. You said she dipped in and out of focus yesterday. What if all that remonstrating last night about what you actually believe means you can no longer see her?"

Niall stepped back from the glass panel. "Sorry, what d'you mean?"

"This morning, you said over breakfast that you'd started to doubt your beliefs after what Terry had said about the afterlife. Didn't Deana tell Ellen that you had to believe? Otherwise, you wouldn't be able to see her."

"Oh. I took that as to be about believing in ghosts, not referring to my beliefs in God our Father, God the Son and the Holy Spirit."

"No, I don't think so. Terry said that some children and men of the cloth can see Deana. Meaning, as a religious leader, for want of a better word, and being inclusive about it, having your doubts about your beliefs could result in not being able to see her anymore?"

"I'm not sure what I believe at the moment." Niall peered through the glass again. "We both could see Terry, though."

"True. Can you see him?"

"No. I think they must be out. Shall we go … give it another try in the morning?"

"Yeah." I nodded. "If the snow keeps falling at this rate, we're gonna need a blooming sledge and a pack of huskies to get back to yours. Anyway, you've got to collect Ellen from next door soon, so we might as well. I hope she's going to be okay about her new governess-cum-housekeeper."

"I think nanny sounds better, and I don't expect you to keep house. Anyway, you make yourself sound like Mrs Danvers," he chuckled before his expression shifted to a scowl, holding me in a skull-piercing stare.

I shuddered at his expression and, with the mention of Mrs Danvers, now wondered if his life was a pastiche to Daphne Du Maurier's novel. He said his wife had died of cancer, but had he murdered her? Perhaps their marriage was a sham and, in reality, the beautiful Julie Dowding was as manipulative and cruel as Rebecca de Winter.

"Hello … excuse me. What are you doing here?" Niall barked, leaving me somewhat bewildered until I realised he wasn't looking directly at me, but behind me.

"Niall, what—"

"Janice, come here," he hissed, urgently beckoning me to step closer. "I asked who you are … you should know that the police are on their way."

I spun around to see who he was talking to, spotting nothing but the empty driveway from where we'd come, before swivelling back to face him. "Niall, who the hell are you talking to?"

"Him!" Niall jabbed a finger at nothing. A tree or the gate, maybe, but not a person.

"There's no one there!"

"Him! That man with a hood … oh, my sweet Lord, please tell me it isn't."

27

Silent Night, Holy Night

"Darling, there's someone at the door. Do you think you could be a love and get that for me? It'll probably be a gaggle of sticky-fingered urchins from the local estate readying themselves to caterwaul their way through an out-of-tune rendition of 'Hark the Herald' ... and I can tell you this angel is too busy to join in!"

Terry rolled his eyes at her bellowed request.

"Darling, did you hear me? They're persistent little buggers, so you're going to have to bung them a crumb and ask them to go forth. Sorry, darling, but I'm a little indisposed."

Before Deana had hollered from the bedroom, Terry had already switched off the TV, plunging the lounge into darkness after hearing the first knock.

Notwithstanding Deana's ridiculous request, based on the fact dead people ensconced in supposedly empty houses don't answer the front door, Terry crept to the lounge doorway before peering around the frame. Despite the nebulous dark vista of the hallway – Deana and Terry had learned some time ago that illuminated rooms really didn't help to maintain their cover – the reflection of the light from the street lamps bouncing off the carpet of snow made it possible to pick out the shape of a figure with their face pressed up against the obscured glass panel to the left of the door.

"Darling, did you hear me?"

When the face pulled away from the glass, Terry made a dash for the stairs, bolting up them two at a time before barrelling through to Deana's bedroom.

"Oh, no need to knock," Deana sarcastically hissed. "Just bowl straight in, why don't you?" she huffed, slapping the quilt and puffing a lock of hair from her eyes before reaching across to turn on the bedside lamp.

"Don't!" Terry hissed.

"Sorry?" Deana snatched her hand away from the switch as if it had become white hot.

"Deana, I'm aware that you've got your head in the ruddy clouds—"

"Oh, darling, my head's been somewhere far more delicious than the clouds," Deana purred.

"I'm sure—"

"Like you wouldn't believe."

"Deana, we have someone at the door," Terry hissed, wildly gesticulating with his hands to emphasise the gravitas of their situation.

"Yes, carol singers, I suspect. Just tell the halfwit beggars to do one."

"If it is, they're not singing very loudly. Unless, of course, they're humming a quiet version of Silent Night. Which defeats the object of carol singing in the first place. As I'm trying to explain, based on it being a silent night, I don't think it's a bunch of halfwit beggars, as you put it, and I can't—"

"Mansplaining, you mean. You're not explaining. Your tone is condescending, thus treating me like a fool. As I said, mansplaining."

"What?"

"Never mind. Do carry on."

"Dee, honey," came a slow mumble from somewhere under the quilt before the bedding flung back to reveal a thirty-something woman wearing a tacky nine-carat gold bracelet and a cat-got-the-cream grin. "Tel is saying that he can't answer the door because he's dead. We're all dead. We're dead ghosts … all of us. Although, I suppose all ghosts are dead," she tittered, holding an exaggerated grin.

Terry eyed the drained flute and empty bottle of Bollinger on the bedside table, suspecting Clara had sunk the vast majority of the content.

"Oh, bother. Sorry, I forget. As I was saying, I was a little distracted. It's easy to lose oneself in a moment of passion."

"I'm sure it must be," Terry sarcastically threw back.

Deana's mood had improved immensely when they arrived home earlier and found Clara waiting for her. Not that Terry was offered more than a fleeting introduction before he sloped off to watch a film, and the girls disappeared up to the bedroom with a bottle of Deana's favoured tipple.

"Clara, you might want to …" Terry waved a hand and nodded at her naked form.

"Oh, yeah. Sorry, Tel. I'm not used to there being anyone else in the house." Clara lifted and pulled at the quilt to cover her modesty. "Dee said I've got the pertest tits she ever—"

"Yes, alright, my darling." Deana stroked Clara's naked back. "You are a lush, but why don't you pop a sock in it and hop into the shower? I'll come and join you after I've sorted Terry out."

Clara pouted.

"Not sort out in that respect. You know I'm all yours. I mean this little issue with the noisy beggars at the front door."

"O–kay," Clara groaned, emphasising both syllables as she flopped back on the bed. "Don't be long, though."

"Darling. Robe. The silk one," Deana demanded, pointing at the ottoman positioned at the foot of the bed.

Terry huffed, grabbed said garment, and held it out for her.

Deana flung the covers away and stood before him, lingering for a second, wearing just a smirk, before spinning around and holding her arms back, ready for Terry to assist her.

"You want me to dress you?"

"Yes, be a gentleman and help me into my robe."

"I'm not your lady's maid."

"Terence, this isn't the time to start discussing what you may or may not be. Hurry."

"Alright," Terry grumbled, holding the gown out for Deana to slip her arms into.

"And Clara, my darling girl, you need to hop into the shower. Remember, though, lather up your luscious body in the dark. We can't go turning the house into Crystal Palace if we have snoops on the doorstep."

"Dee—"

"Yes, my darling," Deana asked while tying the silk cord, pulling it tight to accentuate her slim waist.

"You're such a turn-on when you're bossy."

"Bossy-Boots-Beacham," Terry muttered.

"Terence, I've warned you about using my turgid first husband's name. I shan't tell you again."

"No, M'Lady."

"None of your cheek, either."

"And, Clara, my sweet, by bossy, I assume you mean authoritative and direct? Then, yes, I am one of life's decision-makers. And if that's the case, you gorgeous thing you, I must have the effect of causing you to be in a perpetual state of horniness."

Clara offered a whiny giggle, waving her arm at Deana. "See, that's what I'm talking about, Hun. You're deffo worth being dead for."

"Quite. Now … shower."

Deana spun around and poked Terry on the sternum. "Right, you grunge, let's have a sneak look-see out of the landing window and see what's afoot, shall we? Hopefully, I'm correct, as in it just being carol singers, albeit quiet ones, and they've moved along the street. With any luck, they're now assaulting Dreary-Drake's ears. That's worth giving the little beggars a couple of quid and a packet of Woodbines."

When positioned behind Deana, Terry snapped down a slat of the blind, the metallic pinging sound causing them both to grimace.

"What's all this Dee and Tel thing?" Terry asked.

"It's just Clara's way, darling. I'm sure you've been called Tel before."

"Yeah, a few mates did back in the day. But Dee, though?"

"No. Never. Clara is the only one I'll allow to call me that, so don't get any ideas."

"Hmm," Terry muttered, peering down at the drive.

"Darling, I can't see anything," Deana whispered when on tiptoes.

"Me neither."

"Perhaps they've buggered off."

"Maybe."

"Oh ... hang on. I can see footprints in the snow. Look."

"Yeah, two sets. Does that mean one person came to the door and then left?"

"No, darling, they're pointing the same way. Inwards."

"Oh ... and there's none going back out."

"What does that mean?"

"It means they must still be at the front door."

"Why would they still be there? They've knocked twice, and we haven't answered. Why haven't they buggered off?"

"I don't know."

"Probably not carol singers, then."

"As I was saying when you accused me—"

"Alright. This isn't a time for point scoring."

Terry tutted.

"Don't tut."

"Look, if we stay quiet, whoever they are, I expect they'll be gone in a minute."

"Who on earth, if not carol singers, and don't give me your 'told you so' response, ventures out in this weather on a Monday evening before Christmas?"

Raising himself on the balls of his feet, Terry snapped down another slat and peered down, trying to grab a better view of the doorstep.

"Anything?" Deana hissed.

"Oh."

"What?"

"I think that's the vicar and Janice."

"Oh, bugger. This isn't a good development," Deana hissed. "How on earth d'you suppose they found us?"

"I told them last night, remember? When we were in the graveyard."

"The general area, not the exact house. Darling, we can't have all and sundry knowing our location. It'll be a catastrophe. I've given assurances to The-Powers-That-Be regarding the continued suitability of this abode as a base for operations. There'll be no more missions if we're exposed, and I'll probably have to end up bunking up with Idi Amin."

"I have no idea what you're on about."

"I'm sure I told you about that conversation I endured last week with that dreadful chap I argued with at the call centre. Trouble is, you're like all men. Selective hearing."

"What?"

"Exactly! And, it's pardon, not what."

Still with the blind's slats depressed, Terry puffed out his cheeks and dismissively shook his head as he glanced down at the top of Deana's bedraggled bed hair. For a fleeting moment, he rued that decision of thirty-odd years ago when chatting up Deana at that work's conference. If he'd known what he knew now, he would have given the then-gorgeous woman a wide berth. Although, to be fair, this older version of Deana had tried to warn him off from going to her hotel room.

"Deana."

"What?"

"We may have made a bit of a howler."

"How so?"

"We got Hallam to drop us home today. He now knows where we live."

"Oh. Bugger."

"Bugger, indeed."

"Don't worry, darling, I have a cunning plan."

"Which is?"

"Simples. We'll nip over to his crummy abode in the morning, and I'll wield my trusty Waitrose carrier bag."

"Kill him?"

"Yes, darling. Nothing else for it, is there? I'll perform the suffocating, so you don't need to worry about racking up any negative points. I know you're super keen to see your little Sharon again."

"Seems a bit drastic. Couldn't we ask the git just to keep schtum?"

Deana turned and peered up at him, offering a frown and a dismissive shake of the head.

"No, that won't work, will it?"

"Correct, darling. We know his sort. We simply have to remove him because Inch-High-Pervert-Eye will not be discreet. Anyway, ridding our corner of the world of that revolting little man will be doing womankind a great service. Men like that do not deserve to take a breath. A man should be chivalrous, attentive, caring, and strong. Not act like some filthy hog rutting around sniffing out truffles."

"I think I'm fully aware that you don't like the man."

"No. We didn't like Inch-High, did we, darling?"

"We most certainly did not."

"Now, back to our current situation. What's happening down there?"

Terry raised himself up on tiptoes. "They've stepped away from the door."

"Good. We're going to have to have a stern word with Janice and the vicar come tomorrow. This is unacceptable, turning up at my house like this. Following a spot of murder, and after tracking down those two horrors, Strachan and Meyer, I suggest we swing by the vicarage, find out where Janice is holed up, and put the girl straight on a few things."

"Good idea."

"What are they doing now, for God's sake? Are they still there? I haven't seen them walk back out of the drive."

"I'm not sure …" Terry peered down to the doorstep again. "They're still there, but—"

"But what?"

"I think they're having an argument."

"Really?" Deana walloped her hand down on four slats in an attempt to see. "Perhaps the dishy vicar's … oh, Gawd, look, darling. There, standing by the bushes."

"Oh, yeah, there's someone else. Who the hell is that?"

"Oh, lordy lord, this isn't good," Deana muttered, shivering as she grabbed Terry's arm.

"What?" Terry asked, surprised by her unusual, jittery demeanour. "What's the matter?"

"Him, showing up like this, the proverbial bad penny who's as welcome as a bout of thrush. Darling, this really isn't a good sign."

28

The Penitent Man

"Niall, this isn't funny. I know we joked about ghosts and spooks, but you're taking it too far."

"Janice, please, just come here," he hissed in a tone that suggested this wasn't some joke, which I wasn't getting.

"Why? Niall …" I paused to spin around and wave my hand about. "There's only you and me here!"

"If I can see him, and you can't, then that can only mean one thing. Now, for the love of God, come here." Niall took a pace towards me, holding out his hand as I remained facing him, keeping his focus on what I now presumed must be another ghost, guardian angel, or whatever, apparently wearing a hood, standing behind me.

"Oh crap," I mumbled, grabbing Niall's outstretched hand before spinning around and staggering backwards. As was the case a moment ago, there still appeared to be no one else on the drive, as Niall implored me to believe. Merely the delicately falling snow. However, similar to what occurred last night, some of that snow appeared to halt its descent mid-fall, settling about five or six feet up in the air. My eyes were drawn to the ground as I watched the snow depress and compact as footprints appeared. "Oh, shit. It's walking towards us," I mumbled, tightening my fingers around Niall's.

"That's far enough, fella." Niall held up his palm. "Don't come any closer."

"Christ, they're everywhere! It's like *The Walking Dead* ... except I can't see them!"

"Tell me about it!"

"And he's wearing a hood ... like the—"

"Yeah, the Grim Reaper—"

"Is he carrying a—"

"No, thank the Lord."

"Sidney! What on earth are you doing here, you ruddy idiot?" Deana hissed after she poked her head through the gap in the half-open front door.

"Hello to you, too," Sidney sarcastically batted back. "I see you haven't lost your viperous tongue since I last saw you."

"Unfortunately, that was only last week! Precisely the point when, for the umpteenth time this month, I told you to bugger off! If it's escaped the attention of that pea brain of yours, you're not supposed to be here!"

"I'm lonely."

"Boohoo. Now, do one!"

"Charming. Nothing like kicking a man when he's down. I'll try not to take offence regarding your unfestive welcome. I'm sure you didn't mean to be so mean ... well, maybe you did. You were a nasty cow when I was married to—"

"Sidney, you utter—"

"Anyway, how come this bloke can see me?"

"Do not interrupt me, you cretinous man. He can see you because he's a vicar. Now, why the hell are you here again? And push your hood back, you twit. You look like the ruddy Angel of Death. Anyway, I thought I made it abundantly clear last week that you've got to stop turning up on my doorstep like some bedraggled, pining, lost puppy."

"I don't have anywhere to go, do I? I just aimlessly wander about with nothing to do and no one to talk to."

"That's because you're not supposed to be here. You're supposed to be in Hell."

"Yeah, I know, but I don't want to go there. And anyway, so what if he's a vicar? How does that mean he can see me?"

"He just can. Some men of the cloth have that ability."

"Niall?" I hissed when noticing the front door ajar, and he'd started to play head tennis from the door to the area just above the footprints.

"Deana's at the door. I can't hear what they're saying but, going by the hand gestures, I'm getting the distinct impression that she's not overly chuffed this chap has turned up."

"Chap? He's a ghost, I take it?"

"He most certainly is! A right royal pain in the arse ghost that's gone AWOL and is presumably top of The-Powers-That-Be's most wanted list."

"Based on the fact I can see him, and you can't, I guess he must be. I reckon he's a bloke in his sixties and looks like he might have been sleeping rough."

"Jesus, this is creepy. How many are there of them? The entire area must be crawling with the dead."

"Janice, Niall … why are you here?"

Niall and I shot a look at the door when Terry appeared.

"Darling, we can't hold this conversation out here. Someone, if not Dreary-Drake, the sour-faced old snoop, will spot a commotion, and then the game's truly up. You'd better invite them in."

"And me?"

"I suppose so," Deana groaned. *"But listen, Sidney, you can come in and warm up, but then you must go. I suggest you do the decent thing and hand yourself in. I can't be seen harbouring a fugitive from Hell … it's just not the done thing."*

"Come on, you two, you'd better come in." Terry opened the door and, with a jerk of his head, gestured for us to step inside.

"Mind Deana, she's standing in the doorway," Niall whispered.

"Oh, right. Which side?"

"I'll move! The last thing I need adding to this debacle is Janice flattening me as the silly girl waltzes in clinging to the vicar."

"It's alright, she's stepped aside."

Niall and I followed Terry into the kitchen at the rear of the property before slipping onto the barstools offered. Terry flicked on the cooker-extractor light, bathing the show-home-styled kitchen diner in a bluish ghostly hue.

"Sorry, I can't put the ceiling lights on. We can't have the neighbours thinking there's anyone living here. The haunted house," Terry chuckled. "This was Deana's home before she died, and it's supposed to be empty."

"Nice place." I surveyed the kitchen diner and the plush Victorian-styled orangery, which I presumed offered unhindered access through to the lounge. Opulent, modern, open-plan living, the stuff of expensive, glossy magazines. The dead Deana had an eye for style, design, and luxury, plus the wealth to bring her visions to life, giving me the green eye of envy. The woman really did have it all. Although I was alive, and she was dead. "Niall, is Deana and … that Grim Reaper bloke in the room?"

"No, I can't see—"

"That's Sidney Statham, not the Grim Reaper," Terry interjected, folding his arms as he leaned his bottom against the worktop. "Deana's second husband, the man who raised mine and Deana's son, Damian."

Niall and I shot each other a look.

"It's a long story."

"He's dead, right?" I asked, tipping my head to the side and running my hand through my ponytail. Despite the events of the last two days, it still sounded like a ridiculous question to ask.

"As a doornail. His wife murdered him."

"Deana?" Niall blurted.

"No, no, his second wife."

"Oh, how awful for the poor man."

"Well, yes, I suppose, but he then murdered her, so we're led to believe."

"Hang on, how … oh, he killed his wife when he was a ghost?" I asked.

"He did." Terry clicked his fingers before waving his finger at me. "A classic case of revenge. All murderers beware … those you kill could very well reciprocate the deed."

"Blimey, what a thought. That's surely got to be a better deterrent than life imprisonment," I mumbled, much to myself, still trying to get my head around the absurd situation.

Last week, although unemployed, I still had my life's savings and a home. A week later, with all lost and despite a killer ghost being in the next room, bizarrely, I felt in a better place. Was that because of Niall's reassurances or the fact that I now had two ghosts batting for my side?

"Is he dangerous?" Niall asked. "Well, obviously he is, but is—"

"You don't need to worry. Deana and I can take care of Sidney."

"Oh." Niall bulged his eyes at me, which I reciprocated with an accompanying shrug of my shoulders.

"Anyway, why are you here? And come to think of it, how did you find us?"

Niall and I exchanged another look, simultaneously reaching for each other's hand.

"A lady a few doors down who helps out at Niall's church. We knocked on her door, and she pointed us in this direction."

"Ah, Dreary-Drake, as Deana likes to call her."

"Yes, I imagine they weren't best buddies."

"What gave you that impression?" Terry smirked. "Don't answer that, I can guess. I take it that Mrs Drake doesn't suspect—"

"No," I shook my head. "She fully believes Deana is still dead. Well—"

"I know what you mean."

"Yeah ... Jesus, this is weird," I muttered as Niall squeezed my hand, which I took as encouragement to continue. "Look ... actually, before I get to the point of our visit, where's Deana and her dead husband?"

"From what I can hear, she's giving her dead ex a verbal mauling before she sticks her foot up his backside and unceremoniously boots him on his way. I can hear her going off on one." Terry nodded to his left, presumably meaning they were in the adjoining room. One of many, I suspected. The house was a mini-mansion.

"Oh, okay ... I take it there's still a touch of animosity between them ... as in being divorced?"

"You could say. Well, I get the distinct impression that Sidney wouldn't mind getting back with her, but Deana's having none of that."

"Yeah ... so, let me get this straight. You can still have a relationship when you're dead, then? How the hell does that work?" When noticing Terry's surprise, I thought it best to clarify. "Oh, no, I don't mean like that. I was more thinking of the living arrangements ... y'know, in Heaven, or wherever."

"Sorry, I can't answer that because I simply don't know. I am aware that if I amass enough points to be allowed entry to the upper level, I can be with my wife, Sharon, who I haven't seen since the day I left home to attend a works conference in '83." Terry picked at a fingernail, losing eye contact with us.

I winced, not knowing if I should say something. He clearly looked upset, but I didn't know the man well enough to comment.

"I miss her. Of course, but after all that business with dying in Deana's bed and the many other affairs, I don't know that she'll take me back … which is fair enough. I've got to try, though," Terry huffed before ramming his hands into the pockets of his jeans that were clearly too tight for him. "I know my unfaithfulness can't be excused, but apart from that, I wasn't an evil man when alive. Not like all these gits who Deana and I have been sent to sort out. All I want is one more chance … a chance to say to her how sorry I am."

After a few seconds of awkward silence, Terry still making an in-depth study of the floor tiles, I squeezed Niall's hand to encourage him to look at me.

"What?" he whispered.

"Could you say something vicar-ish … to comfort him?"

"Oh, um … like?"

"I don't know. Isn't this what you do? Give counsel and comfort to those in need?"

Niall nodded before turning to look at the dead man. "Terry, perhaps I could—"

"Please, don't. I really don't want to hear any platitudes like 'It's God's way' or 'I'm sure it will all be alright in the end'. I'm a big boy, and I will have to accept what's coming to me. Good or bad."

"Sorry, that was my fault for asking about how ghosts have relationships."

"Hey …" Terry looked up. "Not at all. You must have a million questions. I know I still do," he chuckled, attempting to lighten the mood.

However, I could see the watery film coating his eyes.

"Forgive us our trespasses, as we forgive those who have trespassed against us. Terry, find it in your heart to forgive those who have wronged you … you might find that your wife will also forgive you."

Terry offered a tight smile.

"Sorry, I don't want to preach at you. I'm blooming useless at it, anyway."

"Sounded pretty alright to me, vicar."

"Cheers. I'll keep practising, and you never know, I might crack it one of these days. So, tell me, this Statham bloke, I assume he shouldn't be roaming around as a ghost. That's not how it works, is it? It's just, yesterday when you were explaining the afterlife—"

"No." Terry held up his palm to stop Niall's flow. "No, the man's AWOL. I'm not fully au fait with all the details, but you're right … he's not here on an official mission."

"I should hope not. Of course, I understand the principle of an eye for an eye, but killing can't be condoned."

"Ah, well, you see, old Sidders has killed a few times … he's what you might call a natural-born killer."

29

The Revenant

"That ghost … he's killed others?" Niall asked, shooting me a look of concern.

We'd come here tonight to ascertain whether Terry and Deana were in any way involved in the death of my landlord's son. Irrespective of their involvement, this latest revelation about the ghost, who apparently was currently on the receiving end of a lambasting from his dead ex-wife, suggested we were in the house of horrors with at least one deranged psychotic murdering ghost.

"Correct. Sidney not only sent his murdering wife cartwheeling over her fifth-floor hotel balcony, but he murdered two others when intervening in our mission to help my son. I'm not condoning his actions, but the two he dispatched had long ago booked their rooms in Hell. One of them he murdered at your church, would you believe?" Terry chuckled before his face dropped, and the chuckle morphed into an embarrassed whine when clocking our shocked expressions.

"That man … ghost, through there," Niall pointed to where Terry had indicated. "He murdered Lee Parish earlier this year?"

"He did. I suppose, although you weren't the incumbent vicar at the time, him being an older chap, as I recall, you've heard all about it?"

"Terry," I interjected before Niall could answer. "Were you there … well, were you and Deana there that day?"

"Well, um …" Terry shrugged and pursed his lips. "I suppose it doesn't matter saying. We were. Deana and I planned to meet a man who was going to supply information. Unfortunately, he didn't show, but the man who'd been part of a team conning my son did."

"Lee Parish?"

"Yeah."

"And then the ghost of Sidney, because Damian was his stepson, jumped into the action and killed Lee. I'm presuming the other person he murdered was the other one involved in the con?"

"You've joined the dots. A conniving black widow by the name of Bridget Jones, would you believe? Sidney murdered her a couple of weeks later."

"So, you and Deana weren't planning to kill Lee, then?"

Niall shot me a look and raised his eyebrows.

"No, not at all. Look, Deana and I are given missions to correct situations. We're not here to kill people. That's not how it works. We planned to scare Lee into giving back to my son what was rightly his, and that would have been that."

"Oh … well, that's a relief."

"Terry, the reason we came here tonight is because Lee Parish's father is Janice's landlord. Unfortunately, he served notice on her today but, in conversation, it came up about his son. It seems we've put two and two together and got five. Look, we just needed to know you and Deana, although clearly dead, weren't killers."

Terry winced.

"What's that look for?" I blurted.

"Sorry, but Deana did kill the man who killed her."

"Oh."

"There seems to be a lot of revenge killing going on. Is this normal?"

"No … not really. But, hey, look, on a positive note, I haven't killed anyone, dead or alive."

"Terry, you are dead, aren't you?" I asked.

"I'm afraid so. It's a bit of a bugger, really. Of course, I'm chuffed that I'm not lying in that grave but, even so, I feel I've missed out on so much since my heart gave up the ghost back in '83. No pun intended."

"I can imagine. Well, no, clearly, I can't. I mean, the world must seem a smidge different."

"Cor, that's an understatement and a half! Deana was only twenty-five and …" Terry paused and winced as he shot a look towards the next room. "Christ, poor sod," he muttered.

"Sorry?"

"Oh, Deana can have a way with words. Sidney's on the receiving end of a few choice ones as we speak."

"Right, shall we go?" Niall checked his watch. "I need to collect Ellen before it gets too late."

"Yes, we'd probably better," I nodded, hopping off my stool before turning to Terry. "How are you getting on with your list? I am grateful for your help, and I know it's only been one day, but I was just wondering. Y'know, as I'm completely broke … through my own stupidity," I offered an embarrassed whine before continuing. "And jobless, and not to mention homeless now that my landlord's decided to sell up."

"We've made a start. I'm pretty confident we can—"

"Jesus, Tel, what's all the shouting for? Who the hell is that bloke she's giving it large to in the living room? I just stuck my head in, and Dee told me not to interrupt her when in full flow. Bossy cow," Clara snickered, tightening the top of her bath towel into her cleavage when spotting a man and a woman at the breakfast bar. *"Oh, hiya. You dead? Gotta say neither of you look particularly dead."*

"Niall?" I hissed, presuming he was looking at Deana or this Sidney bloke, when the kitchen door opened and, from my point of view, no one was there.

"Clara, this is Janice, the subject of our mission, and her friend, Niall."

"Oh. So they're not dead, then. Err … Tel, he's giving me a funny look. He can't see me, can he?"

"Niall is the vicar at All Saints."

"A vicar! Oh, crap." Clara slapped her hand to her forehead and groaned. *"That's not good, you know."*

"Niall … who the hell is this Clara?"

"A woman wrapped in a bath towel," he mumbled. "I guess she must be a ghost."

"More of them! OMG, the damn house is full of them."

"You're not kidding."

"Are they having a convention or something? What is it, spooks incorporated weekly cheese and wine evening? D'you reckon they congregate here after a tough day scaring the shite out of people, like grabbing a moment to swap stories and decompress?"

"I really wouldn't like to hazard a guess," he muttered, seemingly unable to peel his eyes from the latest ghost to appear. One wrapped in a bath towel, apparently. I suppose even ghosts have to wash.

"Shit, shit, shitty de shit," Clara hissed. *"Not again. Not after all that hassle I had on my last mission. I take it he can see all of us, but this comedian, Janice, can't?"*

"Got it in one."

"Is this gonna be an issue? Have you reported it to the higher-ups?"

"Do we need to?"

"Tel, don't be a numpty! Course you do. That lot up there must be informed of every incident when spectral guides have been spotted by the living. It goes into their database or something or other. I don't know, but they do something with the info. Probably got some big spreadsheet going. Y'know, you're gonna land in all sorts of shite if you don't log a sighting."

"Oh."

"I can't believe Dee never mentioned it."

"Perhaps she had her mind on other things?" Terry raised an eyebrow.

Clara giggled.

"Exactly, that's my point. I'll remind Deana to make that call after she's sorted out old Sidders."

"Oh ... is that Sidney in there? The bloke she's giving a mauling to. Her ex-husband?"

"The very same."

"Dee was on about him last week. Apparently, he keeps turning up out of the blue. I told her to report him, but she was worried about the bolshy higher-ups accusing her of harbouring a fugitive. He's a wanted spook, you know that, don't you?"

"So Deana said."

I cleared my throat and nudged Niall's arm.

"Terry, I don't want to be rude and interrupt, but perhaps we'll leave you to it."

"Oh, of course. Look, both of you. I know Deana and I made it quite clear yesterday that you can't tell anyone about us—"

"Did you?" I blurted, struggling to remember that part of the weirdest day of my life. Today coming in a close second.

"Oh, I thought we did. But, that aside, we are imploring you both regarding what you know about our existence, along with Sidney, remains undisclosed. If we are to be successful and put your life back on track, anonymity is vital. We need a successful mission under our belts, you see, because it'll help tot up our good points. God knows we need a few."

"Tel, they can't blab about me either. I'm right at the business end of mine, and I can ill afford to screw this one up."

"Err ... yeah, as Clara just mentioned, she's reaching the critical phase of her mission, so exposure will cause her all sorts of bother."

"You don't need to worry. Janice and I aren't going to breathe a word. Apart from the very real chance we'll both end up being carted away by the men in white coats, we're aware of what some of you lot are capable of. That's, of course, assuming I don't commit myself to the damn funny farm."

"Yes, I can imagine." Terry grinned. "We've not had a mission where anyone can see Deana before. Breaking new ground on this one."

"Yes, Tel, and you need to report it!"

"Also, there are my parishioners to consider. I can't imagine they'd be too accommodating if I started preaching from the pulpit that I'm now in contact with the dead."

"You talk to God," I suggested.

"Well, yes, but he doesn't answer in words. We don't chat like a couple of blokes chewing the fat up at the pub. And he's not dead."

"Oh ... Jesus, then?"

"He's not dead either. The resurrection."

"Oh, course. Sorry."

"Not exactly the religious type, this one, is she? I mean, frig, surely everyone knows about the resurrection. Has the woman never heard of Easter? What did she think all the Easter eggs were for, eh? Some

marketing ploy by the confectionary manufacturers to boost sales? Dee said she was an odd one. From what I can see, she isn't far off the mark."

"Okay, good. That's settled, then." Terry clapped his hands together. "As you say, we mustn't keep you."

"What did Clara say," Niall asked.

"Nothing relevant." Terry grinned and held his hand out, ushering us to the door.

A grin that was covering a lie if ever I saw one.

"Deana also said that you're a skilled politician. As in, full of shite and can charm your way out of any situation." Clara hopped up on a bar stool, flicked her long dark curls over her shoulder and stuck her tongue in her cheek. "She reckoned when you were alive, you could charm the knickers off any woman, too. A real ladies' man. Course, I'm gay, but if I wasn't, I reckon you and me could have had some fun. Don't get any ideas though, 'cos, unlike Bossy-Boots, I don't do cock."

"Did Clara say something else?" Niall asked, noticing Terry's expression.

Terry shook his head and raised his eyebrow. "Um … just talking about Deana, that's all. Right, we'll be in touch … hopefully tomorrow." He ushered us with his arms as we funnelled out of the kitchen before grabbing Niall's elbow. "Hang on. I'll just let Deana know that you're leaving."

"Is she still … y'know?"

"Giving her ex-husband the benefit of her wisdom?"

"Um, yeah."

"She is. I'm sure she'll come up for air in a moment."

"Deana's quite formidable, isn't she?"

"Oh, like you wouldn't believe."

"Tel! Tel, you'd better get back in here. We've got a situation. Two blokes have just snuck in the back door, and I don't like the look of either of them."

Terry paused and shot a look back at the kitchen before holding a shush finger to his lips and a raised palm with his other hand as a stay-put gesture.

Niall and I exchanged a shrug when Terry hot-footed back to the kitchen, I presumed because of something Clara had said before we both crept to the door and, cheek to cheek, peered through the crack in the doorjamb. From what I could see through the dim light and the few millimetres afforded me, I spied two figures who'd entered the kitchen via the back door. Although a little early for burglars to be on the prowl, their hunched stances suggested they weren't invited guests. Also, the fact I could see them indicated they weren't dead, so not a couple of spooks arriving late for the cheese and wine shindig. In that moment, I couldn't decide if that was a good thing or not.

"Who the hell are … Hallam, what the hell is going on?" Terry exclaimed, shifting his stance, thus blocking my sightline.

Niall and I exchanged a glance before retaking our spying positions.

"So, it is you. The man claiming to be Terry-Bloody-Walton."

Terry stepped to one side, affording us a view of a man in his thirties jabbing an accusing finger at him.

"Tel, who the hell are these two idiots? They don't look like they're dead either."

Again, Niall and I shifted our stance to face one another, our eyes searching each other's for answers. As I suspected would be running through his, my mind whirred as I considered the possibility we'd been taken for fools.

If Terry wasn't Terry, who the hell was he?

30

Hammer House of Horror

"Hallam ... what the—"

"Shut it, Walton. Not that's who you really are." The man doing the talking grabbed the collar of the shorter, older guy to thwart his attempts to skedaddle the way they'd come. "Hallam here's been trying to extort me with threats that you and some psycho bitch are hunting me down. Well, look no further because here I am."

"Hallam?" Terry repeated, addressing the shorter of the two men. The little fella now sporting a ruddy complexion due to his twisted collar acting as a garrotte.

"I ... I can't breathe," he gasped.

His assailant released his grip and shoved him towards the sink before kicking the backdoor closed, then jabbed that finger back at Terry.

"Remember me?"

"I do. Hello, Joseph. I think my wife, Sharon, would be devastated to see you now."

"Meyer ... Joseph Meyer," I hissed under my breath. Now I recognised him. Kim's half-brother. Not that I'd seen him more than a handful of times, but when working at the reception at the care home, Joseph and his father, Sam Meyer, had visited Kim's grandfather. If I remember correctly, they tried to con the old boy and swindle Kim out of her inheritance.

"Don't you spout off about my mum. Anyway, she was an airhead like that stupid sister of mine."

"I think you mean half-sister. Kim was very insistent that you are only her half-brother."

"Whatever. Dad was right about her all along."

"Your father is a rapist, a paedophile, and with any luck, will rot in prison for the rest of his miserable life. Just a pity he survived that heart attack and isn't already in Hell."

"You and your trickery caused my dad to have a heart attack. He's never been the same since."

"Saw the light, confessed to his crimes, and rightly gave my daughter the business. Which, I might add, she's entitled to."

"Bollocks is she. And don't keep trotting out that shite about being Kim's father. Who the frig are you?"

"Sam believes I'm Terry Walton."

"That's because my old man has lost his frigging marbles. I mean, he must have to believe the ghost of his old mate has suddenly risen from the dead before the stupid git gifted everything I've worked for, the business, the damn lot, to that frigging stupid sister of mine."

"Half-sister."

"Whatever."

"Joseph, you're forgetting the events of that day when Sam suffered a heart attack—"

"You mean all those stunts you pulled? All that trickery when making stuff fly around the room." Joseph fanned his hands out, akin to an over-dramatic magician. "Hardly gonna forget that, am I?"

"That's my point. No trickery, just Deana ... a ghost like me, but invisible."

"Piss off ... what the frig d'you take me for?"

"I take you for a weak, pathetic man, who, by the fact you're here with Hallam—"

"Hey, I'm here under duress. He made me come," said the shorter guy, who I presumed to be the Hallam bloke, as he backed up against the sink with his hands held up. I couldn't see Terry's face, but I imagined he sported a similar sneer to that offered by Joseph.

"Where is ..." the man, still holding the surrender position, attempted to swallow before continuing. "Is she here ... in the room?" The tremble in his voice and shifting eyes indicated he was petrified of Deana.

"Tel, d'you want me to get Bossy-Boots. She must have run out of words to lob at her ex by now." Clara slipped off the stool before standing in a hands-on-hip pose in front of Hallam. "He's a weedy little fella. Looks a bit like my dad. Y'know, he was a shot-arse, too. Course, I inherited all my luscious looks from my mum. Frig knows what she saw in my dad. He was a decent bloke, though."

"Hallam, don't be a dick. I told you there's no such thing as ghosts."

"Oh, but there is," I mumbled, still with my cheek pressed against Niall's.

"Hang on, Clara. Meyer is my issue. We'll invite Deana through in a minute."

"Clara's got her nose right up against that chap's face," Niall whispered.

"Who the frig are you talking to? Who's this slag, Clara?" Joseph spat.

"Do what? Who the hell are you calling a slag?"

"What just happened?" I whispered when spotting Joseph stumble backwards, clutching his cheek.

"Clara just slapped him. A right corker across the cheek."

"Oh."

"What the ..." Joseph staggered backwards, only stopping when his back collided with the fridge. "Who's there? Who hit me?" his tone now laced with panic. "Shit!" he hissed when something invisible poked his eye.

"It's the ghosts. I told you. This place is probably full of them," Hallam interjected as he eased his hands down.

"You ain't kidding," I muttered. "Oh, look!" I hissed.

"I know, I can see. She's holding it," Niall whispered.

"How the hell ... who's doing this? What tricks are you pulling?"

Terry slipped onto the stool, taking a moment to make himself comfortable before jabbing a finger at Joseph, who now held a splattered pose against the fridge while feverishly blinking his left eye.

"If you would like to cast your eyes to the right, you'll notice there's a rather scary-looking meat cleaver hovering a few inches from your head," Terry paused to allow Joseph to take in the scene of said levitating hatchet. "That meat cleaver—"

"Tel, I'm not actually gonna chop the git with this. Despite the slap and poke, which the knob deserved, I don't do real violence. So, whatever patter you're planning on trotting out, y'know, that charm Bossy-Boots goes on about, it had better be good. I'm just holding it here to focus the knob's mind."

"Appreciated, Clara. Now, Joseph, let's get down to business. Oh, if you're wondering how that meat cleaver is just hanging in mid-air, one of those ghosts you don't believe exists is holding it. My friend Clara here, dead and very much a ghost, although by the looks of your glowing cheek and red eye, she can still pack a punch, will hack off your …"

"I won't, Tel. I just told you, I don't do violence."

"Nose … she'll hack off your nose if I tell her to. I will only do that if I don't like the answers to the questions I'm about to pose." Terry shot his right arm towards Hallam, who'd edged towards the backdoor. "Don't move. Otherwise, I'll let Deana loose on you."

"Err … righto. That seems fair. I'll just stay where I am."

"You do that."

"Look, whoever you are—"

"Joseph, shut up and listen. I'll ask the questions, and you'll answer them. If I don't like what I hear, I'll give Clara the nod or a raised hand … and chop, your hooter ends up on the tiles. You can confirm you understand with a nod."

"All very dramatic, Tel, but can you get on with it? I only nipped down here to grab a glass of water. Now my arm is starting to ache, and I'm freezing my tits off."

"Okay." Terry raised his hand to accept Clara's plea.

"No! Please don't raise your hand. I'll talk, I'll talk."

"Good. However, I was just gesturing to Clara that I understood what she was saying, not to give the order to chop your nose off. But, anyway, good that we're on the same page."

"He's good, isn't he?" I whispered.

"Gladiatorial," Niall nodded.

"Question one. Have you been posing as an American called Chad Ruger with the sole purpose of conning women?"

Joseph shot his eyes right towards the quivering meat cleaver.

"He has! He told me earlier. It's him. He's been doing all those things," Hallam blurted.

Niall tightened his grip on my hand as I took a sharp intake of breath.

"You're dead, Hallam," hissed Joseph.

"Eyes on me, Joseph. Look at me, not the wimpy private investigator." Terry gave the 'see you' gesture with two fingers. "Well? I'm waiting for an answer."

"That prat just told you."

"Meat cleaver, Meyer. Remember the meat cleaver."

"Yes! I have."

"And did you recently con a really good friend of mine, Janice Keelan?"

Joseph's shoulders sagged. "I knew that one was too easy," he muttered.

"That's a yes, is it?"

"Yeah. The stupid bitch was so gullible. The silly slag got what she deserved."

I bowed my head, unable to watch. Although he'd taken my life's savings, apart from the 'bitch' and 'slag' comments, Joseph was right in what he'd said.

"Tel, I'm just gonna swap hands. And I've changed my mind. If you want me to chop his nose off, I'm up for that. I'll do his cock as well, if you like. In fact, after hearing that misogynistic claptrap, I'll chop the git into bite-sized chunks if you want."

Joseph shivered as the cleaver waved around in the air.

"Don't shit yourself, Meyer. Well, not yet. That's Clara, just swapping hands. That meat cleaver looks pretty hefty to me, so I guess she's developed arm ache. Can you imagine what it would do to your face if she dropped it?" Terry pulled an exaggerated grimace and sucked in a breath. "Doesn't bear thinking about, does it?"

Meyer shook his head meekly.

"Okay, d'you want to tell me why?"

"Why what?"

"Why you conned Janice?"

"Why not? It's a numbers game. I sniff out sad bitches online, run the con and take their cash. Most rumble me before I get near any dough, but the really desperate, stupid ones …" Meyer paused as the tip of the cleaver touched his nose. "… just cough up the cash." The end part of his sentence was said in a less bolshy tone while cross-eyed gawping at the cleaver.

"Frig, Tel, where did you dig this knob up from? My God, I've never met anyone who I wanted to kill sooo much."

"Clara's not liking your tone. When it comes down to it, neither am I. See, although I appreciate your candour, Clara, as the name suggests, is female. Your liberal use of derogatory words like slag and bitch aren't doing it for the girl."

"Sorry," Joseph hissed from the side of his mouth.

"You will be, shit for brains."

"And you run these cons because?" Terry raised his palms in a questioning style.

"Because you, whoever you are, 'cos you sure as hell ain't Terry Walton, caused my father to lose his mind, go all gaga, give my slag of … err, my sister everything, leaving me in a whole heap of debt to the wrong sort of people. This psycho nutter waving around a meat cleaver might be some crazed loon but, believe me, she ain't got nothing on the Gowers. I owed that bunch of headcases thousands. Tens of thousands. If I didn't want to end up with my throat cut and at the bottom of the river, I had to find a way to get my hands on cash … and fast."

"So, you're saying it's my fault?"

"Basically, yeah. Wayne Gower's not the sort you get on the wrong side of. He and his thugs beat the shit out of me. It was a case of getting my hands on the cash I owed them, or I was a dead man."

"Darling, what's all the commotion? Oh, I see we have more guests. How delightful. Clara, my sweet girl, what on earth are you doing? You look like you're about to audition for a leading role in a Hammer film. Put that cleaver down before you do someone an injury."

31

Aesop's Fable

"Oh ... no, I see now. Sorry, darling," Deana affectionately stroked Terry's arm. *"How silly of me. I was just popping through to make a flask of hot soup for Sidders, give the silly old sod something before I send him out into the cold Captain Oates-style, and thus I seemed to have misread the situation. Not to mention all the excitement,"* Deana tittered. *"Clara, my darling girl, be a love and keep that cleaver poised, ready to strike Mr Meyer. It is Joseph Meyer you have that wickedly sharp blade pointed at, is it not?"*

"It is," Terry confirmed. "While you and your ex have been reminiscing—"

"I can assure you, darling, we haven't been reminiscing. I, with a few well-chosen words, have been helping Sidney understand my point of view regarding his continued, and wholly unacceptable, I might add, ghostly nomadic existence. I think he now fully understands where I'm coming from."

"You've been shouting at him."

"Yes ... essentially. Same thing." Deana shot a look over her shoulder towards the conservatory. *"I thought I told you to stay put? Sit in the conservatory, try not to spoil the look of the place, and be quiet! Useless*

lump of no good. Was when he was alive, too." Deana muttered the last sentence as Sidney shrugged and pondered which wicker chair to flop into.

"What's happening?" I whispered, detecting ghosts must be talking due to there being a lull in the conversation.

"Deana and that Sidney chap are there. They must have come in through the conservatory."

"Oh … a right old spooks convention. They'll need name tags and lanyards to know who's who if any more show up."

Niall smirked but kept his focus on the events through the crack in the doorjamb.

"What's going on? Who you talking to now?" Joseph asked, still holding that boss-eyed expression, unable to peel his eyes from the cleaver and the bluish glint that shone from the blade and danced around the kitchen as Clara shifted her stance.

"What's gonna happen if Tel or Bossy-Boots tells me to, you turd, is I'm gonna chop you up for dog food."

"Oh, sweety, please. We're not in the bedroom now. Bossy-Boots, indeed," Deana chortled.

Clara winked at Deana and ran her tongue suggestively across her top lip.

"Oh, you saucy girl, you. Wait until I get you upstairs. I can see I'm going to have to get my whip out."

"Deana, please, can we not discuss whatever you and Clara are planning to do to each other under the covers but focus on our mission? Which, as it so happens, I have nearly solved."

"Have you, by golly? You clever boy. And yes, of course, darling. Do tell all. What's happened?"

"Oh no, she's back, isn't she?"

"Darling," Deana stroked Terry's arm. "Please instruct the pasty Inch-High Pervert-Eye that I am not she, thing, or it. If he can't address me correctly, I will have no choice but to carry out my earlier threat."

"Well?" Hallam asked when slowly inching along the counter while surreptitiously shooting looks at the backdoor.

"Hallam, I said don't move. And yes, Deana is here beside me. If you don't belt up, she will carry out her earlier threat."

Hallam cupped his privates and closed his eyes before muttering at the ceiling.

"Is he praying?" I whispered.

"I can't hear what he's mumbling, but it looks that way. I'm not sure why he feels the need to cover his you-know-whats, though," Niall replied.

"Presumably, the threat Terry just mentioned that Deana must have levied his way sometime earlier involved performing some unmentionable act on his you-know-whats."

Niall raised an eyebrow before we both retook our spying positions.

"What happens now? And for frig sake, get this thing … ghost, whatever, away from me. And for the love of God, who the hell are you talking to?"

"Oh, sorry, Meyer, I almost forgot you were there. This is Deana. She's the ghost who caused all the 'magic', as you called it, that day your father suffered a heart attack."

Deana whipped a carving knife from the block and thrust the point into a wooden chopping board, allowing the handle to sway back and forth when leaving said knife ominously embedded.

"Oh, shit," Hallam hissed when cracking open one eye.

"What the fu …" Meyer paused as his eyes followed the movement of the swaying handle.

"So, what's going to happen now is you're going to log onto your banking website thingamajig …"

"Ooo, get you, darling, you tech wizard. Very on-trend for a man with attitudes and moustaches stuck in yesteryear. You're becoming a right little internet ferret in your old age."

"And?" Meyer hissed, unable to move due to Clara pressing the blade onto his skin.

"Look, I'm listening to Deana, so you'll have to accept pauses in the conversation."

"Course you are. Frigging nutter," Joseph muttered. "Shit, that hurt!" he blurted. "The bitch cut me."

"I ain't even started, you knob," Clara hissed as she pushed the tip of the blade into his soft nasal cartilage.

"Clara, sweety, don't get too hasty. I attest the accusation that you're a bitch was nasty. However, as horrid as that is, we need Joseph Meyer alive for the moment. Anyway, that gash you've made in his nose is causing blood to drip onto my Italian porcelain tiles. Because Mrs Mop, my old cleaner … can't remember the woman's name … is no longer performing her bi-weekly duties, all mess will have to be cleaned by yours truly. I can assure you, I'm not the rubber glove type of woman."

"You've got it, Bossy-Boots," Clara saluted. "However, this git calls me a bitch again, and his knob's coming off."

"Yes, that does seem fair." Deana turned and peered into the conservatory. *"Sidders, you old grunge, would you like cream of tomato or Scotch broth to take with you?"*

"Oh, a nice drop of Scotch broth would be lovely. Thanks." Sidney hollered from the dark depths of the conservatory.

"Walton … what now?" Joseph pleaded.

"Yeah, sorry about that. Deana was just discussing what soup her dead husband would like."

"There … there's more of them?" Hallam blurted when opening his eyes.

"Oh, sorry, how rude of me. I should have introduced everyone. That's Sidney. He's a ghost, too, of course. Now, I should mention …" Terry paused and clicked his fingers, waiting for Joseph to look at him.

"Terry can be so forthright. He's what I call a man's man," Deana cooed, pawing at Terry's muscly biceps.

Clara shot her a look.

"Don't give me that look, my sweet girl. I've been quite clear that I'm all yours."

"Promise?"

"Promise. Cross my heart and hope to die type of promise. Although I am already dead," Deana tittered.

"Okay, cheers, Dee. I love you. You know that?"

"I'm delighted to hear that, and I do you. I'm just saying I love it when Terence becomes all brutish and forthright. Okay, do carry on, darling, you're doing such a sterling job, you clever boy. While you continue to terrorise the revolting excuse of a man, I'm just going to pop the hob on and prepare Sidders' soup so we can get him on his way."

"Joseph, as I was saying. Oh, before I do," Terry raised a finger. "Clara mentioned a moment ago that if you call her a bitch one more time, she will cut your knob off."

Meyer shot a look to his right before cupping his privates Hallam-style.

"Okay, Meyer, you're going to open up your account and transfer all the money you stole back to Janice, with … let's say twenty-per cent interest."

"Piss off. Anyway, I don't have that kind of cash."

"Tel, you want me to cut an ear off?"

"Please try not to make too much mess if you do, sweety," Deana asked as she battled with a tin opener.

"If you don't have that cash in your account, you're not going to leave this house alive," Terry jabbed a finger at Meyer, who remained in position with a red drop of blood precariously hanging from his nostril.

"You wouldn't dare … you ain't killing me."

"Oh, Joseph, I can assure you I will. In fact, I might have to toss a coin to see which one of us has the pleasure of doing the deed. You see, us ghosts just love dabbling in a spot of murder."

"We do, darling, especially when it's the likes of reprobates like him we're murdering. Before you slit his throat, you might have to help me with this thing. Years since I've used a can opener."

"Shit!" I whispered.

"I'm not sure we can stand by and allow these ghosts to kill the man. I know he's done despicable things, but killing him isn't acceptable."

"Perhaps it's just a threat. Terry said he wasn't a killer. Where's Deana and that Sidney now?"

"I can just see Sidney. He's lounging in a wicker chair in the conservatory. Deana's opening a tin of soup. Heinz, I think."

"What the hell is she doing making soup at a time like this? And what's the relevance of the brand?"

Niall shrugged before we again placed our cheeks together and continued to watch events through the doorjamb.

"Voilà! Done it."

"Okay … alright. The twenty grand and ten per cent. Then you let me go."

"No, that's not going to work. See, Janice has had a really shit time of late. I think we'll round it up to—"

"Fifty per cent, darling." Deana spouted when upending the soup into a saucepan. "Oh, yuck, looks a bit lumpy. I wonder if it's past its sell-by date? No bother, it's only for old Sidders. Can't kill him," she snickered.

"Fifty per cent. You'll transfer thirty grand into Janice's account, and then maybe I'll ask Clara not to chop you up for stewing steak. How's that sound?"

"Bastard!"

"No. I know who my parents were. Claire and Mick Walton. I am Terry Walton. I am dead. I am a ghost, like Clara, Sidney and Deana, who you can't see. However, I'm quite sure you've come to realise that they are here with me." Terry nodded to the cooker. "I mean, a wooden spoon doesn't just spin around a saucepan of its own volition, does it?"

"Alright," Meyer huffed. "Thirty grand."

"Good. We'll nip through to the study and fire up that contraption. Don't try anything because Clara will be with you all the way."

"I'm on it, Tel. One false move from this shyster, and he'll wave goodbye to his hand."

Niall and I pulled away from our spying pose. Hovering in position for a second.

"Shall we just go? I think they've forgotten we're here," I suggested.

"Perhaps we ought to. Come on," he whispered, taking my hand as we tiptoed to the front door. "No, second thoughts. Let's hide in there." Niall nodded to where Deana had earlier taken Sidney. "I know we're snooping, but it would be good to stay a while longer to confirm you've got all your money back."

I chewed my lip, weighing up the options: stay hidden in a house full of murdering spooks, remain precisely where we were when they all trooped out of the kitchen and thus join the shindig, or leave now and hope the transfer was completed.

"Janice?"

"All right. We'll stay. But we hide in there," I hissed when hearing the scraping of stool legs across the tiles, suggesting they were on their way.

"Hallam, you're coming, too. Where I can keep an eye on you."

"Okay … err … I was wondering."

"What?" Terry barked.

"Well, it's just that Meyer never paid me for that job when I tracked Daniel Maypole. I was just thinking that maybe while he's doing that transfer, we could force him to pay me too … perhaps, maybe?"

"You're dead when we get out of here. I ain't paying you nothing."

"Hallam, I couldn't give two shits what he owes you. You're as bad as each other. Clearly, you knew Meyer was the man we needed to find, but tried to hoodwink us. I'd count yourself damn fortunate that Deana is otherwise engaged doing her impression of The Galloping Gourmet."

"Oh, yes, the dashingly handsome Graham Kerr. I remember him. Blimey darling, that's a bit retro. I think I'm more Nigella. A delicious woman like me. What were you saying about Inch-High?" Deana raised the spoon and took a sip before grimacing at the taste.

"Hallam tried to warn Meyer. He double-crossed us."

"Please, it wasn't like that."

"Oh, Inch-High is such a whingy wuss, isn't he?" Deana grumbled before hollering into the darkened conservatory. "Sidders … apologies, but it's a bit lumpy. I'll probably strain it before pouring it into the flask."

"Righto, thanks, Deana. I think it's supposed to be lumpy. Whatever, I'm sure it will be lovely."

"I doubt that. Hopefully, you'll choke on it, you turgid old git," she muttered, giving the soup a final stir before rummaging in a cupboard for a sieve.

"It was exactly like that," Meyer spat. "You called me, remember?"

"Yeah, big mistake. I was just giving you the heads-up."

"For a price."

"Nothing's free in this world."

"Perhaps you want to tell them about your plan. What was it, the egg the golden goose laid?"

Hallam's jaw flapped.

"You care to explain?" Terry asked.

"Um … err—"

"I had no idea what he was on about." Meyer cut in, appearing keen to deflect any angst away from himself and on to Hallam. "But he reckoned, knowing where you were, could be a nice little earner. Something about exposing you and … and that thing stirring the soup."

"Good grief, another pleb that wants to call me a thing. And they clearly don't understand the meaning of Aesop's Fable. Truth and honesty lost because of their greed. And not, as they believe, the golden opportunity. Oh, well, more stupid people. God knows the world is full of them." Deana sighed. *"Sidders, I'll give you Dickie's old thermos he used to take when cavorting across the countryside with his foxhunting saboteur friends. My darling boy doesn't need it anymore."*

"I'm assuming, Hallam, you intended to sell us down the river. Claim two ghosts were real, living at this address."

"It wasn't personal. Look, business has been a bit thin recently. I just needed a cash injection. I don't suppose this would be a good time to appeal to your better nature and ask if you could see your way clear to letting me have that laptop back, would it?"

"Sidders … you fancy a sausage to dip in your soup? Pasty Inch-High is determined to part with his."

"That would be lovely, thank you," came the reply.

"I really don't think you would enjoy that," she snickered before turning to face Terry.

"Darling, as much as my threat to do whatever to Hallam holds a certain entertainment value and served its purpose regarding scaring the man into complying with us earlier, in all seriousness, what are we going to do with him and Meyer once poor Janice has her cash back? Whether we like it or not, they do have power over us because they know where we are."

"Dee?"

"Yes, my darling girl. Are you still alright with continuing to wave around that cleaver, or would you like me to step in? Tag team, sort of thing?"

"No, I'm good. But who's that in a hood peering at us through the window?"

32

Satan's Emissary

After nipping into the lounge, hovering just inside the door, Niall held the handle, keeping the door ajar as I squinched my eyes tightly closed as if that would somehow assist me in continuing to hear what Terry, the little fella, and that bastard Meyer were saying. Unfortunately, all that was coming back was muffled, indistinguishable tones further covered by the sound of the back door closing.

Although, before we moved positions, Niall could see the other three ghosts, not being able to hear them made piecing together the conversation tricky. What was clear, though, Terry appeared to be telling the truth. Hopefully, within a few minutes, I would be reunited with my life's savings plus a bonus that I could use to cover a good few months' rent on a new home. That's assuming Meyer hadn't escaped the bath-towel-wrapped ghost wielding a meat cleaver, and that door closing wasn't him making a run for it.

"They're coming," Niall held a shush finger to his lips and pulled the door open another inch so we could spot Terry and the man he called Hallam, closely followed by the odd sight of Meyer with a meat cleaver hovering at the side of his neck as they entered the room opposite which I assumed to be the study.

"The ghost in the bath towel is with them?" I mumbled. As soon as I posed the question, I realised my lunacy based on the fact something, or someone, had to be holding the meat cleaver.

Niall nodded. We both held our breath, watched and waited.

"What was all that about someone at the window? Some bloke in the hood prowling around the back garden, you said. Was it one of your lot?" Hallam asked.

"We don't know, but Deana's sent Sidney out to investigate. Right, Meyer, load up your banking thingamajig and do the transfer. Clara, I assume you'll know if he's completed it correctly?"

"No worries, Tel. I've only been dead since the summer. After ten years working as a data analyst in a media company, I'm pretty au fait with the intricacies of internet banking. Okay, I take it you've got this Janice's bank details?"

Niall and I exchanged a look. The news that another ghost had rocked up sent my mind spinning. My earlier quip that the town was potentially riddled with the walking dead appeared not to have been far off the mark.

"Ah, no. Sorry, do we need them?"

"Err … yeah. Jesus, Tel, how the hell are we gonna force this git to transfer money to her if you ain't got her account and sort-code numbers?"

"Oh, well, I didn't know, did I? It's alright for you, being dead for only a few months. I've been dead for decades. In my day, there was none of this internet thing. If you needed to transfer money, you wrote a cheque or queued outside the bank to see a teller at the counter."

"If you haven't got the stupid slag's account numbers, then that's it. You ain't getting nothing out of me. I suggest you call off the dogs, put this psycho bitch with her meat cleaver back in her box, and I'll be on my way."

The cry of anguish that followed Meyer's claim he wasn't of a mind to play ball suggested the bath-towel-wrapped ghost had wielded her weapon of choice upon parts of Meyer's body. Although he deserved all he got, his wailing, whimpering, and, if I'm not mistaken, a fair bit of hyperventilating caused my guts to twist. Meat cleavers, by their very nature, could do a fair bit of damage to flesh, animal or human.

While I stifled a cry with my fist in my mouth, Niall sprang into action, flinging back the door before hot-footing across the hall and bursting into the office.

"Next time, I'll take your hand off."

After pulling myself together, with a quick bollocking for being a wimp, I scooted across the darkened hallway to join them. As I peered around Niall, who'd blocked the doorway, I eyed the meat cleaver hovering in front of Meyer's contorted face as he slumped in the office chair, clutching his hand.

"What on earth is going on here?" Niall boomed in that public school voice he'd employed when taking Gummy-Harry to task on Sunday.

"Who the frig are they?" Hallam squealed.

"Oh, blimey, I'd forgotten you two were still here," Terry blurted as he swivelled around.

"What's happened to his hand," Niall gesticulated at the wimping Meyer.

"Ah, yeah, Clara had to get a bit forceful, I'm afraid."

"She chopped his hand ... fingers off?"

"Oh, no," Terry chuckled. "She only scraped the blade across the back of his hand. It's probably not even still bleeding."

"What's he whimpering for then?"

"Probably because he's a pathetic toad of a man, who throws his weight around and plays the big I am but, when it comes down to it, he's just like the rest of the low-life scum who think they can take advantage of others. The man's a bully. I know because he intimidated his step-sister, my daughter, for years."

"Yes, that was Kim. She told me all about him, so I know how he treated her." When shimmying around Niall, I stepped towards Joseph before addressing the area where I assumed Clara to be standing. "Clara, would it be all right if I held the meat cleaver?" I asked, feeling a smidge embarrassed to be talking to thin air with an audience behind me.

"Yeah, go for it, girl. I'm happy for you to hack the bastard's hand off. Fill your boots."

"Janice, what are you planning on doing? You know I can't condone violence, whatever's gone before. This has to stop."

"Niall, just trust me." I glanced at Terry. "What did Clara say?"

"She's handing it to you. Look, there ... see?"

As I felt her hand touch mine, her fingers guiding me to take the meat cleaver from her, the hairs on my neck fizzled. Although Deana had touched my hand and cheek, this was altogether different. I could feel the invisible force, human in form, as our fingers and hands exchanged the weapon.

"Thanks," I mumbled before assessing the weight in my hand, holding it over the man who'd willingly duped me and thus taken my savings with no thought or concern of how that left me.

Someone far brainer than me had stated that being human requires creativity, resilience, consciousness, empathy and a fair few others I can't remember. The man before me had no concept of the last on my truncated list. Did that make him non-human or just the product of the evil man who'd raised him? As I formulated what I was about to say, I decided it didn't matter what he was.

"So, you're the shit calling himself Chad Ruger, then?"

"That thing, ghost, she cut my hand … the bitch drew blood."

"I'll chop it off if you don't answer me, you utter bastard."

"And his knob. I warned him about calling me a bitch."

"Janice!"

"Niall, just trust me," I barked, not once losing eye contact with Joseph. "So, you are the man who claimed to be Chad Ruger?"

"Yeah. I said I was earlier."

"I know, I heard you. But I needed to hear you say it to my face."

"Look, lady, it was your fault. You have got to be the most gullible so far," he snorted, shaking his head disparagingly to convey how stupid I'd been. "I thought I'd hit the jackpot with you. Twenty grand in such a short space of time. Not once did you ask to have a video call or question why I said I couldn't show you pictures of where I supposedly lived. I mean, talk about the dumbest bitch going."

I held my free palm up, detecting Niall and Terry preparing to enter the affray, suspecting Niall was loosening his tongue to fire off a verbal lambasting and Terry, going by the balled fists, readying himself to larrup the man.

"Yes, unfortunately, I agree. There's no doubt I was a complete idiot, and I'm not surprised to hear I was a soft target. So, how many women have you conned?"

"Err …"

"How many?"

"A few."

"Joseph, if you think I won't use this—"

"Ten … twenty, I don't know. Maybe thirty."

"I want a list of names—"

"I didn't keep a record—"

"Names!"

"Alright, alright."

"So, let's make that transfer to my account, and then every remaining penny you have will be transferred to Niall's church account."

"Wha—"

"Shut up and listen. Every last penny to Niall."

"Janice?"

"Trust me, please, Niall." I shot a look at the short man cowering in the corner. "I overheard earlier that you're a private investigator."

He nodded.

"Terry, this Sidney ghost. D'you think you could contact them up there and get them to agree to let him work for me for a while? Sort of on a secondment basis, if that's doable? If he does what I ask, he might earn some of those Brownie points you've mentioned. And, based on the fact that the three people he's murdered so far were evil, he might avoid ending up in Hell. "

"Err … well, um, I could get Deana to ask. I don't know, but I guess it's possible. But, what for?"

"Tel, I've heard of cases where this sort of thing has happened. If you like, I'll give my handler a buzz in the morning. She's one of the good ones, and I reckon I can persuade her if the circumstances are right. Anyway, I've got some dirt on her. So, if all else fails, I can just resort to blackmail."

"Oh … right."

"What did Clara say?" Niall asked.

"She said she can swing it, but—"

"Hang on," I interrupted Terry. My newly discovered confidence and self-belief flowed through me, making me feel almost giddy. I now had a purpose, something I'd been missing for years as I'd trundled from day to day, just existing but not living. "Mr Hallam, when we have this list, which Joseph will provide, you're going to track every woman down who this git has conned. Then Niall and I will reimburse them with the money Joseph is about to transfer."

"Right, yeah, I can do that. I charge two hundred a day plus expenses."

"No, Mr Hallam. This will be on a pro bono basis."

"I can't do that—"

"You can, and you will. Sidney, the killer ghost, will accompany you to ensure you comply."

Although in a darkened room, the only light source coming from the PC's monitor, I detected Hallam's complexion pale.

"Shit … right, okay, I guess that seems fair."

"It is. You step out of line, and Sidney notches up his fourth murder. He can already claim serial killer ghost status, so one more won't matter."

"And what about me? You can't take everything I've got."

"We can, and we will. Your life is going to be a living hell. Terry said something earlier about the gits who conned his son had already booked their place in Hell before Sidney killed them. And I think we can now confidently assume such a place exists after what we've witnessed over the last couple of days. You, you bastard, booked your slot down there years ago."

"No, but—"

"Shut up, you snake. I'm talking. Before you end up down there, I think it's only fair that you suffer like I and all those poor women you conned. Mine and their crimes only being gullible, trusting, and maybe a bit desperate." I jabbed the cleaver at Joseph, causing him to jerk his head back.

"Oh, isn't she good? It's like watching a flower blossom ... petals unfolding to show its full potential. Well done, Janice. I'm super impressed, you clever girl you. I always said you were a sharp cookie, isn't that right, darling?"

"Um ... did you, I don't recall—"

"I did so, Terence. Right, talking of cookies and refreshments, anyone for a mince pie? Shop bought, I'm afraid ... well, shop stolen, I should say. Sorry, I haven't had time to bake any this year." Deana offered the plate of mince pies as she shimmied around Niall.

"You ... baking?" Terry scoffed as he took one from the plate.

"No, darling, of course not. I wasn't put on this earth to bake ... or open tins of soup, for that matter. It's just what folk say. Oh, yes, I almost forgot. Sidders, the old grunge, found our prowler; they're both in the kitchen tucking into a bowl of my rather yucky Scotch broth."

"One of us?"

"I wouldn't want to class him in the same category as myself, but if you mean is he dead, then yes ... most definitely. I should know because I killed him."

"Pete? Portly-Pete, the trucker?"

"Yes, darling. The revolting, bloated, bald-headed toad himself."

"What the hell is he doing here?"

"Ah, it's not good news for Joseph, I'm afraid to say. Apparently, Portly-Pete has been seconded to a new outfit that The-Powers-That-Be have recently set up. It's all rather hush-hush, as they say. From what I gather, although difficult to understand the man due to his poor diction and propensity to mumble, he's working for a hit squad that reports directly to the Grim Reaper."

"But … why's he here, at your house?"

"Darling, I would have thought that's obvious."

"Is it?" Terry furrowed his brow, pausing when about to bite into his mince pie.

"Of course it is, darling. He's come for Mr Meyer."

33

Is It Better To Have Loved And Lost?

As I have for a few years, on Christmas morning, I, along with the other volunteers, prepared and served Christmas dinner with all the trimmings, offering the complete festive works, including Christmas pudding, mince pies, and crackers to Fairfield's homeless community. Although I'd always enjoyed the company of the other helpers and the homeless on Christmas morning, in years gone by, I'd dreaded the rest of the day, Boxing Day, and so on, until 'normality' arrived during the second week of the new year.

After my stints at the refuge, my Christmas Days since Mother passed have, as previously stated, been low-key affairs. No, scrub that … frigging awful. However, unsurprisingly, this year was panning out to be very different.

While we'd served the food and tackled the associated washing-up carnage that's a by-product of this sort of mass-catering operation, Terry and Ellen entertained the masses with low-level magician tricks. Of course, Terry wasn't remotely skilled in anything sleight of hand. Still, with his able assistants, Deana and Clara, he managed to pull it off. All of which Ellen found hilarious, resulting in her giggling through the whole affair.

Gummy-Harry behaved himself, although Dawn, or Dawny as he called her, gave the poor old boy a peck on the cheek, which I think made his year. When no one was looking, I'd squeezed another slice of turkey onto Red-Box-Ray's plate, which his usually unseen smile suggested had made his day.

After giving his Christmas Day sermon to the few who'd bothered to turn up on a murky grey, chilly morning, Niall popped down to join us and take the opportunity to have a quiet word with Pervy-Perry. Unsurprisingly, following that chat, the man with wandering hands left early, saying he had to see a man about a dog. I think it's safe to assume *Mr Tickle's* unacceptable groping would no longer be something we volunteers would need to worry about. And on a real plus note, Clara took one for the team when volunteering to clean the facilities after Super-Glue-Steve had enjoyed his weekly turnout. Dawn had been surprised and bemused at how clean the facilities were, knowing I hadn't ventured there.

After we'd completed our kitchen tasks, I'd made a point of chatting with the quiet, large lady whose name I didn't know. I'd always assumed that she was probably like the vast majority of those who rocked up each week: addicted to a substance or alcohol, suffering acute mental health issues, or just couldn't face being part of 'normal' society.

I was wrong.

After a few minutes of chatting, I discovered she'd endured years of domestic abuse and chose to live on the streets rather than suffer a daily beating at the hands of her estranged husband. Not being the sort to ask for help and ashamed about her circumstances, Trish had kept her head down, waiting for the cold, or maybe the Grim Reaper, to take her from a living hell.

By the time the Queen delivered her Christmas address to the Nation and Commonwealth, Trish had left the streets for a basic but warm and safe room at the women's refuge. For the first time in over a year, Trish felt there might be something worth living for.

Last Tuesday morning, Clara made a call – I'm not sure if that was via landline, two cans and a piece of string, or whatever, to her 'handler' up there, wherever that was. Whatever persuasion techniques she used, Sidney was duly assigned to chaperone the pint-sized PI, and we'd already reimbursed eleven of the thirty-two conned by Meyer during his six months of evil deeds.

Not one of those eleven unfortunate women had lost funds amounting to anywhere near half of what I had. Which confirmed, not that I needed any more confirmation, that 'stupid Janice' of a week ago couldn't return. Now that I'd 'grown a pair', as my father used to say, I would never allow myself to be taken for a fool again.

Following my childminding stint – incidentally, less than a week in, Ellen had stated she wanted me to stay, her pleading with her father to make that happen causing me to literally melt into tears – I would move on to the next chapter of my life as a new woman. Whatever the future may bring, with the help of my new friends, Niall and Ellen, I would tackle the challenges head-on, no longer wallowing in self-pity when permanently hiding in the shadows.

After we'd returned to the vicarage, and when dinner was all done and dusted, Niall and Terry had chatted about life, death, and what happens after we leave this mortal existence. Ellen and I played games with Clara and Deana. Deana had suggested Monopoly, but Ellen hadn't been keen, and Terry, although not playing, had groaned at hearing the suggestion for some undisclosed reason. Anyway, despite being the only one of the quartet who couldn't see two of the participants, those few hours were undoubtedly the most fun I'd experienced for many a year.

I was going to miss being with Ellen. Within a few days, she and I had slotted into a 'mother-daughter' relationship that I never thought I'd have the pleasure of experiencing. However, as much as I didn't want it to happen, now that I am no longer 'stupid Janice', I knew this charade would soon end when Lena returned in the new year.

The snow that had fallen steadily and blanketed the town last weekend had melted as quickly as it came, much to Ellen's disappointment. However, the forecast for the afternoon showed great promise and, as the metrological office had predicted, this year was officially categorised as a white Christmas by late afternoon following a few hours of heavy snowfall.

All of us, except Deana, who'd said she had some letters to write – which I thought was an odd activity for a ghost – donned our winter coats and trooped into the back garden. After a snowball fight, which was unfair based on Clara harbouring a distinct advantage, we all mucked in to build a snowman. Ellen called him Sidney because he looked sad and fat, like the ghost who'd visited earlier in the week. A statement that tickled Deana when we piled back inside, cold, wet, but utterly joyful.

Not that I knew it at the time, but when Hallam and Sidney reported in later that week regarding their progress, I learned that the pasty-looking PI and his sidekick ghost, or *Randall and Hopkirk* as Niall now called them, had enjoyed a bottle of Johnnie Walker and a Maccy D's in Hallam's office on Christmas Day. Bizarrely, Hallam reckoned it was the best Christmas he'd had in years. Although in very different circumstances, Hallam and I had enjoyed similar experiences when celebrating the birth of our Lord and Saviour. Not that I believed … but there must be something up there. Right?

Of course, Niall and I had quizzed what happened to Joseph Meyer after we'd left the ghosts to deal with him. Terry thought it best that we didn't know, but he assured us he, Deana, or Clara would do no harm to the man. However, Terry informed us that the ghost who'd rocked up late to the party, a bald-headed, rough-looking sort according to Niall, would deal with Joseph, whatever that meant.

Clara left before eight, informing Terry, who acted as interpreter, that she needed to check in with her ghostly partner regarding the progress of their mission. I had absolutely no idea what that meant, but I thought it better not to ask. Terry and Deana left soon after. Much to my and Ellen's dismay, Terry stated our paths were unlikely to cross again. Deana would be waiting for her new assignment, and he had a meeting planned with a woman ominously named Miss De Ath.

After reading Ellen her bedtime story – Niall read a few pages, then me the next few – we decamped to the comfort of the sofa, the warmth of the hearth and the flickering glow of the dying embers in the grate.

Notwithstanding how much I'd enjoyed the day, the reality of the challenges which lay ahead fought hard to dampen my mood. Of course, Niall had paid the final two months' rent, which I'd reimbursed him as soon as my account swelled by thirty grand. Even so, I wasn't looking forward to going home next weekend. Niall was a good friend, and I felt so lucky to have found him.

I planned to start searching for a new home next week, preferably one without leaky windows, and when I had that sorted, I would be all out to find a job. After my few days with Ellen, I considered childminding as a new career choice. Despite my dreams, I knew the chances of finding *Mr Right*, settling down and starting a family were just a pipe dream. Following last week's events, my head was finally out of the clouds, now prepared to face reality head-on.

When Niall returned to the kitchen to grab the wine, I nipped over to the mantlepiece and studied one of the framed pictures of Julie Dowding. A gorgeous woman who had everything before losing it all when that cruel disease took her so young. I couldn't decide who was the more fortunate. Julie for having loved but lost, or me for being alive but never experiencing the shared love she and Niall had. It only took me a moment to realise that Julie had the better deal.

"'Tis better to have loved and lost than never to have loved at all," I muttered as Niall returned.

"Sorry," he asked.

"Oh, nothing. Sorry, I was just looking at the picture of Julie."

"What's that behind it?" he asked as he joined me at the fireplace.

"Oh," I grabbed the envelope, looking quizzically at Niall. "It's addressed to you and me. Why does it say it must be read together?"

Niall shrugged.

"Shall I open it?"

"Think you'd better."

I tore open the envelope and unfolded the single sheet of paper, instantly noticing the elegant handwriting of whoever had penned it. As we had last Monday when spying through the doorjamb, Niall and I stood cheek to cheek and silently read the letter, which the signature and date at the bottom stated had been written by Deana earlier today.

Dear Janice and Niall,

I am writing to you for two reasons. Firstly, neither of you can hear me, and God love the man as I do, conversing through Terence is not always conducive when conveying one's thoughts in the right tone. Secondly, I wish you to read what I have to say together and in private. (Spook-free, if you like.)

Janice, Terence and I have found it an honour and a privilege to be assigned to assist you. I am so sorry that during our mission to help Kim, our actions led to Joseph becoming the despicable man he was. We'd pushed the rat into the corner, you might say. Which, in turn, resulted in your suffering.

We beg your forgiveness. Hopefully, you can find it in your heart to do so now we've set things straight, so to speak. Janice, I misjudged you horribly, for which, again, I am truly sorry.

I am fully aware of who I was when alive and how some perceived me. Yes, I can be fickle, capricious, and often quite needy. I attest that I display snobbish tendencies, possess the urge to judge others and, as all of my turgid ex-husbands have accused me of, be a super bitch. However, as many of my lovers will vouch, being a woman brimming with passion and desire, I harbour a good heart.

I was fortunate to meet a man (I picked his car keys out of the pot at a swingers' party, but that's by the by) who stole my heart like no other. My darling Dickie Burton taught me that sharing one's life and love with another is the most wonderful achievement that any of us can attain. Also, I have an eye for these things. A sixth sense, if you like. (Please discount my errors regarding my choices of my first six husbands. I was young and impetuous. We're all allowed to make the odd mistake, are we not?). Now, this letter is not about me per se, but rather my experiences in life, which I feel are pertinent to you both.

So, my darlings, here's what I have to say. I am right because I always am regarding such matters.

Don't waste the years you have left. I died too young, and my time with the man I loved was cut horribly short. Janice, I know, and you know, you are in love with the man standing by your side. Also, Niall, you dishy vicar, I know, as you do, you are in love with the woman who stands by your side. Accept this fate, live your life together, and raise Ellen to become the truly exceptional young woman she will be. Look back when you're old and grey with pride in your hearts that you both have lived a fulfilling life brimming with love and companionship.

Toodle pip, my darlings,

Deana

P.S. My darling girl, Clara, agrees with me entirely, and we both expect an invitation to the wedding. If I say so myself, I look even more delicious in a hat. And, of course, it goes without saying we both promise to behave.

Seven years

and seven days later ...

34

New Year's Day 2024

The Kiss of Death

"Mum. Mum!"

"Ellen, I'm not deaf. There's no need to shout."

"Oh ... okay, but why's Dad just standing there, staring into space, looking like a saddo?" Ellen bellowed down the stairs.

"Standing where? He's over at the church," I hollered back, busying myself when clearing the carnage in the kitchen after my husband and I had hosted an evening for a few select friends and acquaintances to see in the new year. "I do wish she wouldn't shout," I grumbled before puffing out my cheeks, wondering where to start when contemplating the heaps of dirty crockery.

"He's in the churchyard ... just standing there."

"Sorry, I can't hear you."

"I said, he's just standing in the churchyard, staring into space like some saddo nutter," Ellen bellowed over the stair bannister.

I lobbed the tea towel onto the worktop and groaned before padding to the bottom of the stairs.

"Ellen, what are you on about?"

"Mum, come up."

I huffed, resigned to the fact that I would have to comply with my daughter's demand, traipse up the stairs and fight my way through the carnage of her teenage bedroom.

Ellen, now fifteen, going on twenty-one, over the course of the last six months, had become obsessed with clothes, make-up, boy bands and social media. All bar the last two in that list were usually strewn across her room, making forays into it akin to fighting through the dense undergrowth of the Amazon rainforest. Of course, her bedroom was markedly different from that December Sunday afternoon when I'd first visited the vicarage. Hello Kitty was long gone, although one on-brand soft toy remained, nestled on a bookcase amongst more of the aforementioned paraphernalia.

Seemingly overnight, as far as Niall and I were concerned, our daughter had blossomed into a beautiful young woman, blessed with the genes of her biological mother, Julie Dowding.

"Mum, look," Ellen repeated as I tiptoed through the carnage, trying to avoid standing on anything that might break or cause pain Lego-brick style. Fortunately, Lego injuries were no longer a concern. Still, I was mindful of the potential injury

I might suffer caused by a pair of tweezers lurking under any of the strewn garments.

"Ellen, what's the chance you could make a New Year's resolution to become tidy?"

"Err … none. I wasn't born with the tidy gene."

"No, you inherited the messy one from your father."

As I reached her bedroom window unscathed, I took in the view of the graveyard when Ellen looped her arm through mine and rested her head on my shoulder.

"Is Dad alright, d'you think? I mean, what's he doing? He's been standing there just like that for ages."

"Is he not just waiting for that family who, by the looks of it, are tending to their loved one's grave?"

"I dunno, but he hasn't moved for at least ten minutes."

"Maybe he's just hanging back to give them some space before going over to talk to them."

"Okay. Yeah, probably. I just thought it was odd, that's all."

"They're probably people he knows from the church. Look, he's walking their way now."

Despite eight years having elapsed since the passing of Julie Dowding, I knew Ellen still harboured deep-rooted concerns she might also lose her father. She'd confided in me about those worries during a heart-to-heart session a few years back. As the years passed, I knew those concerns became less acute. Still, the trauma of her mother's illness and death would probably stay with my daughter for the rest of her life.

Although I couldn't guarantee that I could keep my assurances due to it being out of my control, Ellen had made me promise that Niall and I wouldn't die anytime soon. I guess the dread of losing two mothers was enough to torment anyone's thoughts. I'd nearly broke when I lost mine, so I could fully grasp where my adopted daughter was coming from.

"You alright?" I whispered as we watched my husband approach the group.

Ellen nodded, her jet-black mane scraping on my jumper.

"That's alright then."

"You remember when I asked you to promise …"

"I do."

"I know that was silly, but you do still promise, don't you?"

"Course … what's brought all this on?"

"Nothing, I'm fine." Ellen paused, snuggling tighter to me and gripping my arm as if letting go would result in me drifting away. "Mum … I love you."

"As I do you, my darling girl."

While we remained in position, watching Niall chatting with the four children who stood slightly away from their parents in the graveyard, 'my darling girl' comment made me think of Deana. Specifically, when Niall and I had stood cheek to cheek reading her letter seven years and seven days ago.

That Christmas Day evening, as we stood by the hearth, we both finished reading the ghostly diva's penned words at roughly the same time. I remember staring at the page and thinking, as far as I was concerned, how astute the dead woman was. Although not conscious of the fact before reading her eloquently penned note, written while the dead

Clara used her invisible qualities to pelt us all with snowballs, I hadn't allowed my feelings for Niall to surface due to fear of rejection. However, I knew I'd fallen in love with the man.

Being the forthright man that my husband is, he didn't shilly-shally around. Niall kissed me. A kiss that turned into a protracted snog as I flung my arms around his neck, causing me to let go of Deana's letter. When we broke for air from our first-love-styled embrace, I caught sight of the single sheet of notepaper as it curled and blackened where it lay on the embers in the grate.

Whether Deana ever received our invitation, which Niall and I popped through the 'Ghost House' letter box, I guess we'll never know for certain. However, after we, the newlyweds, stood in line to greet our guests before the wedding breakfast, I was convinced I felt two kisses on my cheeks despite all the guests having already filed past. I remember whispering, 'Deana, are you there?'. Of course, I didn't hear a reply.

Also, and completely unexplainable ... well maybe not, Niall's former mother-in-law, Lady Hesketh, who'd made her feelings about me quite clear, as in me being totally unsuitable to be a stepmother to her granddaughter, was on the receiving end of a few rather odd events.

Firstly, and apparently no one saw it happen, a glass of red wine was poured down her dress. And then, after her histrionics about said ruined frock, the woman's stilettoes seem to just cave in from beneath her. With a ruined dress and broken shoes, a bruised bottom and ego, the feisty woman left before Niall and I took to the dance floor to smooch to the rather apt Righteous Brothers' Unchained Melody.

In my husband's arms, the lyrics that Bobby Hatfield poured out with such emotion when pleading for God to speed their love, I prayed with all my heart that Deana would soon be reunited with the man who stole hers … her darling boy, Dickie Burton. She was a good egg, and I so wanted her to be back in her man's arms, wherever that may be.

"Godspeed to you, Deana. I owe you everything," I mumbled when lost in memories of that wondrous day nearly seven years ago.

"Mum?"

"Oh, nothing. I was just thinking about my wedding day."

"All I can remember about that day was holding your hand during the photographs and then the incident when Grandma went ballistic about her dress. We didn't like Grandma, did we?"

"We most certainly did not."

Ellen giggled, a sound that hadn't changed over the last seven years.

"D'you think it was Deana who ruined her dress?"

"Maybe. You still believe she existed?"

"Yeah, hundred per cent."

"Me too. Right, talking of ghosts, I might take a walk over there and catch up with your father in the graveyard before tackling that mess in the kitchen. You coming?"

"Okay … we could say hello to Deana while we're there."

"Sorry," I furrowed my brow when turning to look at her.

"Her grave, silly. Not Deana herself."

"Oh, course."

"We're never going to see her again, are we?"

"No ... funny thing is, though, I'm pretty sure the grave that family are tending to is Terry's."

"Coincidence ... probably. I just need to find my blue scarf, and then I'll be ready to come with you." Ellen turned and pondered the carpet of clothes scattered liberally across her room.

"Will this take long?" I asked, raising my eyebrows at the mess.

"No, Mum. I have a system."

After Ellen had plucked said scarf from under a heap, we donned our winter coats and, arm in arm, headed out into the January chill to find my husband.

"Come on, I see Dad's still talking to that group," Ellen grabbed my hand, almost dragging me along as we weaved our way through the headstones heading their way. "You were right, Mum ... look, it is Terry's grave they're all standing around."

"Okay, I'm coming. I think that's Kim. You know, Kim Verratti. I wasn't aware she tended to Terry's grave."

"You used to be friends, didn't you?"

"We still are. Not that we have much contact these days. Your father used to support that women's refuge over on Chapelfield Road, so he and I were involved with Kim when she set up her charity to support women who'd suffered domestic abuse."

"You never told Kim that you met her father?"

I pulled on Ellen's hand to halt her progress.

"Mum?"

"Ellen, no. We must never—"

"I know," she huffed.

"Nor about what happened to her half-brother. Kim believes Joseph just took off after all that business with her stepfather. As we don't actually know what happened to him, although I could have a good stab at it, I think it's best she continues to believe he's just disappeared."

"I was just … oh, I don't know. It seems sad that we can't tell her about Terry."

"I know, but I don't think we can go there with that one. We know Deana and Terry helped Kim, but I got the impression from Terry that she never believed the man who helped expose her stepfather's wickedness could actually be her real father. It was different for us because your father can see ghosts. From Kim's point of view, it's asking a lot to believe your dead parent has suddenly risen from the grave."

Ellen took a long, ragged breath.

"Bugger," I hissed, pulling my daughter close before affectionately stroking her cheek. "Oh, me and my bloody big mouth. Sorry, Ellen, I didn't mean—"

"No, Mum, it's alright. I know my mum is in Heaven. She would have passed straight through unhindered."

"Yes, I'm sure you're right. Terry told your father that some of the dead zip through 'clearing' without needing to be assessed. Whatever that means."

"He said the best people go through, didn't he? Mum would deffo be in that category."

"Yes, sweety. Top two per cent, if my memory serves me correctly. I'm quite sure Julie was well inside that."

Ellen offered me a tight smile.

"As I was saying, it's much easier for us to understand what happened because your dad could see them. I imagine for Kim, it must have been all quite bewildering."

"And me ... I could see Deana and Clara."

"I know, but I presume now you're older, you can no longer see them."

"Probably not."

"You can't, can you? I mean, you haven't seen any more since Deana?"

"Who knows?" she shrugged. "They're not see-through, so I may have, but not known about it."

"Yes, I suppose."

"What about Dad?"

"What about him?"

"Has he seen any more?"

"No ... well, he said there's been the odd occasion in the church when he's been given a funny look, but your father reckons he gets that sort of reaction from his parishioners from time to time. Especially when he's delivering a sermon."

"Oh, Dad hates doing those, doesn't he?" Ellen giggled.

"It's not his favourite part of the job, that I can say."

"What does he like best?"

I waved my gloved hand toward the group about a hundred yards ahead. "Doing exactly that. Talking to people."

"Yeah, Dad can talk for England. Do we wait here or go and join them?"

"No, come on, let's go and say hello. I haven't seen Kim for such a long time. I'm sure her family won't mind."

As we made our way, arm in arm, up the gentle incline to the final resting place of Terry Walton – perhaps I should say his grave because who the hell knew where the man was hiding out these days – Niall turned and beckoned for us to join them. I thought my husband looked somewhat excited and pleased with himself, suggesting the hangover he awoke with this morning must have worked its way through his system.

"Janice, Janice! Look who's here!"

35

It's That Time Again

"Janice, I said, look who's here," Niall announced enthusiastically while jabbing a finger at Kim.

"So I see," I called out as we approached. Although always lovely to see my old friend, I couldn't quite grasp what had caused my husband to become so animated. "Niall, are you alright? Ellen was worried about you."

"Worried? What for?" he asked our daughter after kissing my cheek before squeezing Ellen's arm affectionately.

"Nothing." Ellen shot me a shut-up-Mum glare as I offered a wave to the group.

"Hi, Kim. Nice to see you again. It must be blooming ages. Did you have a nice Christmas?"

"Hi, Janice. Yes, thanks. You?"

"Yes … err, it was lovely, thanks. Quiet one, but lovely. Anyway, happy New Year."

Although a pleasant exchange, with Kim and the others all mumbling 'Happy New Year' in reply, there seemed to be an edge to the atmosphere as if Ellen and I had butted in. As I cast my eyes around the gathering, offering a hello nod to Vinny, Kim's husband, I detected the other two couples, who I didn't know, weren't feeling comfortable. I couldn't second guess why my husband would encourage us to join a conversation that wasn't as congenial as expected.

I wondered if there'd been some altercation amongst the three couples, and Niall had watched from afar before stepping in. That would explain his staring, saddo stance that Ellen had suggested earlier.

When I spotted Ellen looking towards Deana's grave and the four children who gathered near it, one being Alessia, Kim's daughter, all hopping about and giggling when gazing up at … well, nothing, I nudged her arm to break her trance.

"Ellen, what's the matter?"

"Err … nothing, Mum. I'll be back in a mo," Ellen mumbled before releasing her grip on my arm and taking a couple of steps towards where the children continued to dance around excitedly.

"Poppet … can you?" Niall asked, grabbing hold of her elbow.

"Yeah … I can. Well, just about," whispered our daughter without turning around. "She keeps fading in and out, but she's there."

"It's amazing, isn't it?" Niall grinned.

"Dad … it's the best!" Ellen turned and beamed a smile that suggested whatever they were talking about was the best Christmas present she'd had in years. And that was going some because, as an only child, Niall and I were guilty of sometimes spoiling our daughter.

"Ehm ... Niall, what's amazing?" I hissed before casting my eyes around the group, all of whom remained somewhat awestruck. "What's going on?"

As Ellen approached the children, Niall laid his hand on the small of my back to guide me a few yards away from the others.

"Niall? Are you gonna tell me what's going on?"

"She's here ... she's actually here!"

"Who's here?" My mouth gaped when glancing from my husband's grinning mug to watch Ellen wrap her arms around nothing. "Oh, my God ... Julie—"

"Julie?" Niall furrowed his brow.

"Is Julie ... the ghost of Julie there? Hugging Ellen?" Although my adopted daughter called me Mum, Niall and I ensured we kept Ellen's real mother's memory alive. However, I wasn't sure how I felt about Julie, dead or otherwise, being here and back in the arms of *my* daughter.

"No ... that's not Julie."

While still sporting that shocked pose, I swivelled my head from watching my daughter in that rather peculiar stance to look up at my husband.

"It's her ... you know who!"

"OMG, you've got to be joking!" I hissed. "Why? How?"

"I'm not really sure. She just mentioned something about wanting to catch up with everyone."

"Deana?"

"The very woman herself," he chuckled. "In her usual way, she's currently entertaining those four little ones. Well, she was … now she's hugging Ellen."

As I tried to compute that our matchmaker had shown up again after all these years, in my peripheral vision, I spotted Vinny making the sign of the cross.

I glanced around the group. Kim had closed her eyes and now seemed to be mumbling something incoherent. The handsome black man, a chap oozing a gentle-giant aura, wrapped a tree trunk arm around the tall, stunningly gorgeous woman's waist, who, like Kim, had her eyes closed while muttering to herself.

Describing her as stunningly gorgeous left no adequate words in the English language to describe the blonde woman with her hands on a buggy as she gently rocked it to soothe the toddler snuggly wrapped inside. This woman, clearly much younger than the others, must have got stuck in the section where good looks are dished out, not only grabbing her fair share, but I can only assume that of thousands of others. As she looked up at me and smiled, her true beauty beamed akin to the awe-inspiring effect of the sun hitting the west-facing stained-glass window behind the altar. The woman's beauty was captivating … almost mesmerising.

"Hang on." I peeled my eyes from the group and looked up at Niall again. "Sorry, Niall, but did you just say that Deana's here because she wanted to catch up with everyone?"

"Yes. I've just been trying to convince all of them that she's actually here. It's a bit of a tough sell, I have to say."

"So … you're telling me you can actually hear her? You can hear what Deana is saying."

"Absolutely, I can. I don't know why, but I can only assume because I'm now fully bought into accepting the existence of ghosts wandering around, it means I can see and hear her. Remember, Deana said some small children and religious types with unwavering belief can see and hear her. Just like Ellen could when she was little. Seven years ago, I could only see her because … well, perhaps I wasn't so convinced of her existence then."

"Ellen's not a child anymore."

"That's probably why, for Ellen, Deana keeps fading in and out." Niall followed my gaze to our daughter as she maintained that odd pose.

"I can't believe she's actually here."

"Well, believe it … because Deana is right there hugging our daughter."

I puffed out my cheeks and shook my head. Like the others, a little lost for words.

"Janice?" Niall grabbed my hand. "You alright?"

"I think so. Besides Kim and Vinny, who are the other two couples?"

"That's Damian with his wife, Courteney—"

"The utterly gorgeous blonde?"

"She's a looker, I'll give you that."

"Courteney Statham," I muttered. "Isn't she that famous author?"

"Yes, that's her."

"I'd never made the connection before. It makes sense now. And the other two?"

"That's Ginny and her husband, Viv."

"Terry's three children. Kim, Damian and Ginny?"

"Yeah, with their partners and children."

"I didn't know they all knew each other."

"Well, apparently, they've only just found out they're all related. Crazy, eh?"

"Blimey. I wonder what Terry would make of that?"

"Well, I imagine he'll never find out."

"No … as sad as it is, you're probably right." I gave my husband's gloved hand a gentle squeeze. "It's odd, though … them here with me. The four he and Deana helped."

"Yeah …" Niall rubbed his chin as he pondered that thought.

"What you thinking?"

"Well, as you say, it's odd that she's here today, with all of you here."

"And you say Deana wants them to know she's here?"

"Apparently so."

"And how are they taking it?"

"Not good. It's work in progress, you might say."

"Yeah, I can imagine. But why on earth now? Why does Deana want to show herself after all these years?"

"I'm not sure … she said something about preparing them for a bigger revelation."

"What the hell does that mean?"

"I don't know. Deana was a little cryptic on that front. She just said it was fortunate that I'd turned up and asked if I could have a word with them."

"What … convince them there's a ghost entertaining their children?"

"Yeah," he chuckled. "That's about the size of it."

"Janice, my darling. Isn't this wonderful! It's simply spiffing to see you again."

"Niall? What's happening?" I asked as he shot a look over his shoulder towards Ellen.

"She's heading our way."

"Deana?"

"My darling, Janice. Oh, how truly delightful," Deana halted and turned to the four children. *"Now, be good for Aunty Deana. I simply must give Janice a big, ghostly hug. I'll be back in a jiffy."*

"Stand still and be prepared," Niall hissed.

"For what?"

"I think Deana's about to hug you."

"Oh … right. Blimey."

"Janice, my darling girl. My absolute favourite of all time. I'm so proud of you. You know, I was only just saying to the dishy vicar here that I wouldn't mind a catch-up. I'm so thrilled!"

Seven years ago, I'd experienced touching a real live ghost. Well, okay, perhaps I should say dead ghost. Anyway, that day outside the refuge, Deana had touched my hand, and then later I'd patted her down like an airport security officer might. And not forgetting when Clara and I handed over the meat cleaver. However, this was altogether a very different experience.

As my husband had suggested, Deana flung her arms around me. When I closed my eyes, it felt like I was just in an embrace with a close friend. And, on the subject of friends, new me, after marrying Niall, and with his help to convince me I was someone worth knowing, I was blessed with many.

We stayed in that position long past the point when it felt comfortable. Deana eventually pulled away before what felt like giving me a peck on the cheek. As she took hold of my hand, I experienced that feeling of déjà vu when thinking about my wedding day. As I peeked open my eyes, going by the position of one of Ellen's hands, I presumed she was holding one of my daughter's, too.

"Mum, I think Deana's crying."

"Deana, what's wrong?" I whispered.

"Oh, my darling girl, nothing's wrong."

I felt my hand shake as Deana wiggled it before glancing at my husband for translation services.

"Darling, these are tears of pure joy! I really can't remember a mission that has filled me with such jubilation."

"Deana said there's nothing wrong. She's just so happy for you."

"Deliriously! All three of you."

"You, me, and Ellen."

"Oh," I chuckled. "Um, Niall, I would like to know that she's alright, though."

"I can hear you, my darling girl. And, yes, couldn't be better. Clara and I are now a team. Spooks incorporated!" she tittered. "That lot up there, The-Powers-That-Be, old men with beards and outdated attitudes, who couldn't be trusted to organise an orgy in a whorehouse, have finally bowed to my will. I gave it to them double-barrelled, and believe you me, I can be quite the formidable one when I've got a bee in my bonnet. I made it abundantly clear that my darling Clara and I would be running joint operations. No ifs, no buts. And listen to this, after …"

"Niall?" I quizzed when no answer appeared to be forthcoming.

"Mum, I think Deana's still talking."

"Oh, Sorry."

"No bother, deary. Now, after they buckled to my demands, I had a good old chinwag … more of me telling her than a two-way conversation with that Miss De Ath. She's a right prickly one, she is. Anyway, I got a message through to my darling Dickie, and he was quite insistent that I should enjoy myself down here. It may seem a long time to be away from each other, but when you're dead, time is meaningless. My delicious boy said he's having a whale of a time and was looking forward to all eternity with me when I eventually crossed over. Such a lush, my Dickie. So, to sum up, my death couldn't be better!"

"Deana, perhaps I should update my wife before I forget half of what you said."

"Of course, sorry, darling. One does tend to get carried away when excited," she chortled.

"Niall?" I asked again as I detected Deana rubbing the back of my hand with her thumb.

"Basically, everything's fine. Deana and Clara are still here, in the land of the living, running missions to help people."

"Over thirty successful missions completed, I'll have you know. Clara and I are now very highly regarded in the spectral guide department. We're the official trainers for new recruits."

"And Terry? Did Deana say what happened to Terry?"

"Tetchy Terence is the reason I'm here today. The wanderer has returned with a new recruit in tow, I'm afraid to say. He'll be here very soon."

"Dad, what did Deana say?"

"Um … Terry is here, apparently. Or will be at any minute."

Niall, Ellen and I swivelled around, searching the graveyard when trying to spot a man sporting a 1980s retro moustache.

"I can't see him," I mumbled after letting go of Deana's hand and scanning around before my attention settled on Kim, Vinny and the two other couples who now shot worried looks in our direction.

Fair enough, I suspect our actions must have appeared rather odd.

"Deana, where is he?" Niall hissed. "There's no one here apart from us and that couple standing by the church door."

"What couple?" I asked, squinting into the distance, following where my husband was now pointing. "I can only see a bloke standing there with his hands in his pockets."

"Mum?" Ellen copied my husband, jabbing her arm in the same direction. "There's two of them, see? A man and a woman. Although she looks strange. Almost see-through."

"Sorry? What d'you mean? That man by the door is there on his own."

"Ah, yes, there he is. Better late than never, I suppose. Or, better late than pregnant, as I always used to say when dishing out the condoms at our little parties. Swinging is such fun, but one must always take precautions, you know."

Niall shot a look of surprise at where I thought Deana was still standing. His bushy raised eyebrows now appeared to be frozen in that lofty position.

"Oh, sorry, vicar, I can often be guilty of forgetting my audience," she tittered.

"Dad? What did Deana say?"

Ellen and I exchanged a glance when we noticed my husband seemed a little lost for words.

"Niall?" I prompted him, now a little concerned because speechless wasn't a state that usually could be attributed to my husband.

"Now, unfortunately, as I just mentioned, Terence didn't come alone. Apparently, Terry found it all rather tedious up there while lolling about on a fluffy cloud playing his harp, so he asked if he could return to the land of the living and run a few missions. Would you believe those idiots, The-Powers-That-Be, also agreed to let the boy bring his dead wife with him ... the new recruit Clara and I have been saddled with to train in the art of being a spectral guide. Ridiculous!"

"Ehm ... Deana said that is Terry standing over by the church door. He's returned with his dead wife."

Once more, Ellen and I exchanged a look before I grabbed my husband's hand again. "Niall, did you say his dead wife?"

"Yeah ... that's what she said."

"My God, there's more of them," I mumbled.

"Indeed, deary. Now, I can tell you, with her here, it's been like tiptoeing around on damn eggshells. When considering how Terry died, awkward really doesn't do it justice when describing the atmosphere in our household. It's certainly not much fun for Clara and me. And, as totally idiotic as it may seem, Terence and his perfect annoying little Sharon requested to meet up with Kim. Somewhat ill-thought-through, if you ask me. I'm mean, look at the woman holding the hand of her dashing Italian husband. Kim looks in a right old state at the idea of me being here, and she hasn't even met her dead parents yet!"

What's next?

Thanks for reading Deana and Terry's latest adventure. There will be more from our ghostly duo in 2025. In the meantime, please check out my other series … I've listed them below.

Can you help?

I hope you enjoyed this book. Could I ask for a small favour? Can I invite you to leave a rating or review on Amazon? Just a few words will help other readers discover my books. Probably the best way to support authors you like, and I'll hugely appreciate it.

Free book for you

For more information and to sign-up for updates about new releases, please drop onto my website, where you'll get instant access to your FREE book – Beyond his Time.

When you sign up, you get a no-spam promise from Adrian, and you can unsubscribe at any time.

You can also find my Facebook page and follow me on Amazon – or, hey, why not all three?

<u>Adriancousins.co.uk</u>

Facebook.com/Adrian Cousins Author

Books by Adrian Cousins

The Jason Apsley Series
Jason Apsley's Second Chance
Ahead of his Time
Force of Time
Beyond his Time
Calling Time
Borrowed Time

Deana – Demon or Diva Series
It's Payback Time
Death Becomes Them
Dead Goode
It's That Time Again
Deana – Demon or Diva Series Boxset

Standalone Novels
Eye of Time
Blink of her Eye

Acknowledgements

Thank you to my Beta readers – your input and feedback is invaluable.

Tracy Fisher

Brenda Bennett

Adele Walpole

Patrick Walpole

Also, thank you to Steve Payne, who, after I reached out to my email subscribers to suggest a title for this book, came up with *It's That Time Again*. With Terry and Deana returning for Christmas, I thought it suited the story perfectly!

And, of course, a massive thank you to my editor, Sian Phillips, who makes everything come together. None of this is possible without Sian, and I'm so grateful.

Printed in Great Britain
by Amazon